THE PENGUIN CLASSICS

FOUNDER EDITOR (1944–64): E. V. RIEU

Théophile Gautier was born at Tarbes, on the French side of the Pyrenees, on 31 August 1811. He was the son of a minor tax-official. When he was three and a half, his father's nomination as receiver of taxes led the family to Paris. Gautier was educated, briefly, at the Collège Royal de Louis-le-Grand, and then at the Collège Charlemagne; before he finished his course, he was also learning painting in Rioult's studio in the rue Saint-Antoine. It was here, by chance, that he read *Les Orientales* by Victor Hugo, turned from art to literature, and became a fervent Romantic. In 1830 he attended the historic first night of Hugo's Romantic drama, *Hernani*, and published his own first book, his *Poésies*. This was followed by other Romantic works, poems and short stories, and, in 1835, by the supreme Romantic novel, *Mademoiselle de Maupin*.

In 1836 he was obliged to become a journalist. For nineteen years he wrote for *La Presse*; he then became a contributor to *Le Moniteur universel* and to *Le Journal officiel*. A critic of art and literature, theatre and music, he knew many of his famous contemporaries, and he left some brilliant portraits of them. He was an eager traveller, and the author of *Voyage en Espagne* and *Voyage en Italie*. He was also a lover of ballet, and he wrote *Giselle* and *La Péri*. He continued to produce novels, among them *Le Capitaine Fracasse* (1863); but he was above all a poet, and *Émaux et Camées* (1852) is his most distinguished and influential work.

A supporter of the Second Empire, Gautier was appointed librarian to the Emperor's cousin, Princess Mathilde. The fall of the Empire, and the Franco-Prussian war, largely destroyed his way of life. His *Tableaux de Siège* gives a moving account of the Siege of Paris (1870–71); but the privations which he himself had suffered in the Siege had their effect on his health. He died on 23 October 1872.

Joanna Richardson read Modern Languages at Oxford, and she is a Fellow and Member of Council of the Royal Society of Literature. She is the author of *Théophile Gautier: His Life and Times* (and a member of the Comité d'honneur, Société Théophile Gautier). Her other publications include *Princess Mathilde* (1969), *Verlaine* (1971), *Victor Hugo* (1976) and *Zola* (1978); she has translated selections of poems by Verlaine and Baudelaire for the Penguin Classics.

THÉOPHILE GAUTIER

Mademoiselle de Maupin

*Translated with an Introduction
by Joanna Richardson*

PENGUIN BOOKS

Penguin Books Ltd, Harmondsworth, Middlesex, England
Penguin Books, 625 Madison Avenue, New York, New York 10022, U.S.A.
Penguin Books Australia Ltd, Ringwood, Victoria, Australia
Penguin Books Canada Ltd, 2801 John Street, Markham, Ontario, Canada L3R 1B4
Penguin Books (N.Z.) Ltd, 182–190 Wairau Road, Auckland 10, New Zealand

—

This translation first published 1981

—

Copyright © Joanna Richardson, 1981
All rights reserved

—

Set, printed and bound in Great Britain by
Cox & Wyman Ltd, Reading
Set in Garamond

INTRODUCTION

PIERRE-JULES-THÉOPHILE GAUTIER was born at Tarbes, within sight of the Pyrenees, on 31 August 1811. He was the son of Pierre Gautier, a minor tax official, and his wife, the former Antoinette-Adélaïde Cocarde. For the first few years of his life, Théophile and his parents lived in this sunlit southern town; and when he was three and a half, and his father's nomination as receiver of taxes led them to Paris, Théophile made no secret of his regret. Though he spent nearly all the rest of his life in Paris, he remained a southerner. 'The memory of blue mountains in silhouette at the end of every alley has never left me, and has often touched me in my pensive moods.' His abiding sense of form and colour was no doubt to owe something to the fortuitous setting of his early years.

This frail and gentle child, who looked 'like some little Spaniard from Cuba, cold and homesick', was later to give a glimpse of his sheltered childhood in *Mademoiselle de Maupin*. In 1822 he entered the Collège Royal de Louis-le-Grand; but he grew so miserable and thin that after three months he was sent instead, as a day-boy, to the Collège Charlemagne. Before he finished his course, he was learning painting in Rioult's studio in the nearby Rue Saint-Antoine. It was here that he learned the art of close observation, developed his sense of form and colour; he owed to Rioult, he recorded, his ability to see and to appreciate. And he owed, perhaps, to his master in the Rue Saint-Antoine, to the artist whose own painting has been forgotten, the quality that would dominate and distinguish his prose and poetry, and, through him, profoundly affect the course of French literature: the quality he would signify to the Goncourts when he told them: 'I am a man for whom the visible world exists.'

His short sight and his merely conventional canvases may have indicated to Gautier that painting was not his vocation. But in 1829, in the Rue Saint-Antoine, the decisive revelation was accorded him. 'I should probably have turned artist,' he wrote, 'had it not been for a book by Victor Hugo which fell into my hands in the studio; it was *Les Orientales* ... From that moment the master played a more important part in my life than the most intimate of my friends.'

On 25 February 1830, wearing a flamboyant and now legendary pink doublet, Gautier joined Hugo's supporters at the Théâtre-Français. It was the first night of *Hernani*: the night that was to determine the prestige – one might almost say the supremacy – of the new Romantic literature. It was the decisive encounter between traditional and progressive, past and future, Classicism and Romanticism. 'The twenty-fifth of February 1830!' wrote Gautier, not long before he died. 'The date remains written in flame in the depths of our past: the date of the first performance of *Hernani*! That evening decided our destiny. There we received the impulse that spurs us on, even now, after so many years, the impulse that will make us march on until the end of our days.'

Gautier's first book, his *Poésies*, appeared five months after the *bataille d'Hernani*; it burst upon Paris at the same time as the July Revolution, and naturally it went almost unnoticed. But the young poet was now living with his family at 8, Place Royale – now Place des Vosges – and, soon after the Revolution, Hugo himself came to live next door. Slowly Gautier's painting was abandoned, gradually his writing increased. In 1832 he published *Albertus*, the tale of a witch turned woman who persuades her lover to sell his soul to the devil. The theme is carried through more than a hundred stanzas; it shows a wide technical vocabulary and a developing consciousness of visual detail, and it anticipates a little of the vigorous description which we shall find in *Mademoiselle de Maupin*.

Hugo's interest in his work had inspired Gautier to write *Albertus*. Hugo's introduction led him to write his first short stories; for it was at 6, Place Royale that he met Eugène Renduel, the pre-eminent Romantic publisher. Renduel asked him to write something for him. The first result was a kind of *Précieuses ridicules* of Romanticism, *Les Jeunes-France*.

Les Jeunes-France must have fulfilled all Renduel's expectations; it is a collection of satirical short stories which shows Gautier at his youthful best: vigorous, paradoxical, light-hearted and original. The stranger excesses of his artistic contemporaries are parodied in *Onuphrius: ou les vexations fantastiques d'un admirateur d'Hoffmann*. The medieval cult is exploited in the most sympathetic, most poignant of his tales, *Elias Wildmanstadius*; while *Daniel Jovard ou la conversion d'un classique* is a manual for all who would qualify as '*maître passé en la gaie science du romantisme*'. *Celle-ci et celle-là, ou la Jeune-France passionnée* already shows the Gautier of *Mademoiselle de Maupin*: sensual, assured, appreciative, Romantic, and, as he repeatedly tells us, Turkish in his sexual freedom. These tales, which more than once satirize the author himself, are written with sympathy as well as amusement. They remain among his most spirited works.

At the end of 1834 he rented two tiny rooms in the Impasse du Doyenné, and enjoyed his first independence. The Impasse du Doyenné was a dead-end of dilapidated buildings in a corner of the Carrousel, a few yards from the Louvre. It was all that remained of a *quartier* being demolished, and the houses seemed to Balzac like living tombs. The ruins of the church of Saint-Thomas-du-Louvre, which, in the eighteenth century, had collapsed, killing six canons in its fall, added to the general desolation. But the gloom was charming to the Romantic mind; and if Gautier's own foothold in the Impasse was small, he was living next door to Camille Rogier, the artist, and his endearing friend from the Collège Charlemagne, Gérard de Nerval. They had installed themselves in a large apartment, where Rogier had embellished the walls with a portrait of Neptune strangely like himself, while Gérard had provided tapestries, two Fragonard panels, and a Renaissance bed for some nebulous divinity (he himself slept in a tent on the floor). The colony and the festivities grew: Arsène Houssaye, the future director of the Comédie-Française, installed himself with Gérard, paying his rent, in times of opulence, by dinners at the Restaurant des Trois Frères Provençaux. It was the time of Musard's intoxicating music, the time of febrile carnivals; they gave their balls in the Doyenné ('our Louvre', as Gérard called it) and danced till morning, when they sallied out in daylight, in fancy dress, to breakfast in the Bois de Boulogne.

In this Bohemia, in his microscopic writing, Gautier scribbled away. His renown was already spreading. The pupil of Rioult had begun to be known as a Salon critic with his articles in *La France littéraire*. He had also become a critic of literature. *Les Grotesques*, his studies of 'grotesque' and unfamiliar French poets, had begun in *La France littéraire* in January 1834, with an article on Villon. It was, for the time, an audacious article, for Gautier wrote with enthusiastic admiration – an admiration that would do much to resurrect Villon in France. The immediate result was that Théophile Gautier and *La France littéraire* had both been attacked by *Le Constitutionnel*; and in May 1834, enlarging his diatribe against *Le Constitutionnel*, Gautier had demolished utilitarian literature and the whole tribe of journalists and critics, recited the creed of Art for Art's Sake which he would profess all his life, and, with all the unrestraint and fire of a passionate youth in a wildly exciting age, produced the finest example of rhodomontade in French literature. It was the Preface to *Mademoiselle de Maupin*.

Despite the outrageous manner, the glittering pyrotechnics, the enormous paradoxes, the astonishing, constant rain of conceits, the Preface to *Mademoiselle de Maupin* contains much that remained deep in Gautier's soul all his days. Many of his theories as a critic of literature (and, indeed, as a critic of the arts in general) are found in the Preface and text of this novel. The Preface bears little relation to the novel itself, and is probably included on its own brilliant merits as a polemic. To posterity it has more than polemical interest; for when Gautier derides the whole conception of utility and declares, with all the ardour of his early manner, all the categorical certainty of youth, that 'nothing is really beautiful unless it is useless', he is for the first time professing the creed that he will profess, as poet and as critic, throughout his life. The Preface to *Mademoiselle de Maupin*, written at the outset of his career, is an impressive declaration of the sovereignty of art, of its independence of moral and social conditions. It insists upon the supreme importance of beauty; it is an early expression of the philosophy that Gautier will express, more than twenty years later, in his poem 'La Nue': 'Aime, c'est l'essentiel!'

It is only this belief in beauty and in love that relates the Preface to *Mademoiselle de Maupin*. The novel is, in fact, much less a novel than an admirable series of visual descriptions, an honest, full-blooded likeness of Gautier in his early twenties, a Gautier already possessing many of the beliefs and emotions that will inform his criticism. The story is the least important part of the book: it is only important in so far as the equivocal position of the heroine, her ability to rouse a double passion, enables Gautier to suggest that beauty may be loved independently of sex, for itself alone. His personal worship of loveliness is seen here not merely in his delicate and emotional portraits of women but in his lyrical invocation to ideal beauty ('whomsoever thou be, angel or demon, virgin or courtesan . . .') and in his hymn to beauty, 'pure personification of the thought of God'.

Time and again in *Mademoiselle de Maupin* we are made aware of the author's religion of beauty, his Greek worship of loveliness. In his attitude to beauty, Gautier is pagan; and there remains profound truth in his comment: 'I have looked at love in the classical light, as a more or less perfect piece of sculpture.' If he could consider a woman as her sculptor, this showed no inhumanity: it showed, rather, the Greek attitude, the attitude of the artist and idealist; and, in his search for beauty and love, Gautier was a confirmed idealist: 'There is something great and fine in loving a statue,' he proclaims in his novel. 'The impossible has always pleased me.' This Romantic love of the impossible recurs throughout his work and – as we shall see – it dominates his life. It is the love that he describes when he writes: 'If Don Juan had once found his ideal, he would have been the most faithful of lovers; but his greatness lay in not meeting it, for he sought absolute beauty, and absolute beauty is God.'

Mademoiselle de Maupin was published by Renduel late in 1835. It is a version of *As You Like It* written with all the naïveté of a Romantic in his early twenties. It is based on a premise that does not bear the scrutiny of reason: that a woman could pass, consistently, as a man. Once we accept this wild impossibility, we accept every conceivable *quid pro quo*; perversion becomes innocent or mitigated, love grows hesitant or guilty, and morality becomes strangely contorted. It is not surprising that the novel shocked contemporary opinion: the emotions it revealed were far from the conventional, idealized emotions of *La Nouvelle Héloïse*. Yet *Mademoiselle de Maupin* is more than an exploration of forbidden pleasures. If it impresses us by its unrestrained sensuality, its detailed, appreciative physical description, it impresses us too by its impulse and enthusiasm; its fire, momentum and vivacity transform it into a testament of youth. *Mademoiselle de Maupin* is a book that is written once in a lifetime, when dreams have not dissolved and disillusion is still unknown. None of Gautier's later prose is driven by the same energy; no novel better embodies the careless rapture of the young Romantic.

A few months after its publication, on 30 August 1836, the day before his twenty-fifth birthday, Théophile Gautier became a journalist. His journalism would produce a ceaseless flood of novels and short stories and more than two thousand articles during the next thirty-six years. It would shape and fill his life. It would weigh upon his shoulders all his days.

The author of *Mademoiselle de Maupin* had an unsurprising fascination for women, and he had already charmed them to good effect. We know little about Eugénie Fort, except that she came of good family, was passionate by nature and Spanish in appearance. But what more was needed to attract the partisan of *Hernani*? Eugénie grew wildly enamoured of Gautier's poetry and of himself, and Gautier grew enamoured of Eugénie. On 27 November 1836 she gave birth to Théophile Gautier *fils*. Eugénie implies in her diary that she refused a proposal of marriage from Gautier. It is doubtful whether he ever proposed. One suspects that he continued to wait, like d'Albert in *Maupin*, for some impossible Romantic ideal.

Giselle was first performed at the Opéra on 28 June 1841. Carlotta Grisi was revealed to the world that night, in the ballet that Théo-

phile Gautier had written; and he himself watched the first performance of the most popular of all his works, the greatest triumph of
the 'blonde Italian with forget-me-not eyes'. Gautier recognized
his ideal as instinctively as d'Albert had recognized his in Madelaine
de Maupin. His adoration for Carlotta is evident from this moment.
Countless appreciations and asides scattered throughout his criticism reflect the love that shines from his ballets and his poems, from
his novel *Spirite* and from his letters; and when, in so many of his
works to come, he wrote of an impossible passion, the love of a
statue, a spirit, a woman far removed in place and time, the
Romantic love of the unattainable, it was not only the Romantic
love of *Mademoiselle de Maupin*: it seemed a reflection, now, of his
own predicament. Carlotta had married Jules Perrot, her master
and partner; it was for her a marriage of pure convenience. But
when in time she chose a lover, bore his child, accepted his villa on
the shores of Lake Geneva, she chose a Polish nobleman, Prince
Radziwill. To Gautier she was the statue that never came to life;
and she rewarded her Pygmalion for his devotion, for ballets,
poems, novel, for creating her career, with that bitter consolation,
lasting affection.

Gautier's second ballet, *La Péri*, in which she also danced, was
first performed at the Opéra on 17 July 1841. It is a development of
d'Albert's quest for ideal beauty in *Mademoiselle de Maupin*. It also
strangely anticipates *Spirite*, the novel that Gautier would write
twenty-two years later. It has the same theme of the love of a spirit
and a mortal being; and in the ballet, as in the novel, one seems to
see the author himself: the youth who has exhausted temporal
pleasures and, 'like all great voluptuaries, fallen in love with the
impossible'.

Théophile Gautier, wrote Arsène Houssaye, 'is in love with the
three Grisis'. Gautier's admiration of the beauty of Julia Grisi
shines from the Preface to *Mademoiselle de Maupin*. Gautier's adoration of Carlotta is evident throughout his work, and in the record
in later years, of his constant pilgrimages to the Villa Grisi-sur-
Saint-Jean. But it was neither la Diva nor Giselle who was to dominate his daily existence: it was the sister of Giselle, Ernesta Grisi.

Was it her likeness to Carlotta that first attracted Gautier? Was it her passionate contralto as she sang at the Théâtre-Italien? Was Gautier drawn to her by her physical beauty? All these reasons may help to explain why, by 1844, he had become the lover of this fiery singer. Yet probably the strongest influence was Ernesta's comforting and practical nature. She was not merely attractive; unlike Eugénie Fort, she made herself domestically essential. That was why the liaison was marriage in all but name, and lasted for two decades.

A superb, arresting figure, bearded and exotic, Gautier continued to move in a magic world. He shone with Hugo at the soirées of the Duc de Nemours, he dined with Gérard de Nerval, he ate hashish with Balzac and Baudelaire at the gilded Hôtel Pimodan on the Île Saint-Louis. He travelled to London, to Spain, and to Venice where, in 1850, he had an intense love-affair with an exquisite, mysterious Italian, Marie Mattei. She alone, of all the women Gautier had known, gave him the passionate, dramatic love he needed.

Marie Mattei made a discreet appearance in his *Voyage en Italie*, the travel book which might well be called *Séjour à Venise*. He followed Ernesta to Turkey; and on 17 July 1852, while he was smoking a nargileh in Pera, there appeared his most famous book of poems, *Émaux et camées*. Domestic cares weighed heavily upon him. His son was nearing manhood, but he kept a certain responsibility for Eugénie; he had to support Ernesta and their two young daughters. His two sisters were ageing and both remained unmarried. He desperately needed a sinecure. In 1853 he asked for a post as Inspecteur des Beaux-Arts, and asked (as he had asked three years earlier) in vain.

In 1855 he left *La Presse* to become a critic on the government paper, *Le Moniteur universel*. He was growing increasingly sombre. Early in 1857 he assured the Goncourts: 'It bores me, it's always bored me, writing, and then it's so useless! . . . I don't go fast, but I keep on going, because, you see, I don't try to improve things. An article, a page, is something instantaneous: it's like a child. Either it works or it doesn't. I never think what I'm going to write. I take my pen and write. I am a man of letters, I should know my job.

There I am, in front of the paper, like a clown on the springboard
... And then, I have a very orderly syntax in my head. I throw my
phrases into the air like cats, I know they will always fall on their
paws. It's very simple, you only need good syntax.' His cynicism
was probably momentary, his boredom was sincere. He was now an
Establishment figure, but his Romanticism remained. Years ago,
with his stories *Une Nuit de Cléopâtre* and *Le Pied de Momie*, he had
established his poetic dreams of Egypt. In the autumn of 1856 he
had set to work on a novel, *Le Roman de la Momie*. If the novel was
too clearly written with reference books at hand, it still remains a
loving recreation of an age. It is drawn by the vigilant pupil of
Rioult, the lover of form and colour, contour and shade. It is
modelled by the d'Albert of *Mademoiselle de Maupin*, who 'liked to
follow the curves of contours into their most hidden folds'. And
Gautier recognized the nature of his distinction. 'People damn me
or praise me,' so he told the Goncourts, 'without understanding
the first thing about my talent. My whole importance, and they've
never mentioned it, is that *I am a man for whom the visible world exists.*'

'I've regretted all my life that I gave up my first occupation ...
Since then I've done nothing but make transpositions of art.' So
Gautier confessed to Princess Mathilde. The longing to give
permanence to transient arts, to passing beauty, is one of the basic
themes of his criticism, and it is evident again in his poem 'L'Art'.
His tastes and preoccupations had not changed much with the
years. *Le Capitaine Fracasse*, which appeared in 1863, is an un-
distinguished novel, but it remains a *tour de force*, an example of the
descriptive art; it is, as Gautier intended, a purely picturesque work,
and though the fire and lyricism of *Mademoiselle de Maupin* have long
since died, the visual descriptions are marked by beautifully detailed perception, by language which has some of the untrammelled
spirit of Rabelais, and by a plastic quality which is found in Gautier
alone. If the characters are pale and the plot is thin, the language –
effervescent, prodigal, precise – commands admiration.

In the summer of 1865, staying with Carlotta at Saint-Jean,
Gautier worked at another novel which recalls the theme of *Giselle*,
of *La Péri*, of *Arria Marcella*: the theme of the love of mortal and

immortal, the love of present and past, of impossible passion. *Spirite* – like *Mademoiselle de Maupin* – is the story of a man in love with an ideal. It is also the most personal reflection. When the first instalment of *Spirite* appeared in *Le Moniteur universel*, Gautier wrote to Carlotta: 'Read, or rather read again, for you know it already, this poor novel whose only merit is to reflect a graceful image, to have been dreamed beneath your great chestnut trees and written, it may be, with a pen touched by your hand ... The idea that your charming eyes will rest awhile on these lines where, beneath the veil of fiction, breathes the true, the only love of my heart, will be the sweetest recompense for my work.'

What he wanted – what he had wanted since the days of *Mademoiselle de Maupin* – was some unattainable Utopia. 'I don't know what to do with myself ... I'm as bored as a trunk left behind on a railway station ... How I long for a little cobalt blue in these fogbound skies!' Princess Mathilde, the Emperor's cousin, appointed him her librarian. Sainte-Beuve declared that 'all the imperial government's debt to Théo has now been paid, thanks be to you, Princess; it remains for the Académie to acquit the debt of literature to one of the most charming of our writers.' But the rose-coloured doublet, *Mademoiselle de Maupin*, Gautier's rhodomontades, and no doubt his unorthodox way of life still remained against him. The Académie repeatedly rejected him.

He died on 23 October 1872. A congregation of three hundred filled the church at Neuilly, and the hearse was escorted by a detachment of troops, Gautier's privilege as an Officier de la Légion d'honneur. The Cimetière Montmartre was crowded with admirers, with nameless colleagues 'escorting the journalist – and not the poet, not the author of *Mademoiselle de Maupin*'.

In this they were mistaken. *Mademoiselle de Maupin* is more than a Romantic novel, more even than a testament of youth: it is a profession of faith. If the Preface is a *tour de force* as much as a declaration of the principle of Art for Art's Sake, the text itself is a dazzling though unconscious development of the Keatsian theme: 'I have lov'd the principle of Beauty in all things.' *Mademoiselle de Maupin* is not merely the earliest and best-written of Gautier's novels. It is the first, the most sustained, and one of the most brilliant of Gautier's professions of his creed.

I have used the edition of *Mademoiselle de Maupin* published by Charpentier in 1859. I have chosen not to annotate the numerous literary and historical references because they are principally used as decoration, and they are not germane to the narrative.

Joanna Richardson

Mademoiselle de Maupin

PREFACE

ONE of the most ridiculous things in the glorious epoch which we have the happiness to live in is undoubtedly the rehabilitation of virtue. It is undertaken by every paper, whatever its political hue, red, green, or tricolour.

Virtue is certainly most respectable, and, heaven knows! we shouldn't want to show her disrespect, good and worthy woman that she is! Her eyes are shining through their spectacles, her stockings aren't put on too awry, she takes a pinch from her golden snuff-box with all imaginable grace, and her little dog makes its bow like a dancing-master. All this is true. We even agree that she isn't in too bad a shape for her age, and that she couldn't carry her years better than she does. She is a very agreeable grandmother – but a grandmother she is . . . It seems to me natural, especially when you're twenty, to prefer some immoral little thing who is very sprightly, flirtatious and obliging, with her hair somewhat ruffled, her skirt on the short side, her feet and eyes provocative, her cheeks slightly flushed, a laugh on her lips and her heart on her sleeve. The most monstrously virtuous journalists couldn't be of any other opinion; and, if they say the contrary, it's very probable that they don't think it. To think one thing and to write another happens every day, especially to virtuous people.

I remember the insults which were hurled before the Revolution (I'm talking of the July Revolution) at the unfortunate and virginal Vicomte Sosthène de La Rochefoucauld, who lengthened the dresses of the dancers at the Opéra, and, with his patrician hands, stuck a modest plaster on the middle of every statue. M.le Vicomte Sosthène de La Rochefoucauld has been far surpassed. Modesty has been much improved since those days, and we achieve refinements which he wouldn't have imagined.

Personally I am not in the habit of looking at certain parts of statues. Like other people, I found the vine-leaf cut out by the Minister's scissors the most ridiculous thing in the world. Apparently I was wrong, and the vine-leaf is among the most praiseworthy of institutions.

I have been told, but I have refused to believe it, because it seemed so extraordinary to me, that there were people who, confronted with Michelangelo's fresco *The Last Judgement*, saw nothing in it except the episode of the licentious prelates, and veiled their faces, crying abomination and desolation!

Those same people also know nothing about the romance of Rodrigue, except for the couplet about the serpent. If there is any nudity in a picture or a book, they go straight to it like a pig to filth, and they pay no heed to the flowers in bloom, or the luscious golden fruit that is hanging from every bough.

I must admit that I am not virtuous enough for that. Dorine, the shameless lady's maid, may of course display her ample bosom in front of me, I shall certainly never pull my handkerchief out of my pocket to cover the breast that one ought not to see. I shall look at her breast as well as her face, and if it is white and shapely I shall take pleasure in it. But I shall not feel to see if Elmire's dress is soft, and I shan't push her devoutly against the table, as that poor wretch Tartuffe did.

Nowadays there is a great affectation of morality, and it would be very laughable, if it wasn't very boring. Every newspaper serial turns into a pulpit; every journalist becomes a preacher. All that are missing are the tonsure and the dog-collar. These are dull times when it positively rains sermons; we preserve ourselves by only going out in a carriage and by re-reading *Pantagruel* between our bottle and pipe.

Holy Jesus! What a wild outburst! What fury! What's bitten you? What's stung you? Why the devil do you cry out so loudly, what has poor vice done to you, that you bear it such a grudge? Vice is so amiable and easy-going, and it only asks to enjoy itself and not to annoy other people, if that can be done. Behave to vice as Serre behaved to the gendarme: kiss, and be friends. Believe me, you will be better off that way. Good God! my dear preachers, what would you do yourselves without vice? You would have to go begging from tomorrow, if people became virtuous today.

The theatres would be shut this evening. What would you write your articles about? No more Opéra balls to fill your columns, no more novels to analyse; for balls, novels and comedies are all the devil's work, if we are to believe our holy mother the Church. The actress would dismiss her protector, and she could no longer pay you for your praise. People would stop subscribing to your papers; they would read St Augustine, go to church and tell their beads. All of which might be very fine, but you would certainly not gain by it. If people were virtuous, where would you publish your articles about the immorality of the age? You see quite well that vice has its uses!

But it is the fashion nowadays to be virtuous and Christian, it is the attitude that people strike; they play the part of St Jerome as they used to play that of Don Juan. People are pale and mortified, they wear their hair apostle-style, they walk with their hands joined and their eyes cast to the ground. They act their little pious act to perfection; they have an open Bible on their mantelpiece, a crucifix and some holy box-leaves beside their bed; they don't swear any more, they rarely smoke, and they hardly ever chew tobacco. And then they are Christian, they talk about the holiness of art, about the lofty mission of the artist, about the poetry of Catholicism, M.de Lamennais, the painters of the angelic school, the Council of Trent, progressive humanity and a thousand other splendid things. Some infuse a little republicanism into their religion; they are not the least extraordinary. They couple Robespierre and Jesus Christ in the most jovial way, and – with a gravity worthy of praise – they amalgamate the Acts of the Apostles and the decrees of the *holy* convention, that is the sacramental epithet. Others, as a last ingredient, add some Saint-Simonian ideas; these people are your copper-bottomed Christian republicans; they are the absolute limit. Human ridiculousness can go no further – *has ultra metas . . .**, etc. These are the Pillars of Hercules of the ludicrous.

* 'Beyond this point . . .'

Christianity is so in vogue in the present mood of hypocrisy that even neo-Christianity enjoys a certain favour. They say that it has as many as one adept, including M. Drouineau.

An extremely curious variety of the so-called moral journalist is the journalist with a female family.

He carries the sense of chastity to the point of cannibalism, or very nearly.

His manner of proceeding is, at first glance, simple and straight-forward. None the less, it is ludicrous, and superlatively amusing, and I believe it is worth preserving for posterity – for succeeding generations, as the old fogies of the so-called Great Century used to say.

If you are setting up as this kind of journalist, you need a little equipment for a start – such as two or three legitimate wives, a mother or so, as many sisters as you can manage, a complete assortment of daughters and innumerable female cousins. Then you want an ordinary play or novel, pen, ink, paper, and a printer. You should also have an idea and a few subscribers; but you can do without these if you have much philosophy and the shareholders' money.

When you have all this, you can set yourself up as a moral journalist. The following two recipes, with suitable variations, are enough for writing articles.

Models of virtuous articles about a first performance

'After the literature of blood, the literature of the dunghill; after the mortuary and the prison, the alcove and the brothel; after the rags stained by murder, the rags stained by debauchery; after, etc [according to need and space, you can go on like this for anything from six to fifty lines and more]. It is only to be expected. That is where they lead, the neglect of rational doctrines and the excesses of Romanticism. The theatre has become a school of prostitution which you tremble to enter with a woman whom you respect. You come on the strength of an illustrious name, and you are obliged to leave at the third act, because your young daughter is thoroughly upset and out of countenance. Your wife is hiding her blushes behind her fan; your sister, your cousin, etc.' (One can diversify the relationships: they just have to be female.)

NB. One man has carried morality to the point of saying: I shan't go and see that drama with my mistress. I admire and love that man; I bear him in my heart, as Louis XVIII bore the whole of France in his. That man has the most triumphant, most pyramidal, most amazing, most Luxorian idea which has struck a man's mind in this sanctimonious nineteenth century which has been struck by so many – and so many curious – ideas.

The method of reviewing a book is very cursory and within the reach of every intelligence:

'If you want to read this book, shut yourself up carefully at home; don't let it lie about on the table. If your wife and daughter chanced to open it, they would be lost. This book is dangerous, this book counsels vice. It might have had a great success, in the time of Crébillon, in the love-nests, at the duchesses' intimate little suppers; but now that behaviour has become more pure, now that the people have overthrown the ruinous edifice of the aristocracy, etc, etc, now that . . . now that . . . Every work must have an idea . . . a moral and religious idea which . . . a deep and lofty view which answers the needs of humanity; for it is deplorable that young writers should sacrifice the most sacred things to success, and waste an estimable talent on salacious paintings which would cause a blush to captains of dragoons [the virginity of captains of dragoons is, after the discovery of America, the finest discovery that has been made for a long time]. The novel which we are reviewing recalls Thérèse the philosopher, Félicia, Matheolus, the tales of Grécourt.' The virtuous journalist is vastly erudite where scabrous novels are concerned; I should be interested to know why.

It is alarming to think that, because of the papers, honest businessmen have only these two recipes to subsist on, they and the numerous family they employ.

I seem to be the most enormously immoral person who can be found in Europe or elsewhere; for I see nothing more licentious in the novels and comedies of today than there was in the novels and comedies of former times, and I cannot really understand why the ears of the gentlemen of the press have suddenly become so Jansenist and sensitive.

I don't think that the most innocent journalist would dare to say that Pigault-Lebrun, Crébillon *fils*, Louvet, Voisenon, Marmontel and all the other masters of novels and short stories are more immoral – since there *is* immorality – than the wildest and most shameless productions of Messrs So-and-so, whom I do not name out of pure regard for their modesty.

One would have to have the most arrant bad faith not to agree about this.

People must not object that the names I have mentioned here are virtually unknown. If I have not quoted the brilliant, monumental names, it isn't that they can't support my assertion with their great authority.

Merit apart, the novels and tales of Voltaire are certainly not much more suitable for being awarded as prizes, with little speeches, at boarding-schools, than the immoral tales of our friend the lycanthrope, or even the moral tales of the mealy-mouthed Marmontel.

What do we see in the comedies of Molière? The sacred institution of marriage (to adopt the style of the catechism and the journalist) is flouted and ridiculed in every scene.

The husband is old, ugly and doddery; he puts on his wig askew; he has a hooked cane, his nose smeared with snuff, short legs, and a belly as fat as a carpet-bag. He stutters and utters nothing but stupidities, he does as many stupid things as he says; he sees nothing, hears nothing; people kiss his wife before his eyes, and he doesn't understand; and so it goes on, until he is well and truly proved a cuckold to himself, and to all the audience, which couldn't be more edified, and applauds as loudly as possible.

Those who applaud most are the people who are most married.

Marriage, in Molière, is called George Dandin or Sganarelle.

Adultery is called Damis or Clitandre; no name is honeyed and charming enough for it.

Adultery is always young, handsome, well turned out and at

least a marquis. He comes in humming the latest *courante* to somebody off stage; he takes a step or two with the most assured and the
most triumphant air in the world; he scratches his ear with the pink
nail on his little finger, and he coyly sticks his little finger out. He
combs his fair hair with his tortoiseshell comb, and adjusts the
lower trimming – a most voluminous trimming – on his breeches.
His doublet and trunk hose disappear under the tags and bows of
ribbon, his bands come from a first-class band-maker; his gloves
smell sweeter than benzoin and civet; his feathers have cost a louis
a tuft.

How fiery his eye is, how pink his cheek! How smiling his lips!
How white his teeth! How soft and well washed his hands!

He speaks, it is nothing but madrigals, gallantries perfumed with
delicate preciosity, and in the most excellent style; he has read
novels and knows poetry, he is brave and quick to unsheath his
sword, he scatters gold by the handful. And so Angélique, Agnès,
Isabelle can hardly restrain themselves from casting their arms
around his neck, however well brought up, however ladylike they
may be; and so the husband is regularly deceived in the fifth act,
and he is very fortunate when he isn't deceived in the first.

That is how marriage is treated by Molière, one of the noblest
and most serious geniuses that have ever existed. Do people find
anything more powerful in the indictments of *Indiana* and *Valentine*?

Paternity is respected even less, if that is possible. Look at Orgon,
look at Géronte, look at them all.

How they are robbed by their sons, and how they are beaten by
their valets! How they are stripped, without pity for their age, to
reveal their avarice, their stubbornness and their stupidity! How
they are shoved out of life by the shoulders, these poor old men who
are a long time dying, and have no wish at all to give up their
money! How people talk about the eternity of parents! What special
pleadings against heredity, and how much more convincing it is
than all the Saint-Simonian declamations!

A father is an ogre, an Argus, a jailer, a tyrant, something which
at most can delay a marriage for three acts until the recognition at
the end. A father is the ridiculous husband made more ridiculous

still. Never is a son ridiculous in Molière; for Molière, like all the authors of all possible times, paid court to the young generation at the expense of the old one.

And the Scapins, with their cape striped in Neapolitan style, and their cap on one side, and their feather sweeping through the air, are they not very pious people, very chaste, and worthy of being canonized? The prisons are full of honest men who have not done a quarter of what they have done. The double-dealings of Trialph are poor double-dealings in comparison with theirs. And the Lisettes and the Martons: Zounds! what determined women! The common prostitutes are far from being so smart, so quick with the smutty answer. How well they know how to deliver a note! How well they stand on guard at the secret meeting! Upon my word, they are precious wenches, obliging and wise in counsel.

It is a charming society which flutters and saunters through these comedies and imbroglios. Duped tutors, cuckolded husbands, libertine waiting-maids, sharper valets, young ladies mad with love, debauched sons, adulterous women; isn't that well worth the handsome, melancholy young men and the poor feeble oppressed and passionate women of the dramas and novels of our fashionable authors?

And for all that, apart from the final dagger-thrust, the obligatory cup of poison, the endings are as happy as the endings of fairy-tales, and everyone, including the husband, is as satisfied as they can be. In Molière, virtue is always shamed and belaboured; it is she who wears the horns and offers her back to Mascarille; morality makes at most one appearance at the end of the play in the somewhat bourgeois character of the sergeant, M. Loyal.

Nothing that we have just said is meant to chip Molière's pedestal. We are not mad enough to go and shake that bronze colossus with our little arms. We should simply like to demonstrate to the pious journalists who are alarmed by the new romantic works that the old classics, which they recommend for reading and imitation every day, greatly surpass them in wanton language and immorality.

To Molière we might easily add Marivaux and La Fontaine, those two such opposite expressions of the French genius, and

Régnier, and Rabelais, and Marot, and many others. But, speaking of morality, we don't mean to provide a course of literature for the use of the virgins of journalism.

It seems to me that people shouldn't make such a commotion about so little. We are happily not in the time of fair Eve, and we cannot, with a good conscience, be as primitive and patriarchal as they were in the Ark. We aren't little girls preparing for their first communion; and, when we play crambo, we don't answer cream cake. Our innocence is quite passably sophisticated, and our virginity has gone around the town for quite a while; those are things which you don't have a second time, and, whatever we do, we can't get them back again, for nothing in the world goes faster than a virginity which is departing, or an illusion which is being destroyed.

And perhaps there is no great harm in that, and knowing everything may be better than knowing nothing. That is a question which I leave to be debated by those who are more learned than myself. None the less, the world has passed the age at which one can pretend to be chaste and bashful, it is too much of a greybeard to play the childlike and the virginal without making itself ridiculous.

Since its marriage with civilization, society has lost the right to be ingenuous and bashful. There are certain blushes which are still appropriate on the wedding-night, and cannot be used any more the following day; for perhaps the young woman no longer remembers the young girl, or, if she does, she remembers something which is very indecent, and something which gravely compromises the husband's reputation.

When I happen to read one of those fine sermons which have replaced literary criticism in the public prints, I am sometimes overcome by great remorse and apprehension, for I have a few little broad jokes on my conscience, a few such jokes which are rather too strongly spiced, such as a young man with fire and spirit may have to reproach himself with.

Beside these Bossuets of the Café de Paris, these Bourdaloues of the dress circle of the Opéra, who reprove the century in such fine fashion, I find myself quite the most dreadful scoundrel who has ever sullied the face of the earth; and yet, God knows, the list of my sins, both capital and venial, with the necessary blanks and spaces, would scarcely, in the hands of the most skilful publisher, form one or two volumes in octavo a day. This is not much for someone who does not claim to be going to paradise in the other world, or to win the Prix Monthyon or the rose for the best-behaved girl in her village in this one.

Then, when I think that I have met under the table, and even elsewhere, quite a number of these dragons of virtue, I have a better opinion of myself, and I consider that with all the faults that I may possess, they have another which, to me, is the greatest and worst of all: I mean hypocrisy.

If we look hard, we may find another little vice to add; but this is so hideous that, to be honest, I hardly dare to name it. Come closer, and I'll whisper the name to you: it's envy.

Envy, pure and simple envy.

It is envy which goes crawling and winding through all these hypocritical homilies. However it tries to hide itself, from time to time, above the metaphors and the rhetorical figures, one sees the glint of its little viper's head; one catches it licking its lips all blue with venom, with its forked tongue, one hears it whistling softly, and very low, in the shadow of an insidious adjective.

Of course I know that it is intolerably fatuous to claim that people envy you; it is almost as nauseating as a fop who boasts of a good fortune. I am not boastful enough to believe that I have enemies and enviers. This happiness is not given to all the world, and it will probably be a long time before I enjoy it. I can therefore speak freely and without ulterior motive, like someone quite dis-interested about it.

One thing is certain, and it is easy to demonstrate to those who might doubt it, and that is the critic's natural antipathy for the poet – the antipathy of the person who does nothing for the person who does something – of the drone for the bee, of the gelding for the stallion.

You only become a critic when it is well proved in your own eyes that you cannot be a poet. Before you degrade yourself to the wretched task of looking after the coats and noting the moves like a billiard-boy or a ball-boy, you have long courted the Muse, you have tried to possess her; but you lack the strength for it. Breath has failed you, and you have fallen weak and pale at the foot of the holy mountain.

I understand this hatred of critic for poet. It is oppressive to see someone else at the banquet to which you yourself are not bidden, someone else sleeping with the woman who has rejected you. From the depths of my heart I sympathize with the unfortunate eunuch obliged to watch the sport of the Grand Signor.

He is admitted into the innermost recesses of the Oda; he leads the Sultanas to the bath; he sees them glow beneath the silver waters of the great pools, these lovely bodies all streaming with pearls and smoother than agates; the most secret beauties appear unveiled before him. People are not troubled by him. He is a eunuch. The Sultan caresses his favourite in his presence, and kisses her on her pomegranate mouth. It really is an impossible situation, and he must find it very hard to put a good face on it.

It is the same for the critic who sees the poet strolling in the garden of poetry with his nine lovely odalisks, and lazily disporting himself in the shade of the great green laurels. It is very difficult for him not to pick up stones from the highway and throw them across the wall and hurt him, if he is skilful enough to do so.

The critic who has produced nothing is a coward; he is like an abbé who is paying court to a layman's wife: the layman cannot do the same to him, or fight with him.

I think it would be a history at least as curious as that of Teglath-Phalasar or Gemmagog who invented long pointed shoes, the history of the different ways of depreciating some or other work for the past month.

There is enough matter for fifteen or sixteen folio volumes; but we shall take pity on the reader, and restrict ourselves to a few lines – a benefit for which we shall ask more than eternal gratitude. At a far-off time, which is lost in the night of ages, it must have been some three weeks ago, the medieval novel was flourishing, mainly in Paris and in the suburbs. The blazoned coat of mail was greatly honoured; people did not scorn hennins, they had high esteem for particoloured pantaloons; the long pointed shoe was adored like a fetish. It was nothing but ogives, turrets, little columns, stained-glass windows, cathedrals and strongholds. It was nothing but damsels and young squires, pages and varlets, vagrants and mercenaries, gallant knights and fierce lords of the manor. It was certainly all more innocent than innocent games, and it did no harm to anyone.

The critic did not wait for the second novel before he began this work of depreciation; the moment the first one appeared, he had wrapped himself up in his camel-hair shirt, and had emptied a bushel of ashes over his head; then, assuming his great voice of lamentation, he had begun to cry:

'Still the Middle Ages, always the Middle Ages! Who will deliver me from the Middle Ages, these Middle Ages which are not the Middle Ages, these cardboard and terracotta Middle Ages which are Middle Ages only in name? Oh! the iron barons, in their iron armour, with their iron hearts in their iron breasts! Oh, the cathedrals with their rose-windows eternally in bloom and their stained-glass windows in flower, with their granite lace, with their openwork trefoils, their fretwork gables, their stone chasuble embroidered like a bridal veil, with their candles, their chants, their sparkling priests, their kneeling congregations, their booming organs and their angels hovering and beating their wings beneath the vaults! How they have spoiled my Middle Ages, my delicate and vivid Middle Ages! How they have hidden them under a crude coat of whitewash! What gaudy illuminations! Oh! ignorant daubers, who think you have created colour by laying red on blue, white on black and green on yellow, you have nothing medieval except the shell, you have not divined the soul of the Middle Ages, the blood does not circulate in the skin with which you clothe your phantoms, there is no heart in your steel corselets, there are no legs in your mesh pantaloons, no stomach or breast behind your emblazoned tunics; there are clothes which have the form of men, and that is all. So, down with the Middle Ages as the charlatans have created them (the great word is out! the charlatans)! The Middle Ages are now irrelevant, we want something else.'

And, seeing that the journalists were crying out against the Middle Ages, the public developed a great passion for these Middle Ages which they had claimed to have killed at a blow. Helped by the objections of the press, the Middle Ages invaded everything: dramas, melodramas, romances, novels, poems. There were even medieval vaudevilles, and Momus discovered feudal tol-de-rols.

Beside the medieval novel there decayed the carcass-novel, a most agreeable kind of novel, which was gobbled up by neurotic women of affected elegance and by hardened cooks.

The journalists picked up the scent at once, like crows pick up their quarry, and they dismembered the novel with their pen-nibs and wickedly put it to death: this poor kind of novel which only asked to prosper and to putrefy in peace on the greasy shelves of reading-rooms. What did they not say? What did they not write? Literature of the mortuary and the prison, an executioner's nightmare, the hallucination of a drunk butcher and a convict-warder with a burning fever. They kindly let it be understood that the authors were assassins and vampires, that they had contracted the vicious habit of killing their father and mother, that they drank blood from skulls, and used tibias for forks and cut up their bread with a guillotine.

And yet they knew better than anyone, because they had often had *déjeuner* with them, that the authors were nice young gentlemen, compliant and well-born, white-gloved and fashionably short-sighted, eating beefsteak rather than human cutlets, and more accustomed to drinking wine from Bordeaux than the blood of a young girl or a new-born child. Since they had seen and handled their manuscripts, they knew quite well that they were written with the ink of great virtue, on English paper, and not with blood from the guillotine on the skin of a Christian flayed alive.

But, whatever they said or did, the century was in favour of the carcass, and the charnel-house pleased it better than the boudoir; the reader was only caught by a hook which was baited with a little corpse already turning blue. This was very understandable; put a rose on the end of your line, and the spiders will have time to come and spin a web in the crook of your elbow, you won't catch the tiniest little fish; put on a worm or a piece of old cheese, and carp, young barbel, perch and eels will jump three feet out of the water to catch it. Men are not as different from fish as people generally seem to believe.

One would have said that the journalists had turned Quakers, Brahmins, Pythagoreans, or bulls, they had such a sudden horror of red and blood. Never had one seen them so melting, so emollient; they were cream and whey. They admitted only two colours, sky blue or apple green. Pink was just tolerated, and, if the public had allowed them, they would have led them to graze spinach on the banks of the Lignon, side by side with Amaryllis's sheep. They had changed their black frock-coats for the dove-coloured jackets of Céladon or Silvandre, and wreathed their goose-quills with rosebuds and favours like a shepherd's crook. They let their hair loose like a child's, and created themselves virginities according to the recipe of Marion Delorme, in which they had succeeded as well as she did.

They applied to literature the article in the Ten Commandments:

Thou shalt not kill.

People could no longer allow themselves the least little dramatic murder, and the fifth act had become impossible.

They found the dagger exorbitant, poison monstrous, and no name bad enough for the axe. They would have liked dramatic heroes to have lived to the age of Methuselah; and yet it has been known, since time immemorial, that the purpose of every tragedy is to kill some poor devil of a great man who can do nothing about it! In the same way the purpose of every comedy is to join in matrimony two idiotic lovers each about sixty years old.

It was at about this time that I threw into the fire (after taking a copy first, as one always does) two superb and magnificent medieval dramas, one in verse and the other in prose, the heroes of which were quartered and boiled on stage, which would have been very jolly and quite original.

In order to conform with their ideas, I then composed a classical tragedy in five acts, called *Héliogabale*. The hero of this threw himself into the latrines, an extremely new situation, which had the advantage of demanding a setting never seen before in a theatre. I also wrote a modern drama extremely superior to *Antony*. This was *Arthur ou l'homme fatal*, in which the providential idea occurred in the form of a *paté de foie gras* from Strasbourg, which the hero ate to the last crumb, after raping several women. This, added to his remorse, gave him appalling indigestion, from which he died. A moral ending if ever there was one. It proves that *God is just* and that vice is always punished and virtue always rewarded.

As for the monstrous class of writing, you know how the critics have treated it, how they have dealt with Hans of Iceland, that eater of men, Habibrah the sorcerer, Quasimodo the bellringer, and Triboulet, who is only a hunchback – all this swarming and extraordinary family, all these gigantic toad-like creatures created by my dear neighbour to crawl and skip through the virgin forests and cathedrals of his novels. Neither the grand features in the manner of Michelangelo, nor the curiosities worthy of Callot, nor the effects of light and shade in the style of Goya: none of these has found favour in the critics' sight. They have sent their author back to his odes, when he has written novels, and back to his novels when he has written dramas: the usual tactics of journalists who always prefer what you did before to what you are doing now. Yet my neighbour is a fortunate man, all the same, for he is recognized as superior even by the journalists in all his works – except, of course, the one they are reviewing – he would only have to write a theological treatise or a cookery book to make them find his theatre wonderful!

As for the love story, the ardent and passionate novel, which has Werther the German for its father, and Manon Lescaut the Frenchwoman for its mother, we wrote a few words, at the beginning of this preface, on the moral louse which desperately attached itself to it on the pretext of religion and good conduct. The lice of criticism are like the lice of the body, which abandon corpses for living people. From the corpse of the medieval novel the critics have passed to the living body of the love story. It has a tough and durable skin and might well break their teeth for them.

In spite of all the respect we feel for the modern apostles, we think that the authors of these so-called immoral works, though they aren't as married as the virtuous journalists, very frequently have a mother. Some of them have sisters, and they are provided with an abundant female family. But their mothers and sisters don't read novels, even immoral novels; they sew, embroider and busy themselves with housework. Their stockings, as M. Planard would say, are – absolutely white; you can look at their legs – they are not *blue*, and the good Chrysale, who so hated learned women, would set them up as an example to the learned Philaminte.

I come to the *wives* of these gentlemen, since they have so many of them. However virginal their husbands may be, it seems to me that there are certain things which they ought to know. It may well be that their husbands haven't shown them anything. If so, I understand if they decide to keep them in this precious and blessed ignorance. God is great and Mahomet is his prophet! Women are curious; may heaven and morality grant that they satisfy their curiosity in a more legitimate manner than their grandmother, Eve, and not go and ask questions of the Serpent!

As for their daughters, if they have been to a boarding-school, I don't see what these books might teach them.

It is as ridiculous to say that a man is a drunkard because he describes an orgy, a rake because he describes debauchery, as to claim that a man is virtuous because he writes a moral book. Every day one sees the contrary. It is the character who speaks and not the author. His hero is an atheist, that doesn't mean that he himself is an atheist; he makes the brigands act and speak like brigands, he is not a brigand for that reason. At that rate, one would have to guillotine Shakespeare, Corneille, and all the authors of tragedies; they have committed more murders than Mandrin and Cartouche. This has not been done, though, and in fact I don't believe it will be done for a long time, however virtuous and however moral the critics may become. It is one of the manias of these little scribblers with tiny minds, always to substitute the author for the work and to turn to the personality, to give some poor scandalous interest to their wretched rhapsodies. They know quite well that nobody would read them if they just contained their personal opinion.

We can hardly imagine the purpose of all this wrangling, the point of all this raging and baying. We can hardly imagine what pushes the nimble-footed Messrs Geoffroy to make themselves the Don Quixotes of morality, to set themselves up as the policemen of literature, and to apprehend and cudgel, in the name of virtue, every idea which strolls through a book with its mob-cap a little askew or its skirt pulled up a little too high. It is very singular.

Whatever they say, the age is immoral (if that word means anything, which we very much doubt), and we need no proof except the quantity of immoral books that it produces and the success which they enjoy. Books follow manners and manners don't follow books. The Regency made Crébillon, it wasn't Crébillon who made the Regency. The little shepherdesses of Boucher were painted and bare-breasted because the little *marquises* were painted and bare-breasted. Pictures are done from models, and not models from pictures. Someone or other said somewhere or other that literature and the arts had an influence on manners. Whoever it was, he was certainly a great fool. It is as if one said: green peas make the spring grow; green peas grow, on the contrary, because it is the spring, and cherries grow because it is the summer. Trees bear fruit, it is certainly not the fruit that bears the trees, and that is an eternal law, and unchanging in its variety; centuries follow one another, and each one bears its fruit, which is not the fruit of the previous century; books are the fruit of manners.

Beside the moral journalists, under this rain of homilies, as under a summer shower in a park, there has sprung up, between the planks of the Saint-Simonian platform, a series of little mushrooms of a new and rather curious kind, whose natural history we are going to write.

These are the utilitarian critics. Poor people who had such short noses that they couldn't wear spectacles on them, and yet didn't see as far as their noses.

When an author tossed some or other book, novel or poetry, on to their desk – these gentlemen lay back nonchalantly in their arm-chairs, balanced them on their back legs, and, rocking to and fro with a knowing look, a superior air, they said:

'What is the use of this book? How can one apply it to moralization and to the wellbeing of the largest and poorest class? What! Not a word about the needs of society, nothing civilizing and progressive! How, instead of making the great synthesis of humanity, and following, through the events of history, the phases of regenerating and providential inspiration, how can one produce poems and novels which lead nowhere, and do not advance the present generation along the path to the future? How can one be concerned with style and rhyme in the presence of such grave matters? What do we care, ourselves, about style, and rhyme, and form? This is the real question (poor foxes, they are too green)! Society is suffering, it is suffering from great inner anguish (in other words, no one wants to subscribe to useful periodicals). It is for the poet to seek the cause of this uneasiness, and cure it. He will find the means by sympathizing, heart and soul, with humanity (philanthropic poets! That would be something rare and delightful). We await this poet and invoke him with all our prayers. When he appears, he will deserve the acclamations of the crowd, the palms, the wreaths, the prytaneum . . .'

Well and good; but as we hope our reader will stay awake till the end of this happy preface, we shall not continue this very faithful imitation of the utilitarian style. By its nature, it is pretty soporific, and it might with advantage replace laudanum and academic speeches.

No, imbeciles, no, idiotic and goitrous creatures that you are, a book does not make jellied soup; a novel is not a pair of seamless boots; a sonnet, a syringe with a continuous spurt; a drama is not a railway, though all these things are essentially civilizing, and they advance humanity along the path of progress.

By the bowels of all the Popes, past, present and future, no, and two hundred thousand times no!

You don't make yourself a cotton cap out of a metonymy, you don't put on a comparison instead of a slipper; you can't use an antithesis as an umbrella; unfortunately you couldn't lay a few multicoloured rhymes on your stomach by way of a waistcoat. I have a deep conviction that an ode is too light an apparel for the winter, and that one wouldn't be better dressed with a strophe, an antistrophe and epode, than the cynic's wife who contented herself with her virtue alone for shift, and went about stark naked, so the story goes.

However, the celebrated M. de La Calprenède once had a coat, and, when someone asked him what it was made of, he answered: Silvandre. *Silvandre* was a play that he had just had successfully performed.

Such reasoning makes one shrug one's shoulders above one's head, and higher than the Duke of Gloucester.

People who claim to be economists, and want to rebuild society from top to bottom, seriously suggest such nonsense.

A novel has two uses: one is material, the other spiritual, if you can use that expression about a novel. The material use is, for a start, the several thousand francs which go into the author's pocket, and ballast him so that the wind or the devil doesn't bear him away; for the publisher it is a fine thoroughbred horse which paws the ground and trots in front of his cabriolet of steel and ebony, as Figaro says. For the paper-merchant, the material use is another factory on another stream, and often the means of spoiling a fine site; for the printers, it is a few barrels of logwood, to colour their gullets every week; for the reading-room, a heap of coppers, covered with very proletarian verdigris, and a quantity of grease which, if it were duly collected and used, would make whale-fishing superfluous. The spiritual use of novels is that, while people read them, they sleep, and don't read useful, virtuous and progressive periodicals, or other similar indigestible and stupefying drugs.

Let people say after this that novels don't contribute to civilization. I shan't talk about tobacconists, grocers, and sellers of fried potatoes; they have a very great interest in this branch of literature, since the paper it's printed on is generally of superior quality to that of the newspapers.

It is really enough to make one laugh fit to burst, just to listen to the utilitarian republicans or Saint-Simonians. I should very much like, for a start, to know exactly what it means, this great gawky noun with which they stuff the emptiness of their columns every day, the noun which serves as a shibboleth and a sacramental expression. Utility: what does the word mean, and what do we apply it to?

There are two kinds of utility, and the meaning of the term is always relative. What is useful for one is not useful for another. You are a cobbler, I am a poet. It is useful for me that my first line rhymes with my second. A rhyming dictionary is very useful to me; it is no use to you, except to cobble an old pair of boots, and it's fair to say that a shoemaker's knife wouldn't help me very much to make an ode. You will now object that a cobbler is much above a poet, and that people can more easily do without one than without the other. I have no wish to disparage the illustrious profession of cobbler, which I honour as much as the profession of constitutional monarch, but I humbly admit that I should rather have my shoe unsewn than my line ill-rhymed, and that I'd rather do without shoes than do without poetry. As I hardly ever go out, and walk more skilfully on my head than I do on my feet, I wear out fewer shoes than a virtuous republican who does nothing but run from one ministry to another to have some appointment thrown to him.

I know that there are those who prefer mills to churches, and the bread of the body to that of the soul. To them, I have nothing to say. They deserve to be economists in this world, and in the next.

Is there anything absolutely useful on this earth and in this life which we are living? To begin with, there is very little use in our being on earth and being alive. I defy the most learned of the company to say what purpose we serve, unless it is not to subscribe to *Le Constitutionnel* or to any kind of paper whatever.

And then, if we admit *a priori* the usefulness of our existence, what do we really need to maintain it? Soup and a bit of meat twice a day is all we need to fill our stomachs, in the strict sense of the word. A coffin two feet wide and six feet long is more than enough for man after his death; he does not need a much larger space in his lifetime. A hollow cube seven or eight feet square, with a hole to breathe through, a single cell in the hive, that is all he needs for lodging and for shelter from the rain. A blanket, suitably rolled round the body, will protect him as well as – and better than – the most elegant and the best-cut frock-coat from Straub's.

With that, he will be able literally to subsist. They say in fact that one can live on twenty-five sous a day; but preventing oneself from dying is not living; and I don't see how a town which is planned for its usefulness would be pleasanter to live in than Père-Lachaise.

Nothing beautiful is indispensable to life. If you suppressed the roses, the world would not materially suffer; yet who would wish there were an end of flowers? I would rather give up potatoes than roses, and I believe that there is only one utilitarian in the universe who could tear up a bed of tulips to plant cabbages.

What is the use of women's beauty? Provided that a woman is physically well formed, and that she is capable of bearing children, she will always be enough for economists.

What is the use of music? What is the use of painting? Who would be mad enough to prefer Mozart to M.Carrel, and Michelangelo to the inventor of white mustard?

Nothing is really beautiful unless it is useless; everything useful is ugly, for it expresses a need, and the needs of man are ignoble and disgusting, like his poor weak nature. The most useful place in a house is the lavatory.

For myself – and I hope it does not displease these gentlemen – I am among those to whom the superfluous is necessary – and I prefer things and people in the inverse ratio to the services that they perform for me. I prefer to a certain useful pot a Chinese pot which is sprinkled with mandarins and dragons, a pot which is no use to me at all, and the talent of mine which I most esteem is guessing logographs and charades. I should most joyfully renounce my rights as a Frenchman and as a citizen to see an authentic picture by Raphael, or a beautiful woman naked: Princess Borghese, for example, when she has posed for Canova, or Julia Grisi, when she enters the bath. I should very readily agree, myself, to the return of that cannibal, Charles X, if he brought me back a hamper of Tokay or Johannisberg from his castle in Bohemia, and I should find the electoral laws broad enough, if some streets were wider, and other things less wide. I was not born a dilettante, but I prefer the sound of screeching fiddles and tambourines to that of the President's little bell. I should sell my trousers to have a ring, and my bread for jam. The most becoming occupation for a civilized man seems to me to be inactivity, or cogitating as one smokes one's pipe or cigar. I also have much esteem for those who play skittles, and those who write good verses. As you see, the utilitarian principles are far from being mine, and I shall never be editor of a virtuous paper, unless I am converted, which would be rather funny.

Instead of creating a *prix Monthyon* as a reward for virtue, I should prefer, like Sardanapalus, that great philosopher who has been so misunderstood, to give a handsome prize to the man who invented a pleasure – for enjoyment seems to me to be the end of life, and the only useful thing in the world. God has willed it so, He who created women, perfumes and light, lovely flowers, good wines, lively horses, greyhounds and angora cats: He who said not to His angels 'Be virtuous', but 'Be loving', He who has given us a mouth more responsive than the rest of our skin so that we may kiss women, eyes looking upwards that we may see the light, a subtle sense of smell to draw in the souls of flowers, strong thighs to grip the flanks of stallions and fly as swift as thought without railways or steam-boilers, sensitive hands to caress the long heads of greyhounds, the velvet backs of cats, and the satin shoulders of creatures of little virtue, and Who, in short, has given us alone the triple and glorious privilege of drinking without thirst, of striking light, and of making love in every season, which distinguishes us from the brute far more than the habit of reading papers and making charters.

My God! What a stupid thing it is, this so-called perfectibility of the human race! I am sick and tired of hearing about it. You would really think that man was a machine which could be improved, and that a cog which was better engaged, a counterweight more appropriately placed, could make it work in an easier and more convenient way. When they come to giving a double stomach to man, so that he can ruminate like an ox, eyes on the other side of his head so that, like Janus, he can see those who put out their tongues at him behind his back, and contemplate his *indignity* in a less uncomfortable position than that of the Callipygian Venus in Athens, when they fix wings on his shoulderblades so that he is not obliged to pay six sous to go by omnibus; when they have created a new organ for him, then well and good! The word *perfectibility* will begin to mean something.

For all these fine improvements they have made, what have they done which was not done as well, and better, before the Flood?

Have they managed to drink more than they drank in the days of ignorance and barbarity (to write in the old style)? Alexander, the equivocal friend of the handsome Ephestion, didn't drink too badly, although in his day there was no *Journal des connaissances utiles*, and I don't know which utilitarian could drain the great winecup which he called the cup of Hercules without becoming bibulous and more bloated than Lepeintre *jeune* or a hippopotamus. The Maréchal de Bassompierre, who emptied his great top-boot to the health of the thirteen cantons, seems to me to be singularly estimable in his way and very difficult to improve upon. What economist will enlarge our stomach so that it will hold as many beefsteaks as the late Milo of Crotona, who ate an ox? The menu of the Café Anglais, or Véfour, or any other culinary temple of fame, seems to me very meagre and very ecumenical, compared to the menu of Trimalcio's dinner. At what table, nowadays, do they serve a sow and her twelve young wild boars on a single dish? Who has eaten eels and lampreys fattened on human flesh? Do you really think that Brillat-Savarin has improved on Apicius? Would that great offal-eater, Vitellius, find the wherewithal at Chevet's to fill his famous shield of Minerva with pheasants' and peacocks' brains, phenicoptera's tongues and scarrus' livers? Your oysters at the Rocher de Cancale are really something very choice beside the oysters of Lucrinus, for which they had expressly created a sea. The little houses on the outskirts of Paris, kept by the *marquis* of the Regency, are miserable country cottages if one compares them to the villas of the Roman patricians, at Baiae, Capri and Tibur. The cyclopean splendours of those great voluptuaries who built eternal monuments for the pleasures of a day: should they not make us prostrate ourselves before the antique genius, and strike the word *perfectibility* out of our dictionaries for evermore?

Have they invented any one new capital sin? There are, alas, as there used to be, only seven of them, a total which is very unimpressive. I do not even think that after a century of progress, at the rate at which we are going, any lover could renew the thirteenth labour of Hercules. Can one oblige one's divinity once more than in the days of Solomon? Many highly illustrious scholars and very respectable ladies maintain exactly the opposite opinion, and claim that amiability is decreasing. Well, then, what do you mean by progress? I know that you will tell me that people have an Upper and Lower House, that they hope that everyone will soon have the vote, and that the number of representatives will have doubled or trebled. Don't you think that there are enough errors of French as it is, in Parliament, and that they are enough for the wretched job that they have to get through? I hardly understand the point of shutting up two or three hundred provincials in a wooden shed, with a ceiling painted by M. Fragonard, to make them mess about with and bungle countless silly or dreadful little laws. What does it matter whether it's a sabre, a holy-water sprinkler or an umbrella that governs you? It's always a stick, and I am astonished that progressive men should argue about which cudgel is to chastise their shoulders. It would be much more progressive and less expensive to break it and send the pieces to the devil.

The only one of you who has common sense is a madman, a great genius, an imbecile, a divine poet who is well above Lamartine, Hugo and Byron. Charles Fourier the Phalansterian is all that in one; he alone has been logical, and he has had the audacity to carry his arguments to the limit. He has no hesitation in saying that men would soon have tails fifteen feet long, with an eye at the end; and that, undoubtedly, is progress, and allows people to do a thousand fine things that they could not do before, like killing elephants without striking a blow, swinging from trees without swings, as comfortably as the most practised Macaco, and doing without an umbrella or a sunshade, by spreading out one's tail like a plume, as squirrels do – and they manage without brollies very nicely – and other prerogatives which would take too long to enumerate. Some Phalansterians even claim that they already have a little tail which will grow larger, if God grants them life.

Charles Fourier has invented as many kinds of animals as Georges Cuvier, the great naturalist. He has invented horses which will be three times as big as elephants, dogs as big as tigers, fish which will satisfy more people than the three fish of Jesus Christ which the incredulous Voltaireans believe to be a catch for April fools, and I myself consider a splendid parable. He has built cities beside which Rome, Babylon and Tyre are only molehills; he has heaped up Babels on top of one another, and sent up into the clouds more endless spirals than there are in all the engravings of John Martin. He has imagined I know not how many orders of architecture and new embellishments. He has planned a theatre which would seem grandiose even to the Romans of the Empire, and drawn up a menu for a dinner which Lucius or Nomentanus would perhaps have found enough for a dinner among friends. He promises to create new pleasures, and to develop the organs and the senses; he will make women lovelier and more voluptuous, and men more robust and more vigorous; he guarantees you children, and proposes to reduce the number of the inhabitants of the earth, so that everyone should be comfortable there. This is more reasonable than pushing the proletariat into creating more proletarians, and then shooting them down in the street when they breed too fast, and despatching them bullets instead of bread.

This is the only means of progress. All the rest is a bitter mockery, a witless buffoonery which doesn't even dupe idiotic simpletons.

The Phalanstery is indeed an advance on the Abbey of Thelema, and it finally relegates the earthly paradise to a place among those things which are quite outmoded and old-fogyish. Only the Thousand and One Nights and the Tales of Mme d'Aulnoy can compete to advantage with the Phalanstery. What fecundity! What inventiveness! There are enough wonders there for three thousand cartloads of romantic or classical poems; and, academic or not, our versifiers are very paltry inventors, if one compares them with M.

Charles Fourier, the inventor of passionate attractions. This idea of using instincts which people have hitherto tried to repress is a high and mighty idea indeed.

Ah! you say that we are making progress! If, tomorrow, a volcano opened its jaws at Montmartre, and turned Paris into a shroud of cinders and a tomb of lava, as Vesuvius once did to Stabia, Pompeii and Herculaneum, and if, in a thousand years or so, the antiquaries of the day made digs and exhumed the corpse of the dead city, tell me which monument would remain standing to attest the splendour of the great capital which had been interred. The Gothic Notre-Dame? They would certainly have a fine idea of our arts when they uncovered the Tuileries as touched up by M. Fontaine! The statues on the Pont Louis XIV would have a fine effect, transported into the museums of the time! And were it not for the pictures of the old schools and the classical or Renaissance statues piled up in the gallery at the Louvre, that long and shapeless passage; were it not for the ceiling by Ingres, which would prevent them thinking that Paris was only a camp for the Barbarians, a village of Huns or Topinambous, what they pulled out from the excavations would be very curious. Some National Guardsmen's sabres and firemen's helmets, some coins struck with a shapeless stamp, that is what they would find instead of those noble weapons, so curiously engraved, which the Middle Ages leave in the depths of their ruined towers and tombs, those medals which fill Etruscan vases and pave the foundations of all Roman buildings. As for our miserable veneered wooden furniture, all these poor, bare, ugly, shabby boxes that we call chests of drawers or writing-desks, all these misshapen, fragile implements, I hope that time would have the compassion to destroy the very last vestige of them.

The fancy took us, once, to build a grandiose and splendid monument. We were obliged, for a start, to borrow the plan from the ancient Romans; and, even before it was finished, our Pantheon staggered on its legs, like a rickety child, and tottered, like a dead-drunk invalid, so much so that we were obliged to give it stone crutches, or else it would pitifully have fallen its full length in front of everyone, and would have taught the nations to laugh for more than a hundred years. We wanted to set up an obelisk in one of our squares; we had to go and steal it from Luxor, and it took us two years to bring it home. Old Egypt lined her roads with obelisks, as we line ours with poplars; she carried bunches of them under her arms, as a market gardener carries his bunches of asparagus. She sculpted a monolith out of the flanks of her granite mountains more easily than we carve a toothpick or an earpick. Some centuries ago, they had Raphael or Michelangelo; now they have M. Paul Delaroche, and all because we are making progress. You boast of your Opéra; ten Opéras like yours danced a saraband in a Roman circus. M. Martin himself, with his tame tiger and his poor lion as gouty and drowsy as a subscriber to the *Gazette*, is a wretched creature indeed beside a gladiator of antiquity. Your benefit performances last till two o'clock in the morning. What are they when one thinks of those performances when real ships actually fought on a real sea; when thousands of men conscientiously cut one another to pieces? Turn pale, oh heroic Franconi! And think of those performances when the sea would draw back, and the desert would come with its roaring tigers and lions, terrible dumb actors which were used only once. The leading part was played by some robust Dacian or Pannonian athlete whom they would very often have found it awkward to bring back at the end of the play; his paramour was some beautiful and greedy lioness from Numidia which had been on an empty stomach for three days. Doesn't the elephant on the tightrope seem to you to be superior to Mademoiselle Georges? Do you believe that Mademoiselle Taglioni dances better than Arbuscula, and Perrot better than Bathyllus? I am convinced that Roscius would have given points to Bocage, however excellent he may be. Galeria Coppiola played the part of an *ingénue* when she was more than a hundred years old. It is fair to say that the oldest of our lovers is hardly more than sixty, and that Mademoiselle Mars is not even making progress in that direction. They had three or four thousand gods, in whom they believed, and we have only one, and hardly believe in him; that is a strange way of making progress. Isn't Jupiter stronger than Don Juan, and a very different kind of seducer? I really don't know what we have invented or even perfected.

After the progressive journalists, and as if by way of antithesis, there are the hardened journalists who are always twenty or twenty-two, who have never left their neighbourhood and have only so far slept with their charwomen. As for them, everything bores them, everything wearies them, everything plagues them, they are sated, hardened, worn, unapproachable. They know in advance what you're going to tell them; they have seen, felt, experienced, heard, all that one can see or feel, experience or hear; the human heart has no corner so unknown that they have not taken a lantern to it. They tell you with wonderful assurance: 'The human heart is not like that; women are not made like that; this character is false; this character is good.' Or else they say: 'What! always loves or hates! always men and women! Can't you talk about anything else? But man is threadbare and woman still more threadbare since M. de Balzac got mixed up with them.'

Who will deliver us from men and women?

'So you believe, sir, that your fable is new? It is as new as the Pont-Neuf; nothing in the world is more common; I read that somewhere or other when I was out at nurse or elsewhere; I have been sick to death of it for the past ten years. For the rest, sir, you must learn that there is nothing I do not know, that everything is stale to me, and that if your idea were as virginal as the Virgin Mary, I should still maintain that I had seen it prostituting itself at the street corners to the most inferior scribblers and the most vulgar pedants.'

These journalists have been the cause of Jocko, the Green Monster, the Lions of Mysore and a thousand other fine inventions.

They themselves constantly complain that they are obliged to read books and see plays. Speaking of a bad vaudeville, they talk of almond trees in flower, lime-trees which scent the air, the spring breeze, and the smell of the young leaves; they make themselves nature-lovers in the style of the young Werther, and yet they have never set foot outside Paris, and would not know a cabbage from a beetroot. If it is winter, they will tell you of the delights of the domestic hearth, the crackling fire, the firedogs and the slippers, the half-sleep and the daydream. They will not fail to quote the famous line by Tibullus:

*Quam juvat immites ventos audire cubantem.**

By quoting this they will give themselves an air both disillusioned and naïve, which is the most charming air in the world. They will pose as men who are no longer affected by the work of men, who are left as cold and dry by dramatic emotions as the penknife which they use to cut their pens, and yet men who still cry, like J.-J. Rousseau: 'There's the periwinkle!' These journalists profess a fierce antipathy for the colonels of the Théâtre du Gymnase, for uncles from America, for cousins, male and female, for sentimental old soldiers and romantic widows, and they try to cure us of the vaudeville by proving every day, in their articles, that not every Frenchman is born clever. In truth, we find no great harm in that, quite the contrary, and we gladly admit that the extinction of the vaudeville or the comic opera in France (national species) would be one of the greatest blessings from heaven. But I should certainly like to know what kind of literature these gentlemen would want to see established in its place. It is true that it could not be worse.

Others preach against false taste, and translate the tragedies of Seneca. Finally, to bring up the rear, a new battalion of critics has been formed of a species hitherto unknown.

Their formula of appreciation is the most convenient, the most extensible, the most malleable, the most peremptory, the most superlative and the most triumphant that a critic has ever been able to imagine. Zoilus would certainly not have lost by it.

Until now, when people wanted to depreciate some work or other, or to discredit it in the eyes of the patriarchal and innocent subscriber, they produced quotations which were wrong or perfidiously out of context; they truncated phrases and mutilated lines, so that the very author would have thought himself the most ridiculous person in the world; they charged him with imaginary plagiaries; they compared passages from his book with passages from ancient or modern authors, which had not the least relation to them; they accused him, in the style of a cook and with many

* What a pleasure it is to hear the gentle breezes as one lies in bed!

solecisms, of not knowing his native tongue, of distorting the French of Racine and Voltaire; they asserted, gravely, that his work verged on cannibalism, and that its readers would invariably become cannibals or raging madmen in the course of the week. They insisted that it was all poor, antiquated, superannuated, and as fossil as could be. The accusation of immorality was so often dragged through articles and gossip columns that it became inadequate. Indeed, it became so worn that there was hardly anything left but *Le Constitutionnel*, a progressive political paper, as we know, which had the desperate courage to go on using it.

They therefore invented the critic of the future, the progressive critic. Just imagine, the very first time, how charming that is, and how delightfully imaginative! The formula is simple, and we can give it to you. The great book and the praiseworthy book is the book which is not yet published. The one which appears is always detestable. The one which appears tomorrow will be superb; but it is always today. This critic is like the barber who had the following words written in large letters on his sign:

THERE WILL BE FREE SHAVING HERE **TOMORROW**

All the poor devils who read the placard promised themselves for next day the ineffable and sovereign sweetness of being shaved once in their lives without opening their purses; and the hair on their chins grew six inches with pleasure during the night which preceded this happy day. But, when they had the towel round their neck, the sawbones asked them if they had some money, and told them that, if they didn't cough up, he would deal with them like nut-stealers or apple-thieves; and he swore a great oath that he would cut their throats with his razor, unless they paid him; and when the poor beggars, all miserable and piteous, quoted the placard and the sacrosanct inscription: 'Aha! poor wretches,' said the barber, 'you are not great scholars, and you really ought to go back to school. The placard says *tomorrow*. I am not such a fanciful fool as to shave free today; my colleagues would think that I was losing trade. Come another time, or come when there's a week with three Thursdays, you will find yourself wonderfully satisfied. May I become a green leper if I don't do it free for you then, on my word as an honest barber.'

The authors who read a prospective article, in which they libel a current work, always flatter themselves that the book they write will be the book of the future. They try as hard as they can to come to terms with the critic's ideas, and they make themselves social, progressive, moralizing, palingenesic, mythical, pantheistic, Buchezist, believing that by doing so they will escape the formidable curse; but for them, as for the barber's customers, today is not the eve of tomorrow. The morrow so often promised will never dawn on the world; for this formula is too useful to be given up so soon. While you decry the book you are jealous of, and would like to destroy, you don the gloves of the most generous impartiality. You appear to ask no better than to discover virtues and to praise, and yet you never do so. This recipe is much superior to the one that we might describe as retrospective. This consists in only praising old books which are no longer read and do not inconvenience anybody, at the expense of the new books with which you are concerned, for these are quicker to wound self-esteem.

Before we began this review of the critics, we said that there would be material enough to furnish fifteen or sixteen folio volumes, but that we should content ourselves with a few lines; I'm beginning to be afraid that the few lines are each about a thousand yards long. They are like those brochures so fat and thick that one couldn't pierce them with a cannonball, those publications which bear the perfidious title: A word on the revolution, a word on this or that. The history of the sayings and doings, the manifold loves, of the celebrated Madelaine de Maupin ran a great risk of being dismissed, and you can imagine that an entire book is not too much in which to praise the adventures of that lovely Bradamante. That is why, however much we should like to continue to criticize the illustrious Aristarchuses of the age, we shall content ourselves with the pencil sketch we have just made of them, and add a few reflections on the simplicity of our meek brothers in Apollo who, stupid as Cassandre in the pantomime, just stay there to be hit by Harlequin's broadsword and to have their backsides kicked by Paillasse, and remain as motionless as idols.

It is as if a fencing master clasped his hands behind his back when he was attacked, and took all his adversary's thrusts at his bare breast, without ever trying to parry them.

It is like a lawsuit in which only the public prosecutor could speak, like a debate where no answers were allowed.

The critic advances this and that. He lords it, regardless of the cost. It is absurd, detestable, monstrous; it is like nothing on earth, and like everything else. You stage a drama. The critic goes to see it. It happens not to correspond in any particular with the drama which he had imagined under the same title. In his article, he therefore substitutes his own drama for the author's, he writes long slabs of erudition; he rids himself of all the learning which he had gone and picked up in a library the previous evening, and he gives shameful treatment to people from whom he should be learning, the least of whom would teach better men than himself.

Authors endure this with a magnanimity which seems to me really inconceivable. After all, who are these critics with so peremptory a tone, such laconic words, that one would imagine them to be the true sons of the gods? They are quite simply men with whom we have been to college, men who have clearly profited less from their studies than ourselves, since they have produced no work and can only feed on and destroy other people's as if they were veritable Stymphalides.

Wouldn't it be something to write the criticism of the critics? For these utterly surfeited men, who act so grand, and so hard to please, are far from being as infallible as our Holy Father. There would be enough to fill a daily paper, and a paper of the largest format. Their blunders, historical or otherwise, their invented quotations, their errors of French, their plagiaries, their twaddle, their well-worn jokes, their jokes in bad taste, their poverty of ideas, their lack of intelligence and tact, their ignorance of the simplest things which makes them ready to take the Piraeus for a man and M. Delaroche for a painter: all this would furnish ample material for authors to take their revenge, simply by underlining passages in pencil and textually reproducing them; for the brevet of critic does not always carry the brevet of a great writer, and in order to reproach other people for their errors of language and taste it is not enough just to write correctly oneself; our critics prove as much every day. If Chateaubriand, Lamartine and other people like that wrote criticism, I should understand if people fell on their knees and worshipped; but that Messrs Z., K., Y., V., Q., X., or any other letter of the alphabet between alpha and omega should play the little Quintilian and rebuke you in the name of morality and the honour of literature, that always revolts me and sends me into absolute rages. I should like them to make a police regulation which forbade certain names to come into contact with certain others. It's true that a dog may look at a bishop, and that St Peter's in Rome, gigantic though it is, cannot prevent the Transteverians from fouling it below in a curious fashion; but I believe, all the same, that it would be mad to write alongside certain monumental reputations:

NO RUBBISH TO BE DUMPED HERE

Only Charles X really understood the question. When he ordered the suppression of the newspapers, he did a great service to the arts and to civilization. The press is a sort of agent or go-between which interposes itself between the artists and the public, the King and the people. We know the wonderful things that happened as a result. This perpetual barking dulls inspiration, and casts such mistrust in people's hearts and minds that they don't dare to trust a poet or a government. This means that royalty and poetry, the two greatest things in the world, become impossible, and this in turn is a great misfortune for the nations, which sacrifice their wellbeing to the poor pleasure of reading a few bad sheets of bad paper, scrawled over with bad ink in bad style, every morning of their lives. There was no critic of art under Julius II, and I know no articles on Daniel de Volterre, Sebastian del Piombo, Michelangelo, Raphael, or on Ghiberti delle Porte, nor on Benvenuto Cellini; and yet I think that, for people who had no papers at all, who did not know the word *art* or the word *artistic*, they had enough talent as it was, and did not acquit themselves too badly in their profession. Reading papers prevents the existence of real scholars and real artists. It is a daily excess which makes you enervated and exhausted when you reach the bed of the Muses. Those hard and difficult women want fresh and vigorous lovers. The newspaper kills the book, as the book has killed architecture, as artillery has killed courage and muscular strength. We don't know what pleasures the papers deprive us of. They take the virginity of everything; they ensure that we have nothing of our own, and that we cannot possess a book just for ourselves. They deprive us of the surprise in the theatre, and tell us all the endings in advance; they deprive us of the pleasure of chat, tittle-tattle, gossip and slander, of inventing a piece of news or spreading a true one for a week round all the salons in the world. They instil ready-made judgements into us in spite of ourselves, and they bias us against things that we should like. They ensure that, provided they have a memory, matchbox-sellers talk literature as impertinently as provincial academicians; they ensure that, all day, instead of innocent ideas or individual blunders, we hear tatters of undigested newspaper which are like omelettes raw on one side and burnt on the other. They ensure that we are mercilessly surfeited with news which is three or four hours old, and news which children at the breast already know; they blunt our taste, and make us like those drinkers of spiced brandy, those swallowers of files and rasps, who no longer find any savour in the most generous wines and cannot catch their rich and aromatic bouquets. If Louis-Philippe suppressed all the literary and political papers, once and for all, I should be infinitely obliged to him, and I should immediately rhyme him a fine extravagant dithyramb in free verse and alternate rhymes, signed: your most humble and most faithful subject, etc. Don't imagine that one would no longer be concerned with literature; at the time when there were no papers, a quatrain occupied Paris for a week, and a first performance for six months.

It is true that one would lose by this the advertisements and the eulogies at thirty sous a line, and notoriety would be less prompt and less stunning. But I have thought up a very ingenious way of replacing the advertisements. If, between now and the publication of this glorious novel, my gracious monarch has suppressed the papers, I shall most certainly make use of it, and I promise myself no end of wonders. When the great day comes, twenty-four mounted heralds, in the livery of the publisher, with his address on their backs and breasts, bearing a banner embroidered on both sides with the title of the novel, each of them preceded by a drummer and a kettle-drummer, would cry out loud and clear: 'It is today and not yesterday or tomorrow that they are publishing the admirable, the inimitable, the divine and more than divine novel by the most celebrated Théophile Gautier, *Mademoiselle de Maupin*, the novel which Europe and even the other parts of the world and Polynesia have awaited with such impatience for a year and more. They are selling five hundred copies a minute, new editions are appearing every half-hour. They have already reached the nineteenth. A picket of municipal guards is at the door of the shop, controlling the crowd and preventing any disturbance.' That would certainly be quite as good as a three-line announcement in the *Débats* and the *Courrier Français*, between the elastic belts, the crinoline collars, the feeding-bottles with incorruptible teats, Regnault paste and cures for the toothache.

May 1834

I

You complain, my dear friend, that I rarely write. What do you want me to write to you, except that I am well and I'm as fond of you as ever? These are things which you certainly know already, and they are so natural at my age and with the virtues people find in you, that it is almost ridiculous to send a wretched sheet of paper a hundred leagues merely to say them. I have searched in vain, I have nothing worth reporting; my life is the simplest in the world, and nothing occurs to break its monotony. Today brings tomorrow, just as yesterday brought today; and, though I have no pretentions to be a prophet, I can boldly predict in the morning what will happen to me in the evening.

This is the order of my day. I get up, that goes without saying, indeed it is the beginning of most days. I have lunch, I fence, go out, come in, I dine, I pay a few visits or occupy myself with a book. Then I go to bed exactly as I did the previous night; I go to sleep, and my imagination, which is not excited by new things, gives me only worn and threadbare dreams, which are as monotonous as life itself. It isn't very amusing, as you see. None the less, I tolerate this existence better than I should have done six months ago. I'm bored, it's true, but I'm bored in a serene and submissive way. Life has a certain sweetness, and I should very readily compare it to those pale warm autumn days which have a secret charm after the excessive heat of summer.

Yet though I accept it, in appearance, this life is hardly made for me. At least it bears only a very faint resemblance to the one I dream of, the one I think is suitable for me. Perhaps I'm wrong, perhaps I am made only for this way of life; but I find it hard to believe, for, if it were my proper destiny, I should fit into it more easily, I shouldn't have been bruised by its corners so painfully and in so many places.

You know that strange adventures have an overwhelming attraction for me. I adore everything which is singular, dangerous and excessive. You know how avidly I devour novels and travel stories; perhaps there is not a wilder, more vagabond fancy than mine in all the world. Well! I have never set out on a journey. For me, the voyage round the world is the journey round the town where I live; I touch my horizon on every side; I rub shoulders with reality. My life is that of the shell on the sandbank, the ivy round the tree, the cricket on the hearth. In fact, I am surprised that my feet have not yet taken root.

They paint Love blindfold; it is Fate which they should paint like that.

My valet is a rather crude and stupid sort of oaf. He has travelled as widely as the north wind, he has been God knows where, he has seen with his own eyes everything which I imagine to be so beautiful, and he doesn't care a damn about it. He has found himself in the most extraordinary situations. He has had the most astounding adventures that one can have. I sometimes make him talk, and it makes me furious to think that all these wonderful things have happened to a dolt who is capable neither of feeling nor of thinking, a dolt who is only good for doing what he does, that is to say for brushing clothes and taking mud off boots.

It is clear that this rascal's life should be mine. As for him, he thinks me very lucky, and he is astonished to see me so sad.

None of this is very interesting, my poor friend. It is hardly worth writing, is it? But, since you are absolutely determined that I should write to you, I must tell you what I think and feel, and I must relate the history of my ideas, for want of events and actions. There may not be much order or much novelty in what I shall have to tell you; but you will have only yourself to blame. You will have chosen it.

You are my childhood friend, I was brought up with you; for a long time we led the same life, and we have grown used to exchanging our most intimate thoughts. And so I can tell you without embarrassment all the nonsense which passes through my idle mind; I shan't embroider, I have no vanity where you are concerned. I shall therefore tell you the exact truth – even about the little, shameful things; I certainly shan't strike poses in front of you.

Under this shroud of nonchalant and overwhelming boredom which I mentioned a moment ago, there sometimes stirs a thought which is torpid rather than dead. I do not always have the sad and gentle calm which melancholy brings. I have relapses, and once again I fall into my old restless moods. Nothing in the world is as tiring as these whirlwinds without reason, these transports without aim. On these days, though I have nothing to do, any more than I have on other days, I rise very early in the morning, before the sun, I feel in such a hurry, I feel I shall never have the time I need. I get dressed with all possible speed, as if the house were on fire, I put my clothes on at random and deplore every minute lost. Anyone who saw me would think I was going to meet my mistress or to look for money. Not at all. I don't even know where I am going; but go I must; and I should feel that my salvation was compromised if I stayed. It seems to me as if someone were summoning me from outside, as if my destiny were passing at that moment in the street, as if the question of my life were about to be decided.

I go downstairs, startled and terrified, my clothes in disorder, my hair all wild; people turn round and laugh when they see me, and think I'm a young rake who has spent the night in the tavern or elsewhere. I am certainly drunk, though I haven't had a drink, and I even have the drunkard's uncertain step, sometimes slow and sometimes fast. I go from street to street like a dog which has lost its master, seeking everywhere, very anxious, very alert, turning round at the slightest sound, slipping into every group of people, oblivious of the rebuffs of those I jostle, and looking everywhere with a clarity of vision which at other times I do not possess. Then, suddenly, it is clear to me that I am mistaken, that it certainly isn't there, that I must go further on, to the other end of the town, perhaps beyond. And I hasten on as though the devil were bearing me away. I only touch the ground with the tips of my toes, I don't weigh an ounce. I must really look very odd with my intent, wild expression, my gesticulating arms and my inarticulate cries. When I reflect on my behaviour, I laugh wholeheartedly at myself. This doesn't prevent me, I assure you, from beginning again the next time.

If someone asked me why I ran like that, I should certainly find it extremely difficult to answer. I am in no hurry to arrive, because I am not going anywhere. I am not afraid of being late, because I have no fixed time. No one is waiting for me; and I have no reason to make haste.

Is it an opportunity for love, an adventure, a woman, an idea or a fortune, something which I lack and am seeking without understanding, urged on by some vague and confused instinct? Is it my life which needs to be complete? Is it the wish to escape from my house and from myself, the tedium of my situation and the desire for another? It is something of all that, and perhaps all that at once. None the less, it is a very unpleasant state, a febrile irritation which is usually followed by utter debility.

Often I feel that if I had set out an hour earlier, or if I had quickened my step, I should have arrived in time; that, while I was going down this street, what I was seeking passed down another, and that a carriage hold-up was enough to make me miss what I have sought everywhere and for so long. You cannot imagine the great depressions and the profound despairs which I fall into when I see that it all ends in nothing, and that my youth is passing by and no vista opens before me; then all my idle passions growl, deep down in my heart, and devour each other for want of proper food, like the animals in some menagerie when the keeper has forgotten to feed them. For all the stifled and suppressed disappointments of every day, something in me resists and will not die. I have no hope, for in order to hope you must have a desire, a certain tendency to wish that things will turn out in one way rather than another. I want nothing, because I want everything. I do not hope, or rather I don't hope any more – that is too stupid – and it is exactly the same to me if something happens or doesn't happen. I am waiting – for what? I don't know, but I am waiting.

I wait in trembling, full of impatience, with nervous fits and starts, like a lover waiting for his mistress. Nothing happens. I go into a rage, or begin to weep. I wait for the heavens to open and an angel to come down and make a revelation to me; for a revolution to break out and for someone to offer me a throne; for a virgin by Raphael to step down from her picture and embrace me. I am waiting for relatives whom I do not have to die and leave me enough to let my fantasy drift on a river of gold; I am waiting for a hippogriff to take me and bear me away to regions unknown. Whatever I am waiting for, it is certainly nothing ordinary or commonplace.

This reaches such a point that, when I return home, I always ask: 'Hasn't anyone called? Isn't there a letter for me? Any news?' I know perfectly well that there isn't anything, that there can't be anything. That doesn't matter; I'm always very surprised and very disappointed when they answer, as usual: 'No, sir, absolutely nothing.'

Sometimes – but this is rare – the idea becomes more precise. It will be some beautiful woman whom I do not know, a woman who does not know me, a woman whom I have met in the theatre or at church, who has never taken the slightest notice of me. I go right through the house, and until I have opened the door of the last room, I hardly dare say so, it's so mad, I hope that she has come and that she is there. It isn't self-conceit on my part. I am so unconceited that several women have taken the very kindest interest in me, so other people have told me, and I thought that they were quite indifferent to me, and had never thought particularly about me. This idea is something quite apart.

When I am not dulled by boredom and discouragement, my soul awakes in all its former vigour. I hope, love, and desire, and my desires are so violent that I imagine they will draw everything towards them as a powerful magnet attracts iron particles even when they are very far away. That is why I am waiting for the things I want, instead of going to them, and I quite often neglect the opportunities which offer themselves most favourably to me. Another man would write the most amorous note in the world to the divinity of his heart, and seek the occasion to meet her. As for me, I ask the messenger for the answer to a letter I haven't written, and spend my time devising the most marvellous imaginary situations to present myself to my loved one in the most unexpected and most favourable light. They would make a fatter and more ingenious book than the stratagems of Polybius, with all the stratagems that I imagine to introduce myself into her presence and reveal my passion to her. It would usually be enough to say to one of my friends: 'Introduce me to Madame So-and-so,' and to pay a mythological compliment suitably punctuated with sighs.

To hear all this, you would think me fit to be sent to the lunatic asylum; and yet I am a reasonable young man, and I have not put many of my follies into action. They all take place in the vaults of my soul, all these far-fetched ideas are very carefully buried in the depths of my being. You see nothing from the outside, and I have the reputation of being a calm and cold young man, very little concerned with women and indifferent to the occupations of youth. This is as far from the truth as the judgements of the world usually are.

And yet, despite all the things which have disheartened me, some of my desires have been realized, and, from the little pleasure which their fulfilment has given me, I have come to fear the fulfilment of the others. You remember the childish ardour with which I longed for a horse of my own. My mother very recently gave me one. It is ebony black, with a little white star on its forehead, spirited, with gleaming coat and fine withers, exactly as I had wanted it. When it was brought to me, it gave me such a turn that I went quite pale; it was a quarter of an hour and more before I could recover. Then I mounted it, and, without a word, I left at full gallop, and rode straight on across country for more than an hour with a delight you can hardly conceive. I did the same thing every day for more than a week, and I really don't know how I didn't kill the horse or at least leave it broken-winded. Gradually all this burning ardour was appeased. I set my horse at a trot, then at a walking pace, then I came to ride so nonchalantly that he often stops, now, and I don't notice it. The pleasure has turned into a habit much more quickly than I should have believed. As for Ferragus, that is what I call him, he is certainly the most delightful animal that you could see. He has tufts on his feet, like eagles' down; he is as quick as a goat and as gentle as a lamb. You will have the greatest pleasure galloping on him when you come here; and, though my passion for riding has certainly subsided, I still love him very much, because he has a very estimable equine character, and I honestly prefer him to many human beings. If you heard how joyfully he whinnies when I go and see him in his stable, if you saw how intelligently he looks at me! I must say I am so touched by these signs of affection that I put my arm round his neck and kiss him as tenderly, upon my word, as if he were a beautiful girl.

I also had another desire: more urgent, more ardent, more perpetually awake, more lovingly caressed, a desire for which I had built in my soul an enchanting castle of cards, an aerial palace which was very often destroyed, and rebuilt with desperate constancy. This desire was to have a mistress, a mistress entirely mine, like the horse. I don't know if the fulfilment of this dream would have left me cold as soon as the fulfilment of the other. I doubt it. But perhaps I'm wrong, and perhaps I should have tired of it as fast. I am so made that I desire so frantically what I desire – even though I do nothing to procure it – that if by chance, or otherwise, I achieve what I want, I suffer from complete emotional exhaustion. I am so harassed that I have fainting-fits, and I am no longer strong enough to enjoy it. And so the things that come to me without my having wished them usually give me more pleasure than those which I have most ardently coveted.

I am twenty-two; I am not a virgin. Alas! One no longer is a virgin at this age, nowadays, in body or in heart, which is much worse. Apart from those who give pleasure to men for money, and should count no more than a lascivious dream, I have certainly had a few honest or almost honest women, here and there, in some dark corner or other. They were not beautiful or ugly, young or old, they were such women as offer themselves to young men who have no regular affair and whose heart is unemployed. With a little good-will and a fairly strong dose of romantic illusions, you can call that having a mistress, if you choose. Personally, I find it impossible. If I had a thousand women like this, I should still believe my wish to be as unfulfilled as ever.

So I have had no mistress yet, and my whole desire is to have one.

The idea is singularly tormenting; it isn't an excitable temperament, hotbloodedness, the first blossoming of puberty. It isn't women that I want, it is a woman, a mistress; I want her, I shall have her, and have her soon; if I don't succeed, I must confess that I shan't recover from it, I'll always have an inner timidity, a deep discouragement which will affect me seriously for the rest of my life. I should consider myself a failure in certain respects, out of tune or incomplete: malformed in spirit or in heart; for after all, what I want is legitimate, and nature owes it to every man. As long as I don't achieve my end, I shall consider myself as only a child, and I shan't have the self-confidence I should. A mistress is for me like the robe of manhood for a young Roman.

I see so many men, ignoble in every respect, who have beautiful women, when they hardly deserve to be their lackeys. I blush deeply for them – and for myself. It gives me a pitiful impression of women, to see them infatuated with such contemptible men, who scorn them and deceive them, when they could give themselves to some young man, loyal and sincere, who would consider himself very happy, and worship them on his knees: like me, for example. It's true that this species clutter up the salons, strut about in front of every star, and are always leaning over the back of some armchair, while I myself stay at home, with my face pressed against the window, watching the mist rise on the river and the fog thickening, and silently raise up in my heart the perfumed sanctuary, the wondrous temple where I should lodge the idol of my soul. It is a chaste and poetic occupation, for which women show you as little gratitude as possible.

Women have very little taste for thinkers, but they singularly prize those who put their ideas into action. And, when all is said, they are not wrong. They are obliged by their education and social position to be silent and to wait; they naturally prefer the men who come to them and speak, and rescue them from a false and tedious situation. I feel all this; but never in my life shall I take it upon myself, as many do, to get up, cross a salon, and go and say suddenly to a woman: 'Your dress suits you divinely,' or: 'Your eyes look particularly bright this evening.'

None of this alters the fact that I absolutely must have a mistress. I don't know who it will be, but I don't see anyone among the women I know who can suitably assume this elevated rank. I find in these women very few of the qualities I need. Those who are young enough don't have enough beauty or intellectual accomplishments; those who are beautiful and young have an ignoble and discouraging virtue, or lack the necessary liberty; and then there is always some husband around, some brother, mother or aunt, who has big eyes and big ears and either has to be cajoled or thrown out of the window. Every rose has its aphis, every woman has a mass of relatives who must be carefully picked off, like caterpillars, if one day you want to enjoy the fruit of her beauty. Even second cousins, once removed, and living in the provinces, cousins whom you have never seen, want to keep their dear cousin's immaculate purity in all its perfection. That is sickening, and I shall never have the necessary patience to pull up all the weeds and cut down all the briars which, alas, obstruct the path to a pretty woman.

I don't like mothers, and I like little girls even less. I must also confess that married women have only a very mild attraction for me. I dislike the mixing and the confusion; I can't bear the thought of sharing. The woman who has a husband and a lover is a prostitute for one of them, and often for both, and besides I couldn't consent to give up my place to someone else. My natural pride would not accept such humiliation. I should never leave because another man was coming. Were the woman to be compromised and lost, were we to fight with knives, each of us with a foot on her body, I should stay. The hidden staircases, cupboards, closets, all the apparatus of adultery would be useless expedients with me.

I am rather taken with what they call virginal candour, the innocence of youth, purity of heart, and other delightful things which have the finest effect in verse; I simply call them stupidity, ignorance, imbecility or hypocrisy. This virginal candour, which consists of sitting on the very edge of the chair, with your arms close to your sides and your eyes on the top of your bodice, and only speaking with the permission of your grandparents, this innocence which has the monopoly of white dresses and uncurled hair, this purity of heart which wears close-fitting bodices because it doesn't yet have breasts or shoulders, doesn't really seem to me marvellously piquant.

I have very little interest in spelling out the alphabet of love to little simpletons. I am not old or corrupt enough to take great pleasure in that; besides, I should do it badly, because I have never been able to demonstrate anything to people, even the things that I knew best. I prefer the woman who reads fluently, you are sooner at the end of the chapter; and in everything, especially love, what must be considered is the end. In that respect I am rather like those people who take the novel by the tail, read the ending first, and go back to the first page. This way of reading and loving has its charm. You savour the details better when you are happy about the ending; and turning it upside down brings the unexpected.

So little girls and married women are not to be considered, and we must choose our divinity from among the widows. I am very much afraid that that is all that's left, and even there we shan't find what we want.

If I came to love one of those pale narcissi, bedewed with warm tears, and leaning with melancholy grace over the new marble tomb of some husband happily and recently deceased, I am sure I should soon find myself as unhappy as the late husband was in his lifetime. However young and charming they may be, widows have a terrible disadvantage that other women do not possess. Unless you are on the best terms with them and there is not a cloud in the sky of love, they tell you at once with a little superior and disdainful air: 'Look at you today! You're just like my husband. When we used to quarrel, he was just the same; it's extraordinary, you have the same tone of voice and the same expression; when you lose your temper, you've no idea how like my husband you are. It's frightening.' It's nice to be told these things point-blank, and to your face! There are some who carry their impudence so far as to praise the deceased like an epitaph and to extol his heart and leg at the expense of yours. At least, with the women who have had only one or several lovers, you have the advantage that they never talk about your predecessor. This is a consideration of no small importance. Women have too great a love of the proper and legitimate not to take care to be silent on such occasions, and all these things are relegated as quickly as possible to the past. It is very well understood that you are always a woman's first lover.

I don't think there's any serious answer to such an understandable aversion. It isn't that I find widows completely without charm when they are young and pretty and still in mourning. They have little languid airs, little ways of letting their arms droop, of bending their necks and raising their heads like a turtle-dove without a mate; they have a lot of charming affectations gently veiled under transparent crape, a well-considered coquetry of despair, sighs so skilfully contrived, tears which fall so pertinently, and give such a brightness to the eyes! The liqueur which I most like to drink after wine – if not before – is certainly a good, bright, really limpid tear which is trembling on the edge of eyelashes either brown or fair. How can you resist it? You can't. And then, besides, black is so becoming to women! Poetry apart, white skin turns to ivory, snow, milk, alabaster, everything pure that exists for the use of the makers of madrigals. Dark skin has nothing left but a touch of brown, full of vivacity and fire. Mourning is full of promise for a woman, and I shall never marry because I'm afraid that my wife might get rid of me in order to go into mourning for me. However, some women have no idea at all how to take advantage of their grief, and they weep in a way to make their noses red and discompose their faces like the grotesque figures you see on fountains. It is a great danger. You have to have much charm and art in order to weep pleasantly; otherwise, you run the risk of being unconsoled for a long time. Nonetheless, however great the pleasure of making some Artemis unfaithful to the shade of her mausoleum, I certainly don't want to choose from this crowd of mourners the woman whose heart I shall demand in exchange for mine.

I can hear you say: Who will you choose, then? You don't want young girls, or married women, or widows. You don't like mothers; I don't imagine that you prefer grandmothers. Who the devil do you love? That is the word of the charade, and, if I knew it, I shouldn't be so tormented. Until now, I haven't loved any woman, but I have loved and I do love *love*. Although I haven't had a mistress and the women I've possessed have inspired me only with desire, I have experienced and I know love itself. I didn't love this woman or that one, this person rather than the other, but I loved someone I've never seen, someone who must exist, someone whom I shall find, if God wills it so. I know quite well what she is like, and, when I meet her, I shall recognize her.

I have very often imagined the place she lives in, the dress she is wearing, her eyes and hair. I can hear her voice; I should recognize her step among a thousand others, and if, by chance, someone mentioned her name, I should turn round. She must undoubtedly have one of the five or six names which I have assigned her in my mind.

She is twenty-six – neither more nor less. She is no longer ignorant, and she is not yet bored with life. It is a charming age for making love as love should be made, without childishness and without libertinage. She is of medium build. I don't like a giant or a dwarf. I want to be able to carry my goddess, unaided, from the sofa to the bed; but it wouldn't displease me to find her there. When she stands a little on tiptoe, her mouth must reach mine. That is the proper height. As for plumpness, she must be buxom rather than thin. I am a little Turkish on this point, and I'd hardly like to find a skeleton where I sought a contour; a woman's skin must be well filled, her flesh hard and firm like the pulp of a slightly unripe peach. She is made exactly like this, the mistress whom I shall possess. She is blonde, with dark eyes, fair like a blonde, with the colouring of a brunette, something red and sparkling in her smile. Her lower lip is rather full, her eyes are moist, her breasts are round and small and firm, her wrists are thin, her hands long and plump, her walk is undulating like a snake standing up on its tail, her hips are rounded and mobile, her shoulders broad, the nape of her neck is covered with down: a type of beauty both delicate and firm, elegant and vivacious, poetic and real: a Giorgione motif executed by Rubens.

This is how she is attired. She is wearing a dress of black or scarlet velvet with slashings of white satin or silver cloth, an open corsage, a big ruff à la Medici, a felt hat capriciously out of true like Helena Systerman's, and long white feathers, curled and waved, a golden chain or a diamond necklace round her neck, and a quantity of big rings of different colours on all her fingers.

I shouldn't let her off a ring or a bracelet. Her dress must actually be velvet or brocade; at the very most I should allow her to come down to satin. I should rather ruffle a silk dress than a cloth dress, and make pearls or feathers fall from someone's hair rather than real flowers or a simple bow; I know that the lining of the cloth skirt is often quite as appetizing as the lining of a silk skirt; but I still prefer the silk skirt. And so I have given myself many queens and empresses, many princesses, many sultanas, many famous courtesans as my mistresses in my dreams, but never middle-class women or shepherdesses and, in my wildest moments of desire, I have never seduced anyone on a lawn or in a bed with serge hangings. Beauty is to me a diamond which must be mounted and set in gold. I cannot conceive a beautiful woman without a carriage, horses, lackeys and everything that you have with a hundred thousand francs a year; there is a harmony between beauty and wealth. One demands the other: a pretty foot demands a pretty shoe, a pretty shoe demands carpets and a carriage, and all that follows. A beautiful woman with poor clothes in a sordid house is, to me, the most painful sight that you could see, and I couldn't feel any love for her. Only the beautiful and the rich can be amorous without being ludicrous or pitiful. At this rate, there are few who would have the right to be amorous; I myself would be the first to be excluded. However, that is my opinion.

It will be in the evening that we meet each other for the first time. There will be a beautiful sunset; the sky will have those tones of orange, bright yellow and pale green that you see in certain pictures by the old masters; there will be a great avenue of chestnut-trees in flower or of secular elms with many branches – fine trees of a fresh and melancholy green, shadows full of mystery and dampness. Here and there a few statues, a few marble vases of snowy whiteness will stand out against the green background, there will be a stretch of water where the familiar swan disports itself; and in the distance there will be a castle of brick and stone as in the days of Henri IV, a pointed slate roof, high chimneystacks, weathercocks on all the gables, tall narrow windows. At one of these windows, leaning in melancholy on the balcony, will be the queen of my soul in the attire which I described a moment ago; behind her will be a little Negro holding her fan and her parakeet. Nothing is missing, as you see, and it is all absolutely absurd. The beautiful woman drops her glove; I retrieve it, kiss it and bring it back. The conversation begins. I show all the wit that I don't possess; I say delightful things; she replies with others, I answer, it's a firework display, a luminous rain of dazzling words. In short, I am adorable – and I am adored. Then it is time for supper. I am invited, and I accept. What a supper, my dear friend, and what a feast in my imagination! The wine laughs in the glasses, the fair and gilded pheasant steams in the emblazoned dish; the banquet goes on well into the night, and, as you can imagine, it doesn't end at home. Don't you think that that's well imagined? Nothing in the world is simpler; indeed, it is astonishing that it hasn't happened ten times rather than once.

Sometimes it's in a big forest. The hunt is passing; the horn is blown, the pack barks and rushes across the path with lightning speed. The beautiful Amazon is riding an Arab steed, as white as milk, as spirited and lively as can be. She is an excellent horsewoman, but it is restless, it caracoles and rears, it takes the bit between its teeth and makes straight for a precipice. I arrive there, as if from heaven, and hold back the horse, I take the swooning princess in my arms, I restore her to consciousness and take her back to her castle. What well-born woman would refuse her heart to a man who had risked his life for her sake? No woman would do so. And gratitude is a crossroad which very soon leads to love.

You will at least agree that when I embark upon romance, I am not half-hearted, and I am as mad as anyone can be. It's always so, for nothing in the world is more unpleasant than reasonable madness. You will also agree that, when I write letters, they are volumes rather than simple notes. In all things I prefer the excessive. That is why I love you. Don't laugh too much at the nonsense I have scribbled to you. I am setting down my pen to put it into action; for

I always come back to my refrain: I want to have a mistress. I don't know whether it will be the lady in the park or the beautiful woman on the balcony, but I bid you farewell, and set off on my quest. My resolution is made. Were she whom I seek to hide herself in the depths of the kingdom of Cathay or of Samarkand, I should discover her. I shall let you know if my enterprise succeeds or fails. I hope it will succeed. Wish me well, my dear fellow. I shall now put on my best clothes and set out. I am quite determined only to return with my ideal mistress. I have dreamed enough; now it is time for action.

PS. Do send me news of young D—; what has become of him? No one knows anything here; and give my compliments to your worthy brother and to all your family.

II

WELL, my friend, I am home again, and I haven't been to Cathay, or to Samarkand; but it is fair to say that I lack a mistress as much as ever. Yet I had taken myself in hand, and vowed my great vow that I should go to the end of the world. I haven't even been to the end of the town. I don't know how I manage it, I have never been able to keep my word to anyone, not even to myself. The devil must have a hand in it. If I say: I'll go there tomorrow, I am certain to stay; if I decide to go to the tavern, I shall go to church; if I want to go to church, the paths become entangled beneath my feet like skeins of thread, and I find myself somewhere quite different. I fast when I have decided to have an orgy, and so on. And so I believe that what prevents me from having a mistress is that I have determined to have one.

I must tell you every detail of my expedition, for it deserves the honour of narration. That day I spent two whole hours dressing. I had had my hair combed and curled, I waxed and turned up what moustaches I have, and, since the emotion of desire slightly coloured the customary pallor of my face, I really wasn't too bad. At last, when I had carefully considered myself in the mirror in different lights, to see if I was handsome enough and if I looked gallant enough, I went resolutely out of the house with my head held high, my chin up and my glance direct, and one hand on my hip, making the heels of my boots ring out like a lance-corporal, jostling the bourgeois and looking absolutely victorious and triumphant.

I was like another Jason going to conquer his Golden Fleece. But, alas! Jason was more fortunate than I. Apart from the Fleece, he also conquered a beautiful princess, and I had neither princess nor fleece.

Off I went, then, through the streets, observing all the women, and running up to look at them at close quarters when they seemed to me to deserve examination. Some of them assumed their look of unassailable virtue, and passed by without raising their eyes. Others were at first astonished, then smiled if they had nice teeth. Some turned round after a while to look at me when they thought that I wasn't looking at them any more, and blushed like cherries when they found themselves face to face with me. It was a fine day; there were crowds of people walking out. And yet, for all the respect I have for that interesting half of the human race, I must confess that what we have agreed to call the fair sex is devilishly ugly; out of a hundred women, hardly one was passable. One woman had a moustache; another had a blue nose; others had red patches instead of eyebrows; one had a good figure, but she had a blotchy face. Another had a charming face, but she could scratch her ear with her shoulder; a third would have shamed Praxiteles by the roundness and plumpness of certain contours, but she skated along on feet like Turkish stirrups. Another displayed the most magnificent shoulders one could see, but in shape and size her hands recalled those enormous scarlet gloves which are used as signs for mercers' shops. How tired most of these faces were! How withered, etiolated, ignobly worn by envy, spiteful curiosity, avidity, outrageous coquetry! And how much uglier a woman is if she is not beautiful than a man if he is not handsome!

I didn't see anything good – except for a few working girls of little virtue; but there is more cloth to rumple there than silk, and that isn't for me. I really believe that man, and by man I also mean woman, is the most unsightly animal on earth. This quadruped which walks on its hind legs seems to me to be singularly presumptuous to accord itself the first rank in creation. A lion and a tiger are more beautiful than man, and many of their species possess all the beauty due to them. That is extremely rare among men. How many miserable specimens for one Antinous! How many Goths for a Philis!

I am very afraid, my dear friend, that I shall never be able to embrace my ideal, and yet it is not extravagant or unnatural. It is not the ideal of a third-form schoolboy; I don't ask for globes of ivory, or columns of alabaster, or for traceries of blue; I haven't made it of lilies or snow, or roses, or jet, or ebony, or coral, or ambrosia, or pearls, or diamonds; I have left the stars in the firmament in peace, and I haven't taken the sun down out of season. It is an almost bourgeois ideal, it is so simple, and it seems to me that with a sack or two of piastres I should find it exactly realized in the first bazaar in Constantinople or Smyrna; it would probably cost me less than a horse or a thoroughbred dog. And to think that I shan't attain it, for I feel I shan't attain it! It's enough to drive me mad, and it sends me into enormous rages against my fate.

As for you, you aren't as mad as I am; you've gone along quite happily with life, you haven't tormented yourself trying to shape it, you have taken things as they came. You didn't seek for happiness, and it came to seek you; you are loved, and you love. I don't envy you; at least don't believe that of me. But I find myself less happy than I should be when I think of your felicity, and I reflect, with a sigh, that I should like to enjoy such felicity myself.

Perhaps my happiness has passed me by, and I did not see it, blind that I was; perhaps the voice has spoken to me, and the storms within me prevented my hearing it.

Perhaps I have been obscurely loved by some humble heart which I misunderstood or broke; perhaps I myself was the ideal of somebody else, the pole of a suffering soul, the dream of a night and the thought of a day. If I had looked at my feet, perhaps I should have seen some beautiful Magdalen with her urn of perfumes and her sombre hair. I went about raising my arms to heaven, longing to gather the stars that escaped me, disdaining to pick the little daisy which opened its golden heart to me in the dewy grass. I have made a great mistake; I have asked love for something other than love, and for something that it could not give. I have forgotten that love was naked, I have failed to understand the meaning of that magnificent symbol. I have asked it only for robes of brocade, for feathers, diamonds, sublime intelligence, knowledge, poetry, beauty, youth, supreme power – everything that it is not; love can offer only itself, and he who wants to draw something else from it does not deserve to be loved.

No doubt I have hastened too much. My hour has not come. God Who has given me life will not take it back from me before I have lived. What use is it to give the poet a lyre without strings, or to give man a life without love? God cannot commit such a thoughtless act; and no doubt, when the moment comes, He will set on my path the woman I should love, and the woman who should love me. But why has love come to me before the mistress? Why am I thirsty without a fountain where I can quench my thirst? Or why can't I fly, like those birds of the desert, to the place where water is to be found? The world is to me a Sahara without wells, without date-palms. I have no single shady corner in my life where I can take shelter from the sun; I suffer all the ardours of passion and I do not have the ecstasies and ineffable delights; I know the torments, and have not the pleasures. I am jealous of something that does not exist; I am troubled by the shade of a shade; I utter sighs without reason. I have sleepless nights, and no adored phantom comes to make them beautiful. I shed tears, and they fall upon the ground, and there is none who wipes them away. I give my kisses to the wind, they are not returned to me; I tire my eyes in trying to discern in the distance some uncertain and deceiving form; I await something which will not come, and I count the hours with anxiety, as if I had a rendezvous.

Whomsoever thou be, angel or demon, virgin or courtesan, shepherdess or princess, whether thou comest from north or south, thou whom I know not, thou whom I love! Oh, do not let thyself be awaited any longer, or the flame will burn the altar, and thou wilt find in place of my heart only a pile of ashes grown cold. Come down from the sphere where thou art; leave the crystal sky, consoling spirit, come and cast across my soul the shadow of your great wings. Come thou, woman whom I shall love, that I may close around thee my arms which have been open for so long. Golden gates of the palace she dwells in, open wide; humble latch of her little room, arise; branches of the forest trees, briars of the paths, untangle yourselves; spells of the turret, charms of the magicians, be broken; open, ranks of the crowd, and let her pass.

If thou comest too late, oh my ideal! I shall no longer have the strength to love thee. My soul is like a dovecot full of doves. At every hour of the day, some desire or other flies away. The doves return to the dovecot, but the desires do not ever return to the heart. The blue of the sky grows white with their innumerable swarms; they fly off through space, from world to world, from heaven to heaven, seeking some or other love to settle there and spend the night there. Hasten, my dream! or thou wilt find nothing in the next but the shells of the birds which have flown.

My friend, my childhood companion, you are the only one to whom I can tell such things. Write and say that you commiserate with me, and that you don't find me a hypochondriac; console me, I have never needed consolation so much. How enviable they are, the people who have a passion that they can satisfy! The drunkard doesn't find cruelty in any bottle; he falls from the tavern into the gutter, and he is happier on his dunghill than a king on his throne. The sensual man goes to courtesans to find easy loves, or immodest refinements: a painted cheek, a short skirt, a bare breast, or licentious talk, and he is happy; his eyes turn pale, his lips grow moist; he feels the utmost intensity of happiness, the ecstasy of crude sensual pleasure. The gambler only needs a green cloth and a worn and greasy pack of cards to procure the poignant agonies, the nervous spasms, the diabolical pleasures of his horrible passion. These people can be satisfied or diverted; but, for me, it is impossible.

This idea has so taken possession of me that I hardly care for the arts any more, and poetry no longer has any charm for me. Things which once enchanted me no longer make the least impression on me.

I am beginning to believe that I am wrong. I am asking nature and mankind for more than they can give. What I am seeking doesn't even exist, and I shouldn't complain because I don't find it. And yet, if the woman I dream of is outside the bounds of human nature, how is it that I love only her and not the rest, how is it that my instinct leads me there invincibly? Who has given me the idea of this imaginary woman? Of what clay have I modelled this unseen statue? Where have I found the feathers which I have attached to the shoulders of this chimera? What mystic bird has laid in some dim corner of my soul the unnoticed egg from which my dream has been hatched? What, then, is this abstract beauty that I feel, and cannot define? Why, in the presence of a woman who is often charming, do I sometimes say that she is beautiful – even though I still find her very ugly? Where then is the model, the type, the inner pattern which serves me as my point of comparison? For beauty is not an absolute idea, it can only be appreciated by contrast. Is it in heaven that I have seen her – in a star? Or is it at a ball, in the shadow of her mother, the fresh bud of an overblown rose? Is it in Italy or Spain? Is it here or far away, yesterday or long ago? Was it the idolized courtesan, the fashionable singer, the prince's daughter? Was it a proud and noble head weighed down by a heavy diadem of pearls and rubies? Was it a young and childlike face leaning out between the nasturtiums and convolvuluses on the window-sill? What school did it belong to, the picture in which this beauty stood out white and radiant against the sombre shadows? Was it Raphael who caressed the contour which delights you? Was it Cleomenes who polished the marble which you adore? Are you in love with a madonna or a Diana? Is your ideal an angel, a sylph or a woman?

Alas, it has a little of all of these, and it is something different.

This transparency of tone, this delectable and radiant freshness, this flesh in which there courses so much blood and so much life, this fine fair hair unfurling like a golden cloak, this sparkling laugh, these amorous dimples, these figures undulating like flames, this strength, this suppleness, these gleams of satin, these well-filled contours, these plump arms and smooth, fleshy backs: all this good health belongs to Rubens. Raphael alone could have filled so chaste an outline with this pale amber hue. Who else curls those long lashes, so fine and black, who else unravels the fringes of those eyelids so modestly lowered? Do you believe that Allegri has no part in your ideal? It is from him that the lady of your thoughts has stolen this matt warm whiteness which delights you. She paused in front of his canvases for a very long time to surprise the secret of that angelic and ever radiant smile; she has modelled the oval of her face on the oval of a nymph or saint. That undulating and voluptuous line of the hip is taken from the sleeping Antiope. These plump and delicate hands may be reclaimed by Danae or Mary Magdalen. Dusty antiquity itself has furnished much material for the composition of your young dream; these strong and supple loins which you embrace with so much passion have been sculpted by Praxiteles. This goddess specially allowed the very tip of her charming foot to emerge from the ashes of Herculaneum so that your idol should not be lame. Nature, too, has played her part. Here and there, through the prism of desire, you have seen a pair of fine eyes behind a Venetian blind, an ivory brow pressed against a window-pane, a smiling mouth behind a fan. You have guessed an arm from a hand, a knee from an ankle. What you saw was perfect; you imagined the rest accordingly, and completed it with beautiful details taken from elsewhere. Even the ideal beauty realized by the artists was not enough for you, and you went and asked the poets for more rounded contours, more ethereal forms, more heavenly graces, more exquisite refinements; you asked them to give your phantom breath and speech, all their love, all their daydreams, all their joy and sadness, their melancholy and their morbidezza, all their memories and all their hopes, their knowledge and their passion, their wit and their heart; you took all that from them, and added, to crown the impossible, your own passion and wit, your own dream and your own thoughts. The star bestowed its brightness, the flower its scent, the palette gave its colour, the poet his harmony, the marble gave its shape, and you your desire. How could a real woman, who eats and drinks, gets up in the morning and goes to bed at night, however adorable and however composed of the graces she may be, how can she bear comparison with such a creature? You cannot reasonably hope for it, and yet you hope for it, and you seek. What singular blindness! It is sublime if it is not absurd. How I pity and admire those who pursue the reality of their dream through everything, and who die content if they have once kissed their dream upon the lips! But it is a fearful fate, the fate of the Columbus who has not discovered his world, and of the lover who has not found his mistress!

Oh, if I were a poet, I should always sing of those whose existence had been a failure; whose arrows had missed their mark, who had died without pronouncing the word that they had to speak, without pressing the hand which was destined for them. I should consecrate my songs to everything which has failed, and to everything which has passed unseen: to the smothered fire, the genius without expression, the pearl unknown in the depths of the seas, to everyone who has loved without being loved, to everyone who has suffered and not been pitied. It would be a noble task.

How right Plato was to want to banish you from his republic, and what harm you have done to us, you poets! How much more bitter it is, our absinthe, after your ambrosia! How much more arid and desolate our life once we had gazed deep into the prospects of infinity which you opened to us! What a terrible struggle we have had with our realities, after your dreams! And how our heart was trampled on and crushed by those rough athletes during the fight!

We have sat like Adam beneath the walls of paradise, on the steps of the staircase which leads to the world which you have created, and through the chinks in the gate we have seen the sparkle of a light which is brighter than the sun, and heard, confusedly, the occasional notes of some seraphic harmony. Whenever one of the elect enters or comes out in a burst of splendour, we crane our necks to see something through the open gate. The architecture is fairylike, and it has no equal except in the Arabian Nights. Piles of columns, and arcades one upon the other, pillars twisted into spirals, foliage marvellously carved, cut-out trefoils, porphyry, jasper, lapis lazuli, what else? Dazzling transparencies and reflections, profusions of strange precious stones, sardonyx, chrysoberyls, aquamarines, iridescent opals, azerodach, jets of crystal, torches to make the stars turn pale, a wondrous mist full of sound and frenzy, a quite Assyrian magnificence!

The gate shuts once again, and you see nothing any more; and your eyes, full of burning tears, look down at this poor, pale, barren earth, on these ruined hovels, these people in rags, on your soul, an arid rock where nothing grows, on all the miseries and misfortunes of reality. Oh, if we could only fly that far, if the steps of this staircase of fire did not burn our feet! But, alas, Jacob's ladder can only be climbed by the angels!

What a fate is that of the poor man at the rich man's gate! What outrageous irony, a palace opposite a shack, the ideal face to face with reality, poetry opposed to prose! What rooted hatred must twist the knots deep in the poor man's heart! What gnashings of teeth must echo at night on his truckle-bed, while the wind brings to his very ears the sighs of the theorbos and violas of love! Poets, painters, sculptors, musicians, why have you lied to us? Poets, why have you told us your dreams? Painters, why have you fixed on canvas this imperceptible phantom which rose up from your heart to your head with your flowing blood, and said to us: 'This is a woman'? Sculptors, why have you drawn the marble from the depths of Carrara to make it explain eternally, in the eyes of all the world, your most secret and most fugitive desire? Musicians, why have you listened, at night, to the song of the stars and flowers, why have you set it down? Why have you written such lovely songs that the sweetest voice which says to us 'I love you!' seems to us as raucous as the grating of a saw or the croak of a raven? A curse on you, impostors! And may the fire of heaven burn and destroy all the pictures, poems and statues, and all the scores ... Phew! that was an interminable tirade, and rather unepistolary in style. What a rigmarole!

I have waxed lyrical with a vengeance, my very dear friend, and I've already Pindarized rather stupidly for a long time. It's all a very long way from our subject, which is, if I remember rightly, the glorious and triumphant story of the Chevalier d'Albert in pursuit of Daraïde, the most beautiful princess in the world, as the old romances say. But to tell the truth, the story is so poor that I am obliged to have recourse to digressions and reflections. I hope it won't always be so, and I hope that the story of my life will soon be more complex and more intricate than a Spanish imbroglio.

After I had wandered from street to street, I decided to go in search of a friend. He was to introduce me to a house where, so he said, one saw a multitude of pretty women, a crowd of flesh-and-blood ideals, enough to satisfy a score of poets. There are some for every taste: noble beauties with the looks of eagles, sea-green eyes, straight noses, chins proudly lifted up, royal hands, and the bearing of goddesses: silver lilies set on golden stems. There are simple violets with pale colours, gentle perfume, moist and lowered eyes, frail necks and diaphanous flesh; there are lively, piquant beauties, there are precious beauties, indeed there are beauties in every style. For it is a real seraglio, that house – except for the eunuchs and the kislar aga. My friend says that he has already had five or six passions, all the same; that seems to me absolutely prodigious, and I'm much afraid that I shan't be so successful; de C— says I shall, and that I shall soon be more successful than I'd like. According to him, I have only one fault, and that will be corrected with age and experience: I set too much value on the woman, and not enough on women. There might well be some truth in that. He says that I shall be perfectly amiable when I have got out of this little habit. God grant it will be so! Women will have to feel that I disdain them; for a compliment which they would find delightful and utterly charming from someone else, angers and displeases them when it comes from me, as if it were the most cutting epigram. That is probably because of what C— reproaches me with.

My heart was beating a little as I went up the stairs, and I had scarcely recovered from my emotion when de C— took me by the elbow and set me face to face with a woman some thirty years old – rather beautiful – with a rich but quiet dress, and an extreme affectation of childish simplicity. This did not prevent her from being veneered with red like a carriage-wheel. It was the lady of the house.

De C— put on that shrill and sneering voice – so different from his usual voice – which he uses when he plays the social charmer, and, with many demonstrations of ironic respect, through which there clearly showed the most profound contempt, he said to her, half aloud and half in a whisper:

'This is the young man I was telling you about the other day, a man of most exceptional merit; he couldn't be better born, and I think it can only please you to receive him. That is why I have taken the liberty to present him to you.'

'You have certainly done well, monsieur,' replied the lady, simpering in the most excessive manner. Then she turned towards me, and, having summed me up, out of the corner of her eye, like a skilful judge, in a way which made me blush to the roots of my hair, she said to me: 'You may consider yourself as invited once and for all. Come whenever you have an evening to spare.'

I bowed rather awkwardly, and stammered some incoherent words which could hardly have given her a high idea of my abilities; other people arrived, which freed me from the tedium one feels at any introduction. De C— drew me into the embrasure of a window, and began to lecture me with a vengeance.

'What the devil! You're going to compromise me! I've heralded you as a phoenix of wit, a man with a wild imagination, a lyric poet, everything most transcendent and most passionate, and you stand there, like a blockhead, and never utter a word! What a poor imagination! I thought you were more inventive! Come on, now, let your tongue loose, and chatter away about everything; you don't need to be sensible and judicious, in fact that might do you harm. Just talk, that's the essential. Talk a lot, and talk for a long while. Attract attention to yourself. Forget all your fear and modesty, and get this firmly into your head, that everyone here is an idiot, more or less, and remember that an orator who wants to succeed can't have enough contempt for his audience. What do you think of the mistress of the house?'

'I think her very unpleasant already. I hardly spoke to her for three minutes, but I was as bored as if I'd been her husband.'

'Ah, so that's what you think?'

'Yes, it is.'

'Is your repugnance quite insuperable? That's a pity. It would have been civil for you to have had her, even for a month. That is good style, and she is the only one who can launch a young man of some standing in society.'

'Well, I'll have her, since I must,' I answered, with a rather pitiful air. 'But is that as necessary as you seem to think?'

'Yes, alas, it's absolutely indispensable, and I'll tell you why. Madame de Thémines is in fashion, now; she has all the absurdities of the day in a superior manner, sometimes tomorrow's, but never yesterday's. She is perfectly up to date. People will wear what she is wearing, and she doesn't wear things that have been worn already. She is also rich, and her carriages are in the best taste. She has no wit, but a good deal of jargon; she has very ardent likings and little passion. People please her, but they do not touch her; she is cold at heart and she has a libertine head. As for her soul, if she has one, which is doubtful, it is as black as it can be, and there is no malice or base action of which she is incapable; but she is extremely skilful and keeps up appearances just as much as she needs so that nothing can be proved against her. And so she will readily sleep with a man but won't write him the simplest note. And so her closest enemies find nothing to say about her, except that she puts on her rouge too high up, and that certain parts of her person are not really as rounded as they might appear – which is untrue.'

'How do you know?'

'An excellent question. In the way one knows this sort of thing, by making sure of it for myself.'

'So you've had Madame de Thémines, too?'

'Of course! Why shouldn't I have had her? It would have been a gross breach of good manners if I hadn't had her. She has done me great services, and I'm very grateful to her.'

'I don't understand what sort of services she can have done you . . .'

'Are you really an idiot?' said de C—, and he looked at me with the most comical expression. 'My word, I'm very much afraid you are. Do I have to tell you everything, then? Madame de Thémines is said, and rightly, to have special understandings of certain points, and a young man whom she has taken and kept for a certain time may boldly present himself anywhere, and know that he will soon have an affair, and two affairs rather than one. Apart from this unspeakable advantage, there is another which is no less important. As soon as the women here see you as the regular lover of Madame de Thémines, even if they don't fancy you in the least, they will find it their pleasure and their duty to take you away from a fashionable woman like her. And, instead of the advances and overtures that you would have to make, you will only have the problem of choice, and you will of course become the target for all the wiles and enticements imaginable.

'However, if she inspires you with too much repugnance, don't have her. You aren't exactly obliged to do so, though it would have been civil and correct. But make a choice quickly and attack the one who pleases you best or seems to offer the most facilities, for if you hesitate you will lose the benefit of novelty and the few days' advantage it gives you over all the gentlemen here. None of these ladies understands anything about those passions which are born in intimacy and develop slowly in respect and silence. They are for the *coup de foudre* and the occult sympathies; something wonderfully well conceived to spare the tedium of resistance, all those delays and repetitions which sentiment mingles with the tale of love: delays and repetitions which just defer the conclusion to no purpose. These ladies are very careful with their time, and it seems so precious to them that they would be in despair if a single minute went unused. They want to oblige the human race – a wish that could not be too highly praised – and they love their neighbours as themselves, which is perfectly evangelical and meritorious. They are very charitable creatures, and they wouldn't want to make a man die of despair for anything in the world.

'There must already be three or four who are *struck* with you, and I should advise you as a friend to press the point strongly in that direction, and not amuse yourself by chatting with me in the embrasure of a window. That won't get you very far.'

'But, my dear C—, I am absolutely new to these things. I don't have the social experience to distinguish at first glance a woman who is struck from one who isn't struck at all; and I might make some surprising errors, if you didn't help me.'

'You're really a savage without a name. I didn't think anyone could be so pastoral and bucolic in the blessed century we live in! What the devil are you doing with those big dark eyes of yours? They would have the most vanquishing effect, if you knew how to use them. Just look over there, in that corner near the mantelpiece, at that little woman in pink who is toying with her fan. She has had her eye on you for a quarter of an hour with an assiduity and fixity which are quite significant; she is the only woman in the world who is indecent in so superior a manner, and displays such noble effrontery. She much displeases the women, for they despair of ever reaching that height of impudence; however, she greatly pleases the men, who find in her all the piquancy of a courtesan. It is true that she is delightfully depraved, full of wit, verve and sudden fancies. She is an excellent mistress for a young man with prejudices. In a week she rids you of all conscience and scruples, and she so corrupts your heart that you are never ridiculous or elegiac. She has inexpressibly realistic ideas about everything; she goes to the bottom of things with a speed and sureness which astonish you. She is algebra incarnate, that little woman; she is just the thing for a dreamer and enthusiast. She will soon have corrected you of your vaporous idealism; that is a great service which she will do you. Moreover, she will do it with the greatest pleasure, for her instinct is to disenchant the poets.'

My curiosity was roused by de C—'s description. I left my retreat, and, slipping through the groups of people, I approached the lady and observed her most attentively. She could have been twenty-five or twenty-six. She was small, but she had quite a good figure, though it was a little on the plump side; she had plump white arms, rather aristocratic hands, pretty feet – indeed, they were too dainty – and fat and glossy shoulders, and a small bosom, but what there was was very satisfactory and didn't give a bad idea of the rest; as for her hair, it was extremely shiny and blue-black like a jay's wings. The corners of her eyes were turned up quite high towards the temples, her nose was thin and her nostrils very wide, her mouth was humid and sensual, with a slight division on the lower lip, and an almost imperceptible down on each side. And in all of this there was a life, an animation, a strength, an indescribable expression of lust adroitly tempered by coquetry and intrigue, which made her in short most desirable and more than justified the very ardent fancies which she had inspired, and inspired every day.

I desired her; but I understood, all the same, that, however agreeable she might be, she would not be the woman who would realize my wish and make me say: 'At last I have a mistress!'

I came back to de C—, and said to him: 'The lady quite pleases me, and I may come to an agreement with her. But, before I say anything precise which will commit me, would you kindly show me the indulgent beauties who have been good enough to be struck by me? Then I can choose. You would also please me, since you are my mentor here, if you added a little account of them and a list of their faults and virtues, how one should attack them and the tone which one should employ. I don't want to seem too much of a provincial or a man of letters.'

'Very well,' said de C—. 'Do you see that fine melancholy swan which unfolds its neck so harmoniously and moves its sleeves like wings? It is modesty itself, all that is most chaste and most virginal; it is a snowy brow, a heart of ice, the glances of a madonna, the smile of Agnes. She has a white dress and a soul to match; she wears nothing in her hair but orange-flowers or waterlily leaves, and she only holds to the earth by a thread. She has never had an evil thought, and she is profoundly ignorant of the difference between a man and a woman. The Blessed Virgin is a bacchante in comparison. None of this prevents her from having had more lovers than any woman I know, and that is certainly not saying a little. Just take a quick look at the bosom of that decorous lady; it is a little masterpiece, and really it is difficult to reveal so much by hiding more; tell me if, with all her restraint and all her prudery, she is not ten times more indecent than the good lady who is on her left and bravely displaying her two hemispheres which, if they were united, would form a map of the world of actual size? Or that other lady on her right, who has a dress cut down to her stomach and parades her nothingness with enchanting intrepidity? If I am not very much mistaken, that virginal creature has already reckoned in her head what promises of love and passion are contained in your pallor and your black eyes; and what makes me say that is that she hasn't once looked in your direction, at least in appearance; for she ogles you so artfully, and glances so adroitly out of the corner of her eyes, that nothing escapes her; you would think that she had eyes in the back of her head, for she knows exactly what is happening behind her. She is a female Janus. If you want to succeed with her, you must forget your casual and victorious manners. You must speak to her without looking at her, without making a movement, in an attitude of contrition, and in a hushed and respectful tone of voice; in this way, you will be able to tell her everything you want, provided that it is suitably veiled, and she will allow you the greatest liberties at first in words, and then in action. Just be careful to gaze at her tenderly when her eyes are lowered, and speak to her of the sweetness of Platonic love and the commerce of souls, while you are making the least Platonic and least idealistic gestures in the world! She is very sensual and very susceptible; kiss her as much as you like; but, in the most intimate abandon, do not forget to call her *madame* at least three times a sentence. She quarrelled with me because, when I was in bed with her, I said something or other to her and used the intimate form of address. Hang it, one isn't an honest woman for nothing.'

'After what you've said, I have no great wish to risk the adventure. A prudish Messalina! It's a new and monstrous combination.'

'As old as the world, my dear fellow! You see it every day, and nothing is more common. You're wrong not to settle for that one. She has a great accomplishment, which is that with her you always seem to be committing a mortal sin, and the slightest kiss seems absolutely damnable; while with the others you hardly think you're committing a venial sin, and often you don't even think that you're doing anything at all. That is the reason why I kept her longer than any mistress. I should still have her, if she hadn't left me herself; she is the only woman who has forestalled me, and so I have a certain respect for her. She has little refinements of sensuality which are the most delicate in the world, and she has the great art of appearing to make you extort what in fact she grants very freely. This gives every one of her favours the charm of a rape. You will find ten of her lovers who will swear to you on their honour that she's the most virtuous creature in existence. She is precisely the contrary. It is interesting to examine that virtue on a pillow. Now you've been warned, you run no risk, and you won't make the blunder of falling genuinely in love with her.'

'How old is that adorable person?' I asked de C—, for I could not possibly decide, though I studied her with the most scrupulous attention.

'Ah, that's the question! How old is she? That's the mystery, and God alone knows the answer. Personally I pride myself on assigning women their age to within a minute. I've never been able to discover hers. I can only estimate, approximately, that she must be between eighteen and thirty-six. I have seen her in full dress, undressed, and in her petticoats, and I can't tell you anything about it. I just don't know. The age she seems to be most is eighteen, but that can't be her age. She has a virgin's body and a prostitute's soul, and you need a great deal of time or genius to corrupt yourself so deeply and speciously. You need a heart of bronze in a breast of steel. She has neither one nor the other; so I think she is thirty-six, but really I know nothing about it.'

'Hasn't she any close woman friend who could enlighten you?'

'No. She arrived in this town two years ago. She came from the provinces or from abroad, I can't remember which. It's a wonderful position for a woman who can take advantage of it. With a figure like hers, she can give herself whatever age she wants, and only date from the day she arrived here.'

'That is very agreeable indeed, especially when no impertinent wrinkle belies you, and time, the great destroyer, is kind enough to help you falsify the birth certificate.'

He showed me one or two other women, who according to him, would favour all the requests I chose to make them, and treat me with quite unusual philanthropy. But the woman in pink by the corner of the mantelpiece and the modest dove who served as her antithesis were incomparably better than all the rest; and, if they did not have all the qualities that I require, they had some of them, at least in appearance.

I talked to them all the evening, especially to the latter, and I took care to cast my ideas in the most respectful mould; although she hardly looked at me, I thought I sometimes saw her pupils gleaming through their curtain of lashes, and at certain gallantries – somewhat audacious, but clad in the most delicate gauze – there passed just underneath her skin the slightest blush, restrained and repressed, rather like the blush produced by a pink liqueur poured into a half opaque goblet. Her answers, in general, were sober, considered, but still sharp and full of wit, and they suggested much more than they expressed. They were all intermingled with reservations, hints, oblique allusions, every syllable had its meaning, every silence its significance; there was nothing in the world more diplomatic and charming. And yet, whatever momentary pleasure I took in it, I could not bear such a conversation for long. You have to be perpetually awake and on your guard, and what I like best in a talk are freshness and familiarity. We talked at first about music, which led us quite naturally to talk about the Opéra, and then about women, then about love, the subject in which it is easiest to find transitions to pass from the general to the particular. We outdid one another with our *dear hearts*; you would have laughed to listen to me. Amadis de Gaule was just a vulgar fellow in comparison. There were generosities, abnegations, devotions to make that deceased Roman, Curtius, blush with shame. I really didn't believe I was capable of such transcendent gibberish and pathos. Think of me, doing the most quintessential Platonism, doesn't it seem to you one of the most farcical things, the most comical scenes that you could imagine? And then that perfect pious manner, those little sanctimonious and hypocritical ways that I put on! Can such things be? I didn't seem to touch on it, and any mother who had heard my arguments would at once have let me sleep with her daughter, any husband would have trusted his wife to me. It is the evening in my life when I appeared to be most virtuous, and when I behaved with the least virtue. I thought that it would have been more difficult to be a hypocrite and say things that one didn't believe at all. It must be quite easy, or I must have the most remarkable aptitude to have succeeded so well at the first attempt. In fact I had some very fine moments.

As for the lady, she made many highly specific remarks, which, despite the air of candour she assumed, proved the most consummate experience; you cannot imagine the subtlety of her distinctions. That woman would cut a hair in three lengthwise, and she would have all the angelic and seraphic doctors nonplussed. For the rest, from the way in which she speaks, it is impossible to believe that she has even the shadow of a body. It is so immaterial, vaporous and ideal that it confounds you; and, if de C— had not warned me of the creature's behaviour, I should certainly have despaired of my success, and I should have kept miserably aloof. And when a woman tells you, for two hours, in the most dispassionate tone in the world, that love lives only on privations and sacrifices and other noble things of this kind, how the devil can one decently hope to persuade her one day to put herself between two sheets with you, to excite your natural instincts and see if you are both made the same way?

In short, we parted from each other very good friends, congratulating one another on the elevation and the purity of our emotions.

The conversation with the other woman was, as you may imagine, quite different. We laughed as much as we spoke. We laughed, and very wittily, at all the women present; when I say 'We laughed, and very wittily,' I am wrong: I ought to say 'She laughed'; a man never really laughs at a woman. As for me, I listened and approved, for it was impossible to sketch a sharper feature, or to colour it more ardently; it was the most remarkable gallery of caricatures that I had ever seen. Despite the exaggeration, one felt the underlying truth; de C— was quite right: this woman's mission is to disenchant poets. There is a prosaic atmosphere around her in which a poetic idea cannot live. She is delightful and sparkling with wit, and yet, in her presence, one only thinks of ignoble and vulgar things; while I was speaking to her, I had countless wishes, which were incongruous and impracticable where I was, such as to have myself brought some wine, and to get drunk, to sit her on one of my knees and kiss her breasts, to lift up the edge of her skirt and see if her garter was above or below her knee, to sing a ribald song at the top of my voice, to smoke a pipe or smash the window-panes. Lord knows what else. All the animal part of me, all the brute was roused. I should very willingly have spat on Homer's *Iliad*, and I should have gone down on my knees before a ham. I now absolutely understand the allegory of Ulysses' companions, whom Circe changed into swine. Circe was probably a fast woman like my little woman in pink.

It is a shameful thing to say, but I was quite delighted to feel my-self won over by brutishness; I didn't resist it. I encouraged it as hard as I could, corruption is so natural to man, and there is so much mud in the clay of which he is made.

And yet for a moment I was afraid of the gangrene which was spreading through me, and I wanted to leave the corruptress; but the floor seemed to have risen up as far as my knees, and I was as it were set in my place.

In the end I took it upon myself to leave her, and, since the evening was well advanced, I went home most perplexed and troubled, and rather unsure of what I should do. I hesitated between the prude and the flirt. One was voluptuous and the other had zest. And after a self-examination which was very thorough and very deep, I realized not that I loved both of them, but that I desired both of them, the one as much as the other. I did so ardently enough to become dreamy and preoccupied.

According to all appearances, my friend, I shall have one of these two women, perhaps I shall have them both, and yet I must confess to you that their possession would only half satisfy me; it isn't that they aren't very pretty, but nothing cried out in me at the sight of them, nothing trembled, nothing said: These are they. I didn't recognize them. And yet I don't believe that I shall find very much better among those who are beautiful and of noble birth, and de C— advises me to be content with them. I shall certainly be so, and one or the other will be my mistress, or the devil will soon take me; but, in the depths of my heart, a secret voice reproaches me for being unfaithful to my love, for stopping like this at the first smile of a woman I don't love in the least. I should instead seek tirelessly throughout the world, in cloisters and in brothels, in palaces and inns, for the woman who was made for me, for the woman whom God destines for me, princess or servant, nun or courtesan.

Then I say to myself that I'm building castles in the air, that it's all the same in any case whether I sleep with this woman or another, with all or with none; that the earth will not deviate by a fraction from its course, that the four seasons won't reverse their order for that. Nothing in the world matters less, and it is very good of me to torment myself with such nonsense. That is what I say to myself. But, whatever I say, I am not more tranquil or more resolved.

This is perhaps because I live very much alone, and, in a life as monotonous as mine, the smallest details assume too much importance. I fuss too much about living and thinking; I hear the beating of my arteries, the pulsations of my heart; I pay such attention to my most imperceptible ideas that I take them out of the cloudy mist in which they were floating, and I give them body. If I were more active, I shouldn't notice all these little things, and I shouldn't have time to examine my soul under a microscope, as I do all day. The sound of action would dispel all the swarm of lazy thoughts which flutter about in my head and dizzy me with the buzzing of their wings; instead of pursuing phantoms, I should combat realities; I should only ask women for what they can give – which is pleasure – and I shouldn't seek to embrace some fantastic ideal decked out with cloudy perfections. This desperate straining of my soul towards something unseen has distorted my vision. I cannot see reality, I have gazed so hard at something which does not exist, my eyes are so discerning for the ideal and so myopic for the world about me. And so I have known women whom everyone considers ravishing, who appear to me to be anything but that. I have much admired paintings which are generally considered bad, and bizarre or unintelligible poems have given me more pleasure than the most elegant productions. I shouldn't be surprised if after addressing so many sighs to the moon and gazing in the face of the stars, I didn't fall in love with some very low prostitute or some ugly old woman; it would be a fine fall. Perhaps reality may take this revenge since I have taken little trouble to pay court to her; wouldn't it serve me right if I were seized by a fine romantic passion for some slattern or abominable slut? Can you see me playing the guitar under a kitchen window and being supplanted by a scullion, or carrying the little mongrel of an old dowager, who is spitting out her last tooth? Perhaps, finding nothing in the world which deserves my love, I shall end up by adoring myself, like the late Narcissus of egotistic memory. As a guarantee against such misfortune, I look at myself in every mirror and in every stream that I encounter. To tell the truth, I have so many daydreams and aberrations, that I'm terribly afraid of degenerating into the monstrous and the unnatural. That is a serious matter, and one must be careful. Good-bye, my friend. I am setting off here and now for the pink lady, so as not to let myself drift into my usual contemplations. I don't think that we shall be much concerned with entelechy, and, if we do something, I am sure it will not be spiritual, although the creature herself has much spirit. I am carefully rolling up the pattern of my ideal mistress, and putting it away in a drawer, so as not to try it on this one. I want to enjoy her own beauties and qualities in peace. I want to leave her in a dress made to her own measure, and not try to adapt for her the clothing I have cut out in advance and in any event for the lady of my dreams. These are very wise resolutions, I don't know if I'll keep them. Once again, goodbye.

III

I AM the lover-in-chief of the pink lady; it's almost an official position, and that gives one standing in society. I no longer seem like a schoolboy seeking a conquest among the older women, a boy who doesn't dare say sweet nothings to a woman unless she is a hundred years old; I notice that, since I took up office, I am much more highly esteemed, that all the women speak to me with jealous coquetry, and they make great efforts to please me. The men, on the contrary, are colder to me, and there is something hostile and constrained in the few words which we exchange; they feel that in me they have a rival who is already formidable, and may become still more so. It has been reported to me that many of them bitterly criticized my style of dress, and said that my clothes were too effeminate, that my hair was more carefully brushed and curled than was proper; added to which, my beardless face made me look like a fop of the most ridiculous kind. They said that I affected rich and brilliant dress, with a touch of the theatre, and that I was more like an actor than a man: all the platitudes that people say to give themselves the right to be dirty and to wear cheap and ill-cut clothes. But all that only proves me innocent, and all the ladies think my hair the most beautiful hair in the world, and my elegance to be in the best taste, and they seem very much disposed to reward me for the trouble that I have taken for them, because they aren't foolish enough to believe that all this elegance is merely intended for my personal embellishment.

At first the lady of the house seemed a little piqued at my choice, which she thought was bound to fall on her, and for some days she remained rather bitter about it (only towards her rival; she has never changed her tone to me). This showed itself in little 'My dears', said in that dry, sharp tone which only women use, and in unpleasant comments on her rival's appearance which she made as loudly as possible, such as: 'Your hair is dressed too high, it doesn't suit your face at all'; or: 'Your bodice is baggy under the arms; who made that dress for you?'; or: 'You look very tired about the eyes; you seem very much altered'; and a thousand other little observations which the other did not fail to repay with all the malice you could wish when the opportunity offered itself. If the opportunity was too long delayed, she would invent one for her own especial use, and return, with interest, what she had received. But something else soon distracted the attention of the disdained infanta, this little war of words came to an end, and everything went back to normal.

I told you briefly that I was the lover-in-chief of the pink lady. That is not enough for a man as precise as you. No doubt you'll ask me what she is called. As for her name, I shan't give it to you. But if you like, to make the story easier, and to commemorate the dress which she was wearing when I first saw her, we'll call her Rosette. It's a pretty name: the little bitch I had was called Rosette.

Since you like precision in this sort of thing, you will want to hear all the details of the history of my passion for this beautiful Bradamante, and by what successive stages I passed from the general to the particular, from the state of simple spectator to that of actor; how I was promoted from the ranks to be the lover. I shall satisfy your wishes with the greatest pleasure. There is nothing sinister in our romance; it is rose-coloured, and no tears are shed in it except tears of pleasure; there are no wordy passages in it, and it all moves on towards the end with the haste and speed so warmly recommended by Horace; it is a real French novel. All the same, don't imagine that I took the stronghold at the first assault. Though she is merciful to her subjects, this princess is not as prodigal of her favours as one might at first believe; she is too conscious of their worth not to make you buy them; she also knows too well how much a due delay intensifies desire, what spice a certain resistance adds to pleasure, to give herself to you immediately, however urgent the desire you have inspired in her.

If I'm to tell you everything, I must go back a little further. I gave you a fairly detailed account of our first meeting. I had one or two more, even three, in the same house, then she invited me to call on her; I needed no persuasion, as you may imagine. I called on her discreetly at first, then a little more often, then still more often, then finally whenever I wanted to, and I must admit that I wanted to at least three or four times a day. The lady always received me, after a few hours' absence, as if I had come back from the East Indies. Of this I was most sensible, and I was forced to show my appreciation in the most gallant and tender manner possible. She responded as best she could.

Rosette – as we've agreed to call her – is a woman of great intelligence, and she understands men in the most wonderful way. Although she delayed the end of the chapter for some time, I didn't once lose my temper with her. This is really marvellous; for you know the great rages I go into when I don't have what I want immediately, and when a woman exceeds the time I have mentally assigned her to surrender. I don't know how she did it; from the first meeting, she let me understand that I should have her, and I was more certain of it than if I'd had the promise written and signed in her hand. People may say that the boldness and facility of her manners left the field free for audacious hopes. I don't believe that that was the real reason. I've known some women whose prodigious licence excluded, in a way, the very shadow of a doubt, and they did not produce this effect on me, and in their presence I was timid and anxious in a way which was uncalled for, to say the least.

What usually makes me less amiable with the women I desire than the women whom I find indifferent, is my passionate waiting for the moment and my uncertainty as to whether my plan will succeed; that makes me melancholy and throws me into a reverie which harms my abilities and my presence of mind. When I see them escaping, one after the other, those hours which I had destined for a different purpose, I cannot control my anger, I cannot prevent myself from saying very harsh and bitter things. Sometimes they are even brutal, and they put my affairs back a hundred leagues. I didn't feel any of this with Rosette; never, even at the moment when she resisted me most, did it occur to me that she wanted to escape my love. I allowed her to display all her little coquetries in peace, I was patient about the rather long delays which she was pleased to impose on my passion. There was something attractive about her rigour which greatly consoled you for it, and in her most Hyrcanian cruelties you glimpsed an underlying humanity which hardly allowed you to be seriously afraid. Even when they are least honest, honest women have a sullen, scornful manner which I find quite unbearable. They always appear to be ready to ring and have you thrown out by their lackeys; and it really seems to me that a man who bothers to pay court to a woman (which in any case isn't as pleasant as people might believe) doesn't deserve to be looked at like that.

As for dear Rosette, she doesn't look at you that way; and I assure you it's to her advantage. She is the only woman with whom I have been myself, and I am conceited enough to say that I have never been so distinguished. My wit displayed itself freely; and the skill and fire of her replies made me seem wittier than I had thought, wittier perhaps than I had ever really been. It's true that I wasn't very lyrical – that is hardly possible with her; and yet it isn't that she lacked a poetic side, whatever de C— said about her; but she is so full of life and energy and movement, she seems to be so happy in the sphere in which she lives, that one doesn't want to leave it to rise up into the clouds. She fills real life so pleasantly and makes it so amusing for herself and other people, that reverie has nothing better to offer you.

It's miraculous! It's nearly two months, now, since I've known her, and during this time I've only been bored when I wasn't with her. You will agree that she is not an ordinary woman if she produces such an effect, for women usually have just the opposite effect on me, and please me much more from a distance than from close quarters.

Rosette has the nicest nature in the world; with men, I mean, because with women she is as malicious as the devil; she is lively, vivacious, alert, ready for everything, very original in her way of thinking, and she always has some charming, unexpected drollery to tell you; she is a delightful companion, a pretty comrade with whom you sleep; and if I had a few years the more and a few romantic ideas the less, that would be all the same to me, and I should even consider myself to be the most fortunate mortal in existence. But . . . but . . . There is a particle which bodes no good, and this diabolical little qualification is alas the word of all human languages which is most often used. But I am a beardless youth, an idiot, a proper goose, who can't be content with anything and is always looking for the impossible. Instead of being perfectly happy, I am only half happy; half is already quite a lot for this world, and yet I find that it is not enough.

Everyone can see that I have a mistress whom several men desire and envy me, a mistress whom no man would disdain. My desire appears to be fulfilled, I no longer have the right to quarrel with my fate. And yet it seems to me that I have no mistress; my reason tells me that I have, but I don't feel it; and, if someone suddenly asked me if I had one, I believe I'd answer that I hadn't. And yet the possession of a woman who has beauty, youth and wit constitutes what in every age and in every land one has called and calls having a mistress, and I don't think one can call it anything else. That doesn't prevent me from having the strangest doubts about it, and I carry this so far that, if several people got together to convince me that I'm not the favoured lover of Rosette, I should end up by believing them, despite the palpable evidence of the thing.

Don't go and imagine, because of this, that I don't love her, or that she somehow displeases me. On the contrary, I love her very much, and, like everyone else, I find her a pretty, witty creature. It's just that I don't feel I possess her, that's all. And yet no woman has given me such delight, and if ever I have known sensual pleasure, I have known it in her arms. One single kiss from her, the purest of her caresses, makes me tremble to the soles of my feet, it makes all my blood flow back to my heart. Just work that out. Yet things are as I tell you. But the heart of man is full of absurdities like this; and, if one had to reconcile all the contradictions it contains, one would have a difficult time.

What is the explanation? To be honest, I don't know.

I see her all day long, and even all night long, if I want. I give her every caress I want to give her; I have her dressed or naked, in the city or the country. She is inexhaustibly obliging, and enters perfectly into all my whims, however bizarre they may be. One evening, I suddenly took a fancy to possess her in the middle of the drawing-room, with the chandelier and candles lit, the fire in the hearth, the chairs set out in a circle as if for a grand soirée, and with her in evening dress with her bouquet and fan, all her diamonds on her fingers and round her neck, a headdress of plumes, the most splendid costume imaginable, and myself dressed as a bear. She agreed to it. When everything was ready, the servants were astonished to receive the order to shut the doors and not to let anybody come upstairs; they didn't seem to understand in the least, and they went off with stupefied expressions which much amused us. They certainly believed that their mistress was absolutely mad; but what they thought or didn't think hardly concerned us.

That evening was the most comical evening I have ever spent. Just imagine how I must have looked with my plumed hat in my paw, rings on every finger, a little sword with a silver guard and a sky-blue ribbon on the hilt. I approached the lady; and, having made her the most graceful bow, I sat down beside her and laid siege to her in every way. The scented madrigals, the excessive gallantries which I addressed her, all the jargon of the occasion took on a singular relief as it passed through my bear's muzzle; for I had a superb painted cardboard head which I was soon forced to throw under the table, my goddess was so adorable that evening and I so wanted to kiss her hand and more than her hand. The skin soon followed the head; for, since I was not used to being a bear, I was really stifling in it, and stifling much more than necessary. Then the evening dress had fair play, as you may imagine; the feathers fell like snow around my beauty, the shoulders soon emerged from the sleeves, the breasts from the bodice, the feet from the shoes, and the legs from the stockings; the unstrung necklaces rolled on the floor, and never, I think, had a newer dress been more pitilessly rumpled and crushed; it was a dress of silver gauze, with a lining of white satin. On this occasion Rosette displayed a heroism quite above her sex, and it gave me the highest opinion of her. She watched the plunder of her clothes like a disinterested witness, and didn't for a single moment show the slightest regret for her dress and her lace; on the contrary, she was in the wildest spirits, and she herself helped to rend and tear what did not undo or unhook quickly enough for her taste and mine. Don't you think that's fine enough to consign to history with the most brilliant deeds of the heroes of antiquity? It is the greatest proof of love that a woman can give her lover, not to tell him: Take care not to crumple my dress or leave marks on it—especially if her dress is new. A new dress is a better guarantee of a husband's security than people generally believe. Rosette must adore me, or she must have a philosophy superior to that of Epictetus.

All the same I do think that I more than repaid Rosette for her dress in a money which may not be current among merchants, but is none the less esteemed and prized. Such heroism did indeed deserve such a reward. Besides, as a generous woman, she more than returned what I had given her. I had a wild, almost convulsive pleasure, such as I did not believe I could experience. Those sonorous kisses mingled with bursts of laughter, those trembling caresses, full of impatience, all those sharp, provocative delights, that pleasure incompletely enjoyed because of the costume and the situation, but a hundred times more intense than if it had been without impediments, so worked upon my nerves that I was seized by spasms, and had some trouble getting over them. You can't imagine how proudly and how tenderly Rosette looked at me while she was trying to make me come round, and with what joy and anxiety she busied herself about me. Her face still glowed with the pleasure that she felt at having had such an effect on me, and at the same time her eyes, all wet with gentle tears, expressed the fear she had felt when she saw me ill, the interest she took in my health. Never had she seemed more beautiful to me than she did at that moment. There was something so maternal and so chaste in her glance that I completely forgot the more than anacreontic scene that had just occurred, and I fell on my knees before her, begging for permission to kiss her hand. This she granted me with a singular seriousness and dignity.

That woman is certainly not as depraved as de C— pretends, and as she has often appeared to me; her corruption is in her mind and not in her heart.

I have described one scene among twenty; it seems to me that, after that, without excessive self-conceit, one can consider oneself a woman's lover. Well, I can't. I had hardly returned home when this thought took hold of me again and began to work upon me as usual. I perfectly remembered everything that I had said and heard, everything that I had done and witnessed. The slightest gestures, the most transient poses, all the smallest details were very clearly etched in my memory; I remembered everything down to the slightest inflexions of the voice, the most indiscernible gradations of sensual pleasure. Only it didn't appear to me that it was to me, and not someone else, that all these things had happened. I wasn't sure that it wasn't an illusion, a phantasmagoria, a dream, or that I hadn't read it somewhere, or even that it wasn't a story which I'd made up, as I've often done. I was afraid of being the dupe of my credulity, the victim of a hoax; and, despite the evidence of my lassitude, the material proofs that I'd slept away from home, I should willingly have believed that I'd gone to bed at my usual time, and that I had slept until morning.

I am very unhappy that I can't acquire the moral certainty of something of which I am physically sure. It's usually the opposite which happens, it's the fact which proves the idea. I'd like to prove the fact to myself by the idea. I cannot do so. It's something quite singular, but there it is. It depends on me, up to a certain point, to have a mistress; but I cannot force myself to believe that I have one even while I have one. If I lack the necessary faith within myself, even for so evident a thing, it's also impossible for me to believe in so simple a fact, just as it is for someone else to believe in the Trinity. Faith is not acquired, and it is a pure gift, a special grace from heaven.

Never did anyone want, as I do, to live the life of others, and to assimilate another nature; never was anybody less successful. Whatever I do, other men are hardly anything but phantoms to me, and I do not feel that they exist; yet it isn't the desire to recognize their life and to share in it which is lacking in me. It is the power or the want of real sympathy for anything whatever. The existence or non-existence of a thing or a person doesn't interest me enough to affect me in an appreciable and convincing way. The sight of a real man or woman doesn't leave stronger traces on my soul than the fantastic vision of the dream; there moves around me, murmuring indistinctly, a pale world of shades and of false or real appearances, in the midst of which I find myself as completely alone as I can be, for no one affects me for good or ill, and they seem to me to be of a quite different nature. If I speak to them and they answer something which is more or less common sense, I'm as surprised as if my dog or my cat had suddenly begun to speak and joined in the conversation; the sound of their voice always astounds me, and I should very readily believe that they are only fugitive appearances and that I am the objective mirror. There are moments when I recognize only God above me, and others when I consider myself hardly the equal of the woodlouse under its stone, the mollusc on its sandbank; but in whatever state of mind I find myself, high or low, I have never been able to persuade myself that men were really my fellow creatures. When someone calls me sir, or they talk about me and say 'that man', it seems very singular to me. My name itself seems to me to be a name in the air, a name which isn't really my name; and yet, however low it is pronounced in the middle of the loudest noise, I turn round suddenly with a convulsive, febrile vivacity which I have never been able to understand. Am I afraid of finding that this man who knows my name, this man for whom I am no longer anonymous, is an antagonist or an enemy?

It is above all when I've lived with a woman that I have been most aware how much I invincibly repel every alliance and every mixture. I am like a drop of oil in a glass of water. You can stir it and shake it, but in vain, the oil will never be able to mix with it; it will break up into a hundred thousand little globules which will join together and rise again to the surface, the moment that the water is still. The drop of oil and the glass of water: that's my own history. Even sexual pleasure, that diamond chain which links all creatures, that devouring fire which melts the rocks and metals of the soul and dissolves them into tears, as the material fire melts iron and granite:

even that, all-powerful as it is, has never been able to master me or soften me. My senses are very strong; but my soul is a hostile sister of my body, and the unhappy couple, like every possible couple, legal or illegal, lives in a state of perpetual war. A woman's arms, which bind more closely than anything else on earth, or so they say, are a very feeble attachment for me, and I have never been further from my mistress than when she has clasped me to her heart. I was suffocating, that's all.

How often I've been furious with myself! How often I have struggled not to be like this! How I've exhorted myself to be tender, loving, passionate! How often I've taken my soul by the hair and dragged it to my lips in the very midst of a kiss! Whatever I've done, my soul has always recoiled, wiping her face as soon as I've let her go. What a torture for that poor soul to witness my physical debauchery, and always to attend banquets where she has eaten nothing!

It was with Rosette that I determined, once and for all, to prove if I was absolutely unsociable, and if I could take enough interest in someone else's existence to believe in it. I have carried the experiments to the point of exhaustion, and I haven't enlightened myself very much. With her, the pleasure is so intense that the soul quite often finds itself, if not touched, at least distracted, which rather spoils the precision of the observations. After all, I recognized that it didn't go beyond the skin, and that I had only a pleasure of the epidermis in which the soul shared simply out of curiosity. I have pleasure, because I am young and ardent; but that pleasure comes from myself, not from someone else. The cause is in myself rather than Rosette.

I've tried in vain, I couldn't escape from myself for a minute, I'm still what I was, that is to say something very bored and very boring, which I find extremely unpleasant. I haven't managed to make the idea of someone else enter into my brain, the feeling of someone else enter my soul, the grief or delight of another enter my body. I am a prisoner within myself, and any invasion is impossible; the prisoner wants to escape, the walls ask only to crumble, the doors ask only to open to let him pass; some unknown fatality invincibly holds every stone in place, every key in its lock; it is as impossible for me to admit someone to my house as to go myself to other people; I couldn't pay visits or receive them, and I live in the saddest isolation in the midst of the crowd. My bed may not be widowed, but my heart is widowed always.

Oh! to be unable to grow by a single particle, a single atom; to be unable to make the blood of others flow in one's veins; always to see with one's own eyes, not more clearly, or further, or differently; to hear sounds with the same ears and the same emotions; to touch with the same fingers; to perceive different things with an invariable organ; to be condemned to the same tone of voice, the return of the same accents, the same phrases, the same words, and to be unable to go away, to escape oneself, to take refuge in some corner where one isn't followed; to be forced to keep to oneself for ever, to dine and to sleep with oneself, to be the same man for twenty new women; to drag a compulsory personage, whose part you know by heart, through the strangest situations of the drama of our life, to think the same things, to dream the same dreams: what tedium, what torture!

I have wanted the horn of the Tangut brothers, Fortunatus' hat, Albaris' stick, and Gyges' ring; I should have sold my soul to snatch the magic wand from a fairy's hand, but I have never wanted anything so much as to meet on the mountain, like Tiresias the prophet, those serpents that make you change your sex; and what I most envy the monstrous and bizarre gods of India are their perpetual *avatars* and their countless transformations.

I began by wanting to be another man. Then I reflected that I could, by analogy, pretty much foresee what I should feel, and I shouldn't know the changes and surprises which I expected. I should therefore have preferred to be a woman; this idea has always occurred to me, when I had a mistress who wasn't ugly; for an ugly woman is a man to me, and at the moments of pleasure I should readily have changed my rôle, for it is very tiresome not to be conscious of the effect that one is producing and not to judge the pleasure of others except by one's own. These thoughts and many others have often given me a meditative and dreamy air at moments when it was most out of place, and I have been very wrongly accused of coldness and of infidelity.

Rosette, who doesn't know all this, very fortunately, believes me the most amorous man in the world; she takes this powerless *rage* to be a frenzy of passion, and she submits as best she can to all the experimental fancies which pass through my head.

I have done everything I can to convince myself that I possess her. I have tried to go deep down into her heart, but I have always stopped on the first step of the staircase, at her skin or on her lips. For all the intimacy of our physical relations, I am well aware that we have nothing in common. Never has an idea like mine opened its wings in this attractive young head; never has this heart full of life and fire, which beats beneath such firm pure breasts, beaten in unison with my own. My soul has never united with that soul. Cupid, the god with a hawk's wings, has not kissed Psyche on her fine ivory brow. No! This woman is not my mistress.

If you knew everything I've done to force my soul to share the love of my body! How fiercely I have planted my lips on hers, plunged my hands into her hair, how tightly I have clasped the curves of her supple waist! Like Salmacis, in ancient times, in love with the young Hermaphroditus, I tried to fuse her body with mine; I drank in her breath and the warm tears which overflowed from the chalice of her eyes, so intense was her sensual pleasure. The more we embraced each other's bodies, the more intimately we caressed one another, the less I loved her. My soul remained sadly apart and, with an air of pity, she looked at this deplorable wedding to which she had not been invited; sometimes she veiled her face in disgust and wept silently beneath the folds of her cloak. All this is probably because I don't really love Rosette, however much she deserves to be loved, and however much I want to love her.

In order to rid myself of the idea that I was me, I devised the most unlikely settings, where it was quite improbable that I should encounter myself. Since I could not unfrock my character, I tried to take it out of its element so that it didn't recognize itself any more. I had only moderate success. This devil of a self stubbornly follows me; there's no way of getting rid of it. I haven't got the expedient of having it told, like other importunate visitors, that I've gone out or gone to the country.

I have had my mistress in the bath, and I have played the Triton as best I could. The sea was a big marble tub. As for the Nereid, what she displayed reproached the water, perfectly clear though it was, for still not being clear enough for the exquisite beauty of what it concealed. I have had my mistress at night, in moonlight, in a gondola, with music.

That would be very common in Venice, but here it is very unusual. In her carriage, hurtling at full gallop, with all the noise of the wheels, the bumps and jolts, sometimes lit up by the lanterns, sometimes plunged into utter darkness . . . That is a way which doesn't lack a certain piquancy, and I advise you to try it; but I was forgetting that you are a venerable patriarch, and that you don't indulge in such refinements. I have entered her house through the window, though I had the key to the door in my pocket. I have made her visit me in broad daylight, and finally I have compromised her in such a fashion that nobody now (except myself) doubts that she is my mistress.

Because of all these inventions – if I weren't so young, they would look like the expedients of a hardened rake – Rosette adores me more than anyone, more than all the world. She sees in them the ardour of an eager love which nothing can contain, a love which never changes in spite of the diversity of time and place. She sees in them the endlessly renewed effect of her charms and the triumph of her beauty; and, in truth, I should like her to be right, and, if she isn't right, it really isn't my fault, or her fault, either.

Once – it was at the beginning of our liaison – I thought I had attained my end, and for a minute I thought that I had loved. I have loved. Oh, my friend! I have lived that minute alone, and if that minute had been an hour, I should have become a god. We had both gone out on horseback, me on my dear Ferragus, she on a snow-coloured mare which looked like a unicorn, it was so light of foot, so slim of neck. We were going down a great avenue of elms of prodigious height; the sunlight fell upon us, warm and gold, as it filtered through the fretted leaves; lozenges of ultramarine sparkled here and there in the dappled clouds, great lines of pale blue were piled up on the verge of the horizon and changed into the most delicate apple-green when they touched the orange tones of the setting sun. The sky had a charming, singular appearance; the breeze brought us an indefinable scent of wild flowers which could not have been more ravishing. From time to time a bird took off in front of us and crossed the avenue with a burst of song. The church bell from an unseen village sweetly rang out the Angelus, and the silvery tones, which only reached us attenuated by distance, had an infinite sweetness. Our horses went at a walking pace, side by side, neither was ahead of the other. My heart swelled out, and my soul overflowed into my body. I had never been so happy. I said nothing, and Rosette said nothing, either, and yet we had never understood one another so well. We were so close to each other that my leg touched the flank of Rosette's horse. I leaned towards her and put my arm round her waist; she made the same movement on her side, and she leant her head on my shoulder. Our lips met; oh, what a pure and delicious kiss! Our horses went on walking, with their reins floating loose on their necks. I felt Rosette's arm relax and her body bending more and more. I was weakening, too, and I was nearly fainting. Oh! I assure you that at that moment I was hardly thinking whether I was myself or someone else. We went on like this to the very end of the avenue, where the sound of footsteps made us abruptly sit up straight again. Some people we knew were out riding, too, and they came and talked to us. If I had had pistols, I think that I should have fired at them.

I looked at them with a sombre fury, which must have seemed to them very singular. And indeed I was wrong to grow so angry with them, because they had unwittingly done me the service of cutting off my pleasure at the moment when, by its very intensity, it was going to become a pain or to collapse under stress. It is a science which people don't consider with due respect, the science of stopping in time. Sometimes, when you're in bed with a woman, you put your arm round her waist; at first it is a great physical pleasure to feel the gentle warmth of her body, the soft velvet flesh of her loins, the polished ivory of her thighs, and to close your hand over her erect and trembling breast. The fair lady falls asleep in this position; the arch of her loins becomes less pronounced; her breast subsides; her muscles relax, her head rolls over in her hair. Meanwhile your arm is more crushed, and you begin to be aware that this is a woman and not a sylph; but you wouldn't take your arm away for anything in the world. There are many reasons for that. The first is, that it is rather dangerous to wake up a woman you're sleeping with; you must be able to replace her delightful dream with a reality more delightful still. The second is that, by asking her to rise up to release your arm, you are telling her indirectly that she is heavy and that she's making you uncomfortable, which isn't polite, or else you are giving her to understand that you are weak or tired, something extremely humiliating for you which will do you infinite damage in her mind. The third thing is that, as you have had some pleasure in this position, you believe that by maintaining it you'll be able to feel more, and here you are wrong. The poor arm finds itself imprisoned under the mass of flesh, the blood stops flowing, the nerves are affected, and you are pricked by cramp, with its million pins; you are a kind of little Milo of Crotona, and the mattress of your bed and the back of your divinity represent fairly exactly the two halves of the tree which have reunited. Day comes, at last, to deliver you from your martyrdom, and you leap down from this wooden horse more eagerly than any husband climbs down from the nuptial scaffold.

This is the history of many passions.

It is that of every pleasure.

However this may be – in spite of the interruption or because of the interruption – never had I known such sensual pleasure; I really felt that I had become someone different. The soul of Rosette had completely entered my body. My soul had left me, it filled her heart as her soul was filling mine. No doubt they had met one another in this long equestrian kiss, as Rosette has since called it (incidentally, this has annoyed me), and they had gone through one another and merged with one another as completely as the souls of two mortal creatures can do on a grain of perishable clay.

The angels must no doubt embrace each other like this, and the true paradise is not in heaven, it is on the lips of a woman you love.

I have awaited a similar moment in vain, and I have tried to contrive it, without success. We have often gone riding in the avenue in the forest, in beautiful sunsets; the trees had the same greenness, the birds sang the same song, but we found the sun lacklustre, and the foliage turned sere. The song of the birds seemed to us shrill and discordant, the harmony was no longer within us. We set our horses at a walking pace, and we attempted the same kiss. Alas! only our lips were joined, and it was only the ghost of the kiss of old. The beautiful, sublime and heavenly kiss, the only real kiss I have given and received in my life, had flown away for ever. Since that day I have always come back from the forest with a deep and inexpressible sadness. However light-hearted and wanton she usually is, Rosette cannot escape from this impression, and her reverie is betrayed by a delicate little pout which is at least as good as her smile.

There is hardly anything except the fumes of wine and the dazzling brilliance of candles which can draw me out of such melancholy moods. We both drink as if we were condemned to death, silently, glass after glass, until we have had the dose we need; then we begin to laugh and to ridicule ourselves wholeheartedly for what we call our sentimental natures.

We laugh – because we cannot weep. Oh, who will be able to make a tear well up in the depths of my dry eyes?

Why did I have such pleasure that evening? I'd find it very difficult to say. And yet I was the same man, and Rosette was the same woman. It wasn't the first time that I'd ridden out on horseback, and it wasn't the first time that she had done so. We had seen the sun set before, and the sight hadn't touched us any more than the sight of a picture that one admires, according to whether the colours are more or less bright. There is more than one avenue of elms and chestnut-trees in the world, and this one was not the first we had travelled through; what then had made us find such a sovereign enchantment there, an enchantment which had transformed every dead leaf into a topaz, every green leaf into an emerald, which had gilded all those fluttering atoms, turned into pearls all the drops of water strung out on the lawn, and given so sweet a harmony to the sound of a bell which was unusually discordant, and to the chirping of some little birds? There must have been a most penetrating poetry in the air, since our very horses seemed to feel it.

Yet nothing in the world was simpler or more pastoral: a few trees, a few clouds, five or six sprigs of wild thyme, a woman, and a ray of sunlight set across it all like a golden chevron on a shield. Moreover, there was neither surprise nor astonishment in what I felt. I recognized myself quite clearly. I had never come to this place before, but I perfectly remembered the shape of the leaves and the position of the clouds, and the white dove which flew across the heavens flew in its usual direction; that little silvery bell, which I heard for the first time, had very often rung in my ears, and its voice seemed to me a familiar friend; I had never passed that way, but I had been down that avenue many times with princesses riding unicorns; the most voluptuous of my dreams had strolled there every evening, and my desires had given each other kisses just like the kiss which I had exchanged with Rosette. This kiss was nothing new to me; but it was just as I had expected. It is perhaps the only time in my life that I have not been disappointed, and that reality has seemed as beautiful as the ideal. If I could find a woman, a landscape, a building, something which fulfilled my desire as perfectly as that minute fulfilled the minute which I had dreamed of, I should have nothing to envy the gods, and I should very willingly renounce my place in paradise. But, in truth, I don't believe that a flesh-and-blood man could endure such intense physical pleasures for an hour; two kisses like that would drain a whole existence, they would absolutely empty body and soul. That consideration itself wouldn't stop me; for since I can't prolong my life indefinitely, it is all the same to me if I die, and I'd rather die of pleasure than die of old age or boredom.

But this woman doesn't exist. And yet she does exist; perhaps there is only a partition between us. Perhaps I brushed against her yesterday or today.

What is lacking in Rosette, that she isn't that woman? She lacks my belief in it. What fate always makes me have as my mistress a woman I don't love? Her neck is smooth enough to be decked with the most exquisite necklaces; her fingers are slender enough to do honour to the richest and most beautiful rings; the ruby would blush with pleasure to shine on the pink tip of her delicate ear; her waist might be girded with the cestus of Venus; but only love could tie his mother's sash.

All the merit which Rosette possesses is in her alone, I have given her none. I haven't cast upon her beauty that veil of perfection with which love envelops the beloved. The veil of Isis is transparent compared to that veil of perfection. Only satiety may lift the corner of it.

I don't love Rosette; at least the love I have for her, if I have any, isn't like my own idea of love. Apart from that, my idea may not be right. I don't dare to decide anything. All the same she makes me quite insensible to the merits of other women, and I haven't desired anyone else with any consequence since I've possessed her. If she has cause for jealousy, she is only jealous of phantoms, which she isn't very anxious about, and yet my imagination is her most formidable rival; that is something which, acute though she is, she will probably never perceive.

If women knew that! How often the least inconstant lover is unfaithful to the most adored mistress! We must presume that women more than repay us; but, like ourselves, they say nothing about it. A mistress is a necessary theme which usually disappears under decorations and embroideries. Very often the kisses you give her are not for her; it is the thought of another woman you're kissing in her person, and she profits more than once (if you can call it profit) from the desires inspired by someone else. Oh, how often, poor Rosette, you have served to embody my dreams and given reality to your rivals; how often I have been unfaithful, and you have been the unwitting accomplice! If you had thought, when my arms clasped you so tightly, when my lips were most fiercely pressed against your own, that your beauty and your love were irrelevant, that the thought of you was a thousand leagues away! If someone had told you that those eyes, veiled with the languor of love, were only lowered so as not to see you, not to dissipate the illusion which you merely served to complete! If someone had told you that you were not a mistress, but only an instrument of sensual pleasure, a means of deceiving a desire which could not be fulfilled!

Oh, celestial creatures, lovely virgins, frail and diaphanous, who cast down your periwinkle eyes and join your lily hands in the golden backgrounds of pictures by old German masters! Oh, saintly women in stained-glass windows, martyrs in missals who smile so sweetly among the scrolls of the arabesques, and come out so fair and fresh from the bells of flowers! Oh, lovely courtesans lying naked in your golden hair on beds sown with roses, under great purple curtains, with your bracelets and your necklaces of big pearls, with your fan and your mirrors in which the setting sun hitches a blazing spangle of gold in the darkness! Brown-haired maidens of Titian, who voluptuously display your rippling hips, your firm, hard thighs, your satin bellies and your supple, muscular loins! Antique goddesses, who raise up your white phantoms in the shadows of the garden! You are part of my seraglio; I have possessed you all in turn. St Ursula, I have kissed your hands in the lovely hands of Rosette. I have caressed the black hair of the woman from Murano, and never did Rosette find it harder to do her hair again; virginal Diana, I have been more than Actaeon with you, and I have not been changed into a stag: it is I who replaced your handsome Endymion! These are all rivals whom one cannot guard against, rivals on whom one cannot take revenge. And they are not always painted or sculpted!

Women, when you see your lover grow more than usually tender, clasp you in his arms with extraordinary emotion; when he buries his head in your lap and raises it to gaze at you with tearful, searching eyes; when pleasure only increases his desires, when he silences your voice with his kisses, as if he were afraid of hearing it, be assured that he doesn't even know if you are there. At that moment he has a secret meeting with a dream which you make palpable, a dream whose part you play. Many chambermaids have profited from the love which queens inspired. Many women have profited from the love which goddesses inspired, and a rather vulgar reality has often served as pedestal for the ideal deity. That is why poets usually take rather dirty sluts for mistresses. You can sleep for ten years with a woman without ever having seen her; that is the history of many men of genius whose ignoble or obscure connections have astonished the world.

I have only been unfaithful to Rosette in that fashion. I have only deceived her for pictures and statues, and she has been half responsible for the betrayal. I don't have the slightest little material sin on my conscience to reproach myself with. I am, in this respect, as white as the snow of the *Jungfrau*, and yet, without being in love with anyone, I'd like to be in love with somebody. I don't seek the occasion, and I shouldn't be vexed if it came; if it came, I mightn't take advantage of it, for I am profoundly convinced that it would be the same thing with someone else, and I'd rather it was like this with Rosette than with anyone else; for, mistress apart, I still have at least a pretty companion, full of wit, and delightfully immoral; and this isn't one of the least important reasons which hold me back, for, if I lost the mistress, I should be desolate to lose the friend.

IV

Do you know that it will soon be five months – yes, five months, one might say five eternities – that I have been Celadon-in-waiting to Madame Rosette? It's perfectly splendid. I shouldn't have believed myself so constant, and nor would she, I'm sure. To tell the truth, we're a couple of turtle-doves, for only turtle-doves show such tenderness. How we have billed, and how we have cooed! What ivy-like embraces! What a life for two! Nothing in the world has been more touching. Our two poor little hearts could have been displayed on a coat of arms, on a single spike, burning with one flame.

Five months alone together, so to speak, for we see each other every day and nearly every night – the door is always closed to everyone; doesn't it give you gooseflesh just to think of it? Well, that's something that must be said to the glory of the incomparable Rosette, I haven't been too bored, and this time will no doubt be the most agreeable time of my life. I don't believe it is possible to occupy in a more constant, more amusing way a man who is entirely without passion, and God knows the terrible idleness which comes from an empty heart! You cannot imagine this woman's resources. At first she drew on her wit, and then she drew on her heart, for she loves me to the point of adoration. How artfully she takes advantage of the slightest spark, how well she turns it into a conflagration! How skilfully she controls the slightest instincts of the soul! How she turns languor into loving dreams! And by how many devious paths she guides home the mind which is straying from her! It's wonderful! And I admire her as one of the greatest geniuses in existence.

I arrived at her house very sullen, in very bad humour, looking for a quarrel. I don't know what the enchantress did, but after a few minutes she had obliged me to pay court to her, although I hadn't the slightest wish to do so; she had obliged me to kiss her hands and laugh wholeheartedly, though I was in an appalling temper. Can you imagine such tyranny? And yet, however skilful she is, the tête-à-tête cannot go on any longer. During this last fortnight, it has often happened – and it had never happened before – that I opened the books on the table, and read a few lines during the gaps in the conversation. Rosette noticed this, and she took fright. She found it difficult to disguise her fear, and she had all the books taken out of her closet. I must admit that I regret it, although I don't dare to ask to have them back. The other day – an alarming symptom! – someone came when we were together, and, instead of getting into a rage like I did at the beginning, I felt rather glad. I was almost agreeable; I kept up the conversation which Rosette was trying to drop so that the man would go away, and, when he had gone, I began to say that he had a certain wit and that I found him quite pleasant company. Rosette reminded me that two months earlier I had thought the same man stupid and the most senseless bore in the world. I had no answer, because in fact I'd said so. However, I was right, in spite of my apparent contradiction. The first time he had interrupted a charming tête-à-tête, and the second time he came to the rescue of a conversation which was exhausted and flagging (on one side at least), and he spared me, anyway for that day, a loving scene which was rather tiring to perform.

This is what we have come to; the situation is serious, especially when one of us is still in love and desperately attached to what remains of the other's passion. I'm greatly perplexed. Although I'm not in love with Rosette, I have a very great affection for her, and I shouldn't want to do anything which would hurt her. I want her to believe, as long as possible, that I love her.

I want it in gratitude for all the hours which she made timeless for me, in gratitude for the love which she has given me in exchange for pleasure. I shall be unfaithful to her; but isn't an agreeable fraud preferable to a distressing truth? For I shall never have the heart to tell her that I don't love her. The vain shadow of love which she feasts upon seems to her so adorable and dear, she embraces the pale spectre with such rapture and effusion, that I do not dare to make it vanish; and yet I am afraid that she will discover in the end that it is only a phantom after all. This morning we had a conversation, and I'm going to record it in dramatic form for the sake of accuracy. It makes me afraid that I can't continue our love-affair much longer.

The scene is Rosette's bed. A ray of sunlight is slanting through the curtains. It is ten o'clock. Rosette has an arm round my neck, and she isn't moving, in case she wakes me up. From time to time she raises herself a little on her elbow, and holds her breath, and bends over my face. I can see all this through the lattice of my eyelashes, for I haven't been asleep for the past hour. There is a tucker of Mechlin lace on Rosette's nightdress, which is torn to shreds. The night has been tempestuous. Her hair is coming out here and there from her little nightcap. She's as pretty as a woman can be if you don't love her at all and you've slept with her.

ROSETTE [*seeing that I am no longer asleep*]: You wretched sluggard!

ME [*yawning*]: Haaa!

ROSETTE: If you yawn like that, I shan't kiss you for a week.

ME: Oh!

ROSETTE: Apparently, sir, you don't mind very much if I kiss you or not?

ME: On the contrary.

ROSETTE: You're very casual about it. All right. You can rely on it, I shan't give you the merest peck for a week. Today is Tuesday. Till next Tuesday, then.

ME: Nonsense!

ROSETTE: What do you mean, nonsense?

ME: I mean nonsense! You'll kiss me before this evening, or I'll die.

ROSETTE: You'll die! How conceited can you be? I've spoilt you, sir.

ME: I shall survive. I'm not conceited and you haven't spoilt me, on the contrary. In the first place, you can drop the sir; I know you well enough for you to call me by name and use the intimate form of address.

ROSETTE: I've spoilt you, d'Albert!

ME: All right. Now kiss me.

ROSETTE: No, next Tuesday.

ME: Come on! Aren't we going to caress each other now unless we've got a calendar at hand? We're both a little too young for that. Kiss me, my infanta, or I'm going to get a stiff neck.

ROSETTE: Not a kiss.

ME: Ah, so you want to be raped, my love! Very well! You shall be raped. It's possible, though it may not have been done yet.

ROSETTE: What impertinence!

ME: Observe, my beauty, that I've been polite enough to say *may not have been*; that is very civil of me. But we're getting away from the subject. Bend down. Now what's all this about, my favourite sultana? And how sullen you look! We want to kiss a smile, not a pout.

ROSETTE [*leaning over to kiss me*]: How do you expect me to smile? You say such harsh things to me!

ME: I mean to say very tender ones. Why do you think I say harsh ones?

ROSETTE: I don't know, but you say them.

ME: You take meaningless jokes as harsh comments.

ROSETTE: Meaningless! You call that meaningless! Everything has a meaning in love. Look, I'd rather you beat me than laughed like that.

ME: So you want to see me cry?

ROSETTE: You always go from one extreme to the other. No one's asking you to cry, they're asking you to talk reasonably and to drop that slightly bantering tone. It doesn't suit you at all.

ME: I can't talk reasonably and not banter; so I'm going to beat you, since you have a taste for it.

ROSETTE: Go on.

ME [*giving her a few taps on the shoulders*]: I'd rather cut off my own head than spoil your adorable little body and beat those charming white buttocks black and blue. In fact, my goddess, however much a woman may enjoy being beaten, you aren't going to be beaten at all.

ROSETTE: You don't love me any more.

ME: Now that doesn't follow straight on from what we were saying. It's about as logical as saying: 'It's raining, so don't give me my umbrella'; or: 'It's cold, so open the window.'

ROSETTE: You don't love me, you've never loved me.

ME: Ah! Things are getting complicated. You don't love me any more, you've never loved me. That is rather contradictory. How could I stop doing something I hadn't begun? You see, my little queen, that you don't know what you're saying, and you're absolutely absurd.

ROSETTE: I wanted you to love me so much that I helped to create the illusion for myself. It's easy to believe what you want to believe; but now I can see quite well that I was wrong. You have deceived yourself; you've mistaken an inclination for love, and desire for passion. It's something which happens every day. I don't blame you; it didn't depend on you not to be loving. I must blame myself for not being attractive enough. I should have been more beautiful, more animated, more of a coquette; I should have tried to rise up to you, my poet! instead of wanting to make you come down to me; I was afraid of losing you in the clouds, and I was afraid that your head would take your heart away from me. I have imprisoned you in my love, and I believed that if I gave myself to you entirely, you would keep something of it . . .

ME: Rosette, move back a little; your thighs are burning me – you're like a red-hot coal.

ROSETTE: If I disturb you, I'm going to get up. Oh, heart of rock, drops of water wear away a stone, but my tears can't touch you. [*She weeps.*]

ME: If you cry like that, you're going to turn our bed into a bath. A bath? I mean a sea. Can you swim, Rosette?

ROSETTE: You scoundrel!

ME: There you are, now I'm a scoundrel! You flatter me, Rosette, I don't have that honour. I'm afraid I'm a good-natured bourgeois. And I haven't committed the smallest crime; perhaps I've done something stupid, and loved you madly; that's all. Are you determined to make me repent it? Since I have been your lover, I've always walked in your shadow; I've given you all my time, my days and nights. I haven't spun fine-sounding phrases with you, because I only like them when they're written; but I've given you a thousand proofs of my affection. I'm not speaking of the most complete fidelity, that goes without saying; and finally I have lost a pound and three quarters since you have been my mistress. What more do you want? Here I am in your bed; I was here yesterday, and I'll be here tomorrow. Is this how you behave with the people you don't love? I do everything you want; you say 'let's go', and I go; 'let's stay', and I stay. It seems to me that I'm the most wonderful lover in the world.

ROSETTE: That is exactly what I'm complaining of. You really are the most wonderful lover in the world.

ME: What are you reproaching me with?

ROSETTE: Nothing, and I'd rather I had got something to complain about.

ME: That's a strange quarrel.

ROSETTE: It's much worse than that. You don't love me. I can't do a thing about it, and nor can you. What could anyone do about it? I'd certainly rather have some fault to forgive you. I should reproach you; you would excuse yourself as best you could, and we should make it up with each other.

ME: All the advantage would be on your side. The greater the crime, the more splendid the atonement.

ROSETTE: You know perfectly well, sir, that I haven't yet been reduced to that expedient, and that if I had wanted to a moment ago, although you don't love me, and although we quarrelled with each other ...

ME: Yes, I agree that I owe it entirely to your mercy ... So show me a little kindness; that would be better than producing endless syllogisms as we're doing.

ROSETTE: You want to break off the conversation, because you find it embarrassing. If you don't mind, we'll content ourselves with talking, my dear.

ME: It's an inexpensive feast, and I assure you that you're wrong. You're ravishingly pretty, and I have certain feelings for you ...

ROSETTE: Which you will express another time.

ME: I say, you're a little Hyrcanian tigress, aren't you? Divine one,
   you are unbelievably cruel today! Have you got a sudden itch to
   become a vestal virgin? It would be an original caprice.
ROSETTE: Why not? There have been more bizarre caprices. But,
   certainly, I shall be a vestal to you. You must learn, sir, that I only
   give myself to people who love me or people whom I believe are
   in love with me. You aren't in either position. Let me get
   up.
ME: If you get up, I shall get up, too. You'll just have the trouble
   of going to bed again.
ROSETTE: Leave me alone!
ME: Like hell I will!
ROSETTE [*struggling*]: You will let me go!
ME: I venture, madam, to assure you of the contrary.
ROSETTE [*seeing that she is not the stronger*]: Well, I'll stay; you're
   gripping my arm so tight . . . What do you want from me?
ME: I think you know. I shan't allow myself to say what I shall
   allow myself to do; I respect decency too much.
ROSETTE [*finding it impossible to defend herself*]: On condition that
   you'll love me very much . . . I surrender.
ME: It's a little late to capitulate, when the enemy is in the fortress.
ROSETTE [*throwing her arms round my neck, and half fainting*]: Un-
   conditionally . . . I leave it to your generosity.
ME: You're quite right.

Here, my dear friend, I think it would be appropriate to put a
line of dots, for the rest of this dialogue could hardly be translated
except by onomatopoeias.

. . . .

Since this scene began, the ray of sunlight has had time to go round
the room. A smell of lime-tree flowers comes in from the garden,
delicate and penetrating. The weather is as fine as can be; the sky is
as blue as the pupils of an Englishman's eyes. We get up, and eat
our *déjeuner* with a great appetite; then we set out on a long country

walk. The transparency of the air, the splendour of the countryside and the joyful aspect of nature have cast enough sentimentality and tenderness into my soul to make Rosette agree that, after all, I have a kind of heart like everyone else.

Have you ever noticed how the shade of the woods, the murmur of fountains, the song of birds, the pleasant prospects, the smell of leaves and flowers, all the stock-in-trade of eclogues and descriptions which we have agreed to disdain, still have a secret power over us, however depraved we may be: a secret power which we cannot resist? I shall confide in you under the seal of the greatest secrecy, that I caught myself the other day in the most provincial sentimental mood about a nightingale which was singing. It was in —'s garden; night had long since fallen, but the sky was so bright that it was almost like the most beautiful day; it was so deep and so transparent that your glance easily penetrated to God. I seemed to see the last folds of the angels' robes floating on the white bends in the path of St James. The moon had risen, but a big tree completely hid it. It riddled its black foliage with a million little luminous holes, and stuck more spangles on it than there ever were on the fan of a marquise. A silence full of sounds and stifled sighs could be heard all through the garden (this may look like pathos, but it isn't my fault); although I saw nothing but the blue light of the moon, I felt as if I were surrounded by a population of unknown and beloved phantoms, and I didn't feel I was alone, although I was the only person left on the terrace. I wasn't thinking, I wasn't dreaming, I was made one with the nature around me, I felt myself tremble with the leaves, glisten with the water, shine with the moonbeam, blossom with the flower; I was no more myself than the tree, the water or the marvel of Peru. I was all that, and I don't believe that one can be more absent from oneself than I was then. Suddenly, as if something extraordinary were about to happen, the leaf paused at the end of the branch, the drop of water in the fountain remained suspended in mid air and didn't fall. The silver thread which had set out from the edge of the moon, stopped on its path. Only my heart was beating – and beating so loudly that it seemed to fill the whole great expanse with sound. My heart stopped beating, and

there was such a silence that you could have heard the grass growing and a word being whispered two hundred leagues away. Then
the nightingale, which was probably only awaiting this moment to
begin its song, sent forth from its little throat a note so sharp and
brilliant that I heard it with my heart as much as with my ears. The
sound spread suddenly through the crystalline sky, empty of sounds,
making a harmonious atmosphere, while the other notes which
followed it fluttered and beat their wings. I understood perfectly
what it was saying, as if I had possessed the secret of the language of
birds. It was the history of the loves that I had not known which
this nightingale was singing. Never was a history more accurate and
more true. It didn't omit the tiniest little detail, the most imperceptible nuance. It told me what I had been unable to tell myself, it
explained to me what I had been unable to understand; it gave a
voice to my reverie, and it drew an answer from the phantom which
until that moment had been silent. I knew that I was loved, and the
most langorously spun roulade taught me that I should soon know
happiness. Through the trills of its song, underneath the rain of
notes, in a shaft of moonlight, I seemed to see the white arms of my
beloved stretching out to me. She rose up slowly with the perfume
from the heart of a large rose with a hundred petals. I shall not try
to describe her beauty to you. There are things for which no words
suffice. How can one express the unutterable? How can one paint
what has neither form nor hue? How can one note a voice without
tone, a voice without words? I have never had so much love in my
heart; I should have pressed nature to my breast, I embraced the
void as if I had closed my arms round a virgin's waist; I kissed the
air which passed across my lips, I floated in the effluvia which ema-
nated from my radiant body. Ah! if Rosette had chanced to be
there! What divine gibberish I should have recited to her! But
women never know how to arrive opportunely. The nightingale
stopped singing; the moon, who was worn out for want of sleep,
drew her nightcap of clouds over her eyes, and I myself left the
garden. I was beginning to feel the cold of the night.

As I was cold, I very naturally thought that I should be warmer
in Rosette's bed than mine, and I went to sleep with her. I let myself

in with my master-key, for everyone in the house was asleep. Rosette was herself asleep; and I had the satisfaction of seeing that she slept over an uncut copy of my last book of poetry. Her arms were stretched above her head, her lips were smiling and half-open, one leg was stretched out and the other was slightly bent. Her pose was full of grace and abandon; she looked so beautiful that I felt a mortal regret that I was not in love with her.

As I looked at her, I thought that I was as stupid as an ostrich. I had what I'd desired for so long, a mistress who belonged to me like my horse and sword, a mistress who was young, pretty, amorous and amusing. She didn't have a high-principled mother, a father who was decorated with the Legion of Honour, a crabbed aunt or a swashbuckling brother. She had the unspeakable advantage of a husband duly sealed and nailed up in a fine oak coffin lined with lead, which is something not to be disdained; for, after all, it is hardly entertaining to be caught in the middle of an orgasm, and to finish the sensation on the pavement, having described a curve of forty to forty-five degrees, according to which floor you chance to be on. I had a mistress as free as the mountain air, and rich enough to enjoy the most exquisite refinement and elegance; a mistress who, moreover, had no kind of moral ideas, never talked to you about her virtue while she was trying out a new position, or about her reputation as if she had ever had one, a mistress without any close women friends, disdaining womankind almost as much as if she were a man. I had a mistress who had small esteem for Platonism and who didn't disguise the fact at all, yet was always moved by the heart; a woman who, if she had found herself in another sphere, would undoubtedly have become the most wonderful courtesan in the world, and made the glory of the Aspasias and the Imperias turn pale!

And that woman was mine. I did what I wanted with her. I had the key of her room and her drawer; I broke the seals of her letters; I had taken her name away from her and given her another. She was my chattel, my property. Her youth, her beauty, her love all belonged to me, I used it and abused it. I made her go to bed by day and get up at night, if I had a fancy to do so, and she simply obeyed me without appearing to make a sacrifice, or putting on little airs like a resigned victim. She was attentive, affectionate, and – which was outrageous – she was absolutely faithful; that is to say that, six months ago, if someone had given me even a distant glimpse of such happiness, I should have gone mad with delight, and tossed my hat up into the heavens with joy! Well! now that I have it, this happiness leaves me cold. I hardly feel it, in fact I don't feel it, my situation affects me so little that I often doubt if I have changed it. If I left Rosette, I am deeply convinced that, at the end of a month, perhaps less, I should have forgotten her so completely and so carefully that I should no longer remember if I'd known her or not! Would she do the same for me? I don't think so.

I was reflecting on all this and, out of a kind of feeling of repentance, I kissed the brow of the sleeping beauty. It was the most chaste and melancholy kiss that a young man had ever given to a young woman, on the stroke of midnight. She made a slight movement; her smile became a little more pronounced, but she did not wake. I got undressed slowly, slipped under the bedclothes, and stretched out beside her like a snake. The coolness of my body surprised her; she opened her eyes and, without a word, she pressed her lips on mine, and wound herself round me so tightly that I was warmed up in no time. All the lyricism of the evening turned into prose, but at least it was poetic prose. That night is one of the finest sleepless nights I have ever spent; I can no longer hope for others like it.

We still have our pleasant moments, but they have to have been induced and prepared by some external circumstance like this, and at the beginning I did not need to have my imagination stirred by looking at the moon and listening to the nightingale, in order to enjoy all the pleasure you can enjoy when you aren't really in love. There aren't yet broken threads in our woof, but there are occasional knots, and the warp isn't anything like smooth.

Rosette, who is still in love, does what she can to remedy all these disadvantages. Alas, there are two things in the world which cannot come to order: love and boredom. As for me, I make superhuman efforts to master the somnolence which comes over me in spite of myself, and, like those provincials who doze off at ten o'clock in urban drawing-rooms, I keep my eyes as wide open as I can, and I prop up my eyelids with my fingers. It's no good, and I'm developing the most unpleasant marital indifference.

Since the dear creature felt happy the other day with rural life, she took me yesterday to her country house.

It might not be irrelevant if I gave you a little description of the aforementioned country house, which is rather pretty; it would lighten all this metaphysics a little, and besides you need to have a setting for the characters; figures don't stand out against a void or against that vague brown tone with which artists fill up the backgrounds of their canvases.

The approaches are very picturesque. You go along a wide road lined with old trees, and come to a crossroads, the middle of which is marked by a stone obelisk surmounted by a gilded copper ball. The rays of the star are formed by five paths. Then the ground suddenly dips, and the road plunges into a rather narrow valley, the bottom of which is occupied by a little river. The road crosses it by a bridge with a single arch, then it rises steeply up the opposite side. This is the setting of the village (one can see its slate belfry rising up between the thatched roofs and the round tops of the apple-trees). The horizon isn't very broad, because it is bounded, on both sides, by the crest of the hill, but it is pleasant, and restful to the eye. Beside the bridge, there is a mill and a red stone factory in the shape of a tower; the almost endless barking, a few brachs and a few young bassets with twisted legs, warming themselves in the sun outside the door, would tell you that this is where the gamekeeper lives, if the buzzards and martens nailed to the shutters could leave you in doubt for a moment. An avenue of service-trees begins here, and their scarlet fruits attract clouds of birds. Since people don't pass by very often, there's only a white strip down the middle; the rest of the road is covered with a short, fine moss, and, in the two ruts traced by carriage wheels, there hum and hop small frogs as green as chrysoprase. When you've gone on a little way, you find yourself in front of an iron grille which has been gilded and painted; its sides are decorated with artichokes and *chevaux de frise*.

Then the path goes on towards the château which you don't yet see, because it is hidden in foliage like a bird's nest. The path goes on, still unhurried and quite often turning aside to visit a stream and a fountain, an elegant kiosk or a fine view, crossing and recrossing the river over Chinese or rustic bridges. The uneven ground and the embankments built to serve the mill explain why in several places the river falls four or five feet, and there is nothing more agreeable than hearing all these little waterfalls babbling beside you, usually unseen, because the osiers and elders which line the bank form an almost impenetrable curtain. But all this part of the park is in a way only the anteroom of the rest. A highway crosses the property, and unfortunately cuts it into two; this inconvenience has been remedied in a most ingenious manner. Two high crenellated walls, full of barbicans and loopholes in imitation of a ruined fortress, rise up on either side of the road; a tower with a great swag of ivy on it lets down a real drawbridge with iron chains on the bastion opposite, and this is lowered every morning. You go through a fine Gothic arcade into the interior of the keep, and from there into a second enceinte, where the trees, which have not been cut for more than a century, are of an extraordinary height, with knotted trunks swathed with parasitic plants, the finest and most singular trees that I have ever seen. Some of them only have leaves at the top, and end in huge parasols; others ravel out into tufts of plumes; others have a big clump near their trunk, from which the bare trunk soars up towards the sky like a second tree planted in the first; they seem like the foreground of some formal landscape, or the side-scenes of a stage set, they are so curiously deformed. The ivy goes from one to the other, and strangles them in its embrace, and mingles its black hearts with the green leaves, like their shadows. There is nothing in the world more picturesque. The river widens, here, so as to form a little lake, and it is so shallow that, under the clear water, you can make out the beautiful aquatic plants which carpet the bed. There are waterlilies and lotuses floating nonchalantly in the purest crystal with the reflections of the clouds and the weeping willows which lean over the bank. The château is on the other side, and this little boat, here, painted apple green and red, will allow you to avoid a rather long detour in search of the bridge. The château is a collection of buildings erected at different periods, with irregular gables and a crowd of little bell-turrets. This wing is built of brick with stone corners; the main part of the building is of a rustic order, full of bossages and vermiculated work. That other wing is quite modern; it has a flat roof in the Italian style with vases and a tiled balustrade and a vestibule draped with ticking in the shape of a tent; the windows are all of different sizes, and they don't correspond with each other; there are windows of every kind: you even find trefoils and lancets, for the chapel is Gothic. Some parts of it are trellised, like Chinese houses, with trellises painted in different colours, and they are covered with honeysuckle, jasmine, nasturtiums and Virginia creeper whose sprays come familiarly into the rooms, and seem to hold out their hands when they bid you good morning.

In spite of this irregularity, or rather because of this irregularity, the building looks charming. At least, you haven't seen it all at a glance. There is something to choose from, and you always notice something you haven't seen before. I didn't know this château, because it is some twenty leagues away. It pleased me from the first, and I was extremely obliged to Rosette for having had the triumphant idea of choosing a nest like this for our love.

We reached it at dusk, and ate our supper with great appetite. Since we were tired, what we wanted most was to go to bed (separately, of course), because we meant to have a proper sleep.

I was having some rosy dream or other, full of flowers, perfumes and birds, when I felt a warm breath on my brow, and a kiss settle there, with a flutter of wings. A delicate splash of lips and a pleasant dampness on the place which was touched upon led me to decide that I wasn't dreaming; I opened my eyes, and the first thing I saw was the sweet white neck of Rosette, who was leaning over the bed to kiss me. I threw my arms round her waist, and returned her kiss more amorously than I had done for a long time.

She went to draw the curtains and open the window, then she came back and sat on the edge of my bed, holding my hand between both of hers and playing with my rings. Her attire was most coquettish in its simplicity. She had no bodice and no skirt, she had nothing on at all except a great cambric peignoir as white as milk, very full, with generous folds; her hair was put up on top of her head with a little white rose of the kind which have only three or four leaves; her ivory feet disported themselves in brilliant multi-coloured slippers, as tiny as could be, although they were still too big, and without a band round the heel, like those of young Roman women. When I saw her like this, I was sorry that I was her lover already and that I didn't have to become it.

The dream I was having when she came to wake me so agreeably wasn't very different from reality. My room looked over the little lake which I described a moment ago. The window was framed with jasmine, which shook its stars in a silver rain on my floor; big exotic flowers balanced their urns on my balcony as if to cense me; a sweet and indefinable fragrance, composed of a thousand different aromas, penetrated as far as my bed, and from there I could see the water glistening and flaking into millions of spangles; the birds were jabbering, chirping and whistling: there was a confused and harmonious sound like the hum of a party. Opposite, on a hillside lit up by the sun, there stretched a lawn of a golden green where a few large oxen were scattered here and there, browsing, and looked after by a small boy. At the very top, and further away, you could see huge squares of forests of a darker green, and from these, twisting round in spirals, there rose the bluish smoke of the char-coal-burners.

Everything in this picture was calm, fresh and smiling, and, wherever I chanced to look, everything I saw was young and beautiful. My room was hung with unglazed chintz, with rush mats on the polished floor. Blue Japanese pots with rounded bellies and slender necks, full of extraordinary flowers, were artistically arranged on the shelves and on the blue, white-veined marble mantelpiece which was itself filled with flowers; there were paint-ings over the doors, daintily drawn and brightly coloured, repre-senting scenes of a rustic or pastoral nature, and there were sofas and divans in every corner. There was also a beautiful young woman all in white, whose flesh faintly flushed her transparent robe in the place where it touched it. One couldn't imagine anything better conceived for the pleasure of the soul, or of the eyes.

And so my satisfied and nonchalant gaze roved, with equal pleasure, from a magnificent pot all scattered with dragons and mandarins to Rosette's slippers, and from there to the corner of her shoulder which was glowing under the cambric; it lit on the trembling stars of the jasmine, on the fair hair of the willows on the bank, crossed the water and wandered on the hill, and then came back into the room to fasten on the rose-coloured bows on the long bodice of a shepherdess.

Through the rents in the foliage, the sky opened a myriad blue eyes; the water was murmuring very gently, and I gave myself up to all this joy, plunged into a tranquil ecstasy, not uttering a word, my hand still between Rosette's two little hands.

It's no good: happiness is pink and white; one can hardly represent it otherwise. It demands pale colours as its right. It has nothing on its palette but sea-green, sky-blue and straw-yellow; its pictures are all in clear colours, like pictures by the Chinese painters. Flowers, light, aromas, a soft and silky skin touching your own, a veiled and indefinable harmony, and you are perfectly happy; there is no other way of being happy. I myself have a horror of the commonplace, and I dream only of strange adventures, strong passions, delirious ecstasies, bizarre and difficult situations, and I have to find pure and simple happiness that way, and, try as I may, I haven't been able to find another.

I beg you to believe that I wasn't making any of these reflections at the time; they have occurred to me after the event, while I am writing to you; at that moment, I was only concerned with enjoyment – the sole occupation of a rational man.

I shan't describe the life we are leading here, it's easy to imagine. There are walks in the great forests, violets and strawberries, kisses and forget-me-nots, picnics in the fields, readings and forgotten books under the trees; there are boating expeditions with the end of a sash or a white hand trailing in the current, long madrigals and prolonged laughter repeated by the echo from the bank: the most Arcadian life you can conceive.

Rosette overwhelms me with caresses and attentions. She coos more than a dove in May, she twines herself around me and encircles me with her coils; she sees that I have no atmosphere except her breath and no horizon except her eyes; she blockades me very rigorously, and doesn't let anything come or go without permission; she has built herself a little guardroom next to my heart, and from this she watches over it night and day. She says delightful things to me; she sings me the most elegant songs; she sits at my feet and behaves to me just like a humble slave to its lord and master; this suits me quite well, because I like these little submissive ways, and I have a leaning towards Oriental despotism. She doesn't do the slightest thing without taking my advice, and she seems to have sacrificed her own will and pleasure completely. She tries to guess my thoughts and forestall them; she is overwhelming with her wit, her tenderness and her obliging compliance; she is maddening in her perfection. How the devil could I leave such a charming woman, without appearing a monster? It would be enough to discredit my heart for ever.

Oh, how I wish I could find her at fault, discover a weakness in her! How impatiently I wait for a reason to quarrel! But there's no danger that the wretch will give me one. When I speak to her brusquely and harshly, to provoke an argument, she gives me such sweet answers, in so silvery a voice, with such tear-filled eyes, with so sad and loving an air, that I feel worse than a tiger or at least a crocodile, and, while she drives me wild, I am forced to ask for her forgiveness.

She is literally killing me with love; she is torturing me, and every day she tightens the planks I'm caught between by a notch. She probably wants to force me to tell her that I detest her, to tell her that she bores me to death, and that, if she doesn't leave me in peace, I shall slash her face with a whip. Indeed, it will come to that, and, if she continues to be so nice, it won't be long, or the devil take me.

In spite of all these favourable appearances, Rosette is as tired of me as I am of her; but, as she has done the most wildly extravagant things for me, she doesn't want to do herself the wrong of a rupture in the eyes of the honourable corporation of tender-hearted women. Every grand passion claims to be eternal, and it is very convenient to give oneself the benefits of this eternity without suffering its disadvantages. This is how Rosette reasons: Here is a young man who has only a vestige of liking for me, now, and, as he is rather naïve and good-humoured, he doesn't dare to show it openly, and he is at his wits' end; I clearly bore him, but he would rather die in harness than take it upon himself to leave me. As he is a poet of sorts, he has a head full of fine phrases about love and passion, and he believes that he is obliged, in all conscience, to be a Tristan or an Amadis. Now, as nothing on earth is more unbearable than the caresses of someone whom you are beginning not to love any more (and not loving a woman any more is absolutely hating her), I am going to lavish caresses on him so as to give him indigestion, and either he will have to send me to perdition, or he will have to begin to love me again as he did on the first day, which he will take good care not to do.

Nothing is better conceived. Isn't it delightful to play the abandoned Ariadne? People commiserate with you, people admire you, they don't have imprecations enough for the infamous man who has had the monstrosity to abandon so divine a creature; you assume resigned and melancholy airs, you put your hand under your chin and your elbow on your knee, so as to make the pretty blue veins stand out on your wrist. You wear your hair more dishevelled and, for a time, you wear dresses of a more sombre hue. You avoid pronouncing the name of the ungrateful wretch, but you make oblique allusions to it, and you utter little sighs which are wonderfully modulated.

A woman so good, so beautiful, so passionate, a woman who has made such sacrifices, a woman who does not deserve the least reproach, a chosen vessel, a pearl of love, a mirror without stain, a drop of milk, a white rose, an ideal essence to sweeten a life; a woman to worship on one's knees, a woman to be cut up into little pieces, on her death, so as to be made into relics: to leave her like that, iniquitously, fraudulently, wickedly! But a pirate wouldn't do anything worse! To give her her death blow – for she will certainly die of it. He must have a paving-stone in his breast, not a heart, to behave like that.

Oh men, men!

That is what I say to myself; but perhaps it isn't true.

However good an actress a woman may be by nature, I can't believe that women are such good actresses as that; and, besides, aren't all Rosette's demonstrations the exact expression of her feelings for me? However that may be, it is now impossible to continue being alone together, and the beautiful lady of the manor has just sent out invitations to her local acquaintances. We are busy preparing to receive these worthy provincials. Goodbye, dear fellow.

V

I was mistaken. My wretched heart, incapable of love, had found this reason to free itself from the burden of intolerable gratitude. I had seized upon the idea with delight, in order to excuse myself in my own eyes. I had clung to it, but nothing was more wrong. Rosette wasn't playing a part, and if ever a woman was true, it is she. Well! I almost bear her a grudge for the sincerity of her passion, for it is a bond the more and it makes a rupture more difficult or less excusable; I'd rather she was false and inconstant. What a singular passion it is! You want to go, and you stay; you want to say 'I hate you', and you say 'I love you'. Your past pushes you on and prevents you from turning back or stopping. You're faithful and you regret being so. A curious kind of shame prevents you from devoting yourself to other acquaintances, and it makes you compromise with yourself. You give to the one everything that you can steal from the other, and at the same time you save appearances; the times and occasions for seeing each other, which used to occur so naturally, only occur with difficulty now. You begin to remember that you have important business. This situation is full of vexations, and it is particularly painful, but it is still not as painful as the one in which I find myself. When it's a new affection which takes you away from the old one, it is easier to extricate yourself. Hope smiles at you sweetly from the threshold of the house where your young love dwells. A fairer and more roseate illusion with white wings flutters over the tomb, which is hardly sealed, of the sister who has just died; another flower, more open and more scented, with a celestial tear trembling in it, has suddenly sprung up amid the withered blossoms of the old bouquet. Fine azure prospects open before you; avenues of young hornbeams, humid and

131

discreet, stretch out to the horizon. There are gardens with a few pale statues or a bench leaning against a wall hung with ivy, lawns starred with marguerites, narrow balconies where you lean and gaze at the moon, shadows shot with furtive gleams, salons with the daylight stifled by the heavy curtains; there is all the obscurity and isolation sought by a love which does not dare to reveal itself. It is like a second youth which is given you. Besides, you have the change of place, habits and people. Of course you feel a kind of remorse; but the desire which flutters and hums round your head, like a bee in spring, doesn't let you hear its voice; the void in your heart is filled, and your memories are effaced by impressions. But it isn't the same thing here: I don't love anyone, and it is only out of weariness and boredom with myself rather than her that I should like to be able to break with Rosette.

My old ideas had been somewhat assuaged; they are waking, wilder than ever. I am tormented, as I was before, with the idea of having a mistress, and, in the very arms of Rosette, I doubt – as I used to do – if I've ever had one. Once again I see the beautiful woman at her window, in her park of the Louis XIII period. Once again the huntress, riding her white horse, gallops across the avenue in the forest. My ideal beauty smiles at me from the height of her hammock in the clouds, I think I can recognize her voice in the song of the birds, the murmur of the leaves. I feel that I am summoned from every side, and that the angels brush against my face with the fringes of their unseen sashes. Just as I did when I was restless, I feel that if I set out at once, in haste, and went somewhere, very fast and very far away, I should reach a place where something is happening which concerns me, a place where my destiny is being decided. I feel that I am impatiently awaited in some corner of the world, I don't know where; I feel that a suffering soul is calling me ardently, and dreaming of me, and cannot come to me; that is why I am anxious, and that is what prevents me from staying where I am. I am being torn out of my element. My nature isn't one of those where others converge, one of those fixed stars round which other lights revolve; I must wander over the fields of heaven, a meteor out of place, until I have encountered the planet whose satellite I must be, the Saturn round whom I should set my ring. Oh, when will this marriage be? Until then I cannot hope for my proper state, or for rest, I shall be like the quivering, vacillating needle of a compass, seeking its pole.

I allowed my wings to be caught in this treacherous lime, hoping I should leave just a feather there, believing I could fly away when I chose to do so. Nothing is harder. I am covered with an invisible net, more difficult to break than the net which was forged by Vulcan, and the meshes are so fine and so tightly woven that there is no gap through which one can escape. The net is large, and you can move inside it with an appearance of liberty; you hardly feel it till you try to break it. Then it resists and becomes as solid as a wall of brass.

How much time I have lost, oh my ideal! without the slightest effort to make you real! What a coward I have been to let myself be caught by the pleasure of a night! And how little I deserve to find you!

Sometimes I think I shall begin another love-affair; but I haven't anyone in mind. More often I vow that if I manage to break off this liaison, I'll never bind myself like this again. Yet nothing justifies this resolution; this affair has been very happy in appearance, and I haven't the slightest complaint to make of Rosette. She has always been good to me, and she couldn't have behaved better. She has been a model of fidelity, she hasn't even given me room for suspicion; the most vigilant and anxious jealousy wouldn't have found anything against her, it would have been obliged to go to sleep. A jealous man could only have been jealous of the past; it's true that he would have had very good reason to be so. But this kind of jealousy is a refinement which is happily quite rare, and there's quite enough in the present without digging under the ruins of old passions to extract phials of poison and cups of bitterness. Which women could you love, if you thought about all that? You are very vaguely aware that a woman has had several lovers before you; but since the pride of man winds and coils in a tortuous way, you tell yourself that you are the first that she has really loved, and that it was by a series of unhappy coincidences that she found herself tied to people who were unworthy of her, or else that it was the vague desire of a heart which sought satisfaction, and changed because it had not met anyone.

Perhaps you can only really love a virgin – a virgin in body and mind – a delicate bud which has not yet been caressed by any zephyr, a bud whose unseen breast has not received the raindrop or the pearl of the dew, a chaste flower which unfurls its white robe only for you, a beautiful lily gilded only by your sun, swayed by your breath and watered by your hand. The radiance of the moon does not equal the heavenly pallors of the dawn, and all the ardour of a soul tempered by life is nothing to the celestial ignorance of a young heart awakening to love. Oh, what a bitter and shameful thought, that you are wiping away someone else's kisses, that perhaps there is not a single place on this brow, this breast, these shoulders, on the whole of this body, now yours alone, which has not been reddened and marked by alien lips; that these divine murmurs which come to the aid of language when there are no more words have in fact already been heard; that these senses so aroused have not learned their ecstasy and their delirium from you, and that deep down, in a solitary place, in one of those corners of the soul where you never go, there watches an inexorable memory, comparing the pleasures of former times with the pleasures of today!

Although my natural nonchalance leads me to prefer the highroads to the unexplored footpaths, and the public watering-place to the mountain source, I must really try to love some virginal creature as pure as snow, as trembling as the sensitive plant, a creature who can only blush and lower her eyes; perhaps, beneath this limpid wave where no diver has yet descended, I shall fish up a pearl of the finest water, a worthy counterpart of Cleopatra's; but, in order to do so, I should have to untie the bond which binds me to Rosette, for I probably shall not realize this wish with her, and, to tell the truth, I don't feel strong enough to do so.

And then, I must admit, deep down in me there is an unspoken and shameful motive which does not appear in broad daylight, a motive which I must confess, since I promised not to hide anything from you, and, if a confession is to be deserving, it must be complete. This motive has much to do with these uncertainties. If I break with Rosette, it will have to be some time before I replace her, however easy the kind of women amongst whom I shall look for a successor, and I have acquired a habit of pleasure with Rosette which I shall find it painful to break. It's true that you have the resource of courtesans; I liked them well enough, once upon a time, and I shouldn't abstain from them on such an occasion; but today I find them horribly disgusting, and they give me nausea. And so I mustn't think of them, and I am so unmanned by pleasure, the poison has seeped so deep into my bones, that I cannot bear the idea of being a month or two without a woman. There is egoism for you, and egoism of the lowest kind; but I think that, if they wanted to be frank, the most virtuous men would make rather similar confessions.

This is where I am most stuck, and, were it not for this, Rosette and I would have quarrelled irreparably long ago. And then, to be honest, it is so mortally tedious to pay court to a woman that I don't feel I have the heart for it. To repeat all the charming nonsenses which I've already said so many times, to create the new divinity, write notes and answer them; to take lovely women home, at night, two leagues away from where you live; to get cold feet and catch a chill outside the window, on the watch for a beloved shadow; to calculate, on a sofa, how many layers of material separate you from your goddess; to carry bouquets and frequent the ballrooms, all in order to arrive where I am now! It's hardly worth it. You might as well stay in your rut. To get out of it just to fall into another one which is exactly like it, after a great deal of bother and trouble – what's the good? If I were in love, it would all go naturally, and it would all seem delightful to me; but I am not in love at all, though I want to be most eagerly; for, after all, love is the only thing in the world; and, if the pleasure which is just its shadow holds so many temptations for us, what must the reality be? What streams of ineffable ecstasies, what lakes of pure delight they must swim in, those mortals whose hearts are touched by love with his gold-tipped arrows, those mortals who burn with the pleasant ardours of a mutual flame!

With Rosette I only know the dull calm, the kind of lazy well-being which comes from the satisfaction of the senses; and it isn't enough. Often the voluptuous torpor turns into numbness, and the tranquillity turns into boredom; and then I kill time with aimless distractions, and mawkish idle dreams which tire and exhaust me. I must get out of that state at any cost.

Oh, if I could only be like some of my friends who kiss an old glove with rapture, who consider themselves to be blessed by the clasp of a hand, who would not change a sultana's jewel-box for a few wretched flowers half withered by the sweat of the ball! Oh, if I could be like those who cover a note with tears and sew it into their shirt, over their heart: a note which is poorly written, and so stupid that you feel it must have been copied from *The Perfect Secretary*! If I could only be like those who adore women with big feet, and excuse themselves by saying that they have a beautiful soul! If I could tremble as I followed the last folds of a dress, wait for a door to open so that I might see a dear white apparition pass in a flood of light! If a whispered word made me blush or turn pale; if I had the virtue of not dining so that I could arrive sooner at my tryst; if I could stab a rival with a dagger, or fight a duel with a husband; if, by a particular grace of heaven, I was able to find ugly women amusing, and stupid and ugly women good at heart; if I could resolve to dance minuets and listen to the sonatas which young ladies played on the clavichord and harp; if my capacity was such that I could even learn ombre and reversi; if, in fact, I was a man rather than a poet – I should certainly be much happier than I am; I should be less bored and less boring.

I have always asked for one thing only – and that is beauty; I should very readily do without wit and soul. For me, a beautiful woman is always witty; she has the wit to be beautiful, and I don't know of any wit as good as that. You need many brilliant phrases and scintillating flashes to equal the shining glances of lovely eyes. I prefer a pretty mouth to a pretty word, and a well-turned shoulder to a virtue, even a theological virtue; I should give fifty souls for a dainty foot, and all poetry and poets for the hand of Joan of Aragon or the brow of the virgin of Foligno. I adore above all things the beauty of form; beauty, for me, is visible Divinity, palpable happiness descended on earth. There are certain undulating contours, certain subtleties of the lips, certain shapes of eyelids, certain inclinations of the head, certain elongations of ovals which ravish me beyond all expression and fascinate me for hours on end.

Beauty, which alone of all things cannot be acquired; frail and ephemeral flower that grows without being sown, pure gift of heaven! Oh beauty! the most radiant diadem with which chance may crown the brow – thou art admirable and precious like everything beyond the reach of man, like the azure of the sky, the gold of stars, the perfume of the seraphic lily! One may change a footstool for a throne; one may conquer a world, many indeed have done so; but who could not kneel before thee, pure personification of the thought of God!

I ask only for beauty, it is true; but it must be so perfect that I shall probably never encounter it. I have indeed seen, here and there, in various women, wonderful details in an indifferent whole, and I have loved them for the beauty that they possessed, and excluded the rest; all the same it's a rather painful task, a distressing operation to cut off half of your mistress like this, to make the mental amputation of what is ugly or commonplace about her, and restrict your view to what virtues she may possess. Beauty is harmony, and a woman who is absolutely ugly may often be less disagreeable to look at than a woman who is partially beautiful. Nothing is so painful to see as an unfinished masterpiece, a beauty in whom something is lacking; an oil-stain is less shocking on coarse drugget than it is on sumptuous stuff.

Rosette is not at all bad; she can pass as beautiful, but she is far from realizing my ideal; she is a statue of which several parts have been perfectly finished. The others haven't been so clearly cut out of the block; there are parts which are defined with great delicacy and charm, and others sculpted in a more casual and more careless manner. To ordinary eyes, the statue seems completely finished and absolutely beautiful; but a more attentive observer will soon discover places where the work is not precise enough, and contours which need the sculptor's hands to work over them, time and time again, to attain their proper purity. It is for love to polish and perfect this marble statue, which means that I won't be the one to finish it.

Yet I do not limit beauty to one particular sinuous line. Manner, gesture, bearing, inspiration, colour, sound and perfume; to me the whole of life enters into the composition of beauty; everything which smells sweet, sings or shines has its natural place there. I love rich brocades and splendid stuffs with thick and ample folds; I love big flowers and scent-boxes, the transparency of running water and the gleaming brilliance of fine weapons, I love thoroughbred horses and big white dogs like the ones you see in the pictures of Paolo Veronese. I'm a real pagan about this, and I don't worship gods which are badly made. Deep down I'm not exactly what people call irreligious, but nobody is in fact a worse Christian than I am. I do not understand this mortification of the flesh which is the essence of Christianity; to me it is sacrilegious to humiliate the work of God, and I cannot believe that flesh is bad, since He has created it Himself with His fingers and in His own image. I have small time for those long dark-coloured smocks from which there only emerge a head and two hands, and for those canvases where everything is lost in darkness, except some radiant brow. I want sunlight everywhere, I want as much light and as little shade as possible, I want colour to sparkle, lines to wind in and out, nudity to display itself with pride; and I want the flesh not to hide its existence at all, since it is – like the spirit – an eternal hymn to the glory of God.

I quite understand the Greeks' wild enthusiasm for beauty. Personally, I find nothing absurd in the law which obliged the judges only to hear the advocates plead in some dark place, for fear that their good appearance, their graceful gestures and attitudes might predispose them in their favour and tip the scales of justice.

I shouldn't buy anything from a shopkeeper if she were ugly; I should give more readily to beggars if their rags and leanness were picturesque. There is an ailing little Italian, as green as a lemon, with big black and white eyes which fill up half his face. You would think him an unframed Murillo or Espagnolet which a second-hand dealer was showing at the crossroads. He always gets two sous more than the rest. I should never beat a beautiful horse or a beautiful dog, and I shouldn't want a friend or a servant who didn't have a pleasant appearance. It is a real torture for me to see ugly things or ugly people. Some building in poor taste, an ill-shaped piece of furniture, prevent me from being happy in a house, however comfortable and attractive it may otherwise be. The best wine seems to me almost sour in a badly-made glass, and I confess that I should prefer the most Lacedaemonian broth in a plate enamelled by Bernard de Palissy to the finest game on an earthenware dish. Outward appearance has always had a violent effect on me, which is why I avoid the company of old men; it saddens me and affects me disagreeably, because they are wrinkled and deformed, though some of them do have a special beauty; and there is a good deal of disgust in the pity which I feel for them. Of all the ruins in the world, the ruin of man is certainly the saddest to contemplate.

If I were an artist (and I have always regretted that I was not an artist), I should want to people my canvases only with goddesses, nymphs, madonnas, cupids and cherubims. To devote your brush to painting portraits, unless they are portraits of good-looking people, seems to me a crime of lèse-painting; and, far from wanting to copy these ugly or ignoble faces, these insignificant or common heads, I should rather cut them off the originals. Caligula's ferocity, diverted in this direction, would seem to me to be almost laudable.

The only thing in the world which I have wanted with some consistency is to be beautiful. When I say beautiful, I mean as beautiful as Paris or Apollo. Not to be deformed, to have more or less regular features, in other words to have your nose in the middle of your face, and not flat or hooked, eyes which are neither red nor bloodshot, a mouth which is properly shaped, that is not being beautiful: if it were, I should be beautiful myself, and I'm as far from my own idea of manly beauty as one of those jacks-of-the-clock which strike the hour on belfries; I'm as far from it as if I had a mountain on each shoulder, the twisted legs of a basset, and the nose and muzzle of a monkey. I often look at myself in the mirror for hours at a time, with unbelievable fixity and attention, to see if there's been some improvement in my face; I wait for the lines to make a movement and to straighten up, or to round themselves out, to be purer and more delicate; I wait for my eyes to grow bright and swim in a more sparkling fluid, for the curve which separates my forehead from my nose to fill out, and give my profile the calm and simplicity of the Greek profile. I am always very surprised when this doesn't happen. I always hope that some or other spring I shall shed this form that I possess, like a serpent shedding its old skin. To think that it needs so little for me to be beautiful, and that I shall never be so! What! half a fraction, a hundredth, a thousandth of a fraction more or less here or there, a little less flesh on this bone, and a little more on that – an artist or a sculptor would have adjusted it in half an hour. What difference does it make to the atoms which compose me to crystallize in this way or that? Why was it important for that contour to come out here and go in there, why did I need to be like this and not something else? Because it pleased a miserable particle of something or other to fall somewhere or other and coagulate stupidly into the ill-shaped face that I possess, I am eternally unhappy! Isn't it the most idiotic and the most miserable thing in the world? How is it that my soul, with all her ardent desire, can't drop the poor carcass which she animates, and go and quicken one of those statues whose exquisite beauty saddens and enchants her? There are two or three people whom I'd be delighted to murder, taking care all the same not to bruise or spoil them, if I knew how to make a soul transmigrate from one body to another. It has always seemed to me that, in order to do what I want (and I don't know what I want), I needed absolute and perfect beauty, and I imagine that, if I had had it, my life, which is so confused and thwarted, would have been beautiful in itself.

You see so many beautiful faces in pictures! Why isn't one of them mine? You see so many charming heads in the depths of old galleries which vanish in the dust and mist of time. Wouldn't it be better if they left their frames and came to gladden my shoulders? Would Raphael's reputation greatly suffer if one of those angels who fly in swarms in the ultramarine of his canvases gave me his countenance for thirty years? There are so many places in his finest frescoes which have flaked and fallen into decay! No one would notice. What are they doing round the walls, those silent beauties to whom the common run of men hardly give a passing glance? And why didn't God or chance have the wit to make something which a man can contrive with a few bristles on the end of a stick, and a few blobs of paint of different colours mixed on a board?

When I find myself in the presence of one of those marvellous heads whose painted gaze seems to pass through you and to continue into infinity, my first sensation is one of shock. I feel an admiration which is not unmixed with a certain terror. My eyes fill with tears, my heart beats; then, when I have grown a little familiar with it, when I have gone further into the secret of its beauty, I make a tacit comparison between this head and my own. Jealousy writhes in the depths of my soul, coiled into more knots than a viper, and I have all the difficulty in the world not to throw myself at the picture and tear it into shreds.

To be beautiful is to have a charm which makes everything smile upon you and welcome you. It means that before you have spoken everyone is already in your favour and they are disposed to agree with you. It means that you have only to walk down a street or appear on a balcony to make yourself friends or mistresses in the crowd. Not to need to be pleasant in order to be loved, to be exempt from all that expenditure of wit and kindness which ugliness imposes upon you and from the myriad virtues which you must possess to make up for physical beauty: what a splendid and magnificent gift!

And if a man had supreme beauty and supreme strength as well: if, under the skin of Antinous, he had the muscles of Hercules, what more could he desire? I am sure that with these two things and the soul that I possess, I should within three years become the emperor of the world! Another thing which I've wanted almost as much as beauty and strength, is the power to travel as fast as thought from one place to another. If I had the beauty of an angel, the strength of a tiger and the wings of an eagle, I should begin to find that the world was not as badly organized as I had thought. A beautiful mask to seduce and fascinate your prey, wings to swoop down on it and bear it off, and talons to tear it apart: as long as I don't have these, I shall be unhappy.

All the passions and inclinations I've had have just been these three wishes in disguise. I have loved weapons, horses and women: weapons, to make amends for the strength that I didn't have; horses, to give me wings; women, so that I might at least possess in someone else the beauty which was lacking in myself. I particularly sought the most ingeniously lethal weapons, the ones which wounded beyond the hope of cure. I've never had occasion to use any of these krisses or yataghans; all the same, I like to have them round me. I draw them out of their scabbards with an inexpressible feeling of security and power; I fence furiously with them right and left; and if, by chance, I see my face reflected in a mirror, I am astonished by its fierce expression. As for horses, I overwork them so much that they must die or give the reason why. If I hadn't stopped riding Ferragus, he would have died a long time ago, and that would be a pity, because he is a splendid animal. What Arab steed could have legs as quick and as free as my desire? In women I have sought for nothing but the appearance, and until now those I have seen are far from answering my conception of beauty. And so I have fallen back on pictures and statues: which, after all, is a rather pitiful resource when your senses are as ardent as mine. And yet there is something noble and fine about loving a statue, it is that your love is quite disinterested, that you need not fear the satiety or weariness of victory, and that you cannot reasonably hope for a second wonder like the history of Pygmalion. The impossible has always pleased me.

I am still in the fairest months of adolescence, and, far from having abused everything, I have not even had recourse to the simplest things. Is it not singular that I should have grown so surfeited that I am only titillated by the bizarre or the difficult? Satiety follows pleasure. That is a natural and understandable law. If a man who has eaten hugely from every dish at a feast isn't hungry any more, and tries to rouse his sluggish palate with the thousand arrows of sharp spices or wines, nothing is easier to explain. But if a man who has just sat down at table, and has hardly tasted the first dishes, is already affected by this disdainful disgust, if he is sick unless he touches extremely strong dishes, if he likes only gamey meats, cheeses marbled with blue, truffles and wines which savour of flint, that phenomenon can only be the result of a peculiar nature; it is like a child of six months old who found its nurse's milk insipid, and would only be suckled on brandy. I am as weary as if I had accomplished all the prodigious deeds of Sardanapalus, and yet my life has been very chaste and peaceful in appearance. It is a mistake to think that possession is the only path to satiety. You also reach it by desire, and abstinence is more tiring than excess. Desire like mine is infinitely more fatiguing than possession. It surveys and penetrates the object that it wants, the object which shines beyond its reach. Its glance penetrates it faster and more deeply than if it touched it. What more would custom teach it? What experience could equal that constant and passionate contemplation?

I have been through so many things, although I have explored so few, that only the most precipitous summits tempt me any more. I suffer from that malady which takes hold of nations and of powerful men in their old age: the malady of the impossible. Nothing I can do has the least attraction for me. Tiberius, Caligula, Nero, great Romans of the Empire, you who have been so ill understood, you who are pursued by the barking pack of speechifiers, I suffer from your malady, and I pity you with all the pity that remains to me! I too would like to build a bridge across the sea and pave the waves; I've dreamed of setting cities ablaze to illuminate my feasts; I have wanted to be a woman so that I might know new sensual pleasures. Thy gilded house, O Nero! is but a filthy stable beside the palace I have built myself; my wardrobe is better stocked than yours, Heliogabalus, and it is infinitely more magnificent. My circuses are bloodier and more roaring than yours, my perfumes more bitter and more penetrating, my slaves are more numerous and better made; I, too, have harnessed naked courtesans to my chariots, I have walked over men with heels as disdainful as your own. Colossi of the ancient world, there beats beneath my puny ribs a heart as big as yours, and, in your place, I should have done what you have done and maybe more. How many Babels I should have piled one above the other to reach the heavens and insult the stars and from there spit down upon creation! Why then am I not God – since I cannot be a man?

Oh, I believe that it will take a hundred thousand centuries of nothingness to give me rest after the fatigue of these twenty years of life. God in heaven, what stone will You roll on top of my grave? Into what darkness will You plunge me? In what Lethe will You make me drink? Under what mountain will You inter the Titan? Am I destined to blow a volcano with my mouth and to cause earthquakes when I turn over?

When I think that I was born of a mother so gentle, so resigned, of such simple tastes and habits, I am amazed that I did not burst her womb when she bore me. How can it be that none of her thoughts, serene and pure, passed into my body with her blood? Why am I only the son of her flesh and not of her spirit? The dove has brought forth a tiger which wants all creation as a prey for its talons.

I lived in the most serene, most chaste of surroundings. It is hard to imagine an existence so purely enshrined as mine. My years flowed past, in the shadow of my mother's chair, with my little sisters and the dog. I saw nothing round me but the good, kind, tranquil faces of old servants, heads grown white in our service; friends and relations, grave and devout, clad in black, who put their gloves down separately on the brims of their hats; a few aunts, of a certain age, nice and plump, and neat, discreet, with dazzling linen, grey skirts, string mittens, and their hands folded in their laps, like pious people; furniture which was austere to the point of gloom, woodwork of unvarnished oak, leather hangings, a whole interior sombre and suppressed in tone, like some of those which the Flemish masters have painted. The garden was dank and dark; the box-wood hedges which divided it into compartments, the ivy which covered the walls and a few fir trees with stripped branches had been entrusted with representing verdure, and had they succeeded pretty badly. The brick house, with a very high roof, was spacious and in good condition, but it had something dismal and oppressive about it. There was certainly nothing so suitable as such a dwelling for a solitary, austere and melancholy life. It seemed as if every child brought up in a house like this must end by becoming a priest or a nun. Well, in this atmosphere of purity and rest, in this shadow and devout silence, I was rotting, little by little – though it didn't show at all – like a medlar on straw. In the heart of this honest, pious, blessed family, I had reached a horrible degree of depravity. It wasn't contact with the world, since I hadn't seen it; it wasn't the fire of passions, either, since I was benumbed with the icy sweat which oozed from these worthy walls. The worm hadn't crawled from another fruit into my heart. It had hatched by itself in the very centre of my pulp and gnawed it and riddled it in all directions. None of this appeared from the outside and warned me that I had gone bad. There was no bruise or worm-hole; but I was quite hollow inside, and all that was left was a thin pellicle, brilliantly coloured, which would have burst at the slightest touch. How can you explain that a child born of virtuous parents, brought up with care and attention, kept away from everything that was bad, should grow so perverted all by himself, and reach the point which I had reached? I'm sure that if you went back to the sixth generation, you wouldn't find among my ancestors a single atom which was like the atoms which compose me. I don't belong to my family; I am not a branch of that noble trunk, but a poisonous toadstool which has sprung up between its mossy roots on a stormy night; and yet no one has had more aspirations and more yearnings towards the beautiful than I have, no one has tried more persistently to spread his wings; but every attempt has made my fall greater, and what should have saved me has destroyed me.

Solitude is worse for me than society, although I want the first more than the second. Everything which takes me out of myself is salutary for me; society bores me, but it tears me forcibly out of my hollow dream, drags me away from the spiral which I climb and descend, arms folded and head bowed. And so, since the tête-à-tête is over, and we have visitors with whom I must restrain myself a little, I am less apt to abandon myself to my black humours, and I am not so much a prey to these boundless desires which swoop down on my heart like a cloud of vultures, the moment that I am unoccupied. There are some women who are rather pretty and one or two young men who are quite agreeable and very amusing; but, in all this swarm of provincials, the one who charms me most is a young cavalier who arrived two or three days ago; he pleased me from the first, and I felt affection for him, just to see him dismount from his horse. No one could be more graceful; he isn't very tall, but he's slim and shapely; there is something gentle and undulating about his gait and movements which I find extremely agreeable; many women would envy him his hands and feet. His only fault is to be too beautiful, and to have features which are too delicate for a man. He is endowed with the darkest and most beautiful eyes in the world; they have an indefinable expression, and their gaze is difficult to bear. But, as he is very young and has no sign of a beard, the softness and perfection of the lower part of his face somewhat temper the sharpness of his eagle's eyes; his glossy brown hair floats in big curls over his shoulders, and gives his head particular character. There is one of those types of beauty that I dreamed of, realized at last, before my eyes. What a pity that it is a man, or what a pity that I'm not a woman! This Adonis has not only a beautiful face, but a very quick, wide-ranging wit; he is also privileged to have at the service of his wit and humour a voice which it is hard to hear without being moved. He is really perfect. Apparently he shares my taste for beautiful things, for his attire is very rich and elegant, his horse is very spirited and thoroughbred. And, to crown it all, he was followed by a page of fourteen or fifteen, mounted on a little horse: a page who was fair, pink, pretty as a seraphim, half asleep, and so tired by the journey he had just ended that his master was obliged to lift him out of the saddle and carry him to his room in his arms. Rosette greeted him very warmly, and I think that she has decided to use him to stir up my jealousy and to quicken the little flame which is sleeping under the cinders of my dead passion. Yet, however formidable such a rival may be, I am little inclined to be jealous of him, and I feel myself so drawn towards him that I would quite willingly renounce my love in order to have his friendship.

VI

At this point, if the obliging reader will kindly allow us, we shall for a while abandon to his dreams the worthy personage who has so far always held the stage, and spoken for himself. We shall return to the ordinary form of the novel, without however forbidding ourselves to adopt the dramatic form, should the need arise, and also reserving the right to draw again on this kind of epistolary confession which the aforementioned young man addressed to his friend. We are persuaded that, however penetrating, however full of wisdom we may be, we are sure to know less about it than he does.

... The little page was so exhausted that he was sleeping in his master's arms, and his little dishevelled head rolled from side to side as if he were dead. There was quite a distance from the front steps to the room which had been set aside for the new arrival, and the servant who preceded him offered to carry the child in his turn; but the young cavalier – for whom, moreover, this burden seemed as light as a feather – thanked him, and would not give the child up. He set him down very gently on the sofa, and took a thousand precautions so as not to wake him; a mother wouldn't have done more. When the servant had withdrawn and the door was shut, he knelt before him, and tried to take off his half-boots; but his little swollen, painful feet made the operation rather difficult, and from time to time the pretty sleeper uttered a few vague and inarticulate sighs, as if he were about to wake up; then the young cavalier would stop, and wait for him to go to sleep again. The half-boots finally gave in, which was the most important thing; the stockings offered little resistance. When this operation had been performed, the master took the child's two feet, and laid them side by side on

147

the sofa; they were indeed the two most adorable feet in the world, no bigger than that, as white as new ivory and slightly pink from the pressure of the boots in which they had been imprisoned for seventeen hours. They were feet too small for a woman, feet which never seemed to have walked. What you could see of the leg was round, smooth, transparent and veined, and most exquisitely delicate; it was a leg which was worthy of the foot.

The young man, who was still on his knees, contemplated these two little feet with loving and admiring attention; he bent down, took the left one and kissed it, then the right one and kissed that, too; and then, kiss by kiss, he went up the leg to the place where the material began. The page slightly opened his long eyelids, and cast a drowsy and benevolent glance at his master, a glance which revealed no sense of surprise. 'My belt's uncomfortable,' he said, putting his finger under the ribbon, and he went to sleep again. The master unbuckled the belt, raised the page's head on a cushion, and, touching his feet which had been burning and had now grown rather cold, he wrapped them up carefully in his cloak, took an armchair, and sat down by the sofa. Two hours went by, while the young man watched the sleeping child and followed the shadows of the dreams which passed across his brow. The only sounds in the room were his regular breathing and the tick-tock of the clock.

It was really a very graceful picture. The contrast of these two kinds of beauty had an effect which a skilful painter would certainly have turned to advantage. The master was as beautiful as a woman, the page was as beautiful as a young girl. That round pink head, framed by the hair, looked like a peach under its leaves; it had the same freshness and the same bloom, although the fatigue of the journey had deprived it of some of its usual brilliance; the half-open mouth gave a glimpse of little milky white teeth, and below its full and shining temples lay a network of bluish veins. The eyelashes, like those golden threads which glow round the heads of the virgins in missals, came down almost to the middle of the cheeks; the long silky hair was both gold and silver, gold in shadow, silver in the light; the neck was at the same time plump and slender, and it had nothing of the sex indicated by the attire; two or three buttons on the jerkin had been undone to make breathing easier, and they allowed one to glimpse, through the gap in the fine linen shirt, a lozenge of plump and buxom flesh of admirable whiteness, and the beginning of a curve which was difficult to explain on the breast of a young boy; if you looked closely, you might also have found that the hips were a little too developed. The reader may think what he likes; these are mere conjectures which we offer him; we know no more than he does, but we hope to learn more in a while, and we promise to keep him faithfully informed of our discoveries. If the reader is less short-sighted than we are, let him cast his eyes under the lace of that shirt and decide honestly whether that curve is too rounded or not; but we warn him that the curtains are drawn, and that the light in the room is subdued. This doesn't at all help this kind of investigation.

The cavalier was pale, but his pallor was golden, full of strength and life; his eyes were blue, and they were shining bright. His nose was fine and straight, and gave his profile a wonderful pride and vigour, and his skin was so fine that, on the edge, it let the light shine through; he had the sweetest smile, but his mouth was usually curved at the corners, as on some of those heads which you see in pictures by old Italian masters, an inward rather than an outward smile; this gave him something adorably disdainful, a *smorfia* of the most piquant kind, an air of childish petulance and bad temper which was very singular and charming.

What were the links which bound the master to the page, the page to the master? Certainly there was more between them than the affection which can exist between master and servant. Were they friends or brothers? Then why this disguise? Anyone who had observed the scene which we have just described would have found it difficult, anyway, to believe that these two personages were what they appeared to be.

'Dear love, how fast asleep he is!' murmured the young man. 'I don't believe he had ever travelled so far in his life. Twenty leagues on horseback, for someone as delicate as that! I'm afraid he may be ill with fatigue. But no, it will be all right; tomorrow you won't notice anything; he'll have his fine colour back again, he'll be fresher than a rose after the rain. How beautiful he is like that! If I weren't afraid of waking him, I should devour him with kisses. What an adorable dimple in his chin! What a white and delicate skin! Sleep well, my darling. I am really jealous of your mother, I wish that I had given birth to you. He isn't ill, is he? No, his breathing is regular, and he isn't moving. But I think someone's knocked . . .'

Someone had in fact knocked twice, as gently as could be, on the panelled door.

The young man rose. Afraid that he had made a mistake, he waited for another knock on the door before he opened it. There were two more knocks, rather more emphatic, and a woman's voice gently whispered: 'It's me, Théodore.'

Théodore opened; but not so eagerly as a young man does when a woman with a gentle voice comes mysteriously to knock on his door at about nightfall. Through the half-opened door there came – guess who? The mistress of the bewildered d'Albert, Princess Rosette, more roseate than her name, and her breasts as palpitating as those of any woman who had come, at night, to the room of a handsome cavalier.

'Théodore!' said Rosette.

Théodore lifted up a finger and put it to his lips to represent the statue of silence; and, showing her the sleeping child, he led her into the neighbouring room.

'Théodore!' repeated Rosette. She seemed to find a singular sweetness in the repetition of the name, and to seek at the same time to collect herself. 'Théodore,' she continued, still holding the hand which the young man had offered her to lead her to her chair. 'Have you come back to us at last? What have you been doing all this time? Where have you been? Do you know it's six months since I've seen you? Oh, Théodore, that's very bad; you owe the people who love you some consideration and pity, even when you don't love them.'

THÉODORE: What have I done? I don't know. I've come and gone, I've slept and watched, I've sung and wept, I've been hungry and thirsty, I have been too hot and too cold, I have been bored, I have less money and another six months to my credit, I've lived, that's all. And you, what have you done?

ROSETTE: I've loved you.

THÉODORE: Is that all?

ROSETTE: Yes, absolutely all. I've been wasting my time, haven't I?

THÉODORE: You could have used it better, my poor Rosette. You could, for instance, have loved somebody who returned your love.

ROSETTE: I am disinterested in love, as I am in everything else. I don't lend my love at exorbitant interest; it is just a gift that I make.

THÉODORE: That is a very rare virtue of yours, and it can only be found in the elect. I have very often wished that I could love you, at least as you would like; but there is an insurmountable obstacle which I can't explain. Have you had another lover since I left you?

ROSETTE: I've had one, and I still have him.

THÉODORE: What sort of man is he?

ROSETTE: He's a poet.

THÉODORE: The devil take me! Who is this poet, and what has he done?

ROSETTE: I'm not very sure, a kind of book that nobody knows, a book I tried to read myself one evening.

THÉODORE: So your lover is an unpublished poet. That must be strange. Is he out at elbows, with dirty linen, and stockings like the screws of a cider-press?

ROSETTE: No. He's quite well turned out. He washes his hands, and he hasn't got ink-stains on the end of his nose. He's a friend of de C—'s; I met him at Madame de Thémines's: you know, a grand woman who plays the child and puts on little airs of innocence.

THÉODORE: May one know the name of this glorious personage?

ROSETTE: Lord, of course you may, he is called the Chevalier d'Albert.

THÉODORE: The Chevalier d'Albert! I believe that's the young man who was on the balcony when I got off my horse.

ROSETTE: Exactly.

THÉODORE: The one who looked at me so attentively.

ROSETTE: Quite so.

THÉODORE: He isn't bad. And he hasn't made you forget me?

ROSETTE: No. I'm afraid you aren't the kind whom one forgets.

THÉODORE: He's much in love with you, of course?

ROSETTE: I don't really know. At moments you would think he loved me profoundly; but deep down he doesn't love me, and he isn't far from hating me, because he resents the fact that he can't love me. He has done the same as several others who are more experienced than he is; he has acquired a keen taste for passion, and found himself amazed and disappointed when his desire has been satisfied. It is a common error to think that, because you've slept together, you are obliged to adore one another.

THÉODORE: And what do you expect to do with the aforesaid unloving lover?

ROSETTE: What you do with the old quarters of the moon or last year's fashions. He isn't strong enough to leave me of his own accord, and, though he doesn't love me in the true sense of the word, he stays with me from the habit of pleasure, and these are the habits most difficult to break. If I don't help him, he may become conscientiously bored with me till doomsday, and even beyond; for he has within himself the seed of every noble quality; and the flowers of his soul ask only to bloom in the sun of eternal love. Really, I am vexed that I haven't been his ray of sunlight. Of all the lovers whom I haven't loved, this is the one whom I love most; and, if I were less kind, I shouldn't give him back his freedom, I should still keep him. I shan't do that. At the moment I am finishing with his services.

THÉODORE: How long will it take?

ROSETTE: A fortnight, three weeks, but certainly less than it would have taken if you hadn't come. I know that I shall never be your mistress. You say there is a secret reason for that which I should accept if you were allowed to reveal it. And so I am denied all hope in this direction, and yet I can't decide to be someone else's mistress when you're there: it seems to me like profanation, and it seems as if I no longer have the right to love you.

THÉODORE: Keep him for love of me.

ROSETTE: If it gives you pleasure, I shall do so. Oh, if you could have been mine, how different my life would have been! The world has a very false idea of me, and I shall pass through it without anyone suspecting what I was – except you, Théodore, the only person who has understood me, the only one who has been cruel to me. I have never wanted anyone but you for a lover, and I haven't had you. If you had loved me, Théodore, I should have been virtuous and chaste, I should have been worthy of you. Instead of that, if anyone recalls me, they will recall a woman of little virtue, a kind of courtesan who differed from the common prostitute only by her rank and her fortune. I was born with higher inclinations; but nothing depraves you like not being loved. Many of the people who scorn me don't know what I have had to suffer to get where I am. Since I am sure I shall never belong to the person I love above all, I have let myself go with the tide, I haven't taken the trouble to defend a body which you couldn't possess. As for my heart, no one has had it and no one shall ever have it. It is yours, although you have broken it; and, unlike most women, who think themselves honest because they haven't passed from one bed to another, I have prostituted my flesh, but I have always been faithful in heart and soul to the thought of you. At least, I shall have made some people happy, I shall have sent a few pure illusions to dance round a few pillows. I have in innocence betrayed more than one noble heart; I have been so unhappy that you rejected me that I have always been terrified at the thought of inflicting such torture on someone else. That is the only reason for many of the adventures which people have attributed to mere libertinage. Me! A libertine! O world! If you knew, Théodore, how deep a sorrow it is to feel that you have failed in your life, that you have not known your happiness! If you knew what grief it was to see that everyone was mistaken about you, and that you couldn't change the general opinion, that your finest qualities were turned into faults, your purest essences into black poisons, that all that was known of you, was your weakness! If you knew what it was to have found the doors ever open for your vices and ever closed for your virtues, and, among all the hemlock and wolf's bane, not to have grown a single lily or a single rose! You don't know that, Théodore.

THÉODORE: Alas, alas! What you tell me, Rosette, is the history of all the world! The better part of us remains within us, and it is the part which we cannot show. Poets are like that. Their finest poem is the poem which they haven't written; they bear away more poems to their tombs than they leave behind in their libraries.

ROSETTE: I shall bear away my poem with me.

THÉODORE: And I'll take mine. Who hasn't composed a poem in his life? Who is so happy or unhappy that he hasn't written one in his head or heart? Executioners may have written some all damp with the tears of the sweetest sensibility; poets may have written some which would have suited executioners, they are so scarlet and so monstrous.

ROSETTE: Yes. They could put white roses on my tomb. I have had ten lovers – but I'm a virgin, and I'll die a virgin. Many virgins, on whose tombs there snow eternal jasmine and eternal orange-blossom, were really Messalinas.

THÉODORE: I know your worth, Rosette.

ROSETTE: You are the only one in the world who has seen what I am; for you have seen me moved by a love which is very true and very deep, since it is a love without hope. Those who have not seen a woman in love do not know what she is. That is what consoles me in my moods of bitterness.

THÉODORE: And what do you think of this young man who, in the eyes of the world, is now your lover?

ROSETTE: A lover's thoughts are a gulf which is deeper than the bay of Portugal, and it is very difficult to say what there is in the depths of a man; if a sounding-line were attached to a rope two hundred thousand yards long, and you unwound it as far as it would go, it would still pay out without meeting anything. And if I have sometimes touched the depths of this man in several places, and sometimes the plumb-line has brought up mud, sometimes beautiful shells, more often it has brought up mud and fragments of corals mixed up together. As for his opinion of me, it has varied greatly. In the first place, he began where others have ended, by despising me; young men with a lively imagination are apt to do that. There is always an enormous fall in the first step they take, and they cannot make the transition from their chimera to reality without a shock. He despised me, and I amused him; now he esteems me, and I bore him. In the first days of our liaison, he saw only my commonplace side, and I think that the certainty of meeting no resistance played a great part in his determination. He seemed extremely eager to have an affair, and at first I believed that it was one of those overflowing hearts which only seek to run over, one of those vague loves which you have in the Maytime of your youth, those loves which lead you, for want of women, to embrace the tree-trunks, and kiss the flowers and grass of the fields. But it wasn't that; he was only passing through me to reach something else. I was a path for him, and not an end. Under the freshness of his twenty years, under the first down of adolescence, he concealed profound corruption. He was worm-eaten to the heart; he was a fruit which contained only dust. In this young and vigorous body there stirred a soul as old as Saturn – a soul as incurably unhappy as any soul had ever been. I confess that I was terrified, Théodore, and I nearly had vertigo when I leant over the depths of that existence. Your griefs and mine are as nothing in comparison. If I had loved him more, I should have killed him. Something draws him, summons him invincibly, something which is not of this world or in this world, and he cannot rest day or night; and, like heliotrope in a cellar, he twists to turn towards the sun which he cannot see. He is one of those men whose soul was not steeped completely enough in the waters of Lethe before it was bound to his body, a man who keeps from the heaven whence he comes certain recollections of eternal beauty which disturb him and torment him, a man who recalls that he has had wings, and now has only feet. If I were God, I should deprive of poetry for two eternities the angel who was guilty of such negligence. Instead of having to build a castle of brightly coloured cards to house a fair young fantasy for a single spring, one would have to raise a tower higher than the eight superimposed temples of Belus. I wasn't strong enough, I pretended I hadn't understood him, I let him crawl along on his wings and seek a summit whence he could spring into the immensity of space. He believes that I haven't noticed any of all this, because I have lent myself to all his whims without appearing to suspect their purpose. Since I couldn't cure him, I wanted – and I hope one day I shall be given credit before God – to give him at least the happiness of believing that he had been passionately loved. He inspired me with such pity and interest that I could easily adopt a tone and manner which were tender enough to delude him. I've played my part like a consummate actress; I have been bright and melancholy, sensitive and voluptuous; I have feigned anxieties and jealousies; I have shed false tears, and summoned to my lips any number of artificial smiles. I have decked this mannequin of love with the most splendid stuffs; I have taken him for a stroll in the avenues in my parks; I have asked all my birds to sing as he passed, and all my flowers, dahlias and daturas, to welcome him by bowing their heads; I have made him cross my lake on the silvery back of my favourite swan. I have concealed myself within it, and lent it my voice, my spirit, my beauty and my youth, and I have made it look so seductive that reality was not as good as my illusion. When the time comes to smash this hollow statue into fragments, I shall do it in such a way that he believes that all the wrong is on my side and he is spared any remorse. It is I who will give the pinprick to let out the wind from this inflated balloon. Isn't that a blessed prostitution, an honourable deceit? I have a few tears in a crystal urn, I collected them as they were going to fall. There are my jewel-box and diamonds, I'll give them to the angel who comes to fetch me to take me to God.

THÉODORE: They are the finest diamonds which can sparkle at a woman's neck. They are worth more than a queen's regalia. I believe, myself, that the liquor which Magdalen poured on the feet of Christ was made of the old tears of those whom she had consoled, and I also think that it is with such tears that St James's path is sown, and not, as people say, with drops of Juno's milk. Who will do for you what you have done for him?

ROSETTE: No one, alas, since you cannot do it.

THÉODORE: O dear soul, if only I could! But do not lose hope. You are beautiful and you are still very young. You must pass through many avenues of linden-trees and acacias in bloom before you reach that humid path, lined with boxwood and leafless trees, which leads to the porphyry tomb where they will bury your fine dead years: that tomb of rough stone, covered with moss, where they will hasten to inter the remains of what you were, the wrinkled and tottering spectres of your old age. There is still much of the mountain of life for you to climb; it will be a long while before you reach the zone where snow is found. You have only reached the region of aromatic plants, of limpid cascades where the rainbow hangs its tricoloured arches, the region of fine green oaks and sweet-smelling larch-trees. Climb up a little further, and then, in the broader horizon which will spread out at your feet, perhaps you will see the bluish smoke rising from the roof under which sleeps the man who will love you. You must not despair of your life from the very first; prospects appear like that, in our destiny, perspectives which we no longer expected. Man, in his life, has often reminded me of a pilgrim climbing the spiral staircase in a Gothic tower. The long granite serpent winds its coils in the obscurity, and every scale on them is a step. After a few circumvolutions, the little daylight which came in through the door has disappeared. The shadow of the houses – you have not yet climbed beyond them – does not allow the airholes to let in the sun; the walls are black and oozing; you feel you are going down into a dungeon from which you will never emerge, rather than climbing up that turret which, from below, seemed so slim and slender, and covered with lace and embroidery, as if it were setting off for a ball. You wonder if you should go up higher, the dank shadows weigh so heavily on your brow. The staircase still winds on, and more frequent skylights pink out their golden trefoils on the opposite wall. You begin to see the scalloped gables of the houses, the sculptures on the entablatures, the bizarre shapes of the chimneys; a few more steps, and the eyes range over the whole of the city. There is a forest of spires, steeples and towers bristling on every side, notched, indented, hollowed out, struck out by a puncher, and letting the light through their myriad pinked-out holes. Domes and cupolas round out like the breasts of a giantess or the skulls of Titans. Islands of houses and palaces emerge in shadowy or luminous swathes. A few more steps, and you will be on the platform; and then, beyond the city walls, you will see the verdant farmland, the blue hills, and the white sails on the moiré ribbon of the river. You are inundated with dazzling light, and swallows fly to and fro around you uttering their joyful little cries. The distant sound of the city reaches you like a friendly murmur or the hum of a beehive; all the bell-towers unstring their ropes of sonorous pearls in the air; the winds bring you the scents of the neighbouring forest and the mountain flowers; all is light and harmony and perfume. If your feet had grown weary, or discouragement had taken hold of you, and you had stayed and sat on a lower step, if you had gone right down to the bottom again, this sight would have been lost to you. Sometimes, however, the tower has only one opening in the middle or at the top. The tower of your life is built like that; then you need more dogged courage, a perseverance armed with more hooked nails, to hang on to the projecting stones in the shadow, and reach the dazzling trefoil through which your glance goes out over the landscape; or else the loopholes have been filled in, or they have forgotten to pierce them, and then you have to go to the very top; but the higher you have gone without seeing, the more vast the horizon seems, the greater the pleasure and the surprise.

ROSETTE: O Théodore, God grant that I shall soon reach the place where the window is! For a very long time I have followed the spiral through unbroken darkness. I am afraid that the opening has been blocked up, and I shall have to climb to the top; suppose this staircase with the countless stairs only ended in a walled-up door or a freestone arch?

THÉODORE: Don't say that, Rosette; don't think it. What architect would build a staircase which didn't lead anywhere? Why should the placid architect of the world be more stupid and improvident than an ordinary architect? You cannot imagine that it has amused Him to play a trick on you: to shut you up in a long stone tube without an opening and without an exit? Why should you think He would dispute with miserable ants like ourselves their wretched momentary happiness, the one imperceptible canary-seed which belongs to them in this vast creation? To do that He would need to be as ferocious as a tiger or a judge; and, if we so displease Him, He would only have to tell a comet to turn a little out of its path and strangle us all with a hair of its tail. Why the devil should you think that God would enjoy Himself by spiking us one by one with a golden pin as the Emperor Domitian spiked flies? God is not a door-keeper or a churchwarden, and, although He is old, He is not yet senile. All these spiteful little actions are beneath Him, and He isn't stupid enough to play the wit with us and trick us. Take heart, Rosette, take heart! If you're out of breath, pause for a little, recover your breath, and then go on climbing; perhaps you have only another twenty steps or so to climb to reach the embrasure from which you will see your happiness.

ROSETTE: Never! Oh, never! If I reach the top of the tower, it will only be to throw myself down from it.

THÉODORE: My poor sufferer, cast away those ill-omened thoughts which are fluttering round you like bats, and casting the dark shadows of their wings on your lovely brow. If you want me to love you, be happy, and do not weep. (*He draws her gently to him, and kisses her on the eyes.*)

ROSETTE: What a misfortune for me that I've known you! And yet, if it had to be done again, I should still want to know you. Your harshness has been sweeter to me than the passion of other people; and, though you have made me suffer much, all the pleasure I have had has come from you; through you, I have glimpsed what I might have been. You have been the lightning of my night, you have lit up many sombre places in my soul; you have opened quite new perspectives in my life. I owe it to you that I know the meaning of love, unhappy love, it's true; but in unreciprocated love there is profound and melancholy charm. It is fine to remember those who forget us. It is already a happiness to be able to love even when you are the only one who loves, and many people die without having it, and often those who love are not those who are most to be pitied.

THÉODORE: They suffer and they feel their wounds, but at least they live. They cling to something. They have a star round which they gravitate, a pole to which they ardently turn. They have something to wish for; they can say to themselves: 'If I achieve that, if I have that, I shall be happy.' They have fearful agonies, but when they die they can at least say: 'I am dying for him. To die like that is to be reborn.' The true, the only people who are irreparably unhappy are those whose wild embrace contains the world, those who want everything and nothing, those who, if the angel or the fairy should come down and suddenly say: 'Wish something, and you shall have it,' would find themselves perplexed, at a loss for words.

ROSETTE: If the fairy came, I know quite well what I should ask her.

THÉODORE: You know, Rosette, and that is why you are much happier than I am, for I don't know. Within me move many vague desires, entangled with each other, creating new desires which then devour them. My desires are a cloud of birds which wheel and fly around without an aim; yours is an eagle, gazing on the sun, prevented by the lack of wind from rising on outspread wings. Oh, if I could know what I want! If the idea which pursues me could stand out clear and precise from the mist around it; if the propitious or fatal star appeared in the depths of my heaven; if the light that I must follow came to shine in the night, treacherous will-o'-the-wisp or hospitable beacon; if my pillar of fire walked before me, even if it were across a desert without manna and without fountains; if I knew where I was going, if I were only to end at a precipice! – I should prefer those wild rides of the accursed hunters over the quagmires and the thickets to this absurd and monotonous pawing the ground. To live like this is to have an occupation like those blindfolded horses which turn the wheel of a well, and do thousands of leagues without seeing anything and without changing place. I have been going round for quite a long time, and the bucket should have come up to the surface.

ROSETTE: You have much in common with d'Albert, and, when you talk, it sometimes seems to me as if he's speaking. I'm sure that, when you know him better, you will find yourself very attached to him. You can't fail to suit each other. He is wracked, like you, by these aimless aspirations; he loves immensely, but he knows not what, he would like to go to heaven, for the earth seems to him a stool which is hardly good enough for one of his feet, and he is prouder than Lucifer before his fall.

THÉODORE: I was afraid at first that he was one of those countless poets who have driven poetry from the earth, one of those stringers of artificial pearls who see nothing in the world but the final syllable of a word, one of those poets who, when they have rhymed *gloom* with *tomb*, *goal* with *soul*, and *God* with *plod*, conscientiously fold their arms and cross their legs, and allow the spheres to go on turning.

ROSETTE: He isn't one of those at all. His poems are beneath him, they don't contain him. You'd get a very false idea of his person from what he's done; his real poem is himself, and I don't know if he'll ever produce another. Deep down in his soul he has a seraglio of beautiful ideas; he surrounds them with a triple wall, and he is more jealous of them than ever sultan was of his odalisks. His poems only include the ones he doesn't care about, or the ones that displease him; that is the door through which he discards them, and the world has only the ones he doesn't want any more.

THÉODORE: I understand this jealousy and modesty. In the same way, many people don't acknowledge the love that they have had until they lose it, and they acknowledge their mistresses when they're dead.

ROSETTE: You have such trouble in this world possessing something of your own! Every flame attracts so many moths, every treasure draws so many thieves! I like those silent men who take their ideas into their tombs, and refuse to surrender them to the squalid kisses and the immodest pawings of the crowd. I like those lovers who don't carve their mistress's name on any bark, don't entrust it to any echo; those lovers who, when they go to sleep, are pursued by the fear that they mustn't pronounce it in a dream. I am one of those; I haven't spoken my thought, and no one will know my love ... But it is nearly eleven o'clock, my dear Théodore, and I'm keeping you from the rest which you must need. I always feel a pang when I have to leave you, and it seems to me it's the last time I shall see you. I am delaying it as long as I can; but the day will come when I must go. Goodbye, then. I'm afraid that d'Albert is looking for me. Goodbye, my friend.

Théodore put his arm round her waist, and led her to the door; there he paused, and followed her for a long while with his eyes. The corridor was punctuated at long intervals by little windows with small panes, lit up by the moon, and they created the most fantastic alternate light and shade. At every window the pure white figure of Rosette gleamed like a silver ghost; then it vanished to appear again, more brilliant, a little further on; finally it disappeared completely.

Théodore remained for a moment motionless with folded arms, as if he were sunk in profound reflections. Then he passed his hand across his brow, and tossed his hair back with a movement of his head. He went into his room again, and he retired to bed when he had kissed the page on the forehead: the page who was still fast asleep.

VII

As soon as day dawned at Rosette's, d'Albert made his appearance with an eagerness which was unusual for him.

'There you are,' said Rosette. 'I should say you were very early, if you could ever arrive early. I shall reward you for your politeness. I grant you my hand to kiss.'

And she drew from under the linen sheet adorned with lace the prettiest hand that was ever seen at the end of a plump fat arm.

D'Albert kissed it with compunction. 'And what about the other, the little sister? Aren't we going to kiss it, too?'

'Lord, yes! Nothing is more possible. I'm in my Sunday-best humour today.' And she took her other hand out from under the sheet and tapped him gently on the mouth. 'Aren't I the most accommodating woman in the world?'

'You are grace itself,' said d'Albert, 'and they should raise white marble temples to you in groves of myrtles. Indeed, I'm very much afraid that it may happen to you as it did to Psyche, and Venus may become jealous of you.' He brought his mistress's two hands together and held them to his lips.

'You do recite it all in one breath!' answered Rosette. 'People would think it a phrase you'd learnt by heart.' And she made a delightful little pout.

'Not at all,' replied d'Albert. 'You deserve to have the phrase freshly minted for you, and you are made to gather the virginities of madrigals.'

'Come, now! There's no doubt that something has spurred you on today! Are you ill, that you're so gallant? I'm afraid you must be dying. Do you know that, when someone changes their character all at once, without apparent reason, it bodes ill? It has been ascertained, by all the women who have taken the trouble to love you, that you're usually as sullen as can be, and it is just as certain that you are at this moment as charming as can be and quite unaccountably polite. In fact, my dear d'Albert, you do look pale; give me your arm, and let me take your pulse.' And she lifted up his sleeve, and took his pulse with comical gravity. 'No . . . You're fine, and you haven't the slightest sign of a temperature. So I must be tremendously pretty this morning! Go and fetch my mirror, so that I may see how far your gallantry is right or wrong.'

D'Albert went and picked up a little mirror which was on the dressing-table. He put it on the bed.

'Actually,' said Rosette, 'you aren't completely wrong. Why don't you write a sonnet on my eyes, Sir Poet? You have no reason for not writing one. Just think how unfortunate I am! To have eyes like that and a poet like this, and not to have sonnets, as if I were one-eyed and had a water-carrier for a lover! You don't love me, sir; you haven't even written me a sonnet in acrostics. And my mouth, what do you think of that? Yet I've kissed you with that mouth, and perhaps I'll kiss you again, my romantic lady-killer; and in truth it's a favour you hardly deserve (what I'm saying doesn't apply to today, for you deserve everything). But don't let's speak just about myself. You have a matchless beauty and freshness this morning, you look like a brother of Aurora; and, though it is hardly day, you are already dressed up and gadrooned, as if for a ball. Do you have designs on me, perchance? And would you have made an unfair attempt on my virtue? Would you want to seduce me? But I was forgetting that that was already done, and an old story.'

'Rosette, don't joke like that; you know perfectly well that I love you.'

'But that depends. I'm not quite sure. Are you?'

'Absolutely certain, and so much so that, if you were kind enough to lock your door, I should attempt to show you. I should do so, I dare flatter myself, in a victorious manner.'

'I'm having none of that. However much I want to be convinced, my door will stay open. I'm too pretty to be pretty in private; the sun shines for everyone, and my beauty will be like the sun today, if you don't mind.'

'To be honest, I do mind very much; but behave as if I warmly approved. I am your most humble slave, and I lay down my wishes at your feet.'

'That couldn't be better; go on feeling like that, and leave the key in your bedroom door this evening.'

'The Chevalier Théodore de Sérannes,' said a big Negro's head, which appeared, round and smiling, between the two halves of the door. 'He asks to pay his respects to you and begs you to deign to receive him.'

'Ask the Chevalier to come in,' said Rosette, pulling the sheet up as far as her chin.

Théodore went straight up to Rosette's bed, and made her the deepest and most graceful bow, which she acknowledged with a friendly nod; then he turned towards d'Albert, whom he also greeted with a frank and courtly air. 'What were you talking about?' asked Théodore. 'Perhaps I've interrupted an interesting conversation. Please go on, and give me the gist of it in a few words.'

'Oh, no!' replied Rosette with a mischievous smile. 'We were talking business.'

Théodore sat down at the foot of Rosette's bed, for d'Albert had seated himself at the head, as he had been the first to arrive. For some time the conversation floated from subject to subject, very witty, amusing and lively, and that is why we don't intend to describe it; we'd be afraid that it might lose too much in transcription. The manner, tone and fire of words and gestures, the thousand ways of pronouncing a word, the wit, so like the froth on the champagne which sparkles and at once evaporates, are impossible things to fix and reproduce. We shall leave the reader to fill the gap, he will certainly perform the task better than we should; let him imagine five or six pages filled with everything that is most delicate and capricious, most curiously fanciful, most elegant and be-spangled.

We are well aware that we are using an artifice, rather like that of Timanthus. He was in despair that he could not render Agamemnon's face, so he threw a drapery over his head. But we should rather be timid than unwise.

It would not perhaps be inappropriate to seek the reasons why d'Albert had risen so early in the morning, and what agitation had led him to come to Rosette as early as if he had still been in love with her. It seems that it was a little twinge of vague and unacknowledged jealousy. Certainly he didn't care very much for Rosette, he would in fact have been greatly relieved to have been rid of her – but at least he wanted to leave her himself, not to be abandoned by her, something which always wounds a man's pride very deeply, however extinct his original fire may be. Théodore was such a handsome cavalier that it was hard to see him arrive unexpectedly in a love-affair without fearing what had actually happened many times, that is to say that all eyes turned in his direction and that the hearts followed the eyes; it was remarkable that, although he had carried away many women, no lover had borne that long resentment against him which you usually feel for the people who have supplanted you. There was so conquering a charm in all his ways, so natural a grace, something so gentle and so proud, that even men were sensible of it. D'Albert had come to Rosette with the intention of speaking very harshly to Théodore, if he should meet him there; he was quite surprised not to feel the slightest anger in his presence, and to abandon himself so readily to the advances that he made him. After half an hour, you would have said that they were two childhood friends, and yet d'Albert was deeply convinced that, if ever Rosette was to love, she would love this man, and he had every reason to be jealous, at least for the future, for as to the present he didn't suppose anything yet. What would he have felt if he had seen his mistress, in a white peignoir, slip into the room of this handsome young man like a moth on a moonbeam, and only leave it three or four hours later, with mysterious precautions? He could, in truth, have thought himself more fortunate than he was, for one rarely sees a pretty and amorous woman who leaves the room of an equally handsome cavalier in the same state as that in which she entered it.

Rosette was listening to Théodore with much attention, as you listen to somebody you love; but what he said was so varied and amusing that her attention was only natural and it was easily explained. So d'Albert did not take great umbrage. Théodore's tone towards Rosette was polite and friendly, but nothing more.

'What shall we do today, Théodore?' asked Rosette. 'Suppose we went on a boating expedition? What do you think? Or suppose we went hunting?'

'Let's go hunting. It's less melancholy than gliding over the water side by side with some weary swan and bending the waterlily leaves to right and left. Don't you agree, d'Albert?'

'I'd be quite as happy to glide downstream in the little boat as to gallop wildly after some poor animal; but I'll go wherever you go. All we need to do now is to let Madame Rosette get up, and to put on some suitable attire.' Rosette made a sign of agreement, and rang for someone to get her up. The two young men went off with their arms round each other, and, seeing them such good friends, it was easy to conjecture that one was the lover-in-waiting and the other the heart's love of the same woman.

Everyone was soon ready. D'Albert and Théodore were already on horseback in the front courtyard, when Rosette, in riding-habit, appeared at the top of the stone steps. In this dress, she had a slight air of sprightliness and audacity which suited her to perfection. She leapt into the saddle with her usual agility, and gave a touch of the switch to her horse, which set off like an arrow. D'Albert galloped after her, and he had soon caught her up. Théodore let them go on ahead, since he was sure that he could catch them up when he wanted. He seemed to be waiting for something, and he often looked back towards the château.

'Théodore! Théodore! Come on! Are you riding a wooden horse?' cried Rosette.

Théodore put his horse to the gallop and lessened the distance which separated him from Rosette, though all the same he didn't catch up with her.

He still looked in the direction of the château which was beginning to disappear from sight. A little cloud of dust appeared at the end of the path. Something still invisible was in it, briskly bestirring itself. A few moments later the cloud was beside Théodore, and, half-opening like the classic clouds in the *Iliad*, it revealed the fresh and rosy face of the mysterious page.

'Théodore, come on!' Rosette cried out again. 'Spur on your tortoise and catch up with us!'

Théodore slackened the reins of his horse, which was pawing the ground and rearing with impatience, and in a few seconds he had gone several heads beyond d'Albert and Rosette.

'If you love me, follow me,' said Théodore, jumping a barrier four feet high. 'Well, Sir Poet!' he said, when he reached the other side, 'aren't you jumping? But your steed is winged, so they say.'

'Upon my word, I'd rather go the long way round,' replied d'Albert, smiling. 'I've only got one head to break, after all. If I had several, I should attempt it.'

'So no one loves me,' said Théodore, 'for no one follows me.' And he turned down the bowed corners of his mouth more than usual. The little page looked up at him reproachfully with his big blue eyes, and brought his heels close to his horse's side.

The horse gave a prodigious leap.

'Someone loves you!' he said to him, from the far side of the barrier.

Rosette cast a singular glance at the child, and blushed up to her eyes. Then, with a furious crack of her whip on her mare's neck, she crossed the apple-green wooden crossbar.

'What about me, Théodore, do you think that I don't love you?'

The child looked at her obliquely, out of the corner of its eyes, and went up to Théodore.

D'Albert was already in the middle of the avenue, and he saw nothing of all this; since time immemorial, fathers, husbands and lovers have had the privilege of seeing nothing.

'Isnabel,' said Théodore, 'you're mad – and so are you, Rosette! Isnabel, you didn't have enough space to jump in; and you, Rosette, nearly caught your dress in the stakes. You could have killed yourselves.'

'What does it matter?' answered Rosette in a tone of voice so sad and melancholy that Isnabel forgave her for having leapt the barrier too.

They continued their way like this for some time, till they reached the crossroads where they were to meet the huntsmen and the hounds. Six arches, cut out of the thickness of the forest, opened on to a small stone tower with six sides, each of which was engraved with the name of the path which had led to it. The trees rose up so high that they seemed to want to card the woolly, fleecy clouds which were blown by the sharpish breeze above their summits; the tall, thick grass and impenetrable bushes offered retreats and strong-holds to the game, and the hunt promised to be a success. It was a real forest of olden times, with ancient, more than secular oaks, the kind you no longer see now that people no longer plant trees, and people are too impatient to wait for trees to grow; it was a heredi-tary forest, planted by great-grandfathers for fathers, and by fathers for grandsons, with avenues of prodigious breadth, an obelisk surmounted by a ball, a rockwork fountain, the obligatory pool, and huntsmen with white-powdered hair, yellow leather breeches and sky-blue coats; it was one of those thick and sombre forests which set off to perfection the white satin croups of Wouvermans' big horses, and the broad banners of those hunting-horns *à la Dampierre*, which Parrocel likes to have shining on the backs of his whippers-in. A multitude of dogs' tails, curved like crescents or bill-hooks, were frisking excitedly in a cloud of dust. The signal was given, the dogs, which had been straining at their leads fit to strangle them-selves, were suddenly unleashed, and the hunt began. We shan't give a very detailed description of the stag's evasions and sudden turns of direction through the forest; we don't even know for certain if it was a full-grown stag, and, despite our researches, we haven't been able to find out, which is really distressing. All the same, we think that in such a forest, so ancient, lordly and um-brageous, there should be only full-grown stags, and we don't see why the one they galloped after, on horses of different colours and *non passibus aequis*, the four principal characters in this illustrious novel, shouldn't have been a stag of that kind.

The stag ran like the real stag he was, and the fifty or so dogs which he had at his heels were no small spur to his natural velocity. The course was so fast that one only heard a few occasional barks.

Théodore, who was best mounted and the best horseman, spurred on the pack with unbelievable ardour. D'Albert was close behind him. Rosette and the little page Isnabel followed, after an interval which grew longer and longer with every minute.

The gap was soon so large that they couldn't hope to draw level with them any more.

'Suppose we stopped for a moment,' said Rosette, 'and let the horses recover their breath? The hunt is going along the side of the lake, and I know a short cut which would bring us there as they arrive.'

Isnabel reined in his little mountain pony; it lowered its head, and shook the locks of its mane over its eyes, and began to dig in the sand with its hoofs.

This little horse was the most perfect contrast with Rosette's. It was jet black, while the other was satin white; it was wild-haired and bristling, while the other had its mane plaited with blue, its tail combed and curled. The second looked like a unicorn, and the first like a barbet.

The same antithesis could be observed in the masters as in the mounts. Rosette's hair was as dark as Isnabel's was fair; her eyebrows were very clearly defined, in a most obvious way; the page's eyebrows were almost as pale as his skin, and they looked like the down on a peach. One had a colouring as bright and strong as the noonday sun; the other one's complexion had the transparency and blushes of the rising dawn.

'Supposing we tried to catch up the hunt, now?' said Isnabel to Rosette. 'The horses have had time to recover their breath.'

'Let's go!' replied the pretty amazon, and they rushed off at a gallop down a rather narrow avenue which led off on one side towards the lake; the two horses were galloping neck and neck and they almost filled it.

On Isnabel's side, a big branch like an arm stuck out from a gnarled and twisted tree, as if it would show its fist to the riders. The child didn't see it.

'Take care!' cried Rosette. 'Lie down on the saddle! You're going to be thrown!'

The advice was given too late; the branch struck Isnabel in the middle of his body. The violence of the blow made him lose his stirrups, and, while his horse galloped on, and the branch was too strong to bend, he was lifted out of the saddle and fell roughly to the ground.

The child lay unconscious from the blow. Rosette, in great alarm, leapt off her horse and went up to the page, who gave no sign of life.

His cap had come off, and his fine fair hair was streaming over the sand. His little open hands looked like wax hands, they were so pale; Rosette knelt down beside him and tried to make him come round. She had no salts or phial on her, and she was much perplexed. At last she caught sight of a rather deep rut where the rainwater had collected and settled; she dipped her fingers into it, to the great alarm of a little frog which was the naiad of those waves, and she shook a few drops over the young page's bluish temples. He didn't seem to feel them, and the pearls of water rolled down his white cheeks like a sylphid's tears along a lily leaf. Thinking that his clothes might constrict him, Rosette unbuckled his belt, undid the buttons of his jerkin, and opened his shirt so that he could breathe more easily. Rosette then saw something which for a man would have been the most agreeable surprise in the world, but it did not appear to give her anything like pleasure – for she frowned, and her upper lip trembled slightly. What she saw was a very white breast, not yet quite formed, but a breast which gave the most admirable promise, and already largely fulfilled it; a round, smooth, ivorine breast, to speak like the Ronsards of today: a breast delectable to see, and more delectable to kiss.

'A woman!' she said, 'A woman! Oh, Théodore!'

Isnabel – we shall keep this name for her, though it is not her own – began to breathe a little, and languidly raised her long eyelids; she was not hurt in any way, she was only stunned. She soon sat up, and, with help from Rosette, she managed to stand on her feet and remount her horse. It had stopped as soon as it felt its rider gone.

They made their way slowly to the lake, where they rediscovered the rest of the hunt. Rosette told Théodore briefly what had happened. The latter changed colour several times while Rosette was giving her account, and he rode beside Isnabel all the time for the rest of the journey.

They went back to the château very early. The day which had begun so happily ended in a sad enough manner.

Rosette was pensive, and d'Albert also seemed to be lost in profound reflections. The reader will soon know what had caused them.

VIII

No, my dear Silvio, no, I have not forgotten you; I am not one of those who walk through life without ever casting a glance behind them; my past follows me, it encroaches on my present, and almost on my future; your friendship is one of those sunlit places which stand out most clearly on the horizon – which is already blue – of these latter years; often, from the summit where I stand, I turn round to contemplate it with a feeling of unspeakable melancholy.

Oh, what a wondrous time it was! How angelically pure we were! Our feet hardly touched the ground; it seemed as if we had wings on our shoulders, our desires carried us away, and the fair halo of adolescence shimmered round our brows in the spring breeze.

Do you remember that little island planted with poplars at that place in the bend of the river? You needed a rather long, very narrow plank to reach it, a plank with a curious sag in the middle. It was really a bridge for goats, in fact it was hardly used except by goats. It was delectable. The short, thick grass, where forget-me-nots opened, winking their pretty little blue eyes, a path as yellow as nankeen which made a belt round the green dress of the island, and hugged its waist, an ever-trembling shadow of aspens and poplars: these were not the least pleasures of this paradise. There were great squares of linen which women used to come and spread out to whiten in the dew; you would have thought that they were squares of snow. There was a little girl, all brown and sunburnt, whose big wild eyes shone brilliantly through her locks of hair: the little girl who looked after the goats, threatening them, and waving her osier switch when they looked as if they were going to walk on the linen she was looking after – do you remember her? And the sulphur-coloured butterflies, with irregular and quivering flight, and the kingfisher which we so often tried to catch – which had its nest in that tangle of alder-trees? And those paths down to the river with their rough-hewn steps, their stakes and poles all green at the bottom and nearly always cut off by a lattice of plants and branches? How clear and sparkling that water was! How it revealed its bed of golden sand! And what a pleasure it was to sit on the bank, and dangle your toes in it! The nenuphars with golden flowers grace-fully unfurled, like green hair floating on the agate back of some or other nymph in the waters. The heavens looked at themselves in this mirror with the most delightful sky-blue smiles and pearl-grey transparencies, and, at every hour of day, there were turquoises, spangles, cotton-wool and watered silk in an inexhaustible variety. How I loved those squadrons of little ducks with emerald necks, which navigated incessantly from one bank to the other and made a few wrinkles on the unbroken glass!

What appropriate figures we were in that landscape! How well we went with that sweet, reposeful nature, how easily we harmo-nized with it! Spring outside, and youth within, sunlight on the grass, a smile on the lips, a snowfall of flowers on all the bushes, and white illusions blossoming in our souls, modest blushes on our cheeks and on the eglantine, poetry singing in our heart, hidden birds twittering in the trees, light, cooing, perfumes, a myriad vague murmurs, a beating heart, the river shifting a stone, a drop of water rolling down a calyx, a tear coursing down an eyelid, a sigh of love, the rustle of a leaf ... What evenings we spent there, walking slowly along the river bank, so near the edge that we often walked with one foot in the water and the other on the ground!

Alas! That did not last for long, at least not for me. As for you, while you acquired the wisdom of the man, you still kept the inno-cence of the child. The seed of corruption which was in me grew very fast, and gangrene ruthlessly devoured all that was pure and sacred within me. The one good thing that remains to me is my friendship for you.

I am accustomed to hide nothing from you – neither deeds nor thoughts. I have bared the most secret fibres of my heart before you; however bizarre, however ridiculous, however eccentric the movements of my soul may be, I must describe them to you; but what I have felt for some time is in fact so strange that I hardly dare admit it to myself. I told you somewhere that I was afraid I had so sought for beauty, I had so bestirred myself to find it, that I should end by degenerating into the impossible or the monstrous. I have almost reached that point. Oh, when shall I emerge from all these conflicting currents which drag me off in every direction? When will the deck of my ship cease to tremble under my feet and to be swept by the waves of all these storms? Where shall I find a port where I can anchor, an immovable rock out of reach of the waves where I can dry myself and wring the foam out of my hair?

You know how ardently I have sought for physical beauty, what importance I attach to outward form, what a love of the visible world possesses me. That has to be, I am too corrupt and too indifferent to believe in moral beauty, and to pursue it for any length of time. I have completely lost the knowledge of good and evil; I have been so depraved that I have almost returned to the ignorance of the savage and the child. In fact there is nothing which seems to me worthy of praise or blame, and the strangest behaviour hardly surprises me. My conscience is a deaf mute. Adultery seems to me the most innocent thing in the world; I find it quite natural that a young girl should prostitute herself; I feel that I should deceive my friends without the least remorse, and I shouldn't have the slightest hesitation in kicking the people who vex me over a precipice if I were walking on the edge with them. I should witness the most atrocious scenes with composure, and in the sufferings and misfortunes of humanity I find something which doesn't displease me. When I see some disaster befall the world I feel the same sharp and bitter satisfaction that you feel when you finally take revenge for an old insult.

Oh world, what have you done to me that I should hate you so? Who has embittered me like this against you? What, then, did I expect of you that I feel such rancour against you for deceiving me? What high hope have you disappointed? What eagle's wings have you clipped? What doors remain shut which you should have opened? Which of us has failed the other?

Nothing touches me, nothing moves me; when I hear the account of heroic deeds, I no longer feel those noble tremors which used to run through me from head to foot. Indeed, it all seems to me rather stupid. There is no accent deep enough to touch the slackened fibres of my heart and make them vibrate: I see the tears flow from my fellow men with the same eyes as I see the rain, unless they are of the first water, or catch the light in a picturesque way, unless they flow down a beautiful cheek. There is almost nothing left but animals for whom I have a slight remnant of pity. I should easily let a peasant or servant be beaten without mercy, and I shouldn't bear it patiently if someone did the same to a horse or dog in my presence; and yet I'm not wicked, I've never harmed anyone in the world, and I shall probably never harm them; but that is more likely due to my nonchalance and to my sovereign contempt for everyone who displeases me, which doesn't allow me to concern myself with them, even to harm them. I abhor everyone in the mass; only one or two at most in the whole lot deserve to be particularly hated. Hating someone is setting them apart from the crowd; it is to be impassioned about them; it is to think about them by day and dream of them at night; it is to bite your pillow and gnash your teeth to think that they exist; what more do you do for someone you love? As for the trouble and anxiety which you undergo to destroy an enemy, would you undergo them to please a mistress? I doubt it; if you hate someone very much, you have to love someone else. Every great hatred serves as a counterweight to a great love; and whom could I hate, since I love nothing?

My hatred, like my love, is a vague and general feeling which wants to take against something and can't do so; I have a wealth of hate and love inside me, and I don't know what to do with it, a wealth of feeling which weighs upon me horribly. If I don't find the means to shed one or the other, or both of them, I shall burst like those sacks which are stuffed too full of money, and split and come unsewn. Oh, if I could abhor somebody, if one of those fools with whom I live could insult me, make my old viper's blood boil in my icy veins, and draw me out of the dismal somnolence I huddle in! If you bit my cheek with your rat's teeth, you old doddering witch, and infected me with your venom and your madness! If someone's death could be my life; if the last heartbeat of an enemy writhing beneath my feet could send delightful shudders through my body, if the smell of his blood grew sweeter to my nostrils than the scent of flowers – oh! how readily I should abandon love, how happy I should feel myself to be!

Mortal kisses, tiger's bites, boa constrictors' embraces, elephants' feet on a cracking and flattening breast, stinging scorpion's tail, milky sap of the spurge, corrugated krisses of Java, sword-blades which shine at night and go out in blood, it is you whom I now invoke! You will replace the overblown roses, damp kisses and embraces of love!

I said I loved nothing; alas! I'm afraid that there is something now that I love. It would be a hundred thousand times better to hate than to love like that! I have now discovered the type of beauty that I had dreamed of for so long. I have found the body of my ghost; I have seen it, I have touched its hand, and it exists; it is not a chimera. I knew that I couldn't be deceived, and that my presentiments were never mistaken. Yes, Silvio, I am near the dream of my life; I am here, and my dream is there; from where I am I can see the curtains quiver in the window and I see the light in the lamp. The shadow of my dream has just passed across the curtain; in an hour's time we shall sup together.

Those fine Turkish eyelids, that deep and limpid gaze, that warm pale amber skin, that long dark lustrous hair, that proud, well-modelled nose, those fine and slender wrists and ankles and extremities in the style of Parmigianino, those delicate curves, that pure oval, which give a head such style and nobility, everything that I wanted, everything which I should have been happy to find disseminated among five or six people, I have it all united in one person!

What I adore above everything in the world is a beautiful hand. If you saw that hand! What perfection! How utterly white it is! What softness of skin! What tapered fingertips! How clearly the moon of the nails is defined! What smoothness and brilliance! They are like the inner petals of a rose. The hands of Anne of Austria, so vaunted and so famed, are, in comparison, just the hands of a turkey-keeper or a scullery-maid. And then what grace, what art in the slightest movements of that hand! How gracefully that little finger bends and keeps slightly apart from its big brothers! The thought of that hand drives me mad, it makes my lips tremble and burn. I close my eyes so as not to see it any more; but with its delicate fingertips it takes my eyelashes and opens my eyelids, and a thousand visions of ivory and snow pass before me.

Oh, no doubt it is the devil's claw gloved in this satin skin; it is some scoffing demon who is mocking me; there is sorcery here. It's too monstrously impossible.

That hand . . . I am going to set off for Italy to see the pictures of the great masters, to study, compare and draw, and become a painter, so that I can render it as it is, as I see it, as I feel it; perhaps this will be a way to rid myself of my obsession.

I have wanted beauty; I did not know what I was asking for. It was wanting to look at the sun without eyelids, wanting to touch the flame. I am suffering horribly. I cannot assimilate that perfection, I cannot pass into it and make it pass into myself. I have no means of rendering it and making it felt! When I see something beautiful, I should like to touch it with my whole self, everywhere at the same time. I should like to sing it and paint it, sculpt it and write it, to be loved by it as I love it myself. I should like what cannot be and cannot ever be.

Your letter hurt me very much. Forgive my saying so. That calm, pure happiness which you rejoice in, those strolls in the reddening woods, those long talks, so tender and so intimate, which end in a chaste kiss on the brow; that life apart and undisturbed; those days that pass so swiftly that night seems to you to be early: they all make me find my inner torments more tempestuous still. So you will be married in two months' time; all the obstacles have been overcome, you are sure now to belong to one another for ever. Your present felicity is increased by all your felicity to come. You're happy, and you have the certainty that you will soon be happier still. What a destiny is yours! Your sweetheart is beautiful, but what you have loved in her is not mortal and palpable beauty, material beauty, it is invisible and lasting beauty, the beauty which does not age at all, the beauty of the soul. She is full of grace and innocence; she loves you as such souls know how to love. You have not looked to see if her golden hair resembled the hair in Rubens or Giorgione; it pleases you because it is her hair. I am sure, you happy lover, that you do not even know if your mistress is of Greek or Asian type, English or Italian. Oh Silvio! How rare they are, the hearts which are content with pure and simple love and do not want a hermitage in the forests, a garden on an island in Lake Maggiore.

If I had the courage to tear myself away from here, I should go and spend a month with you; perhaps I should purify myself in the air you breathe, perhaps the shadow of your avenues would cast some coolness on my burning brow. But no, I should not set foot in that paradise. I should hardly be allowed to look from a distance, over the wall, at the two beautiful angels which stroll there hand in hand, gazing into one another's eyes. The demon can only enter Eden in the shape of a serpent, and, dear Adam, for all the happiness in heaven, I shouldn't want to be serpent to your Eve.

What fearsome change, then, has transformed my soul? What has changed my blood and turned it into venom? Monstrous thought, unfolding your pale green branches and hemlock umbels in the icy shadow of my heart, what poisoned wind set there the seed from which you have blossomed? Was that what was in store for me, was that where they were fated to lead, all those paths so desperately tried? Oh, destiny, how you make game of us! All those soarings, eagle-like, towards the sun, those pure flames burning for heaven, that divine melancholy, that deep and sober love, that religion of beauty, that fantasy so curious and elegant, that ceaseless, ever-rising stream of the soul's fountain, that ecstasy, with ever-open wings, that dream which is more flowering than the hawthorn in May, all that poetry of my youth, all those gifts, so fine and rare, were to serve only to set me lower than the least of men!

I wanted to love. I went round like a madman, summoning and invoking love. I writhed with fury when I thought of my powerlessness. I warmed my blood, I dragged my body to the sinks of pleasures; I clasped to my arid heart, so tightly that I might have stifled her, a woman young and beautiful, who loved me. I pursued passion, and passion escaped me. I prostituted myself. I behaved like a virgin who goes into a place of ill repute hoping to find a lover among the debauched, instead of waiting patiently, in discreet and silent shadows, till the angel whom God intended for me appeared in a pale but glowing light, bearing a heavenly flower in her hand. I have wasted all these years, restless like a child, running here and there, attempting to force nature and force time. I should have spent these years in solitude and meditation, trying to make myself worthy of being loved. That would have been wise behaviour. But I could not see, and I was walking straight to the abyss. I already have a foot poised over the void. I think that I shall soon lift the other. I have resisted in vain, I know, I must fall to the very depths of this new abyss which has just opened within me.

Yes, this is how I had imagined love. I feel now what I'd dreamed. Yes, there are the dreadful, charming, sleepless nights when roses are thistles and thistles are roses; there indeed are sweet pain and wretched happiness. There is the ineffable unease which sets a golden cloud around you and makes the shape of things tremble before you as intoxication will do. There are those hummings in the ears where the final syllable of the beloved name for ever sounds. There are the pallors, the blushes, the sudden tremblings, the burning and icy sweat. It is really this; the poets do not lie.

When I am about to enter the drawing-room where we are accustomed to meet, my heart beats with such violence that it might be seen through my clothes, and I am obliged to hold it down with both hands, for fear that it should burst out. If I see my love at the end of a walk, in the park, I am at once oblivious of distance, and I don't know where the path is leading: the devil take it, but I must have wings. Nothing can distract me from my love. I read, and the image sets itself between the book and my eyes. I mount a horse, and gallop at full speed, and in the wind I still seem to feel the long hair mingling with my own, to hear my love's hasty breathing, and the warm breath touching my cheek. This image obsesses me, and follows me everywhere, and I never see it more than when it isn't there.

You pitied me for not loving. Pity me, now, for loving whom I love. What misfortune, what an axe-blow on my life, which was already cut in so many pieces! What senseless, guilty, hateful passion has taken hold of me! It is a disgrace, and I shall never cease to blush for it. It is the most deplorable of all my aberrations, I can't begin to understand it, I don't comprehend it in the least, everything in me is upside-down and in confusion; I no longer know who I am, or what others are, I wonder if I'm a man or a woman, I have a horror of myself, I feel singular and inexplicable urges, and there are moments when I feel that my mind is going, and the sense of my existence has quite gone. For a long time I could not believe what had happened. I watched and listened to myself attentively. I tried to unravel this tangled skein which had become caught up in my soul. At last, through the veils which shrouded it, I discovered the appalling truth ... Silvio, I love ... Oh, no, I could never tell you ... I love a man!

IX

THAT's how it is. I love a man, Silvio. I've tried to delude myself
for a long time; I've given a different name to the emotion I felt, I
clad it in the garb of pure, disinterested friendship; I believed that
it was only the admiration which I have for everyone and everything that is beautiful; for several days I walked along the treacherous and tempting paths that wander round every budding passion;
but now I recognize the deep and terrible track I have embarked on.
I can't deny it: I've studied myself closely, I have dispassionately
weighed all the circumstances; I have accounted to myself for the
smallest details; I have delved into my soul in every direction with
the sureness which comes from habitual self-examination; I blush
to think of it and write about it, but, alas, the thing is all too plain,
I love that young man, not in friendship, but with love – yes, with
love.

You whom I have loved so much, O Silvio, my good, my only
comrade, you have never made me feel the same, and yet, if ever
there was on earth a close and ardent friendship, it was our friendship. If ever two souls, though different, have absolutely understood each other, they were our two souls. What winged hours we
have spent together! What endless conversations, too soon ended!
How many things we have told each other, which people have
never told! We had a window in our hearts for one another: the
window which Momus wanted to open in the flank of man. How
proud I was to be your friend! I was younger than you, I was so
wild, and you were so rational!

What I feel for this young man is quite incredible; never have I
found any woman so singularly disturbing. The sound of his voice,
so silvery and clear, troubles and moves me strangely; my soul

hangs on my lips, like a bee on a flower, to drink in the honey of his words. I cannot brush against him in passing without trembling from head to foot, and, in the evening, when we say goodnight and he holds out his adorable hand, so gentle and smooth, my whole existence is concentrated in the place that he has touched, and an hour later I still feel the pressure of his fingers.

This morning I watched him a very long time without his seeing me. I was hidden behind my curtain. He was at his window, which is exactly opposite mine. This part of the château was built at the end of the reign of Henri IV; it is half in bricks, and half in ashlar, as was customary at the time; the window is long and narrow, with a stone lintel and a balcony. Théodore – for no doubt you've guessed that he is the man in question – was leaning on the balusters and seemed to be lost in a profound and melancholy dream. A red damask drapery, with big flowers, was half drawn up behind him and fell in big folds like a background for him. How beautiful he was, how wonderfully his brown, pale head stood out against that purple tint! Two big clusters of black and lustrous hair, like the bunches of grapes of ancient Erigone, hung gracefully at the side of his cheeks and charmingly framed the perfect and delicate oval of his lovely face. His round, plump neck was quite bare, and he was wearing a sort of dressing-gown with wide sleeves which looked rather like a woman's dress. He was holding a yellow tulip, and ruthlessly tearing it to pieces in his reverie, and he was throwing the pieces to the winds.

One of the luminous angles which the sun drew on the wall came and struck the window, and it gilded the picture with a warm, transparent tone enough to outdo the most iridescent canvas of Giorgione.

With that long hair gently stirring in the breeze, that bare marble neck, that wide robe drawn in at the waist, those lovely hands emerging from their sleeves like the pistils of a flower from the midst of the petals – he seemed not the handsomest of men, but the most beautiful of women – and in my heart I said to myself: 'It's a woman! Oh, it's a woman!' I have just remembered a piece of folly I wrote to you long ago – you know – about my ideal and the way in which I would undoubtedly encounter it: the beautiful lady in the Louis XIII park, the red and white château, the broad terrace, the avenues of old chestnut-trees and the meeting at the window; I gave you all those details a long time ago. It was exactly that – what I saw was the perfect realization of my dream. It was just the style of architecture, the effect of light, the kind of beauty, the colour and character that I had wished for; nothing was missing, but the woman was a man; but I confess that at that moment I had quite forgotten it.

Théodore must be a woman in disguise; otherwise the thing is impossible. That beauty is excessive, even for a woman. It is not the beauty of a man, were he Antinous, the friend of Adrian, or were he Alexis, the friend of Virgil. It is a woman, I am sure, and I am quite mad to have tormented myself like this. Everything can be explained in the most natural way in the world, and I am not such a monster as I thought.

Would God put such long fringes of brown silk on the wretched eyelids of a man? Would He dye so vivid and delicate a carmine our ugly, thick-lipped mouths bristling with hairs? Our bones, rough-hewn and crudely joined, are not worth enveloping in such white and delicate flesh; our misshapen skulls were never made to be bathed in the waves of such wonderful hair.

O beauty! We are created only to love you and to worship you on our knees, if we have found you – or to seek you eternally through the world, if this happiness has not been given us. To possess you, to be beauty ourselves, is possible only to angels and to women. Lovers, poets, painters and sculptors, all of us seek to raise an altar to you, the lover in his mistress, the poet in his verse, the painter in his canvas, the sculptor in his marble. Our eternal despair is not to be able to make tangible the beauty that we feel, and to be enveloped with a body which does not in the least realize the idea of the body which you understand to be your own.

Once upon a time I saw a young man who had stolen from me the form I should have had. This wretch was just as I should have liked to be. He had the beauty of my ugliness, and beside him I looked like his rough draft. He was my height, but he was stronger and he

was more slender; his figure was like mine, but it had an elegance
and a nobility which I don't possess. His eyes were the same colour
as my eyes, but they had a penetration and a brilliance which mine
will never have. His nose had been cast in the same mould as mine,
but it seemed to have been perfected by the chisel of an accomplished sculptor; the nostrils were wider and more passionate, the
flat parts were more clearly emphasized, and it had something
heroic which that respectable part of my person is totally devoid of.
You would have said that nature had attempted in me to make this
perfected other self, I seemed to be the crossed-out and imperfect
rough draft of a thought, and he was the copy in a fine copperplate
hand. When I saw him walk, stop, greet a woman, sit down and lie
down with that perfect grace which comes from beauty of proportion, I was overcome by fearful sadness and jealousy, the sort that
must be felt by the clay model which dries and cracks obscurely in
a corner of the studio, while the proud marble statue, which would
not exist without it, rises proudly on its sculpted plinth and attracts
attention and praise. For after all this scoundrel is only myself a little
better made, and cast in a less refractory bronze which made its way
more accurately into the hollows of the mould. I find him very bold
to flaunt with my form like that, and to be insolent as if he were an
original type; when all is said, he is only my plagiarist, for I was
born before him, and if it hadn't been for me nature would not have
had the idea of making him like that. When women praised his good
manners and his accomplishments, I absolutely longed to get up
and say: 'How stupid you are, praise me directly, for this gentleman
is me, and it is a pointless subterfuge to give him what you ought
to give to me.' At other times I had a horrible urge to strangle him,
to cast his soul out of the door of this body which belonged to me.
I prowled around him with tight lips, with fists clenched, like a lord
who is prowling round his palace: a family of beggars has settled
there in his absence, and he doesn't know how to throw them out.
Besides, this young man is stupid, and all the more successful for
that. And at times I envy him his stupidity more than his beauty.
The Evangelist's words on the poor in spirit are not complete. They
shall have the kingdom of heaven. I don't know anything about

that, and it doesn't matter to me in the least; but they certainly have the kingdom of the earth. Do you know a man of parts who is rich? Do you know a man of feeling and a certain merit who has a passable mistress? Though Théodore is quite beautiful, I still haven't desired his beauty, and I'd rather he had it than myself.

Those strange loves which fill the elegies of the ancient poets, those loves which so surprised us, those loves which we could not conceive, are, then, probable and possible. In the translations we made of them, we put women's names in place of the names that were there. Juventus ended as Juventia, Alexis was changed into Ianthe. Beautiful boys became beautiful girls, and so we recomposed the monstrous seraglios of Catullus, Tibullus, Martial and gentle Virgil. It was a very gallant occupation which only proved how little we had understood the classical genius.

I am a man of Homeric times; the world in which I live is not my own, and I understand nothing of the society around me. Christ did not come for me; I am as pagan as Alcibiades and Phidias. I have never been to gather the passion-flowers on Golgotha, and the deep river which flows from the side of Him Who was crucified, making a red girdle round the earth, has not bathed me in its waves. My rebel body will not recognize the supremacy of the soul, and my flesh does not in the least understand why it should be mortified. I find the earth as beautiful as heaven, and I think that perfection of form is a virtue. Spirituality does not concern me, I prefer a statue to a ghost, and high noon to twilight. Three things please me: gold, marble and purple, brilliance, solidity and colour. My dreams are made of those, and all the palaces I build for my reveries are made of these materials. Sometimes I have other dreams. There are long cavalcades of pure white horses, with no reins or harness, mounted by handsome naked youths who file past on a dark blue border as they do on the frieze of the Parthenon; there are a series of young girls crowned with bandelets, wearing tunics with straight folds, bearing sistrums of ivory, and seeming to wind round an enormous vase. Never fog or mist, never anything vague or indefinite. There are no clouds in my sky, or, if there are, they are solid clouds, cut out with a chisel, made of the splinters of marble fallen from the statue of Jupiter. Mountains with sharp and clear-cut ridges indent it roughly at the edges, and the sun leans over one of the highest peaks and opens wide its great yellow lion's eye with the gilded eyelids. The cricket chirps and chatters; the ear of corn cracks; shade is vanquished and overcome by heat, it curls up and gathers itself up under the trees; everything is radiant, everything glistens, everything shines. The slightest detail assumes solidity and becomes boldly marked; everything takes on robust form and colour. There is no place there for the softness and idle dreaming of Christian art. That world is mine. The streams of my landscapes fall in sculpted waves from a sculpted urn; between these tall reeds, as green and sonorous as those by the Eurotas, you see the glimmer of the round and silvery flank of some naiad with glaucous hair. Here, in this dark oak forest, Diana passes, her quiver at her back, with her flying sash and her buskins with interlaced straps. She is followed by her pack and by her nymphs with harmonious names. My pictures are painted in four tones, like the pictures by primitive painters, and often they are just coloured bas-reliefs; for I like to touch what I have seen with my finger and to pursue the roundness of contours into their innermost folds; I study everything from every side and I turn around it with a lantern in my hand. I have looked at love in the classical light and as a more or less perfect piece of sculpture. How is the arm? Quite good. What do you think about this foot? I think that the ankle lacks nobility, and the heel is common. But the bosom is well set and well shaped, the contour is quite fluent, the shoulders are fleshy and they have a fine character. This woman would be a passable model, and you could mould certain parts of her. Let us love her.

I have always been like that. I have a sculptor's eyes for women, not a lover's eyes. All my life I have been concerned with the shape of the flask, never with the quality of the contents. If I had had Pandora's box in my hands, I believe I shouldn't have opened it. A moment ago I said that Christ hadn't come for me; Mary, the star of the modern sky, the gentle mother of the glorious child, has not come for me either.

For a very long while, and very often, I have paused beneath the stone foliage of the cathedrals, in the trembling light from the stained-glass windows, at the moment when the organ was murmuring of its own accord, when an invisible finger touched the keys and the wind blew in the pipes – and I have plunged my eyes into the depths of the pale-blue almond eyes of the Madonna. I have piously observed the fined-down oval of her face, the barely indicated line of her eyebrows, I have admired her smooth luminous forehead, her chastely transparent temples, her cheekbones shaded with a restrained and virginal colour, more tender than peach-blossom. I have counted one by one the fine golden lashes which cast their quivering shadow on her cheeks; I have discerned, in the half-light which bathes her, the fleeting lines of her delicate neck, which is modestly bowed; I have even, with an audacious hand, lifted up the folds of her tunic and gazed upon the naked virgin breast, swollen with milk, which has never been pressed except by lips divine. I have followed its thin blue veins in their most imperceptible ramifications, I have laid my finger on it to make the celestial draught flow out in a white stream; I have with my lips brushed against the bud of the mystic rose.

Well! I confess that all this immaterial beauty, so winged and vaporous that you are aware that it will soon take flight, has hardly touched me. I prefer the Venus Anadyomene, I prefer it a thousand times over. Those antique eyes, turned up at the corners, those lips so pure and so clear-cut, so amorous, those lips which invite a kiss, that low, full brow, that hair as wavy as the sea and casually knotted behind the head, those firm and lustrous shoulders, that back with a thousand charming sinuosities, that small, slight bosom, all those round, taut lines, that breadth of the hips, that delicate strength, that sense of superhuman vigour in a body so adorably feminine: they all ravish me and enchant me to a degree which you cannot imagine, you who are Christian and good.

For all the humility she affects, Mary is much too proud for me; the tip of her foot, in white bandelets, hardly brushes against the globe – which is already turning blue – the globe where the antique dragon is writhing. Her eyes are the finest in the world, but they are always turned towards heaven, or cast down; they never look you in the face, they have never served to mirror a human form. And then, I don't like those nimbuses of smiling cherubims, which encircle her head in a pale gold vapour. I am jealous of those angelic youths with floating hair and floating robes who busy themselves so amorously in her assumptions; those hands which entwine to support her, those wings which bestir themselves to fan her, displease and vex me. These celestial dandies, so elegant and so triumphant, in their tunics of light, in their periwigs of golden thread, with their fine blue and green feathers, seem too gallant to me, and, if I were God, I should be careful not to give such attendants to my mistress.

Venus emerges from the sea to land on the earth – as befits a goddess who loves men – quite naked and quite alone. She prefers the earth to Olympus, and she has more men than gods among her lovers; she doesn't envelop herself in the languorous veils of mysticism; she stands erect, her dolphin behind her, one foot on her pearly shell; the sun strikes her smooth belly, and with one white hand she holds aloft the waves of her lovely hair in which old Father Ocean has sown his most perfect pearls. You can see her. She hides nothing, for modesty is only for the ugly, and it is a modern invention, born of the Christian contempt for form and matter.

O ancient world! All that you reverenced is scorned; your idols are cast down in the dust; lean anchorites clad in tattered rags, martyrs covered with blood, their shoulders torn by the tigers of your circuses, have settled on the pedestals of your beautiful and charming gods. Christ has enveloped the world in His shroud. Beauty must blush for herself and take a winding-sheet. Fine young men, with limbs rubbed with oil, who wrestle in the lyceum or gymnasium, under the brilliant sky, in the full sun of Attica, before the marvelling crowd; young Spartan girls who dance the bibase, and run naked to the summit of Taygetus, put on your tunics and your chlamys once again: your reign is past. And you, moulders of marble, Prometheuses of bronze, break your chisels: there will be no more sculptors. The palpable world is dead. Only a dark, lugubrious thought fills the immensity of the void. Cleomenes will see at the weavers' what folds the cloth or linen make.

Virginity, you bitter plant, born of a soil steeped in blood, you whose etiolated and sickly flower opens painfully in the damp shade of the cloisters, under a cold lustral rain: O rose without a scent and all bristling with thorns, you have replaced for us the lovely and joyful roses, bathed with nard and Falernus wine, of the dancers of Sybaris!

The ancient world does not know you, barren flower; never were you twined in its wreaths with their heady perfumes; in that vigorous and healthy society, you would have been scornfully trampled underfoot. Virginity, mysticism, melancholy – three unknown words – three new maladies brought by Christ. Pale ghosts who inundate our world with your icy tears: who, elbows on a cloud, and hand on breast, say but a single word: O death! O death! You could not have set foot on this earth so peopled with indulgent, wanton gods!

I consider woman, in the antique manner, as a beautiful slave who is destined for our pleasures. Christianity has not redeemed her in my eyes. She is still for me something different and inferior, something one adores and plays with, a toy which is more intelligent than if it were made of ivory or gold, and picks itself up of its own accord if one lets it fall to the ground. They have told me, because of this, that I have a poor opinion of women; I consider, on the contrary, that that shows a very good opinion of them.

I really don't know why women are so anxious to be considered as men. I can imagine that one might want to be a boa-constrictor, a lion or an elephant; but that someone should want to be a man is completely beyond my understanding. If I had been at the Council of Trent when they debated the important question as to whether a woman was a man, I should certainly have decided in the negative.

During my life I have written a few love poems, or at least poems which claimed to be so. I have just re-read some of them. The modern feeling of love is completely lacking. If they were written in Latin distichs and not in French rhymes, one would take them for the work of a bad poet of the Augustan age. And I am astonished that the women for whom they were written, instead of being enchanted by them, were not really angry about them. It is true that women don't understand poetry any more than cabbages and roses, which is quite natural and quite simple, since they themselves are poetry or at least the best instruments of poetry: the flute doesn't hear or understand the tune you play on it.

These poems do nothing but talk about the gold or ebony of hair, the miraculous delicacy of skin, the roundness of the arm, the smallness of the foot, and the delicate shape of the hand, and they all end with a humble supplication to the divinity to grant the enjoyment of all these fine things as soon as possible. In the triumphant parts, there is nothing but garlands hung over the threshold, rains of flowers, the burning of perfumes, a Catullan account of kisses, delightful sleepless nights, and quarrels with Aurora, with injunctions to the aforesaid Aurora to go back and hide herself behind the saffron curtains of old Tithonus. There is brilliance without warmth, sonority without vibration. It is precise, polite, and all done in the same curious style. It is not at all like the erotic poems written in the Christian era. There is not a soul which asks another soul to love it, since it loves. There is no blue and pleasant lake which invites a stream to melt into its breast and reflect together the stars of heaven. There are not a pair of doves which open their wings together to fly to the same nest.

Cynthia, you are beautiful; make haste. Who knows if you will be alive tomorrow? Your hair is blacker than the lustrous skin of an Ethiopian virgin. Make haste; a few years hence, fine silver threads will steal among the thick clusters. These roses smell sweet today, tomorrow they will have the smell of death and will only be the carcasses of roses. Let us smell the roses as long as they are like your cheeks; let us kiss your cheeks as long as they are like your roses. When you are old, Cynthia, no one will want you any more, even the lictor's servants if you pay them, and you will run after me whom you now reject. Wait until Saturn has scored with his nail that pure and shining brow, and you will find that your door, so besieged, so warm with tears, so strewn with flowers, will be avoided, accursed, and overgrown with weeds and briars. Make haste, Cynthia; the smallest furrow may serve as a grave for the greatest love.

The whole of the antique elegy is contained in this brutal and imperious formula. It always comes back to this. It is its greatest reason, and its strongest, it is the Achilles of its arguments. After that there is not much to say, and when it has promised a robe of double-dyed byssus, and a string of pearls of equal size, it is at its wits' end. It is also almost all that I find most conclusive myself on such occasions. However, I don't always keep to this rather exiguous programme, and I embroider my poor canvas with silk threads of different colours which I have pulled out here and there. But these bits are short, or knotted together a score of times, and they don't stick to the back of the woof. I talk quite elegantly about love, because I have read many beautiful things about it. All one needs here is a gift for acting. With many women, this appearance is enough; the habit of writing and imagining means that I don't stop short on these subjects, and any mind which is in training can easily obtain this result if it applies itself; but I don't mean a word of what I am saying, and I murmur to myself like the ancient poet: 'Cynthia, make haste.'

I have often been accused of being false and dissembling. No one in the world would like to speak frankly and to open their heart as much as I should; but, as I have no idea or feeling like those of the people round me, as there would be a hullabaloo and a general outcry at the first honest word I let out, I have preferred to be silent, or, if I speak, only to disgorge those stupidities which are accepted and have their civic rights. How welcome I should be if I told the ladies what I have just written to you! I don't think they would much appreciate my manner of seeing and my ways of looking at love. As for the men, I can't tell them either, to their faces, that they are wrong not to go round on all fours; and, in truth, that is the most favourable thing which I think about them. I don't want to start a quarrel with every word. What does it matter, when all is said, what I think or don't think; if I am sad when I seem light-hearted, happy when I look melancholy? People don't take it amiss that I don't go naked: can't I dress my face as well as my body? Why should a mask be more reprehensible than a pair of trousers, and a lie more reprehensible than corsets?

Alas! The earth turns around the sun, roasted on one side and frozen on the other. There is a battle in which six hundred thousand men cut each other to pieces; the weather is absolutely perfect; the flowers are flirting in an outrageous way, and shamelessly displaying their abundant breasts under the very hooves of the horses. Today there have been a legendary number of good deeds; it is pouring with rain, there are snow and thunder, lightning and hail; you would think that the world was about to end. The benefactors of humanity have mud up to their stomachs, and they are covered with dirt like dogs, unless they have carriages. Creation mocks man unmercifully, and it is always shooting blood-stained taunts at him. Everything is indifferent to everything, and everything lives or vegetates according to its own law. Whether I do this or that, whether I live or die, whether I suffer or rejoice, whether I conceal or I am frank, what difference does that make to the sun and the beetroots and even to men? A straw has fallen on an ant and broken its third leg at the second joint; a rock has fallen on a village and crushed it. I don't believe that one of these misfortunes wrings more tears than the other from the golden eyes of the stars. You are my best friend, if the expression isn't as hollow as a bell; if I were to die, I'm sure that, however disconsolate you were, you wouldn't go without your dinner even for two days, and, despite this fearful catastrophe, you would still continue to play backgammon very happily. Which of my friends and which of my mistresses will know my Christian names and surname twenty years hence, and would recognize me in the street, if I chanced to pass in a suit which was out at the elbows? Oblivion and nothingness, that is man.

I feel as completely alone as one can be, and all the threads which joined me to things and joined those things to me have broken, one by one. There are few examples of a man who has remained aware of his own movements and has reached such a degree of brutishness. I am like those bottles of liquor which have been left uncorked, when their spirits have completely evaporated. The drink has the same appearance and colour: taste it, and you will find it as insipid as water.

When I think about it, I am terrified by the rapidity of this decomposition; if it goes on, I shall have to preserve myself in salt, or I shall inevitably rot, and the worms will set about me, since I no longer have a soul, and that is the only difference between the body and the corpse. Only a year ago I still had something human about me; I bestirred myself, I was seeking. One thought above all was dear to me, it was a kind of aim, an ideal: I wanted to be loved, I had the dreams one has at my age – less vaporous, less chaste, it is true, than those of ordinary young men, but none the less contained within proper limits. Little by little what was spiritual about them disengaged itself and vanished, and all that remains deep inside me is a thick layer of crude sediment. The dream has become a nightmare, and the chimera a succubus. The world of the soul has closed its gates of ivory in my face; I only understand now what I touch with my hands; I have dreams of stone; everything condenses and hardens round me, nothing floats, and nothing vacillates, there is no air or breath; matter presses on me, encroaches on me, crushes me; I am like the pilgrim who fell asleep one day with his feet in the water, and woke up in winter with his legs caught and encased in ice. I no longer wish for anyone's love or friendship; even glory, that brilliant aureole which I so longed to have round my brow, doesn't give me the slightest yearning any more. There is, alas, only one thing now which stirs within me, and that is the horrible desire which draws me to Théodore. That is what all my ideas of morality have come to. What is physically beautiful is good, everything that is ugly is bad. If I saw a beautiful woman, and knew that she had the wickedest soul on earth, that she was adulterous and a poisoner, I must say I shouldn't mind in the least, and it wouldn't in any way prevent me from taking pleasure in her, if I found that her nose was the proper shape.

This is how I imagine supreme happiness. It is a big square building with no outside windows. There is a big courtyard surrounded by a white marble colonnade, and in the middle is a crystal fountain with a quicksilver jet in the Arab style; there are tubs of orange-trees and pomegranate-trees set out alternately. Above it all a bright blue sky and a bright yellow sun; big grey-hounds with pike-shaped muzzles lie dozing here and there; from time to time barefooted Negroes with golden rings around their legs, and white serving-women, slim and beautiful, in rich, fantastic attire, pass between the open arcades, bearing a basket on their arm, or an amphora on their head. As for me, I should be there, motionless and silent, under a magnificent canopy, surrounded by piles of cushions, with a big tame lion under my elbow, and the bare breast of a young slave like a stool under my feet, and I should be smoking opium in a big jade pipe.

I do not imagine paradise in any other way; and, if God wants me to go there after my death, He will build me a little kiosk to that design in a corner of some or other star. Paradise, as they describe it, seems to me much too musical, and I confess in all humility that I am quite incapable of bearing a sonata which lasted only two thousand years.

You see what my Eldorado is, my promised land: it is a dream like any other; but one thing is special about it, and that is that I never introduce any known person into it. None of my friends has crossed the threshold of this imaginary palace; none of the women I have had has sat beside me on the velvet cushions; I am there alone in the midst of appearances. As for all these figures of women, all these graceful spirits of young girls with which I people it, it has never occurred to me to love them; I have never imagined that one of them was in love with me. In this fantastic seraglio, I have not created a favourite sultana for myself. There are Negresses, mulatto women, Jewesses with blue skins and red hair, Greeks and Circassians, Spanish women and English women; but for me they are only symbols of colour and line, and I have them just as you have all sorts of wines in your cellar, and all kinds of humming-birds in your collection. They are pleasure-machines, they are pictures which need no frames, statues which come to you when you call them and you want to study them at close quarters. A woman has one incontestable advantage over a statue: she turns round as you want unaided, and you yourself have to go round the statue and find your viewpoint – which is fatiguing.

You can see that, with ideas like these, I can't remain in this era or this world; for one can't subsist like this alongside time and space. I shall have to find something else.

If you think like this, it is simple and logical that you should come to such a conclusion. As you seek only visual satisfaction, smoothness of form and purity of line, you accept them everywhere you meet them. This explains the singular aberrations of ancient love.

Since the time of Christ they have not made a single statue of a man in which adolescent beauty was idealized and rendered with the care which was characteristic of the ancient sculptors. Woman has become the symbol of moral and physical beauty; man has really fallen since the day that the little child was born at Bethlehem. Woman is the queen of creation; the stars meet in a crown round her head, the crescent moon makes it its glory to curve beneath her feet, the sun gives up its purest gold to make into jewels for her, artists who want to flatter the angels give them the figures of women, and I for one should certainly not blame them. Before the courteous and gentle teller of parables, it was quite the contrary; you didn't feminize the gods or heroes you wanted to make seductive; they had their model, it was at once vigorous and delicate, but it was always male, however loving the contours were, however smooth and devoid of muscles and veins the craftsmen had made the heavenly arms and legs. People were more inclined to make the special beauty of women conform to these characteristics. They broadened the shoulders, narrowed the hips, and made the throat more muscular; they gave a stronger emphasis to the wrists and ankles. There is hardly any difference between Paris and Helen. And so the hermaphrodite is one of the dreams most ardently caressed by idolatrous antiquity.

It is indeed among the most subtle creations of the pagan genius, this son of Hermes and Aphrodite. You can't imagine anything more ravishing in the world than these two bodies, both of them perfect, harmoniously fused together: these two beauties, so equal and so different, which now form only one which is superior to them both, because they moderate and set off each other. For someone who worships only form, there is no more pleasant uncertainty than the one you are cast into by the sight of this back, these ambiguous loins, these legs which are so delicate and strong that you don't know if you should attribute them to Mercury about to take flight or to Diana coming from her bathe. The torso is composed of the most enchanting monstrosities: on the full, plump breast of the ephebus, the bosom of a young virgin curves with a curious grace. Under the well-covered sides, of a quite feminine softness, you divine the ribs and denticulations, as you do in the sides of a young boy; the stomach is rather flat for a woman, rather round for a man, and the whole body has about it something nebulous and vague which it is impossible to render, something which has an extraordinary attraction. Théodore would certainly be an excellent model of that kind of beauty; and yet I think that the feminine part is dominant in him, he has kept more of Salmacis than Hermaphroditus did in the *Metamorphoses*.

What is remarkable is that I hardly think about his sex any more, and that I love him with perfect confidence. Sometimes I try to persuade myself that this love is abominable, and I tell myself so as harshly as I can; but I speak only with my lips, it is an argument which I create for myself and do not feel. It really seems to me that it's the simplest thing in the world and that anyone else in my place would feel the same.

I see him, hear him speak or sing – for he is a wonderful singer – and I take indescribable pleasure in it. He seems so like a woman to me that, one day, in the heat of conversation, I dropped the word *madame*. It made him laugh with a rather forced laugh, I thought.

Yet, if he were a woman, what reasons would he have to disguise himself like this? I cannot explain them in any way. If a very young, very beautiful man, still beardless, disguised himself as a woman, I'd understand; by doing so he would open a thousand doors which otherwise would have been firmly closed to him, and the misunderstanding could throw him into complicated adventures which were quite labyrinthine and amusing. In that way you could reach a closely guarded woman or make a rapid conquest thanks to the surprise. But I'm not sure what a beautiful young woman could gain by roaming the world in male attire: she could only lose by it. A woman cannot abandon the pleasure of being courted, serenaded and worshipped; she would rather abandon life, and she would be right, for what is a woman's life without all that? Nothing – or something worse than death. And I am always surprised that women who are thirty or have smallpox don't throw themselves from the top of a church tower.

In spite of all that, something stronger than reason cries out to me that this is a woman, and that she is the one I've dreamed of, the one I should love uniquely, the woman who will love me alone. She has appeared to me in this disguise to test me, to see if I should recognize her, if my loving glance would penetrate the veils which enveloped her, as they do in those fairy-tales where the fairies first appear as beggarwomen, then suddenly rise up resplendent with gold and jewels.

I have recognized you, O my love! At the sight of you, my heart leapt in my breast like St John in the womb of St Anne, when she was visited by the Virgin; a blazing light filled the air; I seemed to smell a fragrance of divine ambrosia; I saw the trail of fire at your feet, and I understood at once that you were not an ordinary mortal.

The melodious sounds of St Cecilia's viol, which the angels listen to in bliss, are raucous and discordant in comparison with the pearly cadences which fly from your ruby lips; the young and smiling Graces dance in a perpetual roundelay about you. The birds, when you pass through the forests, warble and bend down their little feathered heads to see you better, and they whistle you their prettiest refrains; the amorous moon rises earlier to kiss you with her pale silver lips, because she has abandoned her shepherd for you; the wind takes care not to brush from the sand the imprints of your adorable feet; the fountain, when you lean over it, makes itself smoother than crystal, lest it should wrinkle and deform the reflection of your celestial face. The modest violets themselves open their little hearts to you and perform a thousand coquettish tricks before you; the jealous strawberry is spurred on to emulate the celestial crimson of your lips; the imperceptible midge buzzes with pleasure and applauds you, beating its wings; all nature loves you and admires you as its masterpiece!

Oh, now I live! Until now I have only been a corpse. Now I am rid of my shroud, and stretch my two thin hands out of the grave towards the sun; my blue and spectral colour has gone. My blood is coursing fast through my veins. The fearful silence around me is broken at last. The dim black vault which weighed upon my brow is full of light. A thousand mysterious voices are whispering in my ears; enchanting stars are shining above me, and scattering their golden dust on my winding path; the daisies are quietly laughing at me, and the bell-flowers are murmuring my name with their little serpentine tongues. I understand a multitude of things which I didn't understand, I discover wonderful affinities and sympathies, I know the language of roses and nightingales, and I now easily read the book which I couldn't even spell out. I have discovered that I had a friend in that venerable old oak all covered with mistletoe and parasitic plants; I have discovered that this periwinkle, so languorous and frail, whose big blue eye is always overflowing with tears, has long cherished a discreet and restrained passion for me. It is love, O Silvio, it is love which has opened my eyes and given me the key to the mystery. Love came down to the depths of the vault in which my huddled, drowsy soul lay petrified; it took it by the hand and guided it up the steep and narrow steps which led outside. All the locks on the gates were picked, and for the first time this poor Psyche emerged from me – from the self in which she had been imprisoned.

Another life has become my life. I breathe in through another's lungs, and the blow that hurt him would kill me. Before that happy day, I was like those dejected Japanese idols who gaze perpetually at their stomachs. I was my own spectator, I was the audience for the play that I was performing; I watched myself live, and I listened to the oscillations of my heart as if they were the ticking of a clock. That was all. Images appeared before my inattentive eyes, but nothing in the external world touched my soul. There was nothing whose existence was necessary to me; I even questioned any other existence but my own, and of that I was not really sure. It seemed to me that I was alone in the middle of the universe, and that everything else was only phantoms, pictures, vain illusions, fugitive appearances which were meant to people this nothingness. What a difference!

And yet, suppose my presentiment deceived me, and Théodore were really a man, as all the world believes! One has sometimes seen these wondrous beauties; and great youth lends itself to the illusion. It's something I don't want to think about, it would drive me mad; that seed which fell yesterday on to the barren rock of my heart has already sent a thousand filaments through it in all directions; it has clung to it sturdily, and it would now be impossible to tear it away. It is already a flourishing tree, growing green, and twisting its muscular roots. If I came to know for certain that Théodore was not a woman, alas! I am not at all sure that I shouldn't love him still.

X

My dear girl, you were quite right to dissuade me from the plan I had conceived: the plan to see men, and to study them deeply, before I gave my heart to any of them. I have extinguished love in myself for ever, and even the possibility of love.

What poor young girls we are: so carefully brought up, so virginally protected by a fortress of precaution and reticence! We are not allowed to hear anything, to suspect anything, and what we know best is knowing nothing. What strange errors we live in, what treacherous dreams cradle us in their arms!

O Graciosa, three times accursed be the moment when I thought of this disguise; what horror, infamy and grossness I have been obliged to see or hear! What a wealth of chaste and precious ignorance I have squandered in this short time!

It was a fine moonlight night, do you remember? We were walking together at the far end of the garden, in that dismal avenue which is rarely frequented. At one end is a statue of a faun playing a flute; the faun no longer has a nose, and the whole of its body is covered with a thick leprosy of blackish moss. At the other end is an artificial landscape, painted on the wall and half washed away by the rain. Through the leaves of the hornbeam arbour, which were not abundant yet, we saw the stars sparkling here and there and the curving silver billhook of the moon. A fragrance of young shoots and new plants reached us from the flowerbed on the little languid puffs of the breeze; an unseen bird was whistling a strange and sentimental tune; and you and I, like the young girls we were, talked about love and suitors and marriage, and about the handsome young man whom we had seen at mass; we exchanged our few ideas about life and humankind. A hundred times we turned over a phrase which we had chanced to hear, because its meaning seemed strange and obscure. We asked each other a thousand of those ridiculous questions which only perfect innocence can conceive. What simple poetry, what adorable nonsense there was in those furtive conversations between two little ninnies just out of boarding-school!

You wanted your lover to be proud and bold, with dark hair and moustache, and a big sword: a kind of amorous braggart; and you were full of the heroic and the triumphant. You dreamed of nothing but duels and scaling walls, and miraculous devotion, you would readily have thrown your glove into the lions' den so that your Esplandian might fetch it. It was very comical to see a little girl, like you were then, all fair-haired and blushing, blown by the slightest wind, reciting those noble tirades all in one breath, with the most martial air in the world.

As for me, I was only six months older than you, but I was six years less romantic. There was one thing which particularly worried me, and that was to know what men said to each other and what they did when they had left the drawing-room or the theatre. I guessed that there were many dark and imperfect corners in their lives which were carefully hidden from our sight, and that it was very important for us to know them; sometimes, concealed behind a curtain, I watched them from a distance, the young men who came to the house, and it seemed to me then that I discerned something ignoble and cynical in their conduct, a gross indifference or an intense preoccupation which I no longer found in them when they came in, which they appeared to shed as if by magic at the door. All of them, young and old, seemed to me to adopt a uniform conventional mask, conventional feelings and a conventional form of speech when they were in the presence of women. In the corner of the drawing-room where I sat up straight like a doll, not leaning against the back of my chair, I turned my bouquet round and round in my fingers, and I listened and watched; though my eyes were lowered, I saw everything to right and left, before me and behind me: like the fabled eyes of the lynx, my eyes pierced walls, and I could have said what was happening in the next room.

I also noticed a notable difference in the way men spoke to married women; it wasn't with the polite and prudent phrases, childishly embellished, that they addressed to me or to my friends. There was a freer humour, a less constrained and easier manner, there were the evident reticences and sudden subterfuges of a corruption which knows it has met corruption like itself. I was aware that there was a common element between them which did not exist between us, and I should have given anything to know what that element was.

With what anxiety, what desperate curiosity, I followed them with my eyes and ears: the humming, laughing groups of young men who bore down on certain points in the circle and then continued their stroll, chatting and casting ambiguous glances as they passed. Incredulous sneers hovered over their disdainful lips; they seemed to be laughing at what they had just said, and to be retracting the compliments and adoration which they had heaped upon us. I didn't hear what they said; but I understood, from the movement of their lips, that they were speaking a language I didn't know, a language which no one had spoken to me. Even those who looked most humble and submissive held up their heads with a very evident air of rebellion and boredom. A sigh of relief, like the sigh of an actor who has got to the end of a long tirade, escaped from them in spite of themselves; and, as they took leave of us, they half-turned on their heels in a spirited and hurried way. It betrayed a kind of inner satisfaction at being free from the drudgery of showing politeness and attention.

I should have given a year of my life to have heard, unseen, an hour of their conversation. I often understood, from certain attitudes, from occasional indirect signs, from sidelong glances, that it was about me, and that they were talking either about my age or my face. Then I was on tenterhooks. The whispered word or two, the fragments of phrases which reached me from time to time, made me intensely inquisitive, but they didn't satisfy my curiosity, and I felt strange doubts and perplexities.

Usually what they said seemed to be favourable, and that wasn't what worried me: I didn't care very much if they thought me beautiful; but the small particulars, whispered into the ear and almost always followed by long chuckles and peculiar winks – that is what I should have liked to know, and, for one of those phrases whispered behind a curtain or behind a door, I should without regret have left the sweetest and the most flowery conversation in the world.

If I had had a lover, I should very much have liked to know how he would have talked about me to another man, and how he would have boasted of his conquest to his companions in debauchery with a little wine inside him and his elbows on the table.

I know that, now, and to tell the truth I'm sorry I know it. It's always like that.

My idea was crazy, but what's done is done, and you can't un-learn what you have learned. I didn't listen to you, my dear Graciosa, and I regret it; but one doesn't always listen to reason, especially when it comes from such a pretty mouth as yours, for I don't know why one can't imagine that advice is wise, unless it is given by some old hoary greyhead, as if sixty years' stupidity could make you intelligent.

But it all tormented me too much, and I couldn't bear it, I was roasting in my little skin like a chestnut on the stove. The fatal apple was ripening in the leaves above my head, and I had to take a bite in the end, even though I would then throw it away, if it tasted bitter to me.

I did what fair Eve, my beloved grandmother, did: I took a bite.

Since the death of my uncle, my one surviving relation, had left me free to do as I pleased, I did what I had dreamed of for so long. I took the greatest care in my precautions so that no one should suspect my sex. I had learned to use the sword and pistol; I rode a horse to perfection, and with a daring which few professional horsemen would have shown; I very carefully studied the way to wear a cloak and crack a whip, and, in a few months, I managed to turn a girl whom people found quite pretty into a much prettier cavalier, who had almost everything except a moustache. I realized what money I possessed, and I left the town, determined not to come back without the most complete experience.

It was the only way to settle my doubts. Having lovers wouldn't have taught me anything, or at least it would only have given me inadequate insights, and I wanted to study man in depth, to dissect him fibre by fibre with an inexorable scalpel and to have him alive and throbbing on my dissecting table; to do so I had to see him alone at home, informally, follow him on his walks, to the tavern and elsewhere. In my disguise, I could go everywhere without being noticed; people did not hide themselves from me, they cast all reserve and all restraint aside, they trusted me with their secrets and I invented some to provoke real ones. Women, alas! have only read the romance of man, and not his history.

It is terrifying to think – and we don't think about it – how profoundly ignorant we are of the life and behaviour of those who seem to love us, and those we marry. Their real life is as completely unknown to us as if they were the inhabitants of Saturn or some other planet a hundred million leagues from our sublunary sphere: you would say they belonged to a different species, and there isn't the slightest intellectual link between the two sexes; the virtues of one are the vices of the other, and what is admirable in men is shameful in women.

As for us women, our life is plain and it can be seen at a glance. It is easy to follow us from home to school, and from school to home; what we do is no mystery to anyone; everyone can see our poor stump-drawings, our watercolour bouquets composed of a pansy and a rose as big as a cabbage, prettily tied round the stems with a delicate coloured ribbon. The slippers which we embroider for our fathers' or our grandfathers' birthdays have nothing about them which is really occult or really disturbing. Our sonatas and our romanzas are executed with the most desirable frigidity. We are well and truly sewn to our mothers' skirts, and at nine or ten o'clock at the latest we go back to our little snow-white beds, in our neat, discreet cells, where we are virtuously padlocked and bolted in until the following morning. The most vigilant and jealous susceptibility wouldn't be offended.

The purest crystal is less transparent than a life like that.

The man who takes us knows what we have done from the moment we were weaned, and even before, if he wants to carry his

researches as far as that. Our life is not a life, it is a kind of vegetation like that of moss and flowers; the glacial shadow of the
maternal stem floats around us, poor stifled rosebuds, who dare not
blossom forth. Our chief concern is to hold ourselves up very
straight, very stiff and very erect with our eyes suitably cast down,
and to exceed the immobility of dummies and mechanical dolls.

We are not allowed to speak, to join in the conversation except to
answer yes and no, if someone asks us a question. As soon as someone wants to say something interesting, we are sent off to study our
harp or clavichord, and our music masters are all at least sixty and
take a dreadful lot of snuff. The models hanging in our rooms have
a very vague and indeterminate anatomy. When the Greek gods
present themselves in a seminary for young ladies, they take care
beforehand to buy very full box-coats with several capes at the
second-hand clothes shop, and to have themselves portrayed in
stippled engravings. This gives them the appearance of porters or
cab-drivers, and makes them unlikely to kindle our imagination.

People are so determined to prevent us from being romantic that
they make us into idiots. Our education is spent not in teaching us
something, but in preventing us from learning anything.

We are really prisoners, body and soul. As for a young man, free
to behave as he likes, a young man who goes out in the morning and
only comes back the following morning, a young man who has
money, who can earn it and dispose of it as he pleases: how could
he justify the way he spends his time? Where is the man who could
tell his best-beloved how he had passed his day and his night?
There is no such man, even among the ones who have the purest
reputations.

I had sent my horse and clothes to a little farm of mine a few
miles out of town. I got dressed, sprang into the saddle and set off,
not without a singular heaviness of heart. I had no regrets, I left
nothing behind me, no relations or friends, no dog or cat, and yet
I was sad, I almost had tears in my eyes. I had only visited the farm
five or six times, and it meant nothing special, it wasn't dear to me,
and it wasn't the pleasure you take in certain places, which moves
you when you have to leave them, but I turned round two or three

times to take another look at its corkscrew of bluish smoke rising far away from among the trees.

It was there that, with my skirts and dresses, I had left my title to womanhood. In the room where I'd dressed I'd put away twenty years of my life which were not to count any more and no longer concerned me. You might have written on the door: Here lies Madelaine de Maupin; for in fact I was no longer Madelaine de Maupin, but Théodore de Sérannes, and no one was ever to call me by the sweet name of Madelaine again.

The drawer in which I had shut up my dresses, henceforward of no use, seemed to me like the coffin of my pure illusions; I was a man, or at least I had the appearance of a man. The young girl was dead.

When I had completely lost sight of the tops of the chestnut-trees around the farm, it seemed to me that I was no longer myself, but someone else, and I remembered my old deeds like the deeds of an unknown person which I had witnessed, or like the beginning of a novel which I hadn't finished reading.

I happily remembered a thousand small details, whose childlike naïveté sometimes brought a rather amused indulgent smile to my lips, like that of a young rake who is listening to the Arcadian and pastoral secrets of a third-form schoolboy; and, just as I was parting from them for ever, all my childish deeds as a little girl and as a young woman ran up to the side of the road, making a thousand friendly signs to me, and blowing me kisses from the tips of their slim white fingers.

I spurred on my horse, to escape these enervating emotions; the trees filed past rapidly, right and left; but the wanton swarm, more buzzing than a beehive, began to run down the side paths and call out to me: 'Madelaine! Madelaine!'

I landed a great crack of the whip on the neck of my steed, and it doubled its pace. My hair stood out, almost straight, behind my head, my cloak was horizontal, as if the folds had been sculpted in stone, I rode so fast; I looked behind once, and I saw the dust which my horse's hooves had raised, like a little white cloud far behind me on the horizon.

I stopped for a while.

In a wild-rose bush, at the side of the road, there stirred something white, and a little voice as sweet and bright as silver reached my ears:

'Madelaine, Madelaine, where are you going, so far away, Madelaine? I am your virginity, my dear child; that is why I have a white robe, a white wreath and a white skin. But you? Why are you wearing boots, Madelaine? It seemed to me that you had very pretty feet. Boots and breeches, and a big hat with a feather, like a cavalier who is going to war! Why this long sword which is beating and bruising your thigh? You have a singular garb, Madelaine, and I'm not sure if I should come with you.'

'If you are afraid, my dear, go back to the house, go and water my flowers and tend my doves. But in truth you are wrong, you would be safer in this fine cloth attire than you are in your gauze and your linen. My boots stop people from seeing if I have pretty feet; this sword is to defend me, and the feather trembling on my hat is to scare all the nightingales which might come to sing me false love songs.'

I continued on my way; in the sighs of the wind I seemed to recognize the last phrase of the sonata which I had learned for my uncle's birthday, and, in a big rose which raised its full-blown head over a little wall, I seemed to recognize the model of the big rose which had inspired me with so many watercolours; as I passed in front of a house, I saw the ghosts of my curtains fluttering at one of the windows. All my past seemed to cling to me to stop me from going on and reaching a new future.

I hesitated two or three times, and I turned my horse's head the other way.

But the little blue snake of curiosity whispered insidious words to me, and said: 'Go on, go on, Théodore; it's a good chance for you to learn; if you don't learn today, you will never know. Are you going to give your noble heart at random, at the first appearance of sincerity and passion? Men hide some very extraordinary secrets from us, Théodore.'

I galloped on.

The breeches suited my body but not my mind. In a gloomy part of the forest, I felt a certain unease and, to be honest, something like a shudder of fear. A poacher let off a gunshot, and I almost swooned. If it had been a robber, the pistols stuck in my holsters and my formidable sword would certainly not have been of much assistance. But gradually I hardened myself, and I didn't worry any more.

The sun sank slowly below the horizon like the chandelier in a theatre which is lowered after the performance. From time to time rabbits and pheasants crossed the path; the shadows lengthened, and everything in the distance was tinged with red. Certain parts of the sky were a very pale soft lilac, others had a touch of lemon and orange; the night birds began to sing, and a multitude of curious noises rose up from the forest; the little light which still remained faded away, and the darkness became complete, intensified as it was by the shadows of the trees. I had never gone out alone at night; I now found myself at eight o'clock in the evening in a big forest! Imagine it, Graciosa! And I used to die of fright when I'd only reached the end of the garden! I was more alarmed than ever, and my heart was beating terribly; it was a great satisfaction, I must confess, when, on the other side of a hill, I suddenly saw the twinkling lights of the town where I was going. As soon as I saw those sparkling dots, like small terrestrial stars, my fear completely vanished. It seemed as if those indifferent lights were the open eyes of so many friends who were watching out for me.

My horse was no less happy than I was, and, scenting a good stable-smell which he found more agreeable than all the fragrance of ox-eye daisies and wild strawberries, he galloped straight to the Red Lion hostelry.

A pale gold light shone through the leaded windows of the inn. The tin sign was swinging backwards and forwards, and groaning like an old woman, for the wind was beginning to blow fresh. I handed over my horse to an ostler, and went into the kitchen.

An enormous hearth at the end of the room opened wide its red and black jaws, and swallowed a bundle of wood at a time, and on either side of the andirons sat a dog which was almost as big as a man. They let themselves be roasted with the greatest phlegm in the world; they merely lifted their paws a little and uttered a sort of sigh when the heat became more intense; but, certainly, they would rather have been burnt to cinders than move an inch or two away.

My arrival did not seem to please them, and it was in vain that I stroked their heads once or twice to make their acquaintance: they gave me sly looks which boded no good. That surprised me, for animals always come to me.

The innkeeper came up to ask me what I should like for supper.

He was a pot-bellied man, with a red nose, eyes of different colours, and a smile which went all round his face. At every word he spoke, he showed two rows of teeth which were pointed and divided like an ogre's. The big kitchen knife which hung at his side had a doubtful look and seemed as if it could serve several purposes. When I had told him what I wanted, he approached one of the dogs, and gave it a random kick. The dog got up, and went towards a kind of wheel which it entered with a pitiful, sullen air, and it gave me a look of reproach. Finally, seeing that there was no mercy to hope for, it began to turn its wheel, and, as a result, the spit which went through the chicken I was to sup on. I promised myself to throw the scraps to the dog for its trouble, and, while I waited for supper to be ready, I began to look round the kitchen.

There were big oak beams like stripes across the ceiling, all browned and blackened by the smoke from the fire and the candles. On the dressers, in the shadows, shone pewter plates which were brighter than silver, and white earthenware pottery decorated with bunches of blue flowers. Along the walls were many rows of well-scoured casseroles which looked not unlike the ancient bucklers which you see hung in rows along the Greek and Roman triremes (forgive me, Graciosa, for the epic splendour of this comparison). One or two buxom serving-women were busying themselves round a big table, and moving plates and dishes and forks, a more agreeable music than any other when you're hungry, for the hearing of the stomach grows sharper, then, than that of the ears. On the whole, in spite of the innkeeper's money-box mouth and his saw teeth, the inn had a quite respectable and cheerful appearance; and had the innkeeper's smile been six feet broader, his teeth three times longer and whiter, the rain was beginning to tinkle on the windows, and the wind was beginning to howl in such a way that you didn't want to go, for I can think of nothing more lugubrious than this sort of groaning on a dark and rainy night.

I had an idea which made me smile; it was that no one in the world would have come to look for me where I was. Who indeed would have thought that little Madelaine wasn't sleeping in her nice warm bed, with her alabaster night-light beside her, a novel under her pillow, her lady's maid in the next-door room, ready to hasten in at the least alarm during the night? Who would have thought that instead she was rocking in a straw-bottomed chair, in a country inn, with her booted feet propped up on the firedogs, and her little hands boldly plunged into her pockets?

No, Madelinette hasn't stayed, like her companions, leaning idly over the ledge of the balcony, between the convolvulus and jasmine, looking at the violet fringes of the horizon across the field, or at some little rose-coloured cloud rounded by the May breeze. Madelinette has not hung her palaces of mother-of-pearl with lily leaves, as habitations for her chimeras. Unlike you, lovely dreamers, she has not dressed some hollow phantom with every imaginable perfection; she has wanted to know men before she gave herself to a man; she has left everything, her fine silk and velvet dresses of brilliant hues, her bracelets, birds and flowers; she has chosen to renounce adoration, obsequious gallantry, bouquets and madrigals, the pleasure of being found more beautiful and better attired than yourselves, she has renounced the sweet name of woman, everything that she was, and she has set out, the brave girl, all alone, across the world, to acquire a great knowledge of life.

If people knew that, they would say that Madelaine was mad. You have said so yourself, my dear Graciosa; but the women who are really mad are those who cast their soul to the winds, and sow their love at random on stones and rocks, not knowing if a single shoot will grow.

O Graciosa! I have never thought of it without terror: fancy loving someone who was unworthy of it! To bare your soul to lewd eyes, and admit the profane into the sanctuary of your heart! To let your limpid current flow for a while with muddy waves! However completely you separate from it, some of this slime will always remain, and the stream cannot regain its old transparency.

To think that a man has kissed you and touched you; that he has seen your body; that he can say: She is like this or that; she has such and such a mark in such a place; her soul has this particular nuance; she laughs at this, and weeps at that; this is her reverie; here in my pocket-book is a feather from the wings of her dream; this ring is woven from her hair; a little of her heart is folded up in this letter; she caressed me in such a way, and here is her usual term of endearment!

O, Cleopatra, now I understand why you had him killed in the morning, the lover with whom you had spent the night. Marvellous cruelty – which I once could not abhor enough! Great sensualist, how well you understand human nature, and what depths there were in your barbarity! You wanted no living man to reveal the mysteries of your bed; those words of love, flown from your lips, were not to be repeated. So it was that you kept your pure illusion. Experience did not gradually destroy the charming ghost you had cradled in your arms. You chose to be separated from him by the sudden blow of an axe rather than slow disillusionment. What torture, indeed, to see the man whom you had chosen belie your idea of him every minute; to discover a thousand pettinesses in his character; to perceive that what had seemed so beautiful to you through the prism of love was really very ugly, and that what you had taken for a real hero from a novel was, when all was said, only a prosaic bourgeois in dressing-gown and slippers!

I don't have the power of Cleopatra, and, if I possessed it, I should certainly not have the strength to use it. And so, unable and unwilling to cut off my lovers' heads as they leave my bed, and being disinclined to bear what other women bear, I have to look twice before I take a lover; and that is what I shall do three times rather than twice, if I feel inclined for love, which I very much doubt, after what I have seen and heard; unless, however, I should meet in some happy land a heart like my own, as the novels say – a pure and virgin heart which had never loved and was capable of it, in the true sense of the word; which is far from being an easy thing.

Several cavaliers came into the inn; the storm and the darkness had prevented them from continuing on their way. They were all young, and the oldest among them was certainly not more than thirty. Their clothes proclaimed that they belonged to the upper class, and, if their dress had not done so, their insolent ease of manner would quite readily have let it be understood. There were one or two who had interesting faces; all the others, to a greater or lesser degree, had that kind of brutal joviality and careless good nature which men have among themselves, and completely discard when they are in our presence.

If they could only have suspected that this frail young man, half asleep on his chair, at the chimney-corner, was anything but what he appeared to be, that he was in fact a young girl, fit for a king, as the saying goes, they would certainly have changed their tone very quickly, you would have seen them strutting about and preening themselves at once. They would have approached with countless bows, pointing their toes, hands on their hips, smiling with mouth and nose and hair and their whole demeanour. They would have boned the words they used, and spoken only in velvet and satin phrases; at my slightest movement, they would have seemed to prostrate themselves on the floor like a carpet, for fear that its unevenness might offend my delicate feet; every hand would have been extended to support me; the most comfortable chair would have been set out in the best place. But I looked like a pretty boy, and not like a pretty girl.

I confess that I was almost on the point of regretting my skirts, when I saw how little attention they paid me. For a moment I was quite mortified; for, from time to time, I forgot that I was wearing men's clothes, and I had to remember it in order not to get into a bad temper.

I was sitting there, in silence, with folded arms, and (apparently with the utmost attention) watching the chicken which took on shades of deeper and deeper gold; and the wretched dog, which I had so unfortunately disturbed, was rushing about half mad in its wheel.

The youngest man in the company came and gave me a rap on the shoulder which really hurt me very much, and made me give a slight involuntary cry. He asked me if I wouldn't rather have supper with them than all by myself, since you drank better when there were several of you. I replied that it was an unexpected pleasure, and that I should be delighted to do so. They laid our places together, and we sat down at table.

The dog was all out of breath, and when it had lapped up an enormous basinful of water in three gulps, it resumed its place opposite the other dog, which had stayed as still as if it were made of china. By a special dispensation of Providence, the newcomers hadn't asked for chicken.

From a phrase or two which escaped them, I learned that they were going to join the Court, which was then at —, and that they were going to meet some other friends there. I told them that I was a well-to-do young gentleman who was leaving the university, and going to visit relations in the provinces, and I was taking the longest way round. That made them laugh, and, after a few comments on my innocent and ingenuous expression, they asked me if I had a mistress. I answered that I knew nothing about it, which made them laugh still more. The flagons followed each other fast; I took care to leave my glass nearly always full, but I was a little warm, and, keeping my idea in mind, I contrived that the conversation should turn to women. I didn't find it difficult; for, after theology and aesthetics, it is what men discuss most willingly when they are drunk.

My companions were not exactly drunk, they carried their wine too well for that; but they began to enter into endless moral discussions, and to lean across the table without ceremony. One of them had even put his arm round the thick waist of a serving-woman, and he was wagging his head amorously; another swore that he'd die at once like a toad who'd taken snuff, if Jeannette didn't let him kiss both the big red apples which served her as cheeks. And Jeannette, who didn't want him to die like a toad, granted him her cheeks with a very good grace, and did not even stop a hand which boldly insinuated itself between the folds of her kerchief, in the damp cleavage of her bosom, which was very ill protected by a small gold crucifix, and it was only after some brief whispered negotiations that he left her free to remove the dish.

And yet these were courtiers, people who had elegant manners, and certainly, unless I had seen it, I should never have thought of accusing them of such familiarities with serving-women in inns. They had probably just left delightful mistresses to whom they had made the finest promises in the world; in truth, I should never have dreamed of exhorting my lover not to defile, on Maritorne's cheeks, the lips which had been pressed against my own.

The scoundrel seemed to take a great pleasure in this kiss, just as if he had been embracing Philis or Oriane; it was a big kiss, firmly and boldly planted, which left two little white marks on the wench's flushed cheek, and she wiped away the traces with the back of her hand – with which she had just washed up the plates. I don't believe that he had ever given one so naturally tender to the pure deity of his heart. That was apparently what he thought, for he muttered, with a very disdainful shrug of the shoulders:

'To hell with thin women and noble feelings!'

This moral seemed to suit the assembly, and they all nodded in sign of agreement.

'Indeed,' he said, continuing his theme, 'I am unfortunate in everything. Gentlemen, I must confess to you, under the seal of the greatest secrecy, that at this moment I myself have a passion.'

'Oh,' said the others. 'A passion! How absolutely miserable! And what are you doing with a passion?'

'She is a respectable woman, gentlemen. You mustn't laugh, gentlemen. Why indeed shouldn't I have a respectable woman? Have I said something ridiculous? . . . Now look, you over there, I'll throw the whole lot in your face, if you don't stop.'

'Tell us more.'

'She's crazy about me. She has the most beautiful soul in the world; and, as for souls, I know what I'm talking about, I know at least as much as I do about horses, and I promise you that this is a first-class soul. There are nobilities, ecstasies, devotions, sacrifices, refinements of tenderness, everything most transcendent that you can imagine; but she has almost no bosom, in fact she hasn't any bosom at all, like a little girl of fifteen at most. Apart from that she is quite pretty, she has a delicate hand and a small foot; she has too much spirit, and not enough flesh, and I sometimes want to leave her in the lurch. After all, you don't sleep with spirits. I am very unfortunate; sympathize with me, my dear friends.' And, growing maudlin with the wine that he had drunk, he dissolved into tears.

'Jeannette will console you for the misfortune of sleeping with sylphs,' said his neighbour, pouring him out a bumper. 'Her soul is so thick that you could easily make bodies out of it for the others, and she has enough flesh to clothe the carcasses of three elephants.'

O pure and noble woman! If you knew what he said about you, in a tavern, without reserve, and in front of people he doesn't know, the man whom you love best in the world, the man to whom you have sacrificed everything! How indecently he undresses you, how shamelessly he delivers you, quite naked, to the drunken looks of his friends, while you sadly stay at home, chin in hand, your eyes turned towards the road by which he will return!

If someone had come to tell you that, twenty-four hours perhaps after he had left you, your lover was making advances to an ignoble serving-woman, and that he had arranged to spend the night with her, you would have insisted that it was impossible, and you wouldn't have wanted to believe it; you would hardly have believed your eyes and ears. Yet so it was.

The conversation went on for some time longer, as wild and licentious as could be; but, through all the ludicrous exaggerations, the often ribald jokes, there emerged a deep, true feeling of utter contempt for women, and I learnt more that evening than if I'd read twenty cartloads of moral works.

I should only want half an hour of such a conversation to correct a romantic young girl for evermore; that would do her more good than any maternal reproofs.

Some of the company boasted that they had had as many women as they liked, and that they only had to say the word; others gave each other recipes for procuring mistresses, or held forth on the tactics to follow in the siege of virtue; some of them ridiculed the women whose lovers they were, and proclaimed themselves to be the most arrant fools on earth to have been captivated by such sluts. All of them held love very cheap.

So that was the thought they were hiding from us under such fine outward appearances! Who would ever think so, to see them so humble, so fawning, so obliging? Oh, how boldly they raise their heads after the victory, how insolently they put the heels of their boots on the brow that they adored from afar, worshipped on their knees! How they avenge themselves for their passing humility! How dearly they charge for their civilities! And with how many insults they take their rest, after the madrigals that they have sung! What wild brutality of thought and speech! What inelegance of manners and conduct! It is a complete change, and one which is certainly not to their advantage. However far my conjectures had gone, they had not gone nearly as far as reality.

Ideal, blue flower with golden heart, who opens all pearled with dew beneath the springtime heaven, flower whose breath is scented with gentle reveries, O flower whose fibrous roots, a thousand times more free than the silken tresses of the fairies, plunge into the depths of our souls with their thousand long-haired heads, to drink its purest substance; flower so bitter and so sweet, we cannot tear you up without making the heart bleed in all its innermost recesses, and from your broken stem there ooze red drops which, falling one by one into the lake of our tears, help us to measure the halting hours of our vigil by the deathbed of Love.

O, cursed flower! How you had grown in my soul! Your branches had multiplied faster than nettles in a ruin. Young nightingales came to drink from your calyx and sing beneath your shade; diamond butterflies, with emerald wings and ruby eyes, fluttered and danced around your frail pistils, dusted with gold; swarms of blond bees, all unsuspecting, sucked in your poisoned honey; chimeras folded up their swans' wings and crossed their lions' paws under their lovely bosoms, to take their rest beside you. The tree of the Hesperides was not better guarded; sylphs collected the tears of the stars in the urns of lilies, and watered you every night with their magic watering-cans. Plant of the ideal, more venomous than the manchineel or the upas-tree, how dearly it costs me, despite your deceitful flowers and the poison one breathes in with your fragrance, to uproot you from my soul! The cedar of Lebanon, the gigantic baobab, the palm-tree a hundred cubits high, could not together fill the place that you occupied all alone, little blue flower with the golden heart!

The supper finally ended, and it was a question of going to bed; but as there were twice as many sleepers as there were beds, it naturally followed that we had to go to bed one after the other or to sleep two together. It was a very simple matter for the rest of the company, but it was not anything like as simple for me – on account of certain protuberances which the upper coat and doublet rather conveniently concealed, but which a mere shirt would have revealed in all their damnable roundness; and I was indeed hardly prepared to betray my incognito in favour of any of these gentlemen, who at that moment seemed to me pure simple monsters (I have since found them to be very good fellows, worth quite as much as any of their kind).

The man whose bed I was to share was tolerably drunk. He threw himself on to the mattress with one leg and one arm hanging over the side, and fell asleep at once. His sleep was not the sleep of the just, but a sleep so deep that if the angel of the Last Judgement had come and sounded his trumpet in his ear, he would not have woken. This sleep greatly simplified the problem; I just took off my doublet and my boots, stepped across the sleeping man, and lay down on top of the sheets, next to the wall.

And there I was, sleeping with a man! It wasn't a bad beginning! I must admit that, for all my assurance, I was singularly moved and troubled. The situation was so strange, so new, that I could hardly accept that it wasn't a dream. My companion slept wonderfully well and I didn't shut my eyes all night.

He was a young man of about twenty-four, with a quite handsome face, dark lashes and an almost fair moustache; his long hair flowed about his head like the waves spilling out of the run of a river, a slight flush spread across his pale cheeks like a cloud beneath the water, his lips were half open and smiled a vague and languorous smile.

I raised myself up on my elbow and stayed there for a long while, looking at him by the flickering light of a candle. Nearly all its tallow had flowed down in broad sheets, and its wick was all coated with black fungoid excrescences.

There was quite a big space between us. He occupied one extreme edge of the bed; I had thrown myself right on the other edge, as an extra precaution.

Certainly what I had heard was not of a nature to predispose me to tenderness and sensual pleasure; I had a horror of men. All the same I was more troubled and disturbed than I should have been; my body didn't share my spiritual repugnance as it ought. My heart was beating fast, I was hot, and, whichever way I turned I could find no rest.

The deepest silence reigned in the inn; all you heard, at long intervals, was the thud of a horse's hoof striking the stable floor, or the sound of a drop of water falling down the chimney on to the ashes. The candle reached the end of the wick, and it went out smoking.

Utter darkness fell like a curtain between us. You cannot imagine the effect which the sudden disappearance of the light had upon me. It seemed to me that this was the end of everything, and that I should never see clearly again. For a moment I wanted to get up; but what should I have done? It was only two o'clock in the morning, all the lights were out, and I couldn't wander like a ghost through an unknown house. I was obliged to stay where I was and wait for the dawn.

I lay there, on my back, with folded arms, trying to think of something else, and always coming back to this, to wit: that I was in bed with a man. I went so far as to wish that he would wake and discover that I was a woman. No doubt the wine I had drunk, although I had drunk very little, had something to do with this extravagant idea, but I couldn't prevent myself from returning to it. I was on the point of stretching out my hand in his direction, waking him up and telling him what I was. A fold in the bedclothes checked my arm, and that was the reason I didn't carry the thing out to the end. It gave me time for reflection; and, while I was disengaging my arm, the common sense which I had totally lost came back to me, if not completely, at least enough to restrain me.

Wouldn't it have been very strange if a disdainful beauty like myself, if I, who would have liked to know ten years of a man's life before I granted him my hand to kiss, if I had given myself, in an inn, on a trucklebed, to the first comer! And, truth to tell, I had very nearly done so.

Can a sudden excitement, a surge of the blood, so humble the most splendid resolutions? Does the voice of the body speak louder than the voice of the spirit? Whenever my pride becomes too high and mighty, I bring it back to earth by setting the recollection of that night before its eyes. I begin to be of men's opinion: what a poor thing a woman's virtue is! And, good God, what does it depend on?

Oh, it is useless to want to spread our wings, there is too much slime weighing them down; the body anchors the soul to the earth. In vain it opens its wings to the wind of the noblest thoughts, the ship remains motionless, as if all the sucking-fish in the ocean had attached themselves to the keel. Nature likes taunting us like that. When she sees an idea standing erect on its pride like a tall column, she whispers to the blood to flow faster and hurry to the gates of the arteries; she commands the temples to throb, the ears to tingle, and the lofty thought is overcome by vertigo. Everything it sees becomes confused and muddled, the earth seems to undulate like the bridge of a ship in a tempest, the sky turns round and round and the stars dance a saraband; those lips, which uttered only counsels of austerity, now pout and seem to ask for a kiss; those arms, which were so strong in rejection, grow soft, become more supple, more enfolding than sashes. Add to that the touch of a skin, and someone's breath through your hair, and all is lost. Often indeed you don't need so much: the fragrance of leaves which comes to you from the fields through your half-open window, the sight of two birds pecking one another, a daisy opening, an old love-song which comes back to you in spite of yourself and you repeat unconscious of its meaning, a warm wind which disturbs and intoxicates you, the softness of your bed or divan, one of these circumstances is enough; even the solitude of your room makes you think that two of you would be happy there, and that you couldn't find a more delightful nest for a brood of pleasures. These drawn curtains, this half-light, this silence, all bring you back to the fatal idea which brushes against you with its treacherous dove's wings, and warbles very softly around you. The materials which touch you seem to caress you and lovingly hang their folds along your body. And then the young girl opens her arms to the first footman with whom she finds herself alone; the philosopher leaves his page unfinished, and, hiding his head in his cloak, runs in all haste to the nearest courtesan.

I certainly did not love the man who caused me such unusual emotions. His only charm was not to be a woman, and, in the state in which I found myself, that was enough! A man! That most mysterious creature who is so carefully concealed from us, that strange animal of whose history we are so ignorant, that demon or god who can alone realize all the dreams of vague sensual pleasure in which the springtime cradles our sleep, the only thought we have from the time when we are five years old!

A man! The confused idea of pleasure floated about in my heavy head. The little that I knew kindled my desire even more. An ardent curiosity urged me to resolve, once and for all, the doubts which troubled me and constantly recurred to my mind. The solution to the problem was on the other side of the page. I only had to turn over, the book was beside me. A handsome enough cavalier, a narrow enough bed, and a dark enough night! A young girl with a few glasses of champagne in her head! What a suspicious assemblage! Well, the only result of it all was a very respectable nothing.

On the wall where I kept my eyes fixed, the darkness grew less intense, and thanks to that I began to make out where the window was; the panes became less opaque, and the grey light of morning slipped behind them and restored their transparency. The sky lightened gradually; it was day. You cannot imagine how pleased I was by that pale ray of light! It shone on the hangings of green

Aumale serge round the glorious battlefield where my virtue had vanquished my desires! It seemed to me like my crown of victory.

As for my companion, he had fallen right on to the floor.

I got up, rearranged my clothes and ran to the window; I opened it, and the morning breeze revived me. As I combed my hair, I stood in front of the mirror, and I was astonished by the pallor of my face. I had expected it to be purple.

The others came in to see if we were still asleep, and gave their friend a push with their feet. He didn't seem very surprised to find himself where he was.

The horses were saddled, and we went on our way again. But that's enough for today; my pen isn't writing any more, and I don't want to sharpen it; in the meanwhile, love me as I love you, Graciosa, the appropriately named, and, after what I have told you, don't go and have too poor an opinion of my virtue.

XI

MANY things are tiresome. It is tiresome to pay back the money which you have borrowed, and which you have grown accustomed to considering as your own. It is tiresome to caress today the woman you loved yesterday. It is tiresome to go to a house at dinner-time, and find that the owners set off for the country a month ago. It is tiresome to write a novel, and more tiresome to read it. It is tiresome to have a pimple on your nose and cracked lips on the day when you are about to call upon the idol of your heart. It is tiresome to be wearing facetious boots, smiling at the pavement through every seam, and especially to accommodate a void behind the spiders' webs on your pocket. It is tiresome to be a porter. It is tiresome to be an emperor. It is tiresome to be oneself and even to be someone else. It is tiresome to go on foot because you hurt your corns, on horseback because you scorch the antithesis of your front, by coach because a fat man infallibly makes a pillow of your shoulder, by packet-boat because you are seasick and cast up your whole inside. It is tiresome in winter because you shiver, and in summer because you sweat; but the most tiresome thing on earth, in hell or heaven, is certainly a tragedy, unless it is a drama or a comedy.

That really makes me sick. Is there anything which is more stupid and idiotic? Those massive tyrants with bull-like voices, who pace the stage from one wing to the other, moving their hairy arms like windmill sails imprisoned in flesh-coloured stockings, aren't they paltry imitations of Bluebeard or the Bogeyman? Their rhodomontades would send anyone who could keep awake into paroxysms of laughter.

The unhappy mistresses are no less ridiculous. It is entertaining to see them appear, dressed in black or white, with their hair flowing over their shoulders, their sleeves flowing over their hands, and their bodies ready to pop out of their corsets like a nut when you press it between your fingers. They seem to drag the floor along on the soles of their satin slippers, and, in their grand gestures of passion, they push back their train with a little kick of the heel. The dialogue, exclusively composed of *ohs* and *ahs*, which they cluck as they strut about the stage, is indeed agreeable food, and easy to digest. Their princes are very charming, too; they are just a trifle gloomy and melancholy, which doesn't prevent them from being the best companions there are in the world or anywhere else.

As for the comedy which is designed to correct people's morals, it performs its duty, happily, with little success. I find the fathers' sermons and the uncles' eternal repetitions as boring on stage as they are in real life. I don't believe we should double the number of fools by portraying them; there are already quite enough as it is, heaven help us, and the race is nothing like extinct. Why do we need to portray a person who has a hog's snout or an ox's muzzle, or to collect the rubbishy stories of a clodhopper, whom we should throw out of the window if he called? The picture of a vulgar pedant is as boring as the pedant himself, and he is no less of a pedant just because you see him in the mirror. An actor who contrived to give a perfect imitation of the manners and attitudes of a cobbler wouldn't amuse me much more than the cobbler himself.

But there is one theatre which I love, it is the fantastic, extravagant, impossible theatre, which the respectable public would boo without mercy from the first scene, since they couldn't understand a word.

The theatre which I love is a singular theatre. Glowworms take the place of lamps; a scarab, beating time with its antennae, stands at the rostrum. The cricket plays its piece; the nightingale is the first flute; tiny sylphs, in the pink of fashion, hold basses of lemon-peel between their pretty legs, which are whiter than ivory, and with their many arms they move their bows, made of one of

Titania's eyelashes, across their spider's-web strings. The little perriwig with three hammers, worn by the scarab-conductor, is quivering with pleasure, and it casts a luminous dust around it, the harmony is so sweet and the overture is so well rendered.

A curtain of butterfly wings, more delicate than the inner film of an egg, slowly rises, after the indispensable three taps. The auditorium is full of poets' souls, sitting in stalls of mother-of-pearl, and watching the spectacle through dewdrops which are mounted on the golden pistils of lilies. These are their lorgnettes.

The scenery is not like any scenery that is known; the country it represents is more unheard-of than America before it was discovered. The palette of the richest painter doesn't have half its variegated shades; everything is painted in bizarre and singular colours; ash-green, ash-blue, ultramarine, red and yellow lacquers are lavished on it.

The sky is blue and turning green, striped with broad light and tawny bands; little frail and slender trees in the background wave their thinly scattered leaves, the colour of old roses; the distances are not drowned in azure vapours, they are the most beautiful apple-green, and here and there spirals of golden smoke rise up from them. A roving ray of sunlight touches the pediment of a ruined temple or the spire on a tower. Towns full of bell-turrets, pyramids, domes, arcades and steps are set on the hillsides and reflected in the crystal lakes; big trees with broad leaves, deeply cut out by the fairies' scissors, inextricably entwine their trunks and branches to make the wings. The clouds in the sky pile up like snowflakes, over their heads, and in their crevices you can see the twinkling eyes of dwarfs and gnomes; their tortuous roots plunge into the earth, like the fingers on a giant's hand. The green woodpecker taps them in regular time with its horn beak, and the emerald lizards warm themselves in the sun on the moss round their feet.

The toadstool watches the performance hat on head, like the insolent creature it is; the dainty violet rises tiptoe on its tiny feet between two blades of grass, and opens its blue eyes very wide, to see the hero pass.

The bullfinch and the linnet lean over the ends of the branches to prompt the actors.

Through the high grass, the tall purple thistles, the burdocks with velvet leaves, there wind about like silver snakes the streams made of the tears of stags at bay. At long intervals you see anemones shining on the grass like drops of blood, and daisies preening themselves, their heads heavy with pearl coronets, like real duchesses.

The characters belong to no time or place; they come and go, one knows not how or why; they do not eat or drink, they have no home, and they have no occupation. They have no estates or incomes or houses; but sometimes they just carry under their arms a little box full of diamonds as big as pigeons' eggs. When they walk, they do not knock a single drop of rain from the heads of the flowers, and they do not raise a single speck of dust along the roads.

Their attire is the most extravagant and the most fantastic in the world. Pointed hats like steeples with brims as wide as Chinese parasols and enormous feathers plucked from the tail of the phoenix and the bird of paradise; capes striped with brilliant colours, doublets of velvet and brocade, showing their satin or cloth-of-silver linings through the gold-laced openings in the sleeves; breeches as puffed-out and inflated as balloons; scarlet stockings with embroidered clocks, shoes with high heels and big rosettes; delicate little swords, their points up and their hilts down, all full of braids and ribbons: there are the men.

The women are no less curiously attired.

The drawings of Della Bella and Romain de Hooge may serve to represent their style of dress. There are well-lined, flowing dresses with big folds as iridescent as the breasts of turtledoves, reflecting all the changing colours of the rainbow; there are big sleeves with other sleeves coming out of them, lace ruffs with openwork patterns, which rise up higher than the head they frame, bodices laden with bows and embroideries, shoulder-knots, curious jewels, crests of herons' plumes and necklaces of big pearls, fans which are made of peacocks' tails with mirrors in the middle, little mules and pattens, garlands of artificial flowers, spangles, lamé gauzes, rouge, beauty-spots, and everything which can add spice and piquancy to a theatrical costume.

It is a taste which is not exactly English, or German, or French, or Turkish, or Spanish, or Tartar, although it has something of them all, and although it has taken from every country what was most graceful and most typical. Actors dressed like this can say anything they like without offending probability. Fantasy can run in any direction, style can unwind its variegated coils as it wills, like a snake warming itself in the sun; the most exotic conceits may open their curious calices without fear, and spread around them their perfume of musk and amber. There is nothing against it, places, names or costumes.

How entertaining and charming their speeches are! Fine actors like these wouldn't go like those howlers of dramas, and distort their mouths and make their eyes pop out of their heads, to hurry on the sensational tirade; at least they don't appear to be like workmen at their task, like oxen harnessed for action and eager to have done with it; they are not plastered with chalk and rouge half an inch thick. They don't carry tin-plate daggers, and they don't keep a pig's bladder full of chicken's blood in reserve under their cloaks; they don't drag round the same oil-stained rag for acts on end.

They talk without haste, without raising their voices, like well-bred people who attach no great importance to what they do; the lover makes his declaration to his beloved in the most detached way in the world; while he is talking, he strikes his thigh with the end of his white glove, or adjusts the lower trimming on his breeches. The lady nonchalantly shakes the dew from her bouquet, and practises a dance with her abigail; the lover doesn't care very much about affecting his cruel mistress: his chief concern is to allow clusters of pearls and bunches of roses to fall from his lips, and to scatter jewels of poetry like a proper spendthrift; indeed, he often effaces himself completely, and lets the author court his mistress for him. Jealousy is not his weakness, and his temper is most accommodating. Lifting up his eyes towards the sky-borders, he waits obligingly until the poet has finished indulging his fancies, and then he resumes his part and falls down on his knees again.

Everything is tied up and untied again with wonderful carelessness: effects have no cause, and causes have no effect; the wittiest person is the one who talks the most nonsense; the stupidest says the most intelligent things; young girls deliver speeches which would make a courtesan blush; courtesans lay down moral maxims. The most unheard-of adventures follow one another in close succession and no explanation is given; the noble father arrives expressly from China in a bamboo junk to recognize a little girl who was kidnapped; gods and fairies do nothing but go up and down in their machines. The action plunges into the sea under the topaz dome of the waves, and moves about on the ocean bed, through forests of coral and madrepore, or else it rises into the sky on the wings of the lark and the griffon. The dialogue is quite universal; the lion contributes an 'oh, oh,' which is vigorously delivered; the wall talks through its crevices, and, provided that there is a witticism, a riddle or a pun to be thrown in, everyone is free to interrupt the most interesting scene. Bottom's ass's head is as welcome as the blond head of Ariel; the author's wit is revealed in every form; and all these contradictions are like so many facets which reflect its various aspects, and add to them all the colours of the rainbow.

This apparent jumble and disorder finally render the fantastic ways of reality more exactly than a drama of manners based on the most detailed study. Every man contains within himself the whole of humanity, and, if he writes what comes into his head, he succeeds better than if he takes a magnifying glass and copies the things which are outside him.

O wonderful family! Romantic young heroes, vagabond young ladies, obliging abigails, caustic clowns, simple valets and peasants, compliant kings, whose names are unknown to the historian and to the realm of the geographer; motley graciosos, clowns with sharp repartees and miraculous capers; O you who let the fancy free through your smiling lips, I love you and adore you especially and above all: Perdita, Rosalind, Celia, Pandarus, Parolles, Sylvius, Leander and the rest, all those delightful characters, so false and so true, who, on the motley wings of folly, rise above crude reality, and in whom the poet personifies his joy, his melancholy, his love and his most secret dream under the most frivolous and the most unconstrained appearances.

In this theatre, designed for fairies, which should be seen by moonlight, there is one play above all which enchants me. It is a play so errant, so vagabond, whose plot is so vaporous, whose characters so singular, that the author himself, not knowing what title to give it, called it *As You Like It*, an elastic title which embraces everything.

As you read this strange play, you feel yourself transported into an unknown world, of which you still have some vague recollection. You no longer know if you're alive or dead, dreaming or waking; graceful figures smile at you sweetly, and send you a friendly good-morning as they pass; you feel moved and disturbed to see them, as if, as you turned the corner of the path, you suddenly encountered your ideal, or the forgotten phantom of your first mistress suddenly rose before you. Springs are flowing, murmuring their stifled lamentations; the wind is stirring the secular trees in the ancient forest over the head of the old exiled duke, with compassionate sighs; and when the melancholy Jaques sends his philosophic complaints down the stream with the willow leaves, it seems to you that you yourself are speaking, and that the most secret, the most obscure corner of your heart is revealed and illuminated.

O young son of the valiant Sir Rowland de Boys, so ill used by fate! I cannot prevent myself from being jealous of you; you still have a faithful servant, the good Adam, whose old age is so green beneath the snow of his hair. You are banished, but at least you are banished after you have fought and triumphed; your wicked brother has taken all your worldly goods away, but Rosalind gives you the chain of her heart; you are poor, but you are loved; you have left your native country, but the daughter of your persecutor follows you across the seas.

The dark forest of Arden opens its great branches of foliage to receive you and hide you; it piles up its most silken moss in the depths of its grottoes for you to sleep on; it bends its arches over your brow, so as to shelter you from sun and rain; it pities you with the tears of its springs and the sighs of its fawns and its trotting stags; it makes its rocks into obliging desks for your love-letters; it lends you the thorns of its bushes to hang them on, and commands the satin bark of its aspens to yield to the point of your stylet when you want to carve Rosalind's initials upon it.

If only, young Orlando, one could be like you, and have a great shady forest in which to retire and isolate oneself in one's grief; if only, as one turned the corner of an avenue, one met the woman whom one was seeking, recognizable, although disguised! But, alas! the world of the soul has no verdant Forest of Arden, and it is only in the flowerbed of poetry that there grow those little whimsical wild flowers whose scent makes you forgetful of the world. We have shed tears in vain, they do not form these lovely silver cascades; we have sighed in vain, no obliging echo has troubled to send us back our lamentations decked with assonances and conceits. It is in vain that we hang sonnets on the thorns of every briar, Rosalind never collects them, and we carve the initials of love upon the bark of trees without reward.

Birds of the heavens, give me a feather, each of you, the swallow and the eagle, the humming-bird and the roc, so that I may make myself a pair of wings to fly aloft and fast through unknown regions, where I find nothing that recalls the city of the living to my mind, where I can forget that I am myself, and live a strange new life, further away than America, further than Africa, further than Asia, further than the last island in the world, across the sea of ice, beyond the pole where the aurora borealis quivers, in the intangible kingdom to which the divine creations of poets and the symbols of perfect beauty take wing.

How can one bear the ordinary conversations in clubs and drawing-rooms, when one has heard you speak, sparkling Mercutio, whose every phrase bursts into a rain of gold and silver, like a firework under a sky bespangled with stars? Pale Desdemona, what pleasure would you have us find in any earthly music, after the song of the willow? Which women do not seem ugly beside

your Venuses, O sculptors of ancient times, poets who write
stanzas of marble?

O, despite the passionate embrace with which I have wanted to
clasp the material world, for want of the other, I feel I am ill born,
that life is not made for me, and that it rejects me; I cannot mingle
with anything; whatever road I follow, I go astray; the level garden
path, the rocky track, both lead me to the abyss. If I want to take
flight, the air condenses round me, and I am caught, with wings
outstretched, unable to shut them again. I cannot walk or fly; the
sky attracts me when I am on earth, the earth attracts me when I'm
in the sky; up above, the north wind tears out my feathers; down
below, the stones bruise my feet. The soles of my feet are too tender
for me to walk on the broken glass of reality; my wings are too
narrow for me to hover over things, and to rise, from circle to
circle, in the deep azure of mysticism, to the very summits of
eternal love; I am the most wretched hippogriff, the most miserable
mass of heterogeneous fragments which has ever existed, since the
Sea has loved the Moon, and women have been unfaithful to men:
the monstrous Chimera, slain by Bellerophon, with the head of a
virgin, the paws of a lion, the body of a goat and the tail of a
dragon, was an animal of simple composition beside me.

In my fragile breast there live both the daydreams, sown with
violets, of the chaste young girl, and the extravagant ardours of
courtesans at an orgy: my desires, like lions, go sharpening their
claws in the darkness, and seeking for something to devour; my
thoughts, more feverish and nervous than goats, hang from the
most menacing crags; my hate, all swollen with poison, twists its
scaly coils in inextricable knots, and drags itself lengthily along the
ruts and the ravines.

My soul is a strange land, a land of prosperous and splendid
appearance, but more saturated with putrid and pernicious miasmas
than the land of Batavia. The slightest ray of sunlight on the mud
makes the reptiles hatch and the mosquitoes pullulate; the big
yellow tulips, the nagassaris and the angsoka flowers splendidly
conceal rotting carcasses. The loving rose opens her scarlet lips,
and smilingly reveals her little teeth of dew to the gallant nightin-

gales, which recite her madrigals and sonnets; nothing is more charming, but you may wager a hundred to one that, in the grass, underneath the bush, a dropsical toad is crawling on its halting legs, and silvering its path with its slime.

There are fountains there which are brighter and more limpid than the purest diamond; but you would do better to draw the stagnant water from the marsh under its cloak of decaying reeds and drowned dogs than to dip your glass in these waves. A serpent is hidden at the bottom, and spinning round with terrifying speed, disgorging its venom.

You have sown corn; there rise up asphodel and henbane, tares and pale hemlock with its stems covered with verdigris. Instead of the root you have planted, you are amazed to see the hairy, twisted limbs of black mandragora rising from the earth.

If you leave a token of remembrance there, and come to fetch it some time afterwards, you will find it greener with moss, more swarming with woodlice and disgusting insects than a stone on the damp floor of a vault.

Do not attempt to cross the mysterious forests; they are more unpassable than the virgin forests of America and the jungles of Java; lianas as strong as ropes run from tree to tree; plants as sharp and bristling as lances obstruct every path; the grass itself is covered with a scorching down like the thistle. Gigantic bats, like vampires, hang by their nails from the arches of foliage; scarabs of enormous size shake their threatening horns, and beat the air with their quadruple wings; fantastic, monstrous animals, like the ones you glimpse in nightmares, lumber forwards, breaking the reeds before them. There are herds of elephants which crush flies between the folds of their dried-up skin or rub their flanks against stones and trees, rhinoceroses with rugged hides, hippopotami with their swollen snouts bristling with hairs, which go about kneading the mud and the detritus of the forest with their big hooves.

In the clearings, where the sun thrusts in a shining ray, through the damp humidity, like a corner of gold, in the place where you would have liked to sit, you will always find some family of tigers nonchalantly lying down, sniffing the air through their nostrils, winking their sea-green eyes and giving a gloss to their velvet furs with their tongues red with blood and covered with papillas; or else there will be a knot of boa-constrictors, half asleep, digesting the last bull that they have swallowed.

Beware of everything: the grass, the fruit, the water and the air, the sunshine and the shadow, all bring death.

Shut your ears to the babble of the little parrots with golden beaks and emerald necks which fly down from the trees and settle on your fingers with fluttering wings; for the little parrots with emerald necks will end up amiably gouging out your eyes with their pretty gold beaks just as you bend down to kiss them. That's how it is!

The world does not want me; it rejects me like a ghost escaped from the tombs; I am almost as pale: my blood refuses to believe that I am alive, and it will not colour my skin; it drags itself slowly through my veins, like stagnant water in choked-up canals. My heart does not beat for anything which moves the heart of man. My sorrows and my joys are not those of my fellow-men. I have violently desired what nobody desires; I have disdained things that men want with desperation. I have loved women when they did not love me, and I have been loved when I should have liked to be hated: always too soon or too late, too much or too little, one way or the other; never what was needed; either I have not arrived or I have gone too far. I have cast my life out of the windows, or I have concentrated it on a single point, to excess, and from the anxious activity of the ardelion I have come to the dull somnolence of the teriaki and of the stylite on his pillar.

What I do always seems to be as if in a dream; my actions seem the result of somnambulism rather than the result of free will. There is something in me, something I feel obscurely, deep inside me, which makes me act without my own participation and always beyond ordinary laws; the simple and natural side of things is only revealed to me after all the rest, and I always begin by seeing the eccentric and the bizarre. If a line slopes in the least, I shall soon make it into a spiral more twisted than a snake; if contours are not defined in the most precise manner, they are blurred and deformed. Faces take on a supernatural appearance and look at you with terrifying eyes.

And so, by a sort of instinctive reaction, I have always desperately clung to matter, to the external silhouette of things, and in art I have given a very big place to the plastic. I understand a statue perfectly, I don't understand a man; where life begins, I stop and recoil in fear as if I had seen the head of Medusa. The phenomenon of life causes me an astonishment from which I cannot recover. I shall no doubt be an excellent corpse, for I am a rather poor living creature, and the meaning of my existence completely escapes me. The sound of my voice surprises me to an unimaginable degree, and I should sometimes be tempted to take it for someone else's voice. When I want to stretch out my arm and my arm obeys me, it seems to me absolutely prodigious, and I fall into the deepest stupefaction.

On the other hand, Silvio, I completely understand what is unintelligible; the most extravagant ideas seem to me perfectly natural, and I enter into them with singular facility. I easily see the connection of the wildest and most freakish nightmares. That is the reason why the kind of plays I was telling you about a moment ago give me more pleasure than any other.

We have great discussions on this subject with Théodore and Rosette. Rosette has little sympathy for my system, she is in favour of *actual* truth; Théodore gives the poet more latitude, and accepts a truth of convention and appearance. Personally I think one should leave the field quite open for the author, and I think that fantasy should reign like an absolute sovereign.

Many among the company chiefly relied on the fact that these plays were generally outside theatrical conditions, and couldn't be performed; I told them that this was true in one sense and false in another, like most of the things that people say, and that the ideas they had on the possibilities and impossibilities of the stage seemed to me to be incorrect and to be based on prejudices rather than reasons. I also said, among other things, that the play *As You Like It* was certainly quite feasible, especially for men of the world who were not accustomed to other rôles.

That inspired the idea of performing it. The season is getting on, and they have exhausted every kind of amusement; they are weary of hunting, and expeditions on horseback and on the water; the hazards of boston, however they may vary, are not exciting enough to fill an evening, and the proposition was received with general enthusiasm.

A young man with a gift for painting offered to make the scenery; he is working on it now with great ardour, and in a few days it will be finished. The stage is erected in the orangery, and I think that all will go well. I myself am playing Orlando; Rosette was to be Rosalind, that was only fair: as my mistress and the mistress of the house, the part naturally belonged to her; but she didn't want to dress up as a man – a whim which was rather curious for her, since prudery is hardly one of her failings. If I had not been sure of the contrary, I should have thought that she had ugly legs. Actually none of the ladies of the company was ready to be less scrupulous than Rosette, and that nearly ruined the play; but Théodore, who had taken the part of the melancholy Jaques, offered to take her place, since Rosalind is nearly always dressed as a man, except in the first act, where she's dressed as a woman, and with rouge, a pair of stays and a dress, he can create sufficient illusion, since he has no beard yet and he has a very slight figure.

We are in the process of learning our parts, and it is rather curious to see us. In all the solitary corners of the park, you are sure to find someone with a sheet of paper in their hand, muttering phrases under their breath, raising their eyes to heaven, casting them suddenly to the ground, and repeating the same gesture seven or eight times over. If you didn't know that we were going to perform a play, you would certainly take us for a household of lunatics or poets (which is almost a pleonasm).

I think that we shall soon know enough to have a rehearsal. I expect something very singular. Perhaps I'm wrong. I was afraid for a moment that instead of performing with inspiration, our actors would insist on reproducing the poses and vocal inflexions of some actor in fashion; but fortunately they have not studied the theatre closely enough to fall into this inconvenient habit, and I believe that, through the awkwardness of people who have never trodden the boards, they will have rare flashes of truth, and that charming artlessness which the most consummate talent could not imitate.

Our young artist has really done marvels: it is impossible to give a stranger shape to the old tree-trunks and to the ivy which twines around them; he had modelled them on the trees in the park, heightening and exaggerating them, as he should do in painting scenery. Everything has been expressed with wonderful boldness and imagination; the stones, the rocks, the clouds, are mysteriously distorted; shimmering reflections move across the water, more tremulous and a-quiver than quicksilver, and the usual coldness of the leaves is marvellously enhanced by the saffron tints which are cast on it by the brush of autumn; the forest varies from emerald green to cornelian purple; the warmest and coldest tones clash in harmony, and the sky itself passes from the palest blue to the most ardent hues.

He has made all the costumes according to my designs, and he has done so in the finest style. People insisted, to begin with, that they couldn't be translated into silk and velvet, or into any known material, and at one moment it seemed that the troubadour costume was going to be adopted for everyone. The ladies said that these glaring colours would blind them. To which we replied that their eyes were stars which could never be extinguished, and that, on the contrary, their eyes would dim the colours, the lamps, the chandeliers and the sun, if the occasion arose. They had no answer to make to that; but there were a throng of other objections which rose up, bristling, all the time, like the hydra of Lerna; you had no sooner cut the head off one of them than another arose more stubborn and more stupid.

'How do you think that will hold together?' 'It's all right on paper, but it's different when you put it on; I shall never wear it!' 'My skirt is at least four inches too short; I shall never dare appear like that!' 'This ruff is too high; I look as if I'm humpbacked and have no neck. This hairstyle ages me intolerably.'

'Everything will hold together with starch, pins and goodwill.' 'You're not serious! With a waist like yours, narrower than a wasp's, a waist which would slip through my signet-ring! I wager twenty-five louis to a kiss that you will have to take in that bodice.' 'Your skirt is far from being too short, and, if you could see what adorable legs you have, you would certainly agree with me.' 'On the contrary, your neck is wonderfully set off and outlined by its lace halo; that hairstyle doesn't age you at all, and even if you were to seem a year or two older, you are so excessively young that it shouldn't matter to you in the least; in fact, you would make us strangely suspicious, if we didn't know where to find what was left of your last doll . . .' etcetera.

You cannot imagine the prodigious number of compliments which we have been obliged to pay to compel our ladies to wear enchanting costumes which suited them to perfection.

We have also had a good deal of trouble making them put on their beauty-spots properly. What diabolical taste women have! And with what titanic stubbornness a vapourish belle believes that glazed straw-yellow suits her better than jonquil or bright pink! I'm sure that, if I'd applied to politics half the ruses and intrigues I have used to have a red feather worn on the left and not on the right, I should be Minister of State or Emperor at least.

What pandemonium! What an enormous, inextricable *omnium gatherum* a real theatre must be!

Since we have talked about acting a play, everything here is in absolute chaos. All the drawers are open, all the cupboards emptied; everything has been ransacked. Tables, chairs and pier-tables are all cluttered up, you don't know where to step; prodigious quantities of dresses, mantlets, veils, skirts, cloaks, caps, hats, are trailing about the house; and, when you think that this is to clothe seven or eight people, you can't help remembering those mountebanks at fairs who wear eight or ten suits on top of each other, and you can't imagine that, out of all this, there will only emerge one costume apiece.

The servants do nothing but come and go; there are always two or three on the road from the château to the town, and, if this goes on, all the horses will become broken-winded.

A theatre director is too busy to be melancholy, and for some time I have hardly ever been sad. I am so bemused and confounded that I'm beginning not to understand the play any more. As I myself act the part of the impresario as well as the part of Orlando, I have a double task. When a problem arises, they have recourse to me, and since my decisions aren't always accepted like those of the oracles, it degenerates into endless discussions.

If what you call living is to be constantly on your feet, to give answers to a score of people, go up and down stairs, and not have a minute in the day to yourself, I have never lived so much as I have this week; and yet I don't take as great a part in this activity as you might think. The movement is just on the surface, and a few fathoms down you would find the water stagnant and still; life doesn't enter me so easily; and indeed it is now that I live least, although I appear to be busy and involved in what is happening; action dulls me and tires me to an unimaginable degree; when I'm not busy, I'm thinking or at least I'm dreaming, and that is a mode of existence; I no longer have it as soon as I emerge from my repose, the repose of a porcelain idol.

Until now, I haven't done anything, and I don't know if I shall ever do anything. I don't know how to stop my mind, and that is the whole difference between the man of talent and the man of genius; it is an endless ebullition, wave after wave; I cannot control this sort of inner jet which rises from my heart to my head, and drowns all my thoughts because there are no outlets. I can't produce anything, not out of sterility, but out of superabundance; my ideas grow up so thick and dense that they choke and cannot ripen. However fast and eagerly I realize them, I can't do so fast enough. When I write a sentence, the thought which it expresses is already as distant as if a century had passed and not a second, and, in spite of myself, I often mingle it with something of the thought which has taken its place in my head.

That is why I couldn't live, either as a poet or a lover. I can only express the ideas which I no longer have. I only have women when I've forgotten them and I'm in love elsewhere. How, as a man, shall I produce my idea in the light of day, since, however much I hurry, I no longer have a sense of what I am doing, and I only behave according to some dim recollection?

To take a thought in a vein of one's mind, get it out rough at first like a block of marble from a quarry, set it in front of oneself, and, from morn till night, a chisel in one hand, a hammer in the other, knock and carve and scrape, and at night take away a pinch of dust to scatter over one's writing; that is something I shall never be able to do.

In my mind's eye I can easily disengage the figure from the rough block, and I have a very clear vision of it; but there are so many corners to smooth down, so many splinters to knock off, so much scraping and hammering to do to approach the form and catch the exact undulation of the lines, that I get blisters on my hands, and I drop the chisel.

If I persist, I become so absolutely exhausted that my inner vision is quite obscured, and I no longer see the white divinity hidden in the thick white marble cloud. And then I pursue it blindly and at random; I cut too deeply in one place, and not deeply enough in another; I take away what ought to be the leg or the arm, and I leave a solid mass where a void should be; instead of a goddess, I make a monstrosity, and the wonderful block, extracted at such expense, and with such labour, from the bowels of the earth, hammered, cut, hollowed out in all directions, looks as if it had been gnawed away and pierced through by polyps and turned into a ruff, not as if it was made by a sculptor according to a definite plan.

What do you do, Michelangelo, to cut marble into slices, like a child carving a chestnut? Of what steel were your unconquered chisels made? And what robust loins have borne you, all you fruitful and industrious artists, whom no material resists, artists who cast the whole of your dream in colour and in bronze?

It is in a way an innocent and permissible vanity, after the cruel things I've said about myself, and, Silvio, you won't be the one to blame me. But, although the world will never know about it, and my name is destined for oblivion, I am a poet and a painter! I have had ideas as fine as those of any poet in the universe; I have treated thoughts as pure and as divine as those which are most admired in the works of the masters. I see them there before me, as clear, as distinct as if they were really painted, and, if I could open a hole in my head and put a window there so that people could look in, it would be the most wonderful gallery of pictures that had ever been seen. No king on earth can boast one like it. There are Rubens, as blazing and afire as the purest you see in Antwerp; my Raphaels are beautifully preserved, and his madonnas do not have more gracious smiles; Buonarotti does not twist a muscle in a prouder or more terrible fashion; the sun of Venice shines in this canvas as if it were signed *Paulus Cagliari*; the shadows of Rembrandt himself are massed in the depths of this frame, and a pale star of light is trembling in the distance; the pictures which are in my own manner would certainly not be disdained by anyone.

Of course I know that it seems strange for me to say this, and that I'll look as if I'm giddy with the crude intoxication of the most idiotic pride; but so it is, and nothing will shake my conviction about it. No one, of course, will share it; but I can't help that. Everyone is born marked with a black seal or a white one. My seal is apparently black.

Sometimes I even find it hard to veil my thoughts about this properly; I have often chanced to speak too familiarly of those lofty geniuses whose footsteps we ought to worship, whose statue we ought to contemplate from afar, and on our knees. Once I so forgot myself as to say 'we'. Luckily it was in front of someone who took no notice, otherwise I should have been thought the most conceited coxcomb in the world.

Silvio, I am a poet and a painter, aren't I?

It is a mistake to believe that all the people who have been considered to have genius were really greater men than the rest. One doesn't know how much the pupils and the obscure artists whom Raphael employed in his studio have contributed to his reputation; he gave his signature to the spirit and talents of several of them, that's all.

A great painter or a great writer occupies and fills a whole century by himself: his most urgent wish is to attempt every genre at once, so that, if a few rivals should arise, he can promptly accuse them of plagiary, and halt them at the beginning of their careers; the tactics are familiar, and, though they are nothing new, they succeed every day, all the same.

It may be that a man who is already famous has exactly the same sort of talent that you would have had; at the risk of passing for his imitator, you are obliged to divert your natural inspiration and make it flow in another direction. You were born to blow the heroic trumpet loud and clear, or to recall the pale phantoms of ages past; you are obliged to finger the seven-holed flute, or to tie bows on a sofa deep in some or other boudoir, and all because your father didn't take the trouble to cast you into the mould eight or ten years sooner, and because the world can't imagine that two men should till the same field.

So it is that many noble minds are forced deliberately to take a path which is not their own, and continually to run along the border of their own domain, from which they are banished. They are lucky if they can just steal a furtive glance over the hedge, and see, on the far side, blooming in the sunshine, the lovely variegated flowers whose seeds they possess and cannot sow because they have no ground.

As for me, I might have had more or less favourable circumstances, more or less air and sun. Perhaps there was a door which remained shut and should have been open, perhaps there was a meeting I missed, someone I should have known and didn't know. But I'm not sure if I should ever have achieved anything.

I don't have the degree of stupidity which you have to have in order to be what people simply call a *genius*. I don't have the enormous stubbornness which people later glorify as willpower, when the great man has reached the radiant mountain-top – the stubborness which is essential if you are to reach it. I know too well that everything is hollow, and rotten inside, to attach myself for long to anything, and to pursue it ardently and exclusively to the end.

Men of genius are very limited, and that is why they are men of genius. Their lack of intelligence prevents them from seeing the obstacles which separate them from the object which they want to attain; they go on, and in two or three strides they tear through the intervening space. As their minds remain stubbornly closed to certain courses, and they perceive only the things which most closely concern their plans, they waste much less thought and action. Nothing distracts them, nothing diverts them, they move by instinct rather than anything else, and some of them, taken out of their particular sphere, are of an almost incredible nullity.

It is certainly a rare and charming gift to write verse well; few people take more pleasure than I do in poetic matters. All the same I don't want to limit or circumscribe my life in the twelve feet of an alexandrine; there are a thousand things which concern me as much as a hemistich. I don't care about the state of society or the reforms which must be made; I don't care very much whether peasants can read or not, and whether men eat bread or browse on grass; but there pass through my head in the space of an hour more than a hundred thousand visions which haven't the slightest connection with the caesura or the rhyme, and that is why I write so little, although I have more ideas than certain poets who could be burnt at the stake with their own works.

I adore beauty and I feel it; I can express it as well as the most amorous sculptors can express it – and yet I sculpt no statues. The ugliness and imperfection of the rought draft revolt me; I cannot wait for the work to succeed through polishing and repolishing; if I could decide to leave certain things in what I do, in verse or in painting, I might end by producing a poem or a picture which would make me famous, and those who love me (if there is anyone in the world who gives themselves this trouble) would not be obliged to take me at my word, and they would have a victorious answer to the sardonic sneers of the detractors of that great undiscovered genius, myself.

I see many people who pick up a palette and brushes and cover their canvas, only concerned with what caprice creates at the tip of their brush, and others who write a hundred lines in succession without crossing out and without once looking up at the ceiling. I always admire them, although I don't always admire their productions; with all my heart I envy this charming intrepidity, this fortunate blindness which prevents them from seeing their faults, even the most palpable. As soon as I've drawn something wrong, I see it at once, and I'm excessively concerned about it; and, as I am much more knowledgeable in theory than in practice, it very often happens that I cannot correct a fault that I'm aware of; and then I turn the canvas face to the wall and I never go back to it.

The idea of perfection is so present in me that it makes me disgusted with my work from the start, and it prevents me from going on.

Oh, when I compare the sweet smiles of my thought with the ugly grimace it makes on canvas or paper, when I see a dreadful bat pass by instead of the lovely dream which opened its wide wings of light deep in my nights, when I see a thistle grow on the idea of a rose and I hear the braying of an ass where I was expecting the sweetest melodies of the nightingale, I am so horribly disappointed, so angry with myself, so furious at my impotence that I resolve not to write or speak another word in my life rather than commit such crimes of high treason against my thoughts.

I cannot even manage to write a letter as I should wish: I often say something quite different; certain parts are developed out of proportion, others shrink until they are imperceptible, and very often the idea which I had to express isn't there at all or only appears in a postscript.

When I began writing to you, I certainly didn't mean to tell you half the things that I've told you; I simply wanted to let you know that we were going to perform a play. But a word brings a sentence, and parentheses grow fat with other little parentheses which, in turn, have others in their wombs about to be born. There is no reason why it should end and why it shouldn't go on for two hundred folio volumes – which would undoubtedly be too much.

As soon as I take up my pen, there is a humming and buzzing of wings in my mind, as if someone had let loose a multitude of cockchafers. They knock against the walls of my skull, fly round and up and down, and make a horrible din. These are my ideas, wanting to escape and find a way out; they all try to come out at once; more than one of them breaks its legs in the process and tears the crape of its wings: sometimes the door is so obstructed that not one of them can cross the threshold and finally reach the paper.

That is how I'm made: no doubt I'm badly made, but what can I do? The fault lies with the gods, and not with me, a poor devil who can do nothing about it. I don't need to ask for your indulgence, my dear Silvio; I already have it, and you are kind enough to read my indecipherable scrawls, my shapeless idle dreams, to the end. However incoherent and absurd they may be, they are always of interest to you, because they come from me, and everything that is me, even when it's bad, is not without a certain value to you.

I can show you what most revolts the generality of men: honest vanity. But let's have a little respite from all these fine things, and, since I am writing to you about the play we're going to perform, let's come back to that and talk about it a little.

The rehearsal took place today. Never in my life have I been so overwhelmed—not because of the embarrassment which there always is when you recite something to a lot of people, but for another reason. We were dressed up, and ready to begin; only Théodore had not yet arrived. Someone was despatched to his room to see why he was late; he sent a message that he would soon be ready, and he was coming down.

He came indeed; I heard his footsteps in the corridor a long time before he appeared, and yet no one in the world has a lighter step than Théodore; but the sympathy I feel for him is so strong that in a way I can divine his movements through walls, and, when I understood that he was about to touch the handle of the door, I was seized by a sort of trembling, and my heart beat most horribly. It seemed to me that something important in my life was about to be decided, and that I had reached a solemn moment which I had awaited a long while.

The door slowly opened, and slowly it closed.

There was a general cry of admiration. The men applauded, the women turned scarlet. Only Rosette turned extremely pale and leant against the wall, as if a sudden revelation were passing through her mind. She made the same movement as I did, in the opposite direction. I have always suspected her of loving Théodore.

No doubt, at that moment, she believed as I did that the pretended Rosalind was in fact nothing other than a young and beautiful woman, and the fragile house of cards of her hopes suddenly collapsed, while my own rose again on its ruins; at least that is what I thought: perhaps I am wrong, for I was hardly in a state to make precise observations.

There were three or four pretty women there, not counting

Rosette; they appeared revoltingly ugly. In the presence of this sun, the star of their beauty was suddenly eclipsed, and everyone wondered how he could have found them even passable. People who would have been very glad, before, to have had them as mistresses would hardly have wanted them as their servants.

The image which until then had only taken a faint shape and assumed vague contours, the phantom which I had adored and pursued in vain, was there, before my eyes, living, palpable, no longer in a mist or in twilight, but drenched with a flood of white light; not in vain disguise, but in its true attire: no longer with the mocking shape of a young man, but with the features of the most enchanting woman.

I felt an enormous sense of wellbeing, as if someone had taken a mountain or two off my breast. I felt my horror of myself disappear, and I was freed from the sorrow of thinking I was a monster. Once again I conceived a quite pastoral opinion of myself, and once again all the violets of the spring flowered in my heart.

He, or rather she (for I want to forget that I was stupid enough to take her for a man), remained for a minute motionless on the threshold, as if to give the assembly time to make its first exclamation. A sharp ray of light illumined her from head to foot, and against the dark background of the corridor which stretched far into the distance, framed in the sculpted frame of the door, she sparkled as if the light were emanating from her instead of simply being reflected, and you would have taken her for a wonderful creation of the brush rather than a human being made of flesh and blood.

Her long brown hair, intertwined with strings of big pearls, fell in natural curls down her lovely cheeks; her shoulders and her bosom were bare, and I have never ever seen anything in the world that was so beautiful: the most finished marble doesn't approach this exquisite perfection. How you see life flow beneath this transparent shadow! How white this flesh is, yet how coloured, too! How these harmoniously golden tints soften the transition from skin to hair! What enchanting poems in the gentle undulations of those contours more pliant and more velvet than swans' necks! If there were words to render what I feel, I should give you a description fifty pages long; but languages have been created by contemptible fellows who have never looked carefully at a woman's back or at her breast, and we haven't got half the most essential words.

I really and truly think that I must become a sculptor. To have seen such beauty, and to be unable to express it, is enough to drive you mad and desperate. I have written twenty sonnets about those shoulders, but it isn't enough: I should like something which I could touch with my finger, something which was exactly like it; verses only render the ghost of beauty, and not beauty itself. The painter reaches a more exact likeness, but it is only a likeness. Sculpture has all the reality which something completely false can possess; it has many aspects, it casts a shadow, and it allows itself to be touched. Your sculpted mistress only differs from the real one in that she is somewhat harder and that she doesn't speak, which are two very unimportant failings!

Her dress was made of some shot material, blue in sunlight, and gold in shadow. Very narrow, very tight half-boots shod her feet, which had no need of that to be too small, and scarlet silk stockings clung lovingly to the most shapely and most provocative legs. Her arms were bare to the elbows, and emerged round, plump and white from a bunch of lace, as splendid as polished silver and of an unimaginable delicacy of line; her hands, laden with golden rings and jewelled rings, gently waved a big fan of particoloured feathers of singular hues which seemed like a miniature pocket rainbow.

She came forward into the room, her cheeks slightly flushed with a pink which was not rouge, and everyone went into raptures, and cried out with admiration, and asked themselves if it was really possible that this was Théodore de Sérannes, the dashing rider, the determined hunter, and if he was absolutely sure that this was not his twin sister.

But you would think that he had never worn any other costume in his life! He is not in the very least awkward in his movements, he walks very well and he doesn't get caught up in his train; he uses his eyes and his fan to admiration; and what a slim waist he has! You could encircle it with the fingers of one hand! It is prodigious! It is inconceivable! The illusion is as perfect as possible: you would almost think that he had breasts, his bosom is so plump and well filled, and not a single hair of a beard, not one; and his voice is sweet! Oh, lovely Rosalind! Who would not want to be her Orlando?

Yes – who would not want to be the Orlando of this Rosalind, even at the price of the torments which I have suffered? To love as I have loved with a monstrous, unavowable love, a love which even so one cannot tear up from one's heart; to be condemned to keep the deepest silence, not to dare allow oneself what the most discreet and most respectful lover would not hesitate to say to the most strait-laced and prudish woman; to feel oneself devoured by ardours which are insane and inexcusable, even in the eyes of the most incorrigible libertines; what are ordinary passions beside this, a passion shameful in itself, a passion without hope, one whose improbable success would be a crime and would make you die of shame? To be reduced to wishing that you will not succeed, to fear the favourable chances and opportunities, that was my fate.

The deepest discouragement took hold of me; I looked at myself with a horror mixed with surprise and curiosity. What revolted me most was to think that I had never loved before, and that this was for me the first effervescence of youth, the first daisy in my springtime of love.

I had this monstrous love, and not the fresh and chaste illusions of youth. Those dreams of tenderness so gently caressed, at evening, at the edge of the woods, along the little paths tinged with sunset, along the white marble terraces, near the lake in the park: were they to be transformed into this treacherous sphinx, with the doubtful smile, the ambiguous voice, before whom I stood without daring to undertake to explain the enigma! To misinterpret it would have killed me; for, alas, it is the only link which binds me to the world; when it is broken, all will be ended. Take away that spark from me, and I shall be more dismal and inanimate than the mummy imprisoned in bandelets of the oldest of the Pharaohs.

At the moments when I felt myself most violently drawn to Théodore, I threw myself in terror into the arms of Rosette, although I found her infinitely displeasing; I tried to interpose her between him and myself like a barrier and buckler – and I felt a secret satisfaction, as I lay beside her, to think that at least she was a well-proven woman, and that, if I no longer loved her, she still loved me enough for this liaison not to degenerate into intrigue and debauchery.

And yet, deep down, and through it all, I felt a kind of regret that I was thus unfaithful to the idea of my impossible passion; I reproached myself for it as if it were a betrayal, and, although I knew quite well that I should never possess the object of my love, I was dissatisfied with myself, and I resumed my usual coldness with Rosette.

The rehearsal was much better than I had expected; Théodore, in particular, proved to be wonderful; it was also thought that I performed superlatively well. It is not however that I have the qualities I need to be a good actor, and people would be very wrong to believe that I could perform other parts in the same manner; but, by a rather singular chance, the words I had to speak were so appropriate to my situation that they seemed to me to be invented for me rather than learned from a book. If I had lost my memory in certain places, I should certainly not have hesitated for a moment to fill the void with an impoverished sentence. Orlando was myself at least as much as I was Orlando, and it is impossible to find a more marvellous coincidence.

In the challenger's scene, when Théodore took a chain off his neck and gave it to me, as the part demanded, he gave me a glance so sweetly langorous, so full of promises, he said with such grace and nobility:

> Gentleman,
> Wear this for me, one out of suits with fortune,
> That would give more, but that her hand lacks means,

that I was really troubled, and I could hardly continue:

> What passion hangs these weights upon my tongue?
> I cannot speak to her, yet she urg'd conference.
> O poor Orlando!

In the third act Rosalind, dressed as a man, and under the name of

Ganymede, reappears with her cousin Celia, who has changed her name to Aliena.

This made a disagreeable impression on me: I had already become so accustomed to this woman's costume which allowed some hopes for my desires, and kept me in treacherous but seductive error! You very soon grow used to considering your wishes as realities on the strength of the most transient appearances, and I grew all sombre when Théodore reappeared in masculine dress, more sombre than I had been before; for happiness only serves to make one more aware of grief, the sun only shines to make one more aware of the horror of darkness, and the gaiety of white merely serves to emphasize the sadness of black.

Théodore's attire was the most elegant and gallant in the world, of a stylish and whimsical cut, all adorned with aiglets and ribbons, something in the style of the exquisites at the court of Louis XIII; a pointed felt hat, with a long curled feather, shaded his fine curly hair, and a damascened sword raised the back of his travelling-cloak.

And yet he was dressed in a way which suggested that this masculine attire had a feminine lining; something broader about the hips and fuller in the chest, some sort of flow which materials don't have on a man's body, left little doubt of the person's sex.

He had a half-determined, half-timid manner which could not have been more engaging, and, with an infinite art, he made himself appear as embarrassed in a costume which was normal for him as he had appeared at his ease in clothes which were not his own.

My serenity began to return, and I persuaded myself again that it was quite definitely a woman. I regained enough confidence to perform my own part properly.

Do you know the play? Perhaps you don't. In the past fortnight I have done nothing but read and declaim it, and I know it all by heart, and I can't imagine that everyone isn't as conversant with the plot and the intrigue as I am. It is an error I often fall into. I think that, when I'm drunk, all creation is intoxicated and bumping into the walls, and, if I knew Hebrew, I'm sure I should ask my servant for my dressing-gown and slippers in Hebrew, and I'd be quite astonished that he didn't understand me. Read the play if you want to; I'm behaving as if you'd read it, and only touching on the points which are related to my situation.

When Rosalind strolls in the forest with her cousin, she is astonished to see that the bushes don't bear blackberries and sloes, but madrigals in praise of herself. Happily these singular fruits don't always grow on briars; after all, when you're thirsty it's better to find good blackberries than poor sonnets on the brambles. Rosalind is very anxious to know who has spoiled the bark of the young trees like this by carving her name on it. Celia, who has already met Orlando, tells her, after much persuasion, that the rhymer is none other than the young man who has vanquished Charles, the Duke's wrestler, in their struggle.

Orlando himself soon appears, and Rosalind gets into conversation by asking him the time. There indeed is an opening of the most extreme simplicity; there couldn't be anything in the world more bourgeois than that. But have no fear: from this common, ordinary phrase there immediately springs a harvest of unexpected conceits, as full of flowers and bizarre comparisons, as if they sprang from the richest and most nurtured soil.

After a few lines of sparkling dialogue, where every word, as it falls into the sentence, sets millions of wild sparks leaping out left and right, like a hammer on a red-hot iron bar, Rosalind asks Orlando if by chance he knows the man who hangs odes upon the hawthorns, and seems to be affected by the quotidian of love, which she is well able to cure. Orlando confesses that he is the man so tormented by love; and, since she has boasted of having several infallible cures, he asks her if she would kindly suggest one. You are not in love, answers Rosalind; you have none of the signs by which I should recognize a man in love. You don't have lean cheeks or sunken eyes; your hose is not ungartered, your sleeves are not unbuttoned, and the rosettes on your shoes are tied with much grace; if you're in love with anyone, it is certainly with yourself, and you have no need of my remedies.

It was not without real emotion that I answered her literally as follows:

'Fair youth, I would I could make thee believe I love.'

This answer, so curious, so unexpected, had no introduction; it seemed as if, with a kind of foresight, the poet had written it especially for me. It had great effect when I gave it to Théodore. His divine lips were still slightly puffed out by the ironic expression of the sentence he had just spoken, and his eyes were smiling with inexpressible sweetness. A sunlit glow of benevolence gilded all the upper part of his handsome young face.

'Me believe it! You may as soon make her that you love believe it; which, I warrant, she is apter to do than to confess she does: that is one of the points in which women still give the lie to their consciences. But, in good sooth, are you he that hangs the verses on the trees, wherein Rosalind is so admired?'

When she is quite sure that it is he, Orlando, and no other, who has rhymed these admirable lines, that he is as much in love as his rhymes speak, the lovely Rosalind consents to tell him her cure. This is what it consists of: she had pretended to be the beloved of the love-sick swain, and he had been obliged to woo her every day, as if she were really his mistress; 'at which time would I, being but a moonish youth, grieve, be effeminate, changeable, longing, and liking; proud, fantastical, apish, shallow, inconstant, full of tears, full of smiles; for every passion something, and for no passion truly anything, as boys and women are for the most part cattle of this colour; would now like him, now loathe him; then entertain him, then forswear him; now weep for him, then spit at him.' She was never for a moment consistent: simpering, fickle, prudish, languorous, she was everything in turn, and all the wild fantasies that boredom, the vapours and depression could stir up in the empty head of a belle, the poor devil was obliged to bear or to perform. A sprite, a monkey and an attorney combined wouldn't have contrived more mischief. This miraculous treatment hadn't failed to have its effect. 'I draw my suitor from his mad humour of love to a loving humour of madness; which was, to forswear the full stream of the world, and to live in a nook merely monastic.' The most satisfactory result that you could imagine – and one which, moreover, was easy to foresee.

Orlando, as you may imagine, is hardly anxious to be restored to health in such a fashion; but Rosalind insists, and wants to undertake this cure. 'I would cure you, if you would but call me Rosalind, and come every day to my cote to woo me.' She pronounced this phrase with such a marked and evident meaning that it was impossible for me not to attach a broader sense to it than the words suggested, and not to see it as an indirect admonition to declare my real feelings. And when Orlando answered her: 'With all my heart, good youth,' she replied with even more significance, and with a kind of vexation that she didn't make herself understood: 'Nay, you must call me Rosalind.'

Perhaps I was wrong, and I thought I saw what didn't actually exist, but it seemed to me that Théodore had observed my love, although I had certainly never said a word to him about it, and that through the veil of these borrowed words, under this theatrical mask, with these hermaphrodite words, he was alluding to his real sex and to our position towards each other. It is quite impossible that a woman as intelligent as she is, a woman with such knowledge of the world, should not, from the beginning, have discovered what was happening in my soul. The words were lacking, but my eyes and my perplexity were eloquent enough, and the veil of ardent friendship which I had cast over my love was not so impenetrable that an attentive and interested observer could not easily see through it. The most innocent and most pristine girl would not have hesitated for a minute.

No doubt there is some important reason, which I cannot know, which obliges this beautiful woman to adopt this accursed disguise. It has been the cause of all my torments, and it very nearly made me an unnatural lover. Otherwise everything would have gone smoothly and easily, like a carriage with well-oiled wheels on a very smooth road covered with fine sand; I could have abandoned myself in sweet security to the most amorous and vagabond dreams, and taken between my hands the small white silken hands of my divinity, without shuddering with horror, and without stepping twenty paces back, as if I had touched a red-hot iron, or felt the claws of Beelzebub in person.

Instead of despairing, growing distraught like a proper maniac, of beating myself in order to feel remorse, and lamenting that I didn't feel it, I should have said every morning, as I stretched my arms, said with a feeling of duty fulfilled and conscience satisfied: 'I am in love.' This sentence is as agreeable to repeat to yourself in the morning, with your head on a nice soft pillow, under a nice warm eiderdown, as any other sentence of four words that you could imagine – except of course for this: 'I have some money.'

When I'd got up, I should have gone and stood in front of my mirror, and there, considering myself with a sort of respect, I should have been moved, as I combed my hair, by my poetic pallor, and promised myself to make the most of it, and to make it duly appreciated, for there is nothing so ignoble as to make love with a rubicund face; and, when you have the misfortune to be florid and amorous, two things which may coincide, I believe you should cover your countenance with flour every day, or give up being fashionable, and keep to the Maggies and Lizzies.

I should then have had *déjeuner* with solemnity and compunction, to nourish this dear body, this precious casket of passion, to nurture it with the juice of meats and game, with good digestive juices for love, with good warm blood, and keep it in condition to give pleasure to charitable souls.

After *déjeuner*, while I was picking my teeth, I should have interlaced a few irregular rhymes in the form of a sonnet, all in honour of my princess; I should have found a thousand little comparisons, each more original than the last, and infinitely gallant. In the first quatrain, there would have been a dance of suns, and, in the second, a minuet of theological virtues; the two tercets would not have been in inferior taste. Helen would have been dismissed as a barmaid, and Paris as a fool; the Orient would have had nothing to desire in the splendour of the metaphors; the last line, above all, would have been particularly fine and it would have contained at least two conceits per syllable; for the venom of a scorpion lies in its tail, and the merit of the sonnet in its last line. When the sonnet was finished and duly inscribed on glazed and scented paper, I should have set out, a hundred cubits tall, bending down so as not to knock against the sky and get caught up with the clouds (a wise precaution), and I should have gone to recite my new production to all my friends and all my enemies, then to children at the breast and their nurses, then to horses and donkeys, then to walls and trees, to have some idea of the opinion of creation on this latest product of my poetic vein.

In company, I should have talked to women with a doctoral air, and maintained sentimental theses in a grave and measured tone of voice, like a man who knows much more than he is prepared to say about the subject under discussion, a man who has not gained his knowledge from books. This doesn't fail to produce the most prodigious effect, and all the women present who no longer give their ages, and the few young girls whom one hasn't asked to dance, swoon like carps out of water.

I could have led the happiest life in the world, trodden on the pug's tail without drawing too many tears from his mistress, knocked over centre tables laden with porcelain, eaten the tastiest morsels at dinner and not left a scrap for anyone else; everything would have been excused because men in love are renowned for their distraction; and, when they saw me swallow everything like this with a wild expression on my face, everyone would have clasped their hands and said: 'Poor young man!'

And then what a dreamy, plaintive look I should have displayed, what unkempt hair, what ill-drawn stockings, what a loose cravat, what limply hanging arms! How I should have paced the avenues in the park, sometimes with big strides, sometimes with short steps, like a man whose reason has completely flown! How I should have looked the moon full in the face, and made circles in the water with utter tranquillity!

But the gods have ordained things otherwise.

I have fallen in love with a beautiful woman in doublet and boots, with a proud Bradamante who disdains the garb of her sex, and leaves you wavering, at times, in the most disturbing perplexity. Her features and her body are certainly the features and the body of a woman, but her mind is certainly that of a man.

My mistress is a swordsman of the first order, and she would be more than a match for the most experienced fencing-master's assistant; she has had I don't know how many duels, and killed or wounded three or four people; she jumps ditches ten feet wide on horseback, and hunts like an old provincial squireen. These are singular qualities for a mistress! Such things only happen to me.

I'm laughing, but there's certainly nothing to laugh about, because I have never suffered so much, and these last two months have seemed like two years or rather two centuries. The ebb and flow of uncertainties in my head have been enough to stupefy the strongest mind; I was so violently disturbed and pulled about in all directions, I had such wild urges, such dull debility, such extravagant hopes and such profound despairs that I really don't understand how I haven't worked myself to death. I was so full of this idea, so occupied with it, that I was surprised that people didn't see it clearly through my body like a candle in a lantern, and I was in mortal fear that someone might chance to discover who was the object of this senseless love. Yet Rosette, who had more interest than anyone in the world in watching over the movements of my heart, hadn't seemed to notice anything at all; I think that she was herself too busy loving Théodore to notice that I had grown cold towards her; or else I must be a past master in the art of dissimulation, and I am not conceited enough to think that. Théodore himself hasn't given any sign until today that he had the slightest suspicion of the state of my soul, and he has always talked to me in an easy, friendly way, as a well-bred young man talks to another man of his age, but nothing more. His conversation with me ranged impartially over all kinds of themes, the arts, and poetry, and other such matters; but there was nothing intimate and precise which could have related to him or to me.

Perhaps the reasons which drove him to adopt this disguise no longer exist, and he'll soon put on his proper clothes again. I don't know. All the same, Rosalind pronounced certain words with particular inflexions, and she gave a very marked emphasis to all the passages in her part which had an ambiguous meaning and could have tended in that direction.

In the meeting scene, she displayed a miraculous talent, from the moment when she rebuked Orlando for not coming two hours earlier, as befits a veritable lover, but two hours later, to the moment when she uttered a grievous sigh and, fearful of her intensity of passion, cast herself into Aliena's arms: 'O coz, coz, coz, my pretty little coz, that thou didst know how many fathoms deep I am in love!' It was an irresistible mixture of tenderness, melancholy and love; there was something tremulous and warm in her voice, and one felt that behind the laughter the most violent love was ready to burst out; add to that the piquancy and singularity of the transposition, and the novelty of seeing a young man pay court to a mistress whom he takes for a man, a mistress who has every appearance of being one.

Expressions which would have seemed ordinary and common-place in other situations, assumed a special significance in this one, and all the small change of loving comparisons and protests, which is current in the theatre, seemed to have been recoined with a quite different stamp; besides, if the phrases had been more worn than a judge's gown or the crupper of a hired-out donkey, instead of being rare and delightful as they are, the way in which they were pronounced would have made them seem wonderfully subtle and in the best taste in the world.

I forgot to tell you that, after she refused the part of Rosalind, Rosette had obligingly undertaken the secondary part of Phebe. Phebe is a shepherdess in the Forest of Arden, madly loved by the shepherd Sylvius, whom she cannot abide and constantly oppresses with her harshness. Phebe is as cold as the moon whose name she bears; she has a heart of snow which doesn't melt in the fire of the most ardent sighs, its icy crust only becomes thicker and thicker and as hard as a diamond. But she has hardly seen Rosalind in the garb of the handsome page, Ganymede, before all this ice dissolves into tears and the diamond becomes softer than wax. Proud Phebe, who laughed at love, is herself in love; she now suffers all the torments which she made others endure. Her pride is humble enough for her to make all the advances, and she makes poor Sylvius take Rosalind an ardent letter which contains the avowal of her passion in the meekest and most supplicating terms. Rosalind, moved by pity for Silvius, and having, besides, the most excellent reasons possible not to reciprocate Phebe's love, makes her endure the harshest treatment, and ridicules her with unparalleled cruelty and fierceness. Phebe still prefers these insults to her shepherd's most delicate and most impassioned madrigals; she follows the handsome stranger everywhere, and the most she can get by pestering him is the promise that, if ever he marries a woman, it will certainly be her; in the meanwhile, he makes her promise to treat Sylvius kindly and not to indulge in too much hope.

Rosette performed her part with a sad and caressing grace, a resigned and melancholy tone which went to the heart; and when Rosalind said: 'I would love you, if I could,' her tears were about to overflow, and she found it hard to restrain them, for the history of Phebe is her own, as that of Orlando is mine with this difference, that everything ends happily for Orlando, and that Phebe, disappointed in love, is reduced to marrying Sylvius instead of the delightful ideal she wanted to embrace. Life is like that: one person's happiness is bound to be someone else's misfortune. It is very fortunate for me that Théodore is a woman; it is very unfortunate for Rosette that Théodore isn't a man, and that she now finds herself cast into the amorous impossibilities in which I went astray not long ago.

At the end of the play, Rosalind abandons the doublet of the page, Ganymede, for the clothes of her own sex, and she is recognized by the Duke as his daughter, and by Orlando as his mistress; the god Hymen arrives in his saffron livery, bearing his torches. Three marriages are solemnized. Orlando marries Rosalind, Phebe Sylvius, and the clown Touchstone marries the simple Audrey. Then the epilogue comes to bid farewell, and the curtain falls . . .

It all concerned and affected us extremely; it was in a sense a play within a play, a drama invisible and unknown to the other spectators, which we performed for ourselves alone, a drama which, in symbolic words, summed up our whole life and expressed our most secret desires. Had it not been for Rosalind's singular cure, I should have been more ill than ever, and I should have continued to wander sadly in the obscure parts of the gloomy forest.

But I have only a moral certainty; I have no proofs, and I cannot remain in this state of uncertainty any longer; I absolutely must talk to Théodore in a more precise manner. I have approached him a score of times with a sentence all prepared, and I haven't managed to say it – I don't dare; I have many occasions to talk to him alone or in the park, or in my room, or his, because he comes to see me and I go to see him, but I let these occasions pass unused, although a moment later I feel mortal regret, and I fly into terrible rages with myself. I open my lips and, despite myself, I utter different words, and not the words that I should like to say; I don't declare my love, instead I talk about the rain or the fine weather or about some such stupidity. Yet the season will soon be over, and we'll all be going back to town; the facilities which favour my desires while I am here won't be found again anywhere else; perhaps we shall lose sight of one another, and no doubt different currents will bear us off in different directions.

The freedom of the country is so charming and convenient! Even the autumnal trees, with their sparse leaves, offer delightful shades to the reveries of burgeoning love! It is so difficult to resist among the beauties of nature! The birds have such languorous songs, the flowers have such heady perfumes, the slopes of the hills such sunlit, silky grass. Solitude inspires you with a thousand voluptuous thoughts, which the vortex of the world would have scattered or sent flying in all directions, and the instinctive movement of two beings who hear the beating of their hearts in the silence of the deserted countryside is to entwine their arms more tightly and to fall back upon each other, as if in fact they were now the only living creatures in the world.

I went for a stroll this morning; it was mild and damp, the sky didn't show the slightest lozenge of blue; and yet it wasn't sombre or threatening. Two or three tones of pearl grey, harmoniously merged, filled it from end to end, and against this vaporous background fleecy clouds passed slowly by like big pieces of cottonwool; they were driven by the dying breath of a little breeze, hardly strong enough to stir the tops of the most restless aspens; wreaths of mist were rising up between the great chestnut-trees and marked out the course of the river from afar. When the breeze recovered its breath, a few parched and reddened leaves were moved, and scattered, and ran along the path in front of me like swarms of frightened sparrows; then, when the breeze fell, they came down a few steps further on. It was a true image of those minds which seem like birds which are flying with their wings, and, when all is said, are only leaves which are withered by the morning frost, the toy and laughing-stock of the slightest wind.

The distances were so blurred with mists, and the fringes of the horizon so unravelled at the edges, that it was hardly possible to decide where the sky began and the earth ended; a slightly darker grey, a slightly thicker mist, vaguely indicated the distance and the difference between the planes. Through this curtain, the willows, with their ash-coloured heads, seemed more like the spectres of trees than actual trees; the sinuosities of the hills looked more like the undulations of a mass of clouds than a stratum of solid earth. The contours of things quivered in one's sight, and a kind of grey web of inexpressible fineness, like a spider's web, stretched between the foreground of the landscape and its fading depths; in the shadowy places, the cross-hatching was much more clearly de-lineated, and revealed the meshes of the net; in the more illuminated places, the net of mist was imperceptible, and melted into the diffused light. There was something drowsy in the air, something moist and warm, mild and dim, which strangely predisposed you to melancholy.

As I walked on, I thought that autumn had also come for me, and that the radiant summer had gone past hope of recall; the tree of my soul was perhaps more leafless still than the trees of the forest; there hardly remained on the topmost branch one small green leaf, trembling and sad to see its sisters leaving it, one by one.

Stay on the tree, O little leaf, the colour of hope, cling to the branch with all the strength of your ribs and filaments; don't let yourself be frightened, little leaf, by the whistling wind! For, when you have left me, who will be able to discern if I am a dead or a living tree, and who will prevent the woodcutters from gashing my trunk with his axe and making bundles of firewood out of my branches? The time is not yet come when the trees have no more leaves, and the sun may still rid itself of the swathes of mist which surround it.

This spectacle of the dying season made a profound impression upon me. I thought that time was passing swiftly, and that I might die without having clasped my ideal to my heart.

When I got back to my room, I made a resolution. Since I couldn't bring myself to speak, I wrote my whole destiny down on a sheet of paper. Perhaps it is ridiculous to write to someone who is living in the same house as yourself, someone you can see every day, and at any time; but I am past thinking whether things are ridiculous or not.

I sealed my letter, not without trembling and turning pale; then, choosing the moment when Théodore had gone out, I put it in the middle of the table, and I fled, as agitated as if I had done the most abominable deed in the world.

XII

I'VE promised to tell you the rest of my adventures; but really I'm so lazy about writing, that you must be the apple of my eye, and I must know you to be more inquisitive than Eve or Psyche, for here I am sitting down at a table with a large sheet of white paper which I must make completely black, and an inkwell deeper than the sea, every drop of which must turn into thoughts, or at least into something which passes for them. If I didn't write, I should make a sudden resolution to mount a horse, and gallop at full speed for the eighty enormous leagues which divide us, to go and tell you myself what I'm going to send you in my imperceptible hand – otherwise I should take fright at the prodigious volume of my picaresque odyssey.

Eighty leagues! To think that all this space lies between me and the person I love best in the world! I'm very much tempted to tear up my letter and saddle my horse. But I had forgotten – with the clothes I'm wearing, I couldn't come near you, and resume the familiar life we used to lead together when we were very naïve and very innocent little girls. If ever I wear skirts again, this will be the reason.

I left you, I think, at our departure from the inn where I spent such a comic night, and where my virtue thought of being wrecked just as it had come out of port! We all set out together, and went in the same direction. My companions went into constant raptures over the beauty of my horse, which is indeed a thoroughbred, and one of the best coursers that there are; that raised me at least half a cubit in their esteem, and they added all the merit of my mount to my own. However, they seemed to be afraid that it was too spirited and fiery for me. I told them not to worry, and, to prove that there was no danger, I made it do several voltes and curvets; then I jumped quite a high barrier, and set off at a gallop.

The company tried in vain to follow me; when I had gone some distance, I turned back, and returned to meet them hell for leather; when I got very close to them, I reined in my galloping horse, and brought him to a sudden halt: which is, as you know, or do not know, a wonderful feat of equitation.

They passed without transition from esteem to the most profound respect. They did not imagine that a young scholar, fresh from the university, could be so distinguished a horseman as that. This discovery did me more service than if they had found that I had all the theological and cardinal virtues. Instead of treating me as a green youth, they spoke to me in a tone of obsequious familiarity which gave me pleasure.

When I divested myself of my clothes, I didn't shed my pride. As I was no longer a woman, I wanted to be a real man, not to be content with just the external appearance. I'd decided that as a cavalier I should have the successes which I could no longer aspire to as a woman. What worried me most was to know how I should set about having courage; for courage and skill in physical exercises are the means by which a man most easily establishes his reputation. It's not that I'm timid for a woman, and I don't have those idiotic pusillanimities which you see in some of them; but there is still a long way between that and the fierce, indifferent brutality which makes the glory of men, and my intention was to be a little braggart, a bully as fine gentlemen are, to give myself good standing in society and to enjoy all the advantages of my metamorphosis.

However, I came to realize that nothing was easier and that the recipe was very simple.

I shan't tell you, as travellers always do, that I did so many leagues a day, that I went from this place to the other, that the roast which I ate at the White Horse or the Gold Cross tavern was raw or burnt; that the wine was acid and that the bed I slept in had curtains patterned with figures or flowers. These are very important details which it is good to preserve for posterity; but posterity must do without them on this occasion, and you must resign yourself to not knowing how many dishes my dinner consisted of, and whether I slept well or badly during my travels. Nor shall I give you an exact description of the different landscapes, the cornfields and the forests, the various crops and the hills covered with villages which have passed in succession before my eyes. That is easy to imagine; take some earth, plant a few trees and a few blades of grass, daub a little bit of pale-blue or greyish sky behind it, and you will have a very adequate idea of the moving background of our little caravan. If, in my first letter, I entered into a few details of this sort, please forgive me, I shan't do so again; as I had never gone out, the smallest thing seemed enormously important to me.

One of the cavaliers, the companion of my bed, the one whose sleeve I had nearly pulled on that memorable night whose agonies I've told you of in detail, conceived a great passion for me and constantly kept his horse alongside mine.

Except for the fact that I shouldn't have wanted to take him as a lover, even if he had brought me the finest crown in the world, I didn't find him displeasing; he was educated, and he didn't lack wit or good humour. But, when he spoke of women, he did so with a scorn and sarcasm for which I would readily have torn both his eyes out of his head, especially as, for all the exaggeration, there were many things in what he said which were cruelly true, and my male attire forced me to recognize it.

He invited me to go with him and see one of his sisters; she was nearing the end of her widowhood, and at the moment she was living in an old château with one of her aunts. His invitation was so pressing, and so often repeated, that I could not refuse it. I made a few objections for the sake of form, but in fact I could just as well go there as anywhere else, and I could achieve my object just as well in this way as in any other; and, as he told me that I should really offend him very much if I didn't grant him at least a fortnight, I answered that I should be delighted, and I accepted.

At a fork in the road, my companion showed me the straight downstroke of this natural Y, and said: 'It's along there.' The others shook hands with us, and went on their separate way.

After several hours' journey, we reached our destination.

A fairly broad ditch which was filled, not with water, but with thick and abundant vegetation, separated the park from the main road; the facing was of freestone; and, in the corners, there bristled gigantic iron artichokes and thistles which seemed to have grown like natural plants between the disjointed blocks in the wall; a little bridge with one arch went over this dried-up canal, and allowed us to reach the iron gate.

A tall avenue of elms, arched like a bower and dressed in the old-fashioned way, appeared before us; and, after we had followed it for a while, we emerged into a sort of *rond-point*.

The trees looked antiquated rather than old; they seemed to have periwigs and to be powdered white; all that had been left to them was a little tuft of foliage on the tops of their heads; everything else had been carefully lopped, so that you would have taken them for enormous feathers planted at regular intervals in the ground.

After we had crossed the *rond-point*, which was covered with fine and carefully rolled grass, we had to pass under a curious edifice of foliage decorated with cressets, pyramids and pillars of rustic order, all cut out with the aid of shears and billhooks in an enormous thicket of boxwood. Through different openings to left and right, you sometimes saw a half-ruined rockwork castle, sometimes the moss-worn steps of a dried-up cascade, or else a vase or a statue of a nymph and shepherd with noses and fingers broken, and a few pigeons perched on the head and shoulders. A big flower-garden, designed in the French style, stretched in front of the château; all the compartments were outlined with box and holly in the strictest symmetry; it looked as much like a carpet as a garden: big flowers decked for a ball, with majestic bearing and tranquil mien, like duchesses preparing to dance a minuet, gave you a slight inclination of the head as you passed. Others, apparently less polite, remained stiff and motionless, like dowagers working at their tapestry. Shrubs of every possible shape, if however one excepts their natural shape, round, square, pointed, triangular, in green and grey boxes, seemed to walk in procession along the main avenue, and to lead you by the hand to the foot of the steps at the entrance.

A few turrets, half engaged in more recent buildings, projected the

whole height of their candle-snuffer towers above the line of the
château, and their dovetailed sheet-iron weathercocks bore witness
to a quite honourable antiquity. The windows in the centre part of
the building all gave on to a common balcony ornamented with an
iron balustrade of extremely elaborate and most opulent workman-
ship, and the others were surrounded by stone window-frames with
sculpted knots and cyphers.

Four or five big dogs rushed up, barking their heads off, and cutting
the most extraordinary capers. They gambolled round the horses and
leapt up in their faces; they gave a particular welcome to my companion's horse, which they probably often used to visit in the stable,
or accompany on a ride.

At the sound of all this commotion, there finally appeared a kind
of valet, who looked half labourer, half ostler. He took our horses
by the bridles, and led them away. I hadn't yet seen a living soul,
except for a little peasant girl as wild and frightened as a deer, who
had fled at the sight of us and cowered in a furrow behind some
hemp, although we called out to her more than once, and did all we
could to reassure her.

No one appeared at the windows. You would have thought that
the château was deserted, or at least inhabited only by ghosts; for
you didn't hear the slightest sound from outside.

We had begun to walk up the first steps of the perron, stamping
so that our spurs rang out, for our legs had grown rather heavy,
when we heard the sound of doors being opened and shut inside, as
if someone were hurrying to meet us.

And indeed a young woman appeared at the top of the steps, took
one bound across the space which separated her from my companion, and threw her arms round his neck. As for him, he kissed
her with much affection, and, putting his arm round her waist, he
virtually picked her up and carried her to the top of the steps.

'Do you know that you're very amiable and gallant for a brother,
my dear Alcibiades?' 'Perhaps I should assure you, sir, that he is my
brother,' said the beautiful young woman, turning towards me. 'He
really doesn't act very like it.'

To which I replied that one might make a mistake, and that it was in a way a misfortune to be her brother and thereby to be excluded from the category of her worshippers; that, as for me, if I were her brother, I should become both the most unfortunate and the most fortunate cavalier in the world. This made her smile very sweetly.

While we were talking like this, we went into a low-ceilinged room, the walls of which were hung with a high warp Flemish tapestry. On this, there were big trees with sharp leaves which carried swarms of fantastic birds; the colours, changed by time, produced curious transpositions of shades; the sky was green, the trees royal blue with yellow lights, and in the draperies round the figures the shadow was often of a different colour to the ground of the fabric. Flesh tints looked like wood, and the nymphs who strolled under the faded shadows of the forest had the appearance of unswathed mummies; only their mouths, whose crimson kept its original hue, smiled with a semblance of life. In the foreground there bristled tall plants of a singular green with big variegated flowers whose pistils looked like peacocks' crests. Herons with grave and pensive looks, their heads huddled between their shoulders, their long beaks resting on their plump crops, stood philosophically erect on one of their long legs, in black and stagnant water, striped with threads of tarnished silver; through the openings in the foliage, one could see little châteaux in the distance with pepperpot turrets and balconies crowded with beautiful ladies in splendid attire watching processions and hunts as they passed.

Whimsically scalloped rockwork, from which there tumbled torrents of white wool, merged with the dappled clouds on the edge of the horizon.

One of the things which struck me most was a huntress who was shooting at a bird. Her open fingers had just released the bowstring, and the arrow had gone; but, as this part of the tapestry happened to be at a corner, the arrow was on the other side of the wall, and it had completely changed direction; as for the bird, it was flying off on its motionless wings and seemed to want to reach a nearby branch.

This barbed arrow, with its golden tip, always in flight and never reaching its destination, had the most singular effect, for it seemed like a sad and woeful symbol of human destiny, and the more I looked at it, the more mysterious and sinister meanings I discovered in it. The huntress was there, erect, one foot outstretched, and one leg bent; her eye, with silken eyelids, was open wide, and it could no longer see her arrow, which had deviated from its course. She seemed to be looking anxiously for the flamingo with splendid feathers which she wanted to bring down and expected to see fall in front of her, shot through the heart. I don't know if it is an error of my imagination, but I found on this face an expression as dejected and desperate as that of a poet who dies without having written the work he had counted on to establish his reputation, a poet who is mercilessly seized by his death-rattle just as he is trying to dictate it.

I'm talking to you at length about this tapestry, certainly for longer than it deserves; but it's something which has always strangely engrossed me, this fantastic world created by the high-warp artisans.

I passionately love this imaginary vegetation, these flowers and plants which do not exist in reality, these forests of unknown trees in which there wander unicorns, nightjars, and snow-white deer with a golden crucifix between their antlers, generally pursued by huntsmen with red beards and in Saracen dress.

When I was small, I hardly ever went into a tapestried room without feeling a kind of shudder, and I hardly dared to move in it.

All these figures standing against the wall, to whom the undulation of the material and the play of light give a kind of supernatural life, seemed to me like so many spies busy watching my behaviour so as to give an account of it in due time and place, and I shouldn't have eaten an apple or a stolen cake in their presence.

How many things these grave characters might have said, if they could have opened their red thread lips, if sounds could have entered their embroidered ears. How many murders, betrayals, infamous adulteries and monstrosities of every kind they must have witnessed, alert and unmoved! . . .

But let's leave the tapestry and return to our story.

'Alcibiades, I'm going to tell my aunt that you've arrived.'

'Oh, there's no hurry for that, dear sister; let's sit down first, and talk for a little. Let me present a cavalier, Théodore de Sérannes, who is going to stay here for a while. I don't need to ask you to make him most welcome. He is recommendation enough in himself.' (I am repeating what he said; don't hasten to accuse me of vanity.)

The lady gave a little sign of her head, as if in agreement, and we spoke of other things.

While we were talking, I looked at her more attentively than I had so far been able to do.

She could have been twenty-three or twenty-four, and her mourning suited her to perfection; to tell the truth, she didn't look very lugubrious or desolate, and I doubt whether she would have eaten the ashes of her Mausoleus in her soup as a kind of rhubarb. I don't know if she had wept abundantly for her departed husband; but, if she had done so, there was hardly a sign of it, and the pretty cambric handkerchief which she held in her hand was as perfectly dry as it could be.

Her eyes weren't red, on the contrary they were the brightest and most shining eyes in the world, and one would have sought in vain for the furrow on her cheeks down which the tears had passed. To tell the truth, there were only two little dimples hollowed out by the habit of smiling, and, for a widow, it must be said that one very often saw her smile. This was certainly not an unpleasant sight, for her teeth were very white and regular. I respected her from the first for not feeling herself obliged, because some husband or other had died, to dab her eyes and empurple her nose. I was grateful to her, too, for not assuming a rather miserable expression, and for talking naturally in her musical, silvery voice, without drawling the words and punctuating her sentences with virtuous sighs.

This seemed to me in very good taste; I thought her from the first to be a woman of character, which indeed she is.

She had a good figure, and very seemly feet and hands; her black dress was done up in the most elegant fashion you can conceive, and so gaily that the sombreness of the colour completely vanished, and she could have gone to a ball like this, and no one would have thought it was strange. If ever I marry and become a widow, I shall ask her for the pattern of her dress, for it suits her divinely well.

After we had talked for a while, we went upstairs to see the old aunt.

We found her lying back in a big armchair, with a little footstool under her feet; beside her was an old dog, all blear-eyed and sullen, which raised its black muzzle when we arrived, and greeted us with a far from friendly growl.

I have never considered an old woman with anything except horror. My mother died quite young; no doubt, if I had watched her slowly growing old, and had seen her features change imperceptibly, I should have grown serenely accustomed to it. In my childhood, I was surrounded only by young and happy faces, and so I have kept an insuperable objection to old people. I therefore shuddered when the beautiful widow kissed the dowager's parchment-coloured forehead. It was something I couldn't bring myself to do. I know quite well that, when I'm sixty, I shall be like that. It doesn't matter, I can't do anything about it, and I pray God to let me die young like my mother.

However, the old woman had kept certain simple and majestic lineaments of her beauty, and they prevented her from degenerating into that baked-apple ugliness which is the lot of women who have been only pretty or just fresh; her eyes had claws of wrinkles at the corners, and they were covered with big, limp eyelids, but they still kept some sparks of their original fire, and you saw that, in the reign of the other king, they must have shot forth dazzling flashes of passion. Her thin, bony nose, slightly hooked like the beak of a bird of prey, gave her profile a sort of solemn grandeur; this was tempered by the indulgent smile on her Austrian lips, which were tinged with crimson, according to the fashion of the last century.

Her costume was antiquated without being ridiculous, and it harmonized perfectly with her face; she wore a plain white head-dress with a little lace; her hands were long and thin, and one guessed that they must have been very beautiful, and they moved loosely in mittens without thumbs or fingers. A feuillemorte dress, figured with a flower pattern in a deeper tone, a black mantle and an apron of iridescent paduasoy completed her attire.

Old women should always dress like this and have enough respect for their approaching death not to rig themselves out with feathers, garlands of flowers, pale-coloured ribbons and a thousand baubles which only befit the extremely young. It is no use their making advances to life, life doesn't want them any more, they have had their pains for nothing, like those superannuated courtesans who plaster themselves with red and white, and are pushed aside with kicks and insults by drunk muleteers.

The old lady received us with the ease and exquisite politeness peculiar to those people who attended the old court; the secret of it seems to be more lost every day, like so many other good secrets. Though her voice was weak and quavering, it still had a great sweetness.

I seemed to please her greatly, and she looked at me for a very long time and very attentively as if she were much moved. A tear formed in the corner of her eye, and slowly coursed down one of her deep wrinkles, where it disappeared and dried up. She begged me to excuse her, and told me that I was very like a son she had once had, who had been killed with the army.

Because of this likeness, real or imagined, the old lady treated me with extraordinary and quite maternal kindness all the time I stayed at the château. I found more charm in it than I should at first have thought, for the greatest pleasure that the old can give me is never to speak, and to go the moment I arrive.

I shan't tell you in detail and day by day all that I did at R—. If I have dwelt a little on the beginning, if I've given you a fairly detailed sketch of these two or three appearances, either of people or of places, that is because some most singular and yet very natural things happened to me there, and I should have foreseen them when I adopted male attire.

My natural thoughtlessness made me guilty of an indiscretion which I cruelly repent, because it caused anguish to a good and beautiful soul, and I cannot appease that anguish without revealing what I am and gravely compromising myself.

To seem exactly like a man and amuse myself a little I found nothing better than to pay court to my friend's sister. It seemed to me very comical to rush and fall on my knees when she dropped her glove and to give it back to her with very long bows, to lean over the back of her chair with a slight air of adorable languor, and to whisper in her ear a thousand and one of the most delightful madrigals. As soon as she wanted to go from one room to another, I graciously gave her my hand; if she mounted a horse, I held her stirrup, and, when we went walking, I always walked beside her; in the evening I read to her or sang with her; in short I performed with the utmost punctuality all the duties of a cicisbeo.

I assumed all the expressions which I had seen a lover assume; it amused me, and made me laugh uncontrollably, like the mad creature I am, when I found myself alone in my room and reflected on all the impertinences which I had just recited in the gravest manner in the world.

Alcibiades and the old marquise seemed to look on this intimacy with pleasure, and they very often left us alone together. I sometimes regretted that I wasn't really a man and couldn't have taken more advantage of it; if I had been one, it would have depended only on me, for our delightful widow seemed to have forgotten the dear departed completely, or, if she recalled him, she would very readily have been unfaithful to his memory.

Once I had begun in this style, I could hardly decently go back, and it was very difficult to retreat with arms and baggage; however, I couldn't go beyond a certain limit either, and I hardly knew how to be pleasant except in words. I hoped in this way to get to the end of the month which I was to spend at R—, and to withdraw and promise to come back, and to do no such thing. I thought that on my departure the lady would console herself, and that when she no longer saw me she would soon forget me.

But, while I was making game of her, I aroused a serious passion, and things turned out very differently; and this illustrates the old and familiar saying, that you should never play with fire or love.

Until she met me, Rosette had not known love. Married very young to a man much older than herself, she hadn't felt anything for him except a kind of filial affection. No doubt she had been courted, but she hadn't had a lover, however extraordinary that may seem. Either the suitors who courted her were indifferent seducers, or – and this is more probable – her moment had not yet come. Provincial lordlings and squireens, always talking of scents and leashes, punches and antlers, death-flourishes and full-grown stags, and mixing it all up with dated charades and madrigals musty with old age, were indeed hardly made to suit her, and her virtue didn't have to struggle very hard not to surrender to them. Besides, her gaiety and her natural sprightliness were protection enough against love, that indolent passion which has such a hold over the dreamy and the melancholy. Whatever idea of sensual pleasure her old Tithonus had given her, it must have been mediocre enough, for it did not tempt her to try it again, and she was quietly enjoying the pleasure of being widowed so young and having so many years ahead in which to be pretty.

But, on my arrival, everything completely changed. I believed at first that if I had kept within the narrow bounds of dispassionate and rigorous politeness, she would have paid no further attention to me; but, in fact, I was later obliged to recognize that this would have made no difference, and that this supposition, though very modest, was quite gratuitous. Alas! Nothing can change the ascendancy of fate, and no one can avoid the benign or malignant influence of their star.

Rosette was destined to love only once in her life, and to love with an impossible love; she must fulfil her destiny, and she will do so.

I have been loved, O Graciosa! And it is sweet, although I have only been loved by a woman, and, in a love so deviant, there was something painful not to be found in ordinary love. Oh, it's very sweet! When you wake at night you prop yourself up on your elbow and say to yourself: 'Someone is thinking about me; someone is concerned with my life; a movement of my eyes or lips is the joy or sorrow of another person; a word which I let fall by chance has been carefully gathered in, discussed and analysed for hours on end; I am the pole to which a restless magnet turns; my eyes are a heaven, my lips a paradise more desired than Paradise itself; if I should die, a rain of tears would warm my corpse, my grave would be more decked with flowers than a wedding-present; if I were in danger, someone would throw themselves between the point of the sword and my breast; they would sacrifice themselves for me! That is a fine thing; and I don't know what more anyone can possibly want.'

That thought gave me a pleasure for which I reproached myself, because I had nothing to give in exchange for it all. I was like a poor man accepting presents from a rich and generous friend, without the hope that he can ever give presents in return. It delighted me to be so adored and at moments I let it continue with singular complacency. Since everybody called me sir, and I was treated as a man, I gradually forgot that I was a woman. My disguise seemed to me to be my ordinary dress, and I didn't recall ever wearing anything else; I no longer thought that I was in fact just a little hare-brained creature who had made a sword out of her needle, and a pair of breeches by cutting up her skirt.

Many men are more feminine than I am. I have hardly anything of a woman except her breasts, a few more rounded lines, and more delicate hands; the skirt is on my hips and not in my mind. It often happens that the sex of the soul is not the same as that of the body, and this contradiction cannot fail to produce a great deal of confusion. Look at me: if I hadn't made this resolution – mad in appearance, but really very wise – to abandon the clothes of a sex which is only mine materially and by chance, I should have been extremely unhappy. I like horses, fencing, all violent forms of exercise, I like to climb and run about here and there like a young boy; it bores me to sit still with my legs together, my arms glued to my sides, to lower my eyes in modesty, to talk in a little piping, honeyed voice, and to pass the end of a piece of wool ten million times through the holes in a canvas. I don't like obeying in the least, and the words I most often say are: 'I will'. Under my smooth brow and my silken hair there stir strong and virile thoughts; none of the affected stupidities which generally seduce women has ever greatly touched me, and, like Achilles disguised as a young girl, I should willingly exchange the mirror for a sword. The only thing which pleases me about women is their beauty; for all its disadvantages, I shouldn't want to abandon my figure, although it ill befits the spirit which it enfolds.

It was something new and piquant, an intrigue like this, and I should have enjoyed it very much if poor Rosette hadn't taken it seriously. She began to love me with wonderful innocence and con-scientiousness, with all the might of her good and lovely soul – with that love which men don't understand and couldn't even begin to comprehend, delicately, ardently, as I should wish to be loved, and as I should love, myself, if I should meet the reality of my dream. What a beautiful wasted treasure, what white, transparent pearls, the like of which no diver will find among the jewels of the ocean! What sweet breaths and what gentle sighs scattered to the winds, which might have been reaped by pure and loving lips!

This passion could have made a young man so happy! So many unfortunate, handsome youths, charming and well endowed, with sensibility and intellect, have pleaded in vain, and on their knees, with idols which were dull and unfeeling! So many good and tender souls have cast themselves in despair into the arms of courtesans, or else they have quietly died like lamps in vaults, when they would have been saved from debauchery and death by true love!

What so many others had ardently desired was granted to me, and I didn't want it and couldn't want it. A capricious young girl had taken it into her head to roam about the country in men's clothes, to learn a little of what she might expect from her lovers-to-be; she slept in an inn with a worthy brother who politely introduced her to his sister, and the sister promptly fell in love with her like a cat, or dove, or anything sentimental and amorous which you can think of. It is quite clear that if I had been a young man and it could have been some use to me, it would have been completely different, and the lady would have had a horror of me. Fortune is quite fond of giving slippers to people who have wooden legs, and giving gloves to people without hands; the inheritance which would let you live in comfort generally comes to you on the day you die.

I used to go occasionally, not as often as she would have liked, to see Rosette while she was still in bed; though she generally doesn't have visitors till she's dressed, she made an exception in my favour. She would have made many other exceptions, if I had wanted; but, as the saying goes, the most beautiful girl can only give what she possesses, and what I possessed would not have been of great use to Rosette.

She gave me her little hand to kiss. I admit that I didn't kiss it without a certain pleasure, because it is very soft, very white, exquisitely scented, and it is made softer by a slight clamminess. I felt it tremble and contract beneath my lips, and I wickedly prolonged the pressure. Then Rosette, much affected, and with an air of entreaty, gazed at me with her long eyes full of sensuality and flooded with a moist, transparent light, then she let her pretty head – which she'd slightly raised to receive me – fall back again on the pillow. I saw her anxious breast fall and swell under the sheet, and her whole body suddenly quicken. Someone who had been in a condition to dare could undoubtedly have dared a great deal, and his daring would have been gratefully received. It would certainly have been appreciated that he had skipped a chapter or two of the novel.

I stayed there with her for an hour or two, never letting go of her hand, which I had put down on the coverlet; we had endless delightful conversations; for, although Rosette was very preoccupied with her love, she thought herself too sure of success not to keep nearly all her freedom and frivolity. Only from time to time her passion cast a transparent veil of gentle melancholy over her gaiety, and this made her more piquant than ever.

In fact it would have been unheard-of if a young beginner, as I appeared to be, didn't consider himself very happy with such a good fortune, and did not take the utmost advantage of it. Rosette was in fact not made to encounter great cruelty, and, not knowing much about me, she counted on her charms and on my youth to succeed where love had failed.

However, as this situation began to go on rather beyond the ordinary limits, she grew anxious about it, and a reduplication of flattering phrases and fine protests could hardly restore her original security. Two things about me surprised her, and she observed contradictions in my behaviour which she could not reconcile: these were my warmth of speech and my coldness of behaviour.

You know better than anyone, my dear Graciosa, that my friendship has every appearance of a passion; it is sudden, ardent, intense, exclusive, it even has the jealousy of love, and I had a friendship for Rosette almost like the one I have for you. One could easily be mistaken. Rosette was all the more mistaken since the clothes I wore hadn't allowed her a different idea.

As I have not yet loved any man, the excess of my affection has in a way overflowed into my friendship with young girls and young women; I have shown the same passion and the same exaltation in them as I have shown in everything I do, because it is impossible for me to be moderate in anything, especially where the heart is concerned. There are in my eyes only two kinds of people, the people I adore and the people I hate; the others virtually don't exist for me, and I should ride over them as if I were riding along the highway: they are no different in my mind from cobbles and paving-stones.

I am naturally expansive, and I have a very affectionate manner. Sometimes I forgot the significance of such demonstrations, and while I was walking with Rosette I put my arm round her waist, as I did when you and I used to walk together down the secluded path at the bottom of my uncle's garden; or else, while I was leaning over the back of her chair as she did her embroidery, I used to curl round my fingers the little stray fair curls on her round plump neck, or I smoothed her hair, held taut by a comb, with the back of my hand, and I gave it back its lustre – or else it was some other pretty gesture which you know I often make to my women friends.

She took good care not to attribute these caresses to mere friendship. Friendship, as you usually conceive it, doesn't go that far; but, seeing that I didn't go further, she was inwardly surprised and she didn't really know what to think. She decided that it was excessive timidity on my part, a result of my extreme youth and my lack of practice in amorous relationships, and she decided that I must be encouraged by all sorts of advances and favours.

As a result, she took care to contrive a quantity of occasions for private conversations in places which were likely to embolden me because of their solitude and their remoteness from any disturbance or interruption; she made me go for several walks in the great forests, to see if the voluptuous dreams and amorous desires which the dense, propitious shades of the forest inspire in sensitive souls might not be turned to her advantage.

One day, when she had made me wander for a long time through a very picturesque park which stretched out far beyond the château, a park where I only knew the parts that were near the buildings, she led me, by a little path, capriciously twisted and lined with elders and hazel-trees, to a rustic cottage, a sort of charcoal-burner's hut, built of billets placed crosswise, thatched with reeds. The door was crudely made of five or six pieces of wood which had hardly been planed, and the cracks in it were stopped up with moss and weeds; close beside it, between the green roots of big ash-trees with silver bark, speckled here and there with black patches, there gushed a flowing fountain which, a few steps further on, fell over two marble steps into a basin brimming over with watercress greener than emerald. In the patches where there was no cress, you caught a glimpse of sand as fine and white as snow; this water was as transparent as crystal and as cold as ice; springing suddenly from the earth, and never touched by the palest ray of sunlight, under these impenetrable shades, it did not have time to grow warm or to be troubled. For all their crudity, I love these spring waters, and, since this water was so clear, I couldn't resist the desire to drink some; I leant over and cupped some, several times, in the hollow of my hand, for I had no other vessel at my disposal.

Rosette wanted to quench her thirst, and she asked to drink some of this water, too; she begged me to get her a few drops, for she said she didn't dare to lean over so far to reach it. I plunged both my hands into the clear fountain, holding them as close together as possible; then I raised them like a cup to her lips. I held them there until Rosette had drunk all the water they contained, which didn't take long, as there was very little, and this little was dripping through my fingers, however close together I held them. It was a very pretty group, and I should have liked a sculptor to have been there to sketch it.

When she had almost finished, and had my hand close to her lips, she could not refrain from kissing it, in such a way however that I could believe that it was an inhalation to drain the last pearl of water which had collected in my palm; but I wasn't deceived, and the charming blush which suddenly suffused her face was sufficient information against her.

She took my arm again, and we made our way towards the cottage. The fair lady was walking as close as possible to me, and leaning over me as she talked so that the whole of her bosom rested on my sleeve; an extremely artful position, and one which could have troubled anyone but me; I was perfectly aware of the smooth, firm contour and the gentle warmth; I could also feel a hurried breathing which, affected or not, was none the less flattering and enticing.

And so we reached the cottage door, and I kicked it open; I certainly didn't expect the sight which appeared before my eyes. I had imagined that the hut was hung with reeds, with a rush mat on the ground and a few stools to sit on. Not at all.

It was a boudoir furnished with all imaginable elegance. The paintings over the doors and mirrors represented the most gallant scenes in the *Metamorphoses* of Ovid: Salmacis and Hermaphrodite, Venus and Adonis, Apollo and Daphne, and other mythological loves in bright purple camayeu. The walls between the windows were made of pompon roses, very daintily sculpted, and little marguerites in which, with a refinement of luxury, only the centres were gilded and the leaves were silver. There was silver braid edging all the furniture, and it enhanced the hangings, which were the palest possible blue, a colour wonderfully suited to set off the whiteness and brilliance of the skin; the mantelpiece, tables and whatnots were laden with a thousand curios, and there was a profusion of couches, chaises longues and sofas, which clearly suggested that this retreat was not intended for the most austere occupations, and that the flesh was certainly not mortified there.

A fine rococo clock, set on a richly encrusted pedestal, stood opposite a big Venetian mirror, and was repeated in it with singular brightness and curious reflections. It had also stopped, as if it had been unnecessary to tell the time in a place which was designed for forgetting it.

I told Rosette that this refinement of luxury pleased me, that I found it in excellent taste to conceal the greatest elegance under an appearance of simplicity, and that I warmly approved if a woman had embroidered skirts and shifts adorned with Mechlin lace with a plain cloth overcoat; it was a delicate attention for the lover whom she had or might have, and one couldn't be grateful enough, and it was certainly better to put a diamond into a nutshell than a nut into a golden box.

Rosette lifted up her dress a little, to show that she agreed with me, and revealed the edge of a skirt that was richly embroidered with big flowers and leaves; it would only have depended on me to be admitted into the secret of greater inner splendours; but I didn't ask to see if the magnificence of the shift matched that of the skirt: it was probably no less luxurious. Rosette dropped back the fold of her dress, vexed that she had not shown more. However, this exhibition had allowed her to display the beginning of a perfectly shaped calf which gave the best ascensional promises. This leg, which she stretched forward to spread out her skirt better, was quite miraculously delicate and graceful in its neat and well-drawn pearl-grey silk stocking, and the little heeled slipper decked with a bunch of ribbons at the end looked like the glass slipper which fitted Cinderella. I paid her my most sincere compliments, and I told her that I hardly knew a prettier leg or a smaller foot; it would have been impossible for them to have been more shapely. To which she replied with the most delightful and intelligent frankness and innocence: 'That's true.'

Then she went to a panel which had been contrived in the wall, and took out one or two bottles of cordial and a few plates of preserves and cakes, set them all out on a small round table, and came and sat next to me in a rather narrow easy-chair, so that in order not to be too uncomfortable I had to put my arm round her waist. As she had both hands free, and I could only use my left, she poured out my drink herself, and she put fruits and sweetmeats on my plate. Indeed, she soon perceived that I was being rather clumsy about it, and said: 'There now, you leave that; I'm going to spoon-feed you, little child, since you don't know how to eat by yourself.' And she actually put the pieces into my mouth, and obliged me to swallow them faster than I wanted, pushing them in with her pretty fingers, just as you do when you stuff a bird. It made her laugh a great deal. I could hardly fail to return to her fingers the kiss which she had recently accorded to the palms of my hands, and as if to stop me, but really to give me a chance to kiss harder, she tapped my mouth two or three times with the back of her hand.

She had drunk two or three drops of cream of Barbados and a glass of Canary wine, and I had drunk about the same. It certainly wasn't much; but it had been enough to light up two women who were accustomed to drinking only water with the merest tinge of wine. Rosette let herself fall back, and lay most amorously on my arm. She had thrown off her mantlet, and you could see the beginning of her bosom, it was thrust forward and immobile in this arched position. It was ravishingly delicate and transparent in colour; it was marvellously fine and yet solid in shape. I contemplated it for a while with indefinable pleasure and emotion, and the thought occurred to me that men were more favoured than we were in their loves, that we gave them the most enchanting treasures to possess, and that they had nothing like them to offer us. How delightful it must be to let one's lips wander over this smooth and delicate skin, these beautifully rounded contours which seem to meet the kiss and to provoke it! That satin flesh, those flowing lines which envelop one another, that silken hair so gentle to the touch: what inexhaustible sources of exquisite pleasures which we don't have with men! Our own caresses can hardly be anything but passive, and yet there is more pleasure in giving than in receiving.

Those are some observations which I should certainly not have made last year, and I could have seen all the bosoms and shoulders in the world, without being concerned whether they were well shaped or not; but, since I've discarded the clothes of my sex and I have been living with young men, a new sense had developed in me which I hadn't known: a sense of beauty. Women are usually deprived of it, I really don't know why, because at first sight you would think that they could judge it better than men; but, as it is they who possess it, and self-knowledge is the most difficult knowledge to acquire, it isn't surprising that they don't understand a thing about it. Usually, if a woman finds another woman pretty, you can be sure that the latter is very ugly, and that no man will pay her the least attention. On the other hand, all the women whose grace and beauty are admired by men are unanimously considered to be abominable and affected by the whole bevy of petticoats; there are endless protests and commotions. If I were what I appear to be, I should have no other guide in my choice, and I should find the disapproval of women an adequate certificate of beauty.

Now I love and know beauty; the clothes I wear separate me from my sex, and remove any kind of rivalry from me; I am better qualified to judge than other people. I am no longer a woman, but I am not yet a man, and desire will not so blind me that I mistake a mannequin for an idol; I see coldly and dispassionately, neither for nor against, and my position is as completely disinterested as possible.

The length and delicacy of the eyelashes, the transparency of the temples, the limpidity of the eyes, the volutes of the ear, the colour and quality of the hair, the nobility of the feet and hands, the degree of slimness of wrists and ankles: a thousand things which I didn't notice constitute real beauty and prove the purity of race. These guide me in my appreciation, and they rarely fail me. I think that people could accept blindfold a woman of whom I'd said: 'She isn't bad.'

As a very natural consequence, I understand much more about pictures than I used to do, and although I have only a very superficial smattering of the masters, it would be hard to make me accept a bad work as a good one; I take a profound and singular delight in this study; for, like everything else in the world, moral or physical beauty demands to be studied, and it cannot be understood immediately.

But let's come back to Rosette; it isn't a difficult transition from this subject to her, and the ideas follow one another.

As I said, the fair lady was leaning back on my arm, and her head was resting on my shoulder; emotion tinged her lovely cheeks a shade of pale pink which was admirably enhanced by the deep black of a little beauty-spot very prettily placed. Her teeth were shining through her smile like raindrops in the depths of a poppy, and her half-lowered lashes increased even further the moist brilliance of her big eyes. A ray of sunlight made a thousand little metallic diamonds sparkle in her silky, moiré hair, and a few locks had come loose and were curling in ringlets down her long, plump neck, enhancing its warm whiteness; a few little stray hairs, more rebellious than the others, had detached themselves from the rest, and, winding in capricious spirals, gilded with strange reflections, and shot through by the light, they took on all the colours of the rainbow. They were like those golden threads round the heads of the virgins in old pictures. We both remained silent, and I diverted myself by following the little blue veins under her nacreous, transparent temples, and the gentle, imperceptible decline of the down at the end of her eyebrows.

The fair lady seemed to withdraw into herself and to lose herself in dreams of endless pleasure; her arms hung down beside her body as limp and flowing as untied sashes; her head leant further and further back, as if the muscles which held it had been cut or were too weak to support it. She had drawn her two small feet back under her skirt, and she had continued to nestle up in the corner of the little sofa where I was sitting, so that, although this piece of furniture was too narrow for us, there was a big empty space on the other side.

Her body, supple and fluent, modelled itself like wax on my own, and followed its whole external line as closely as possible; water wouldn't have flowed more precisely into its every curve. Fixed to my side like this, she looked like the double line which painters add to their drawing on the shadow side, to make it thicker and stronger. Only a woman in love could undulate and entwine herself like that. Ivy and willows are nothing in comparison.

The gentle warmth of her body penetrated through her clothes and mine; a thousand little magnetic streams radiated from her; her whole life seemed to have passed into me and abandoned her completely. Every moment she was more languishing and dying and drooping; there was a slight sweat glistening on her glossy brow; her eyes were full of tears, and two or three times she made as if to raise her hands to hide them; but, halfway, her weary arms fell back on to her lap, and she couldn't do so; a big tear overflowed and rolled down her burning cheek, where it soon dried.

My situation was becoming very embarrassing and rather ridiculous; I felt I must look enormously stupid, and this vexed me in the highest degree, although it was not in my power to look any different. Bold actions were forbidden me, and they were the only actions which would have been appropriate. I was too sure of meeting no resistance to risk them, and, to tell the truth, I was at my wits' end. Paying compliments and reciting madrigals would have been all right at the beginning, but nothing would have seemed more insipid at the point that we had reached; to get up and go would have been the last word in rudeness; and, besides, I'm not sure that Rosette wouldn't have played Putiphar and held me back by the corner of my cloak. I shouldn't have had any virtuous reason to give her for my resistance; and then, I shall confess it to my shame, this scene, quite equivocal though it was for me, was not without a certain charm which held me back more than it should; this ardent desire was warming me with its flame, and I was genuinely vexed that I wasn't able to satisfy it: I even wished that I were a man, as in fact I appeared to be, so that I might consummate this love, and I much regretted that Rosette was mistaken. My breathing grew faster, I felt myself blushing, and I was hardly less troubled than my poor mistress. The thought of the similarity of sex gradually faded and only left a vague idea of pleasure; my eyes misted over, my lips were trembling, and, if Rosette had been a cavalier instead of what she was, I am sure that she would easily have got the better of me.

At last, unable to bear any more, she got up suddenly, with a kind of spasmodic movement, and began to bustle round the room; then she stopped in front of the mirror, and re-arranged a few locks of hair which had lost their wave. While she was moving about, I cut a poor figure, and I hardly knew what countenance to put on.

She stopped in front of me and appeared to reflect.

She thought that only desperate shyness was holding me back, and that I was more of a schoolboy than she had at first believed. Beside herself, and roused to the highest degree of amorous exasperation, she decided to make a supreme effort and to play neck or nothing, at the risk of losing the game.

She came to me, sat down on my lap quicker than lightning, put her arms round my neck, clasped her hands behind my head, and her mouth clung to mine in a wild embrace; I felt her breasts, half-naked and aroused, buoyant against my breasts, and her interlaced fingers tighten in my hair. A quiver ran all through my body, and my nipples stood out.

Rosette didn't leave my mouth; her lips enveloped mine, her teeth struck against my teeth, our breaths merged with each other. I recoiled for a moment, and two or three times I turned my head away to avoid this kiss; but an invincible attraction made me turn back again, and I returned it almost as ardently as she had given it. I really don't know what would have happened if we hadn't heard a great barking outside the door and a sound of scratching paws. The door burst open, and a fine white greyhound came yapping and romping into the hut.

Rosette looked up suddenly, and, with a bound, she flew to the far end of the room; the fine white greyhound frolicked gaily and joyfully around her, and tried to reach her hands so as to lick them; she was so disturbed that she had a good deal of trouble readjusting her mantlet round her shoulders.

This greyhound was the favourite dog of her brother Alcibiades; he never left him, and, when you saw the dog appear, you could be sure that the master wasn't far away; that is what had so alarmed poor Rosette.

And indeed Alcibiades himself came in a minute later all booted and spurred, and whip in hand. 'Ah, there you are!' he said. 'I've been looking for you for an hour, and I should certainly not have found you if my good greyhound Snug hadn't dug you out of your hiding-place.' And he cast a half-serious, half-playful glance at his sister, which made her blush up to the eyes. 'Apparently you have very ticklish things to discuss, since you have withdrawn into such solitude? I expect you were discussing theology and the dual nature of the soul?'

'Oh Lord, no! Our occupations were nothing like so sublime; we were eating cakes and discussing fashions. That's all.'

'I don't believe a word of it. You looked as if you were deep in the middle of some sentimental dissertation. But I shall distract you from your vaporous conversations, I don't think it would be a bad idea if you came for a little ride with me. I've got a new mare that I want to try out. You can try her, too, Théodore, and we'll see what can be done with her.' The three of us went out together, he gave me his arm and I gave mine to Rosette. The expressions on our faces were singularly different. Alcibiades looked pensive, I looked much relieved, and Rosette appeared extremely vexed.

Alcibiades had arrived most opportunely for me, and most in-opportunely for Rosette, who thereby lost or thought she lost all the fruits of her artful attacks and ingenious tactics. It had to be done again. Another quarter of an hour, and the devil take me if I know how this adventure could have ended – I can't see any possible ending. Perhaps it would have been better if Alcibiades hadn't inter-vened just at the dangerous moment, like a *deus ex machina*. The thing would have had to end in one way or another. During this scene, I was two or three times on the point of confessing who I was to Rosette; but the fear of passing for an adventuress and of seeing my secret divulged held back the confession which was ready to take wing.

Such a state of things couldn't last. The only way to cut short this endless intrigue was to leave; and so, at dinner, I announced officially that I should be leaving the very next day. Rosette, who was sitting beside me, was nearly ill when she heard the news, and she dropped her glass. A sudden pallor spread across her beautiful face; she gave me an anguished look, full of reproach, and it left me almost as moved and disturbed as she was.

The aunt lifted up her old wrinkled hands with a movement of surprise, and in her piping, quavering voice which faltered even more than usual, she said to me: 'Oh, my dear Monsieur Théodore, are you leaving us like that? Yesterday you didn't seem ready to go in the very least. The mail hasn't come; so you haven't had any letters and you have no reason to go. You've granted us another fortnight, and you're taking it back; you really haven't got the right to do so: you can't take back what you have given. See how Rosette is looking at you, how she reproaches you; I warn you that I shall reproach you at least as much as she does, and I shall look on you quite as severely, and a sixty-eight-year-old face is rather more forbidding than a face of twenty-three. See what you choose to expose yourself to: the anger of the aunt and the niece, and all this for some or other whim which has suddenly seized you between the pear and the cheese.'

Alcibiades struck a great blow on the table with his fist, and swore that he would barricade the gates of the château and hamstring my horse, rather than let me go.

Rosette darted me another look, so sad and supplicating that it would have needed all the ferocity of a tiger which had been starving for a week not to be touched by it, and, although I found it singularly vexing, I gave a solemn promise to stay. Dear Rosette would readily have thrown her arms round my neck and kissed me on the lips for this kindness; Alcibiades clasped my hand in his big hand, and shook my arm so violently that he almost wrenched my shoulder off, made my rings oval instead of round, as they had been, and cut three of my fingers quite deeply.

The old lady celebrated by taking a huge pinch of snuff.

However, Rosette did not regain all her gaiety; the idea that I could go away, and that I wanted to do so, cast her into a deep reverie. The colour which the announcement of my departure had driven from her cheeks did not return as bright as before; she was still rather pale about the cheeks and anxious in the depths of her heart. My behaviour towards her surprised her more and more. After the marked advances that she had made me, she didn't understand the reasons which made me so restrained in my relations with her. What she wanted was to bring me to an absolutely decisive promise before I left, because she had no doubt that after that it would be extremely easy for her to keep me as long as she liked.

In this she was right, and, if I hadn't been a woman, her calculation would have proved correct; for, whatever one has said about the satiety of pleasure and the disgust which usually follows possession, any man who has his heart in roughly the right place, and isn't miserably hardened and impoverished, feels his love intensified by happiness, and very often the best way of keeping a lover who is ready to go is to abandon oneself to him completely.

Rosette planned to make me do something decisive before I left. Knowing how difficult it is to resume a liaison later on at the point at which you had left it, and, anyway, being far from sure that she would ever find me again in such favourable circumstances, she neglected none of the occasions which could present themselves to put me in a position to declare myself quite clearly and to drop the evasive manner behind which I was sheltering. I had, myself, the absolutely positive intention of avoiding any kind of meeting like the one in the rustic cottage, but I couldn't, without looking ridiculous, affect too much coldness towards Rosette, and behave to her as prudishly as a little girl; and so I wasn't quite sure what countenance to put on, and I always tried to have a third person with us. Rosette, on the contrary, did everything she could to find herself alone with me, and she fairly often succeeded, since the château was a good way from the town and it was little frequented by the neighbouring nobility. This silent resistance saddened and surprised her; at times she had doubts and hesitations about the power of her charms, and, seeing herself so little loved, she was sometimes not far from thinking that she was ugly. And then she redoubled her attentions and her coquetry, and although her mourning did not allow her to employ all the resources of dress, she still knew how to adorn and vary it so as to be two or three times more charming every day – which isn't saying a little. She tried everything: she was sprightly, melancholy, tender, passionate, attentive, coy, and even affected; she put on, one after the other, all those adorable masks which suit women so well that you no longer know if they are real masks or their actual faces; she put on eight or ten quite different characters, to see which would please me and then adopt it. She alone made me a complete seraglio where I only had to drop a handkerchief; but naturally nothing succeeded with her.

The failure of all these stratagems cast her into an absolute stupor. In fact, she would have outwitted Nestor and melted the ice of the chaste Hippolytus himself – and I seemed anything but Nestor and Hippolytus: I'm young, and I had a proud, determined look, bold conversation, and, everywhere except in a tête-à-tête, I had a most resolute appearance.

She must have thought that the witches of Thracia and Thessaly had cast their spells over my body or that, at least, my shoulder-knot was tangled, and she must have had the most appalling opinion of my virility, which is indeed somewhat insignificant. But apparently this idea did not occur to her at all, and she just attributed this extraordinary reserve to my lack of love for her.

The days flowed past, and her affairs made no progress. She was visibly affected: an expression of anxious sadness had replaced the smile that had always lit up her face; the corners of her mouth, so happily turned up, had visibly turned down, and formed a firm and serious line; a few little veins appeared more clearly defined on her tender eyelids; her cheeks, which had been so like a peach, had only kept their imperceptible velvet. Often, from my window, I saw her cross the flower-garden in her morning gown; she walked, hardly raising her feet, as if she were gliding, her arms limply folded over her breast, her head bent, more deeply bowed than a branch of a willow-tree dipping into the water, with something undulating and weighed-down about her, like a drapery which is too long and trailing on the ground. At such moments, she seemed like some classical woman, a prey to the wrath of Venus, a woman in love whom the ruthless goddess pursues with all her might. This is how I imagine Psyche must have been when she had lost Cupid.

On the days when she didn't strive to conquer my coldness and hesitation, her love had simple, primitive ways which would have charmed me; she showed me a silent and trusting surrender, a simple readiness to caress, an inexhaustible fullness and plenitude of heart, all the treasures of a noble nature scattered without reserve. She had none of those pettinesses and meannesses which you see in nearly every woman, even in those women who are best endowed; she sought no disguise, and she calmly let me see the whole extent of her passion. Her self-love did not rebel for a moment because I did not respond to all these advances, for pride leaves the heart the moment that love comes in; and if ever anyone has been truly loved, it is me by Rosette. She was suffering, but without complaint and without bitterness, and she attributed the failure of her endeavours to herself alone. However, her pallor increased every day, and the lilies had fought a hard fight with the roses on the battleground of her cheeks, and the roses had been finally routed; I was desolate, but, in all conscience, I could do less about it than anyone. The more I spoke to her with gentleness and affection, the more endearing my manner towards her, the further I drove the barbed arrow of impossible love into her heart. By consoling her today, I prepared a much greater despair for her in the future; my remedies poisoned her wound while they appeared to heal it. In a way I repented all the pleasant things that I had been able to say to her, and, because of the extreme friendship which I felt for her, I should have liked to find the means to make her detest me. You cannot take disinterestedness further than that, because I should certainly have been very vexed by it; but it would have been better.

I tried, on two or three occasions, to say a few cutting words; I very soon went back to the madrigal, for I am more afraid of her tears than I am of her smile. On these occasions, although the loyalty of my intention fully absolves me in my conscience, I am more touched than I should be, and I feel something akin to remorse. A tear can hardly be dried except by a kiss, and you cannot decently leave this office to a handkerchief, were it made of the finest cambric in the world. I undo what I have done, the tear is very soon forgotten, sooner than the kiss, and still further embarrassment always follows for me.

Rosette, who saw that I was going to escape her, clung stubbornly and miserably to what remained of her hopes, and my position became more and more complicated. The strange sensation that I had experienced in the little hermitage, and the inconceivable confusion into which the ardent caresses of my fair lady had thrown me, had recurred several times, although less violently; and often, seated by Rosette, with her hand in mine, hearing her speak to me in her gentle, musical voice, I imagine that I am a man, as she believes, and that, if I don't respond, it's pure cruelty on my part.

One evening, by some chance or other, I found myself alone in the green room with the old lady; she had some embroidery in hand, for, despite her sixty-eight years, she was never idle, and she wanted, before she died, so she said, to finish a set of furniture which she'd begun and had already been working on for a very long time. Since she felt a little tired, she set down her work and lay back in her big armchair; she looked at me very attentively, and her grey eyes were sparkling through her spectacles with a curious brightness; she passed her thin hand two or three times over her forehead, and she seemed to be lost in reflection. The memory of times which were no more, and times which she regretted, gave her face a look of melancholy tenderness. I said nothing, for fear of disturbing her in her thoughts, and the silence lasted for some minutes. At last she broke it.

'Those are really Henri's eyes, my dear Henri's: the same moist, shining look, the same bearing of the head, the same proud and gentle face. Anyone would think that it was him. You can't imagine just how like him you are, Monsieur Théodore; when I see you, I can't believe that Henri is dead any more; I think that he's just been on a long journey, and that here he is, back again at last. You have given me much pleasure and much pain, Théodore: pleasure, because you have reminded me of my poor Henri; pain, because you have shown me how great a loss I have suffered; sometimes I've taken you for his ghost. I cannot accustom myself to the thought that you're going to leave us; it seems to me that I am losing my Henri once again.'

I told her that if it were really possible for me to stay longer, I should do so with pleasure, but that my stay had already been prolonged beyond its proper limit; that, in any case, I certainly hoped to come back, and that the château left me with too many happy memories for me to forget it so quickly.

'However sorry I am that you're going, Monsieur Théodore,' she went on, pursuing her idea, 'there's someone who will be sorrier than I am. You know quite well who I mean without my telling you. I don't know what we'll do with Rosette when you have gone; but this old château is very sad. Alcibiades is always out hunting, and the company of a poor old cripple like myself isn't very amusing for a young woman like her.'

'If someone is to have regrets, it isn't you, madame, or Rosette, it is myself. You are not losing much, and I am losing a great deal.

You will easily find someone whose company is more charming than mine, and it is more than doubtful if I can ever replace that of Rosette and yourself.'

'I don't want to quarrel with your modesty, my dear sir, but I know what I know, and I say what is true. We shall probably not see Madame Rosette in good humour again for a very long while, for you dictate the colour of her cheeks. Her mourning is about to end, and it would be most vexing if she abandoned her gaiety with her black dress; that would be a very bad example, and quite contrary to the ordinary laws. It is something which you can prevent without too much trouble, and something which no doubt you will prevent,' said the old lady, and she laid great stress on the last words.

'Certainly, I shall do all I can to ensure that your dear niece keeps her delightful gaiety, since you think I have so much influence upon her. But I hardly see how I could set about it.'

'Oh! you really hardly see! How do you use those beautiful eyes of yours? I didn't know that you were so short-sighted. Rosette is free; she has an income of eighty thousand livres which is hers alone, and people find women pretty who are twice as ugly as she is. You are young and handsome, and, I believe, unmarried; it seems to me the simplest thing in the world, unless you have an insuperable horror of Rosette: which is hard to believe . . .'

'That isn't so and can't be so; for her soul is as lovely as her person, and she is one of those women who could be ugly without your noticing or wanting them to be any different . . .'

'She could be ugly with impunity, and she is charming. That means she is right twice over; I don't doubt what you say, but she has made the wiser choice. As far as she's concerned, I'm prepared to say that there are a thousand people whom she hates more than you, and that, if you asked her several times, she might finally confess that you don't exactly displease her. You have a ring on your finger which would suit her perfectly, for your hand is almost as small as hers, and I am almost sure that she would accept it with pleasure.'

The good lady paused for a moment or two to see what effect

her words would have on me, and I don't know that she was satisfied by the expression on my face. I was cruelly embarrassed, and I didn't know what to answer. From the beginning of this conversation, I had seen where all her insinuations were leading; and though I had almost expected what she had just said, I was surprised and speechless, none the less. I could only refuse; but what valid reasons could I give for such a refusal? I had none, except that I was a woman; that, it is true, was an excellent reason, but it was just the one reason which I didn't want to mention.

I could hardly fall back on very strict and ridiculous parents; all the parents on earth would have accepted such an alliance with rapture. Had Rosette not been what she was, beautiful and good by birth, the income of eighty thousand livres would have removed every difficulty. To say that I didn't love her would have been neither true nor fair, for I really loved her very much, and more than a woman loves a woman. I was too young to claim that I was engaged elsewhere. The best thing I could think of doing was to allow it to be understood that as I was the youngest son of a good family, the interests of the family demanded that I should enter the Order of Knights Hospitallers of Malta, and that did not allow me to think of marriage; this caused me the greatest sorrow in the world since I had seen Rosette.

This answer wasn't worth tuppence, and I knew it perfectly well. The old lady wasn't deceived by it and she didn't take it as final; she thought that I had spoken like that to give myself time to reflect and consult my parents. Indeed, for me such a union was so advantageous and unhoped-for that I couldn't possibly have refused it, even if I'd only loved Rosette a little, or not at all; it was a good fortune that was not to be missed.

I don't know if the aunt made this overture to me at the instigation of the niece, but I incline to think that Rosette had nothing to do with it. She loved me too simply and too ardently to think about anything other than possessing me at once, and marriage would certainly have been the last means that she employed. The dowager had not failed to notice our intimacy, which no doubt she thought much greater than it was, and she had devised the whole of this plan in her own mind. She wanted to keep me near her, and, as far as possible, to replace her dear son Henri, who had been killed with the army, the son to whom she thought I bore so striking a likeness. She was delighted with this plan, and she had taken advantage of this moment of solitude to have it out with me. I saw by her expression that she didn't consider she was beaten, and that she intended to return to the attack before long. This vexed me in the highest degree.

As for Rosette, on the night of that day, she made a final venture which had such serious results that I must write you a separate account of it; I can't describe it in this letter, which is already infinitely too long. You will see what extraordinary adventures were destined for me, and how heaven had cut me out in advance to be the heroine of a novel; I'm not too sure what moral may be drawn from it all – but lives are not like fables, and there isn't a rhymed proverb at the end of every chapter. Very often the meaning of life is that it isn't death. And that's all. Farewell, dear girl, I kiss your lovely eyes. You will soon have the next instalment of my triumphant biography.

XIII

THÉODORE – Rosalind – for I don't know what name to call you by – I saw you just a moment ago, and I am writing to you. How I should like to know your woman's name! It must be as sweet as honey and hover on the lips more suave and more harmonious than poetry! I should never have dared to tell you that, and yet I should have died if I hadn't told you. What I have suffered, no one knows, nobody can know, I myself could only give a poor idea of it; words don't express such anguish; I should appear to have given a wanton twist to my sentences, flogged myself to say new and extraordinary things, indulged in the wildest exaggerations, and I should only be painting what I have felt with images which were hardly adequate.

O Rosalind! I love you, I adore you; why isn't there a stronger word than that? I have never loved, I have never adored anyone but you; I prostrate myself, I humble myself before you, and I should like to compel all creation to kneel before my idol; to me you are more than all creation, more than myself, more than God; indeed it seems strange that God does not descend from heaven to become your slave. Where you are not, all is wilderness, all is dead, all is darkness; you alone people the world for me; you are hope, you are the sun. You are everything. Your smile makes day, your sadness makes night; the spheres follow the movements of your body, and the celestial harmonies take their pattern from you, O my beloved queen! O my lovely real dream! You are clothed in splendour, and you float unendingly in emanations of light.

I have hardly known you for three months, but I have loved you for a very long while. Before I saw you, I was already pining away for love of you; I called you, I sought you, and I was in despair that I never found you on my path, for I knew I could never love another woman. How often, in my dreams, you appeared to me – at the window of the mysterious château, leaning sadly on the balcony, and casting the petals of some or other flower to the wind, or else, a petulant amazon, on your Arab horse, whiter than snow, galloping through the dark avenues in the forest! They were indeed your proud and gentle eyes, your diaphanous hands, your fine wavy hair and your half-smile, so adorably disdainful. But you were less beautiful in my dreams, for the wildest and most ardent imagination, the imagination of a painter and a poet cannot attain this sublime poetry of reality. There is in you an inexhaustible fount of graces, an ever-flowing fountain of irresistible seductions; you are an ever-open casket of the most precious pearls, and, in your slightest movements, your most unmindful gestures, your most careless poses, you cast abroad, at every moment, with royal profusion, inestimable treasures of beauty. If the soft undulations of contours, the fugitive lines of an attitude, could be fixed and preserved in a mirror, the mirrors which you had passed would make men disdain and dismiss as inn-signs the most heavenly canvases of Raphael.

Every gesture, every turn of your head, every different aspect of your beauty, are engraved with a diamond point on the mirror of my soul, and nothing in the world could efface the deep imprint; I know where there was shadow, where there was light, the flat part which was glossed by the sun, and the place where the shifting reflection merged with the more softened tints of the neck and cheek. I could draw you in your absence; the idea of you is for ever posing before me.

As a child, I used to stand for hours in front of the paintings of the old masters, and I used avidly to search in their sombre depths. I looked at those lovely figures of saints and goddesses whose flesh, white as ivory or wax, stood out so marvellously against the dim backgrounds, charred by the decomposition of the colours; I admired the simplicity and the splendour of their figures, the strange grace of their hands and feet, the pride and the fine character of the features, at once so delicate and so firm, the grandeur of the draperies which fluttered round their heavenly forms, the purple folds of which seemed to lengthen as if they were lips to kiss their heavenly bodies. I peered so obstinately under the veil of mist which had grown thicker with the centuries that my sight became troubled, the contours of things lost their precision, and a kind of dead and motionless life animated all these pale ghosts of vanished beauties; I found in the end that these figures bore a vague resemblance to the lovely unknown woman whom I adored in the depths of my heart; I sighed when I thought that the woman whom I was to love might be one of those, and that she had been dead for three hundred years. This idea often moved me to tears, and I became quite furious with myself for not having been born in the sixteenth century, when all these beautiful women had been alive. I considered my blunder and clumsiness unforgivable.

When I grew older, the gentle phantom haunted me more closely than ever. I always saw it between myself and the women whom I had as my mistresses, smiling with an ironic smile and mocking their human beauty with all the perfection of its own divine loveliness. It made me find women ugly who were really charming and made to delight anyone who hadn't been in love with this adorable shade – this shade who had, I thought, no living body, this shade which was only the presentiment of your own beauty. O Rosalind! How unhappy I was because of you, before I knew you! O Théodore! How unhappy I was because of you, after I'd known you! If you want, you can open to me the paradise of my dreams. You stand on the threshold, like a guardian angel enveloped in its wings, and you hold the golden key in your fair hands. Tell me, Rosalind, tell me, do you want to do so?

I await only a word from you to live or to die: will you speak it?

Are you Apollo banished from heaven, or white Aphrodite emerging from the bosom of the sea? Where have you left your chariot of precious stones drawn by its four horses of fire? What have you done with your pearly shell and your dolphins with azure tails? What loving nymph has fused her body with your own in the midst of a kiss, O beautiful young man, more charming than Cyparissus and Adonis, more adorable than all women?

But you are a woman, we are no longer in the age of meta-morphoses. Adonis and Hermaphroditus are dead – and this degree of beauty may no longer be attained by a man; for, since the heroes and the gods have gone, you alone preserve in your statuesque bodies, as in a Greek temple, the precious gift of form which was declared accursed by Christ, and you alone show that the earth has nothing to envy heaven; you represent, with dignity, the first divinity in the world, the purest symbol of the eternal essence – beauty.

The moment I saw you, something was rent inside me, a veil fell, a door opened, I felt I was flooded by waves of light within; I understood that my life was before me, that I had reached the decisive crossroads at last. The dim and invisible parts of the half-radiant figure which I sought to discern in the shadow were suddenly lit up; the darkened tints which drowned the depths of the picture were gently illuminated; a pale pink light spread over the rather greenish ultramarine of the background; the trees which were only confused silhouettes began to emerge more clearly; the flowers, which were heavy with dew, pricked the dull green of the grass with specks of brilliance. I saw the bullfinch with its scarlet breast at the end of an elder-branch, the little white rabbit with pink eyes and upright ears, peering out between two blades of wild thyme and brushing its paw against its face, and the timid deer which came to drink at the spring and reflect its antlers in the water. From the morning when the sun of love rose on my life, everything changed; where vague shapes had wavered in the shades, monstrous or terrible for all their vagueness, groups of flowering trees stood out with elegance, hills rose around in gracious amphitheatres, palaces of silver with their terraces laden with vases and statues bathed their feet in azure lakes and seemed to be swimming between two *skies*; what I had taken in the obscurity for a gigantic dragon with wings armed with claws, crawling through the night with its scaly feet, is only a felucca with silken sail, painted and gilded oars, full of women and musicians, and that fearful crab which I thought I saw moving its claws and nippers above my head is only a fan-shaped palm-tree whose long narrow leaves are stirred by the nocturnal breeze. My chimeras and errors have vanished. I am in love.

I had despaired of ever finding you, I accused my dream of lying and I quarrelled furiously with fate. I told myself that I was quite mad to seek such a symbol, or that nature was very fertile and the Creator was very unskilful not to be able to realize the simple idea in my heart. Prometheus had had the noble pride to want to create a man and rival God; as for me, I had created a woman, and I believed that as a punishment for my audacity an ever-unassuaged desire would, like another vulture, gnaw away at my liver; I expected to be chained with diamond chains to a bleak rock on the shores of the wild ocean; but the lovely sea-nymphs with their long green hair, lifting their pointed white breasts above the waves, and showing the sun their pearly bodies streaming with the tears of the sea, would not have come to lean across the shore to talk to me and console me in my sorrow, as they had done in the drama of old Aeschylus.

It has been different.

You have come, and I have had to reproach my imagination for its powerlessness. My torment was not, as I had feared, the torment of being a constant prey to an idea, on a barren rock; but I have suffered none the less for that. I saw that you did in fact exist, that my presentiments had not deceived me; but you appeared to me with the ambiguous and terrible beauty of the sphinx. Like Isis, the mysterious goddess, you were wrapped in a veil which I did not dare to lift for fear I should drop dead. If you knew with what breathless and anxious attention I watched and followed you, under my apparent distraction, watched and followed the slightest movements which you made! Nothing escaped me. How ardently I looked at what little appeared of your flesh at your neck and wrists to try to determine your sex! I made a thorough study of your hands, and I may say that I know their smallest curves, their most imperceptible veins, their slightest dimples; if you were hidden from head to foot under the most impenetrable cloak, I should recognize you just by one of your fingers. I analysed the undulation of your walk, the way you set down your feet, and put up your hair, I tried to discover your secret by watching your physical habits. I watched you especially in those hours of indolence when the bones seem to withdraw from the body and the limbs sag and bend as if they were loosened to see if the feminine line would be more boldly pronounced in this forgetfulness and nonchalance. Never was anyone watched so vigilantly, so ardently, as you.

I was lost for hours on end in this contemplation. I withdrew into some corner of the salon, holding a book which I wasn't reading; I crouched behind the curtain in my room, when you were in yours, and the shutter of your window had been opened. Then, penetrated through and through by the wondrous beauty which spread around you in a kind of luminous atmosphere, I said to myself: 'She is certainly a woman.' Then, suddenly, in a minute, a brusque, bold gesture, a virile accent or some cavalier gesture destroyed my frail structure of probabilities, and cast me back into my original uncertainty.

I was sailing full sail on the boundless ocean of amorous dreams, and you came to ask me to fence or play tennis with you; the young girl, who had been transformed into a young cavalier, gave me terrible beatings and made the foil leap from my hands as nimbly as the swashbuckler who was most practised in fencing. At every moment of the day, there was some such disappointment.

I was going to approach you to tell you: 'My fair lady, you are the one whom I adore,' and I saw you bending tenderly over a woman's ear and whispering whiffs of madrigals and compliments through her hair. Imagine my predicament. Or else some woman whom, in my strange jealousy, I should have flayed alive with the greatest pleasure in the world, hung on your arm, and drew you aside to confide some or other puerile secret in you, and kept you in an embrasure of the window for hours on end.

I was enraged to see women talking to you, for that made me think that you were a man, and, had you been one, I should have found it extremely hard to bear. When men approached you freely, and with familiarity, I was still more jealous, because I thought that you were a woman, and that perhaps they suspected it like me; I was a prey to the most contrary passions, and I didn't know where to turn.

I was enraged with myself, I reproached myself most harshly for being tormented by such a love, and for lacking the strength to tear out of my heart this venomous plant which had sprung up in it overnight like a poisoned toadstool; I cursed you, I called you my evil genius; for a moment I even believed that you were Beelzebub in person, for I couldn't explain the feeling that I experienced in your presence.

When I was quite convinced that you were in fact only a woman in disguise, the improbability of the reasons with which I tried to justify such a caprice cast me back into my uncertainty, and once again I began to deplore that the form which I had dreamed of for the love of my soul should happen to belong to someone of the same sex as myself; I cursed chance, which had clothed a man in such charming appearances, and, to my eternal misfortune, had led me to meet him at the moment when I no longer hoped to realize the absolute idea of pure beauty which I had so long cherished in my heart.

Now, Rosalind, I am profoundly convinced that you are the most beautiful of women; I have seen you in the attire of your sex, I have seen your shoulders and arms, so pure and so perfectly rounded. The beginning of your bosom which I glimpsed through your ruffle can only be that of a young girl: neither Meleager, the handsome hunter, nor Bacchus the effeminate, with their ambiguous forms, have ever had such suavity of line or such great delicacy of skin, although they are both of Paros marble and smoothed by the loving kisses of twenty centuries. I am no longer tormented about that. But this isn't all. You are a woman, and my love is no longer reprehensible, I can give myself to it without remorse, and abandon myself to the tide which bears me towards you; however great, however wild the passion that I feel, it is permissible and I can confess it. But you, Rosalind, for whom I burned in silence, you who were ignorant of the immensity of my love, you whom this belated revelation may only surprise, do you not hate me, do you love me, will you be able to love me? I don't know – and I tremble, and I am even unhappier than I was before.

At times, it seems to me that you don't hate me; when we performed *As You Like It*, you gave certain lines in your part a particular stress which increased their meaning, and, in a sense, demanded that I should declare myself. I believed I saw gracious promises of kindness in your eyes and in your smile, I believe that I felt your hand return the pressure of my own. If I was mistaken, O God! it's something I dare not think of. Encouraged by all that and urged on by my love, I have written to you, for the clothes you wear lend themselves ill to such confessions, and a thousand times the words have stopped at my lips; although I had the idea and the firm conviction that I was speaking to a woman, this man's dress alarmed all my tender loving thoughts, and prevented them from flying towards you.

I beg you, Rosalind, if you don't yet love me, try to love me, for I have loved you in spite of everything, beneath the veil in which you wrap yourself, no doubt from compassion for us; do not doom the rest of my life to the most fearful despair and the most dismal dejection. Think that I have loved you since the first ray of thought dawned in my head, that you were revealed to me in advance, and that, when I was very small, you appeared to me in a dream with a wreath of dewdrops, a pair of rainbow wings and the little blue flower in your hand. Remember that you are the end, the means and the significance of my life; that, without you, I am only a vain appearance, and that, if you extinguish this flame that you have lit, there will be nothing left deep inside me but a handful of dust finer and more impalpable than the dust which sprinkles the very wings of death. Rosalind, you who have so many prescriptions for curing the malady of love, cure me, for I am very ill. Play your part to the end, cast off the clothes of the beautiful page Ganymede, and hold out your white hand to the youngest son of the brave Sir Rowland de Boys.

XIV

I was at my window, engrossed in watching the stars which blossomed joyfully in the flowerbeds of heaven, and breathing in the fragrance of the marvel of Peru which was brought to me by the dying breeze. The wind from the open window had blown out my lamp, the last that had remained lit in the château. My thought had drifted into a vague reverie, and a kind of somnolence was beginning to come over me; yet I was still leaning on the stone balustrade, either because I was enthralled by the charm of the night, or because I was nonchalant and forgetful. Rosette no longer saw my lamp lit and she couldn't make me out because of a great angle of shadow which fell exactly on the window; she believed, no doubt, that I had gone to bed, and this was what she was waiting for in order to risk a final, desperate attempt on me. She pushed the door open so gently that I didn't hear her come in, and she was two steps from me before I noticed her. She was very surprised to see that I was still up; but she soon recovered from her surprise. She came to me and took my arm and called me twice by my name: 'Théodore, Théodore!'

'What! You are here, Rosette, at this time of night, all alone, without a light, in such complete undress!'

I must tell you that the fair lady had nothing on but a dressing-gown in extremely fine cambric, and the triumphant shift edged with lace which I hadn't wanted to see on the day of the famous scene in the little kiosk in the park. Her arms, as smooth and cold as marble, were completely bare, and the material which covered her body was so clinging and so diaphanous that it showed her nipples, like those statues of bathing women covered with wet drapery.

'Is that a reproach that you're making me, Théodore? Or is it just a simple sentence, a mere exclamation? Yes, here I am, Rosette, the beautiful woman, here, in your bedroom, and not in mine where I ought to be at eleven o'clock or possibly midnight. I have no duenna or chaperone or abigail, I am almost naked, just in a nightgown. It's very surprising, isn't it? It surprises me as much as you, and I don't quite know what explanation to give you.'

As she said this, she put one of her arms round my waist, and she let herself fall on to the bottom of my bed so as to pull me down with her.

'Rosette,' I said to her, as I tried to disengage myself, 'I'm going to try and light the lamp again; there's nothing as dismal as a dark room; and then, it's really murder not to see clearly when you are there and to deprive oneself of the sight of your beauties. Allow me, with a match and a bit of amadou, to make myself a little portable sun. It will enhance all that jealous night effaces with its shades.'

'It isn't worth it; I'd rather you didn't see my blushes; I can feel my cheeks all burning, for it's enough to make me die of shame.' She buried her face in my bosom, she stayed there for some minutes, as if she were choking with emotion.

During that time I passed my fingers mechanically through the long curls of her loose-flowing hair; I sought in my mind for some decent way to get myself out of these awkward circumstances, and I couldn't find any at all, for I was up against the wall, and Rosette seemed absolutely determined not to leave the room as she had entered it. Her clothes were formidably casual, and they boded no good. I had nothing on myself but an open dressing-gown which would have ill-defended my incognito, and so I was as anxious as could be about the result of the battle.

'Théodore, listen to me,' said Rosette. She raised her head and pushed her hair back on either side of her face, as far as I could make out in the pale light which the stars and a very narrow crescent moon, which had begun to rise, cast into the room through the open window. 'I am making a strange overture. Everyone would blame me for having made it. But you are going to go soon, and

I love you. I can't let you go like this without explaining myself to you. Perhaps you'll never come back; perhaps this is the first and last time that I shall see you. Who knows where you'll go? But wherever you go, you will take my soul and my life with you. If you had stayed, I shouldn't have reached this extremity. The happiness of looking at you, hearing you, living beside you would have been enough for me. I should have asked for nothing more. I should have locked up my love in my heart; you would have thought you had nothing in me but a good, true friend. But that cannot be. You say that you absolutely must go. Théodore, you find it wearisome to see me following your steps like this, like a loving ghost which can only follow you and would like to merge into your body; it must displease you to find pleading eyes always behind you, and hands outstretched to catch the hem of your garment. I know that, but I cannot help doing it. Besides, you can't complain about it; it is your fault. I was calm, peaceful, almost happy until I met you. You arrived: handsome, young and smiling, like the delightful god Phoebus. You showed me the most assiduous care, the most delicate attentions; no cavalier was ever more amusing or more gallant. Every moment roses and rubies fell from your lips; everything became for you the occasion for a madrigal, and you knew how to turn the most insignificant sentence into the most enchanting compliment. A woman who had begun by having a mortal hatred for you would have ended up by loving you, and I myself had loved you from the moment I saw you. Why did you then seem so surprised, when you had been so pleasant, that you should be loved so much? Isn't it a quite natural result? I'm not a mad or harebrained creature, or a little romantic girl who falls for the first sword that she sees. I know about people, and I know what life is about. As for what I'm doing, any woman, even the most virtuous or the most prudish, would have done as much. What was your idea, what was your intention? I imagine that you meant to please me, for I can't imagine anything else. How, then, can you seem to be rather vexed that you have succeeded so well? Have I unintentionally done something that displeased you? Please forgive me. Don't you find me beautiful any more, or have

you found some fault in me which repels you? You have the right
to be difficult where beauty is concerned, but either you have lied
most strangely, or I myself am beautiful, too! I am young, like
you, and I love you; why do you now disdain me? You used to be
so assiduous about me, you took my arm with such constant
solicitude, you pressed the hand I gave you so tenderly, you raised
such yearning eyes towards me; if you didn't love me, what was
the point of all this intrigue? Were you by chance so cruel as to
kindle love in someone's heart so that you could then make it a
laughing-stock? Oh, it would be a horrible mockery, it would be
an impious sacrilege! It could only be the amusement of a dreadful
creature, and I cannot believe it of you, however inexplicable your
behaviour towards me. What then is the reason for this sudden
change? I cannot see what it could be, myself. What mystery lies
behind such coldness? I cannot believe that you find me repugnant;
what you have done proves otherwise, for you cannot woo a woman
so intensely if she disgusts you, even if you were the greatest rogue
on earth. O Théodore, what have you against me? Who has
changed you like this? What have I done to you? If the love that
you seemed to have for me has flown, mine, alas, has remained,
and I cannot tear it from my heart. Have pity on me, Théodore, for
I am so unhappy. At least appear to love me a little, and say a few
sweet words to me; it won't cost you much, unless you have an
insuperable aversion for me . . .'

At this touching point in her discourse, her sobs completely
stifled her voice; she laid her hands on my shoulder, and leant her
forehead against them in an attitude of complete despair. Everything
that she said was perfectly true, and I had no good answer to make.
I couldn't treat the thing in a tone of mockery. That wouldn't have
been appropriate. Rosette wasn't one of those creatures whom you
could treat so lightly; besides, I was too moved to do so, I felt
guilty that I had played like that with the heart of a charming
woman, and I felt the most acute and genuine remorse in the
world.

Seeing that I made no answer, the dear girl uttered a long sigh
and made a movement as if to rise, but she fell back, weighed down

by her emotion. Then she put her arms round me – I could feel their coolness through my doublet – laid her face against mine and began to weep silently.

It had a singular effect on me to feel this inexhaustible current of tears flowing down my cheek – these tears which did not come from my own eyes. It was not long before my own tears mingled with them, and there was a real downpour of salt water; it would have caused a second Flood, if it had only lasted forty days.

At that moment the moon arrived exactly opposite the window; a pale ray shone into the room and lit up our silent group with a bluish light.

With her white dressing-gown, her bare arms, her bosom uncovered and almost the same colour as her linen, Rosette looked like an alabaster statue of Melancholy seated on a tomb. As for me, I'm not quite sure what sort of appearance I could have presented, since I didn't see myself and there wasn't any mirror at all to reflect my likeness, but I think that I might very well have passed for a statue of Uncertainty personified.

I was moved, and I caressed Rosette once or twice with more than usual affection; my hand had moved down from her hair to her velvet neck, and from there to her round smooth shoulder which I gently stroked, following its trembling lines. The child was quivering at my touch like a clavichord at a musician's fingers; her flesh was shuddering, and it suddenly moved, and loving tremors ran all down her body.

I myself felt a kind of vague, confused desire, the purpose of which I could not comprehend, and I felt great sensual delight exploring these pure and delicate contours. I left her shoulder and, taking advantage of a gap in the folds, I suddenly enclosed her frightened little breast in my hand. It was palpitating wildly, like a turtle-dove surprised in its nest. From the outer edge of her cheek, which I brushed with an almost imperceptible kiss, I came to her half-open mouth; we stayed like that for some time. But I don't know if it was two minutes, or a quarter of an hour, or an hour; for I had completely lost count of time, and I didn't know if I was in heaven or on earth, here or elsewhere, dead or living. The heady wine of sensual pleasure had so intoxicated me at the first sip that I had drunk that all my reason had gone. Rosette held me tighter and tighter in her arms and enveloped me with her body; she leant over me convulsively and clasped me to her bare and panting breast; with every kiss, all the life in her seemed to rush to the place that I had touched, and to abandon the rest of her body. Singular ideas were passing through my head; if I hadn't been afraid of betraying my incognito, I should have given Rosette complete freedom in her transports of passion, and perhaps I should have made some wild and vain attempt to give a semblance of reality to this shadow of pleasure which my lovely mistress embraced with such ardour. I had not yet had a lover; and these passionate attacks, these repeated caresses, the contact of this lovely body, these terms of endearment lost in kisses, troubled me in the highest degree, even though they came from a woman; and then this nocturnal visit, this romantic passion, this moonlight, it all had a freshness and a charm of novelty for me which made me forget that, after all, I wasn't a man.

However, I made a great effort with myself, and told Rosette that she was compromising herself horribly by coming into my room at such a time, and staying there so long, that her servants might observe her absence and see that she hadn't spent the night in her apartment.

I said this so feebly that Rosette's only answer was to drop her cambric dressing-gown and her slippers, and to slide into my bed like a snake into a bowl of milk; for she imagined that only my clothes prevented me from coming to more precise demonstrations, and that this was all that held me back.

She believed, poor child, that the hour of surrender, which she had so laboriously contrived, was at last to strike for her; but it only struck two o'clock in the morning. My situation could not have been more critical, when the door swung open to make way for the cavalier Alcibiades in person; he was holding a candlestick in one hand and his sword in the other.

He went straight to the bed, tore off the bedclothes, and, holding his light to the face of the confused Rosette, he jeered at her: 'Good morning, sister!' Little Rosette didn't have the strength to find a word in answer.

'It appears, then, my very dear and very virtuous sister, that having judged in your wisdom that my lord Théodore's bed was softer than yours, you came to sleep here? Or perhaps there are ghosts in your room, and you thought that you would be safer in this one, under his protection? An excellent idea. Ah, Monsieur de Sérannes, you have looked lovingly at my sister, and you think that that's all there is to it. I consider it wouldn't be unseemly to cut each other's throats for a while, and I should be infinitely obliged if you would consent. Théodore, you have abused the friendship which I felt for you, and you make me repent the good opinion that I had originally formed of your character. That's bad, very bad.'

I couldn't make any valid defence of myself; appearances were against me. Who, in fact, would have believed me, if I had said (which was perfectly true) that Rosette had only come into my room against my wish, and that, far from seeking to please her, I was doing all I could to turn her away from me? There was only one thing I could say, and I said it: 'My lord Alcibiades, we will cut each other's throats for as long as you please.'

During this conversation, Rosette had not failed to swoon according to the soundest rules of pathos; I found a glass goblet full of water, which contained a big white half-blown rose, and I threw a few drops in her face, which made her come round at once.

She was not too sure what sort of countenance she should put on; and she huddled in bed and buried her pretty head under the eiderdown, like a bird settling down to sleep. She had so gathered the sheets and pillows round her, that it would have been very difficult to make out what was under the pile; a few little fluted sighs, which emerged from time to time, were all that allowed one to guess that it was a young repentant sinner, or at least a sinner who was extremely vexed to be a sinner in intention but not in fact: which was the case with the unfortunate Rosette.

Her brother, who was no longer anxious about her, resumed his dialogue with me, and said in a somewhat milder tone: 'It isn't absolutely indispensable to cut each other's throats at once, that is the ultimate resort, there's always time for that. Listen: it's not an equal match between us. You are extremely young and much less vigorous than I am; if we were to fight, I should certainly kill you or maim you – and I shouldn't want to kill you or disfigure you – it would be a pity; Rosette, who is under the eiderdown over there and saying nothing, would bear me a grudge for it all her life; for she's as nasty and spiteful as a tigress when she sets her mind to it; that dear little dove. You don't know that, for you are her Prince Galaor, and she only grants you charming favours; but it isn't pleasant. Rosette is free, and so are you; it appears that you aren't irreconcilable enemies; her widowhood is about to end, which couldn't be more fortunate. Marry her; she won't need to go back to her own bed, and, as for me, I shall be spared from making you a sheath for my sword, which wouldn't be agreeable for you or for me. What do you think?'

I must have made a horrible grimace, for what he suggested was for me the most impracticable thing in all the world; I should have walked upside-down on the ceiling, on all fours, like flies, and unhooked the sun without taking a pair of steps to reach it, rather than do what he asked me, and yet the second proposition was undoubtedly more agreeable than the first.

He seemed surprised that I didn't accept with enthusiasm, and he repeated what he had said as if to give me time to reply.

'The marriage couldn't do me greater honour, and I should never have dared to aspire to it: I know that it's an unheard-of good fortune for a young man who has not yet acquired rank or consideration in the world, and that the most illustrious would consider themselves very happy with it; and yet I can only persist in my refusal, and, since I am free to choose between the duel and the marriage, I choose the duel. It is a singular choice, and few people would make it, but it is mine.'

Here Rosette uttered the most heart-rending sob in the world, brought out her head from under the pillow, and immediately put it back again, like a snail whose horns are hit, when she saw my set, determined expression.

'It isn't that I don't love Madame Rosette at all, I have boundless love for her; but I have reasons for not marrying at all, which you yourself would consider excellent, if I were at liberty to give them to you. Besides, things haven't gone as far as people might believe from appearances; apart from a kiss or two which are explained and justified by a rather warm friendship, there is nothing between us which could be called improper, and your sister's virtue is certainly the purest and the most intact in the world. I owe her this testimony. Now when shall we fight, Monsieur Alcibiades, and where?'

'We'll fight here and now!' cried Alcibiades, who was beside himself with rage.

'What are you thinking of? In front of Rosette?'

'Unsheath, you wretch, or I shall murder you,' he continued, brandishing his sword and waving it round his head.

'Let us at least go out of the room.'

'If you're not careful, I'm going to nail you to the wall like a bat, my fine Céladon, and it won't be any use beating your wings, you won't unhook yourself, I warn you.' And he rushed upon me with raised sword.

I drew my rapier, because he would have done as he said, and at first I contented myself with parrying the thrusts he made at me.

Rosette made a superhuman effort to come and throw herself between our swords; but her strength failed her, and she fell unconscious on the foot of the bed.

Our weapons sparkled and rang out like an anvil, for we had so little space that we were obliged to engage our swords at close quarters.

Two or three times Alcibiades nearly struck me, and, if I hadn't had an excellent fencing-master, my life would have been in the greatest danger; for he had astonishing skill and prodigious strength. He exhausted all the ruses and feints in fencing to touch me. He was enraged that he couldn't manage it, and two or three times he exposed himself to my rapier. I didn't want to take advantage of it; but he returned to the attack with such a wild and brutal outburst of passion, that I was compelled to seize the openings he left me; and then the noise and the whirl and flash of steel both intoxicated and dazzled me. I didn't think about death, I wasn't in the least afraid; this sharp and deadly point which appeared before my eyes at every moment had no more effect on me than if I had been fencing with foils with buttons on; only I was angry at Alcibiades' brutality, and the sense of my absolute innocence increased my indignation even more. I wanted just to prick his arm or his shoulder to make him drop his sword, for I had tried in vain to make it jump out of his hands. He had an iron grip, and the devil wouldn't have made him loosen it.

At last he made such a sharp, deep thrust that I could only half parry it; my sleeve was cut through, and I felt the chill of the blade on my arm; but I wasn't wounded. At the sight of this, I was overcome by anger, and, instead of defending myself, I attacked in my turn; I no longer thought that it was the brother of Rosette, and I bore down on him as if he had been my mortal enemy. Taking advantage of the wrong position of his sword, I gave him a flanconade so deftly aimed that I touched his side. He gasped 'Ho!', and fell back.

I thought he was dead, but in fact he was only wounded, and he had fallen because he had tripped as he tried to break my move. I cannot express, Graciosa, the sensation I felt. It certainly isn't hard to imagine that if you strike someone's flesh with a fine, sharp point you will pierce a hole in it, and that blood will gush out. And yet I fell into an utter stupor when I saw the red threads streaming down Alcibiades' doublet. Of course I didn't imagine that bran would come out, as if it had been the body of a chubby doll; but I know that never in my life had I felt so surprised, and it seemed that something unheard-of had happened to me.

What was unheard-of was not, it seemed, that blood had flowed from a wound, it was that I had opened that wound, and that a young girl of my age (I was going to write a young man, I have entered so well into the spirit of my part) had felled a vigorous captain, as practised in fencing as the noble Alcibiades; and, what is more, all for the crime of seducing and refusing to marry an extremely rich and charming woman!

What with the swooning sister, the brother whom I thought was dead, and myself (and I wasn't far from swooning like the one or being dead like the other), I was really in a cruel embarrassment.

I clung to the bell-rope, and rang a peal enough to waken the dead, as long as the ribbon remained in my hands; and, leaving the unconscious Rosette and the disembowelled Alcibiades with the task of explaining things to the servants and the old aunt, I went straight to the stable. The fresh air revived me immediately; I had my horse brought out, I saddled it and bridled it myself; I assured myself that the crupper held properly, and that the curb-chain was in good condition; I adjusted the stirrups to the same length, I tightened the saddle-strap by a notch; in short, I completely harnessed it with a diligence which was singular, to say the least, at a moment like this, and with a calm which was quite inconceivable after a fight which had had such an ending.

I mounted my horse, and crossed the park by a path I knew. The branches of the trees, all heavy with dew, struck against my face and made it wet; one would have said that the old trees were stretching out their arms to hold me back and keep me for the love of their châtelaine. If I had been in another frame of mind, or a little superstitious, I could easily have believed that they were so many ghosts who wanted to seize me and that they were showing me their fists.

But really I had no thoughts at all, either this or any other; a leaden stupor, so heavy that I was hardly aware of it, weighed upon my head, like a helmet that was too tight; only it really seemed to me that I had killed someone there and that this was the reason I was going. I also had a terrible longing for sleep, either because of the lateness of the hour or else because the violent emotions that evening had had a physical reaction and had made me bodily tired.

I came to a little postern which opened on to the fields by a secret catch which Rosette had shown me on our expeditions. I dismounted from my horse, pressed the button and pushed open the gate. When I had taken my horse through, I got back into the saddle, and galloped on till I reached the main road to C—, where I arrived just as dawn was breaking.

This is the most faithful and most detailed account of my first good fortune and my first duel.

XV

It was five o'clock in the morning when I entered the town. Households were beginning to put their noses out of the windows; the worthy inhabitants were showing their benevolent faces, topped with pyramidal nightcaps, behind the panes. At the sound of my horse, whose hooves rang out on the uneven, pebbly street, there appeared at every garret window the strangely red fat faces and the early-morning uncovered breasts of the local Venuses who wore themselves out in conjectures about this unwonted apparition of a traveller in C—, at such an hour and in such a garb, for I was very succinctly dressed and wearing clothes which were suspect, to say the least. A little ragamuffin pointed out an inn to me. His hair came right down over his eyes, and he raised his barbet's muzzle to study me more at his ease; I gave him a few sous for his pains, and a conscientious crack of the whip, which made him run off, yelping, like a jay plucked alive. I threw myself on to a bed and fell fast asleep. When I woke it was three o'clock in the afternoon; it was hardly enough to give me a proper rest. It really wasn't excessive after a sleepless night, a conquest, a duel, and a very rapid though very victorious flight.

I was very worried about Alcibiades' wound; but, a few days later, I was completely reassured, for I heard that it had had no serious results, and that he was fully convalescent. That took a singular weight off my mind, for I was strangely troubled by the idea of having killed a man, although it was in my legitimate defence and against my will. I had not yet reached that sublime indifference to human life which I have since attained.

At C— I rediscovered several of the young men we had travelled with. That pleased me; I became more friendly with them, and they introduced me at several pleasant houses. I was perfectly used to my male attire, and the tougher and more active life which I had led, the violent exercises in which I had indulged, had made me twice as robust as I had been. I followed these young Hotspurs everywhere; I rode, and hunted, and I had orgies with them for, gradually, I had made progress in drinking; I hadn't reached the quite German capacity which some of them possessed, but I could certainly empty two or three bottles by myself, and I wasn't too drunk, which was most satisfactory progress. I swore by God excessively often, and I kissed the serving-maids in inns with considerable determination. In short, I was an accomplished young cavalier and exactly like the latest model. I rid myself of certain provincial ideas which I had had about virtue and other such trifles; on the other hand, I became so prodigiously sensitive about the point of honour that I fought a duel nearly every day; indeed, this had become a kind of necessity for me, a kind of indispensable exercise without which I'd have felt ill all day long. And so, when no one had looked at me or trodden on my foot, when I had no reason for a fight, rather than remain idle and not use my hands I acted as a second to my friends or even to people whom I just knew by name.

I soon had a huge reputation for courage, and I had to have it to stop the pleasantries which my beardless face and effeminate appearance would unfailingly have caused. But three or four extra buttonholes which I opened in doublets, a few tags which I cut, very delicately, out of some recalcitrant skins, made most people consider that I looked more virile than Mars himself, or Priapus in person, and you would have met people who swore that they had stood sponsor to my bastards.

Throughout this apparent dissipation, this life which was wasted and squandered away, I never ceased to follow my original idea, that is to say the conscientious study of man and the solution of the great problem of a perfect lover, a problem rather more difficult to solve than that of the philosopher's stone.

It is the same with some ideas as it is with the horizon. This quite certainly exists, because, whichever way you turn, you see it before you, but it persistently eludes you, and whether you go at a walking pace or rush at a gallop, it is always the same distance away; for it can only make itself manifest on condition that it is a certain distance from you; it is destroyed as fast as you go forward, to be formed again, further on, with its fugitive and unassailable blue, and it is in vain that you try to catch it by the edge of its floating cloak.

The further I advanced in my understanding of the creature, the more I saw how impossible it was to realize my desire, and how far the happy love I asked was beyond the conditions of his nature. I became convinced that the man who was most genuinely in love with me would, with the best will in the world, find the means of making me the unhappiest of women, and yet I had already abandoned many of the demands which I had made as a young girl. I had come down from the sublime clouds, not actually into the street and the gutter, but on to a hill of average height, accessible, although a little steep.

The ascent, it is true, was fairly rough; but I was vain enough to believe that I was well worth the trouble of making this effort, and that I should be sufficient reward for the trouble that people had taken. I could never have decided to make an advance; I waited patiently, perched on my summit.

This was my plan. In my male attire I should make the acquaintance of some young man whose appearance pleased me; I should live familiarly with him; by skilful questions and by false confidences which elicited true ones, I should soon acquire a complete understanding of his feelings and his thoughts; and, if I found him as I wished, I should make a pretext of some journey, and keep myself away from him for three or four months to give him a little time to forget my features; then I should come back in my women's clothes, and in some secluded suburb I should fit up a voluptuous little house, hidden away among the trees and flowers; then I should so arrange things that he met me and wooed me; and, if he had shown a true and faithful love, I should give myself to him without restrictions or precautions. The title of his mistress would seem honourable to me, and I shouldn't ask him for any other.

But this plan will certainly not be carried out, for it is the nature of plans not to be carried out, and it is there that you really see the frailty of will and the pure nothingness of man. The proverb – what woman wills, God wills – is no more true than any other proverb, which means that there is little truth in it.

As long as I had only seen them at a distance and through my desire, men had seemed handsome to me, and perspective had created an illusion. Now I find them dreadful in the extreme, and I don't know how a woman can allow that into her bed. As for me, it would make me sick, and I couldn't bring myself to do it.

How coarse and ignoble their features are! They have no elegance or delicacy. What offensive and ungraceful lines! What hard, dark, wrinkled skin! Some are as weather-beaten as corpses six months on the gallows: emaciated, bony, hairy, with violin strings on their hands, big drawbridge feet, a dirty moustache always full of victuals and turned up like hooks towards the ears, hair as coarse as the bristles on a broom, a chin which ends like a wild boar's head, lips cracked and burnt by strong liquors, a neck full of twisting veins, big muscles and projecting cartilages. The others are padded with red meat, and push a belly in front of them which is hardly encircled by their belt; they blink as they open their little sea-green eyes inflamed with lust, and they look more like hippopotami in breeches than human beings. They always reek of wine, or brandy, or tobacco, or with their natural smell, which is much the worst of all. As for those whose shape is a little less disgusting, they look like unsuccessful women. That's all.

I hadn't noticed all that. I lived in life as if it were a cloud, and my feet hardly touched the ground. The perfume of roses and lilies-of-the-valley went to my head like too strong a perfume. I dreamed of nothing but accomplished heroes, faithful and respectful lovers, passions worthy of the altar, wonderful devotions and sacrifices, and I should have thought that I found it all in the first villain who said good-morning to me. However, this first, crude intoxication did not last for long; I began to have strange suspicions, and I had no rest until I had cleared them up.

At first, I carried my horror of men beyond the limit, and considered them as terrible monsters. Their ways of thinking, their behaviour and their casually cynical language, their brutalities and their disdain of women shocked and revolted me in the extreme, the idea I had created of them bore so little resemblance to the reality. They are not monsters, I admit, but they are really much worse than that. They are excellent fellows with the most jovial natures, they eat and drink well, they will do you all kinds of services, they are intelligent and brave, good painters and good musicians, they are fit for a thousand things, except just one for which they have been created, which is to serve as a male to the animal which is known as woman, to whom they bear not the slightest relationship, either physical or moral.

I found it hard at first to disguise the contempt which they inspired in me, but gradually I became accustomed to their way of life. I was no more piqued by the jokes they made about women than if I myself had been a man. On the contrary, I made excellent jokes about women, too, and their success strangely flattered my pride; certainly none of my friends went as far as I did in my gibes and sarcastic remarks. My perfect knowledge of the subject gave me a great advantage, and, apart from the piquant turn they might have, my epigrams were distinguished by an accuracy which was often lacking in their own. For, though all the ill one says of women always has some foundation, it is nonetheless difficult for men to keep the necessary coolness to mock them well, and there is often much love in their invectives.

I have observed that it is the most affectionate men, and those who had the most feeling for women, who have treated them worse than all the others and returned to the subject with a quite unusual furious obstinacy, as if they had borne them a mortal grudge for not being as they had wished them to be, and for belying the good opinion which they had originally conceived of them.

What I wanted most of all was not physical beauty, it was beauty of soul, it was love; but love as I feel it may not be humanly possible. Yet it seems to me that I should love like this and that I should give more than I demand.

What magnificent folly! What sublime prodigality!

To abandon yourself completely and keep nothing of yourself, to renounce your independence and freewill, to put your will into someone else's hands, to see no longer through your own eyes, to hear no longer with your ears, to be only one in two bodies, to fuse and merge your souls so as no longer to know if you are one or the other, to absorb and radiate continually, to be sometimes the moon and sometimes the sun, to see all the world and all creation in a single being, to displace the centre of life, to be ready, at every moment, for the greatest sacrifices and the most complete abnegation; to suffer in the heart of the beloved, as if it were your heart; O miracle! to double yourself by giving yourself: that is love as I conceive it to be.

The fidelity of ivy, the embraces of a young vine, the cooings of a turtle-dove, these go without saying, and these are the first and simplest conditions.

If I had stayed at home, in the clothes of my own sex, sadly turning my spinning-wheel or doing my embroidery at a seat before the window, what I have sought throughout the world might have come to find me of its own accord. Love is like fortune, it doesn't want to be pursued. It prefers to visit those who sleep beside the well, and often the kisses of queens and gods are set upon closed eyes. It is a snare and a delusion to think that all adventures and felicities only exist in the places from which you are absent, and it is a mistaken calculation to have your horse saddled and go post-haste in search of your ideal. Many people make this mistake, and many more will make it. The horizon is always the most delightful blue, although, when you have reached it, the hills which form it are usually nothing but bare cracked clay, or ochres washed by the rain.

I imagined that the world was full of admirable young men, and that on the roads you would encounter populations of Esplandians, Amadises and Lancelots of the Lake in search of their Dulcineas, and I was most surprised that the world was very little concerned with this sublime quest and was content to sleep with the first available strumpet. I have been severely punished for my curiosity and my defiance. I have grown surfeited in the most dreadful possible way, without having enjoyed. In my case, knowledge preceded practice; there is nothing worse than these hasty experiences, which are not the fruit of action. The most complete ignorance would be a hundred thousand times better, it would at least make you do a good many stupid things which would serve to teach you and to rectify your ideas; for, underneath the disgust which I mentioned a moment ago, there is always a deep-rooted and refractory element which produces the strangest disorders: the mind is convinced and the body is not, and it will not accept this proud disdain. The young, robust body frets and kicks under the mind. It is as if a vigorous stallion were ridden by a feeble old man; yet it cannot throw him, because the cavesson is supporting its head, and the bit is cutting into its mouth.

Since I have lived with men, I have seen so many women infamously treated, so many secret love-affairs shamelessly divulged, the purest loves carelessly dragged in the mud, young men hastening to frightful courtesans as they leave the arms of the most charming mistresses, the most established intrigues broken suddenly and without a plausible reason, that I can no longer possibly decide to take a lover. It would be throwing oneself, in broad daylight, and with open eyes, into a bottomless abyss. Yet the secret wish of my heart is still to have one. The voice of nature drowns the voice of reason. I am quite sure that I shall never be happy unless I love and unless I am loved. The misfortune is that one can only have a man as a lover, and if men are not complete devils, they are very far from being angels. It would be no use their sticking feathers on their shoulderblades and putting gold paper haloes round their heads. I know them too well to be deceived. None of the noble speeches which they might deliver would make any difference. I know in advance what they are going to say, and I could finish it for them. I have seen them learning their parts and rehearsing them before they go on stage; I know their most dramatic tirades, and the passages they count on. Neither the pallor of the face nor the change of countenance would convince me. I know that it doesn't prove anything. One night of orgy, a few bottles of wine and two or three prostitutes are enough to make them quite conveniently unrecognizable. I have seen this trick used by a young marquis, who was very fresh and pink-cheeked by nature, and he did as well as possible with it. It was entirely due to this touching pallor, which was so well earned, that he owed the consummation of his love. I also know how the most languorous Céladons console themselves for the cruelty of their Astrées, and find the means to be patient, while they await the happy moment. I have seen the slatterns who served as understudies for the modest Ariadnes.

To tell the truth, man doesn't tempt me very much after that; for, unlike women, he has no beauty: beauty, the splendid garment which so well conceals the imperfections of the soul. That divine drapery, cast by God over the nakedness of the world, means that in a way it is forgivable to love the most despicable prostitute on the streets, if she possesses this splendid royal gift.

For want of the virtues of the soul, I should like at least the exquisite perfection of form, the gloss of flesh, the roundness of contours, the suavity of lines, the delicacy of skin, all that makes the charm of woman. Since I cannot have love, I should like to have sensual pleasure, and as far as possible to replace the brother by the sister. But all the men I have seen appear to me terribly ugly. My horse is a hundred times more beautiful, and I should find it less repugnant to kiss him than to kiss certain fops who think them-selves most charming. I certainly shouldn't find it a brilliant theme to embroider with the variations of pleasure, like a dandy or two whom I know. Nor would a soldier really suit me better; the military have something mechanical about their gait and something bestial about their faces, which makes me hardly consider them human beings; lawyers don't enchant me much more, they are dirty, oily, hirsute, shabby, with tight lips and glaucous eyes; they have an exorbitant smell of rancidness and mustiness, and I should have no wish to lay my face against their lynx's or badger's snouts. As for poets, they are not concerned with anything in the world except the endings of words, and they don't go further back than the penultimate syllable, and it's true to say that they're hard to turn to proper account; they are more boring than the others, but they are just as ugly, and – which is really strange – they haven't the least distinction or elegance in their manner and their clothes. People who busy themselves all day with form and with beauty don't notice that their boots are ill made and their hat ridiculous! They look like provincial apothecaries or unemployed tutors of performing dogs, and they would disgust you with poetry and verse for several eternities.

As for artists, they are also quite enormously stupid; they see nothing except the seven colours. One of them, with whom I'd spent several days at R—, was asked what he thought of me, and he gave this ingenious answer: 'He is quite warm in tone, and you shouldn't use white in the shadows, but Naples yellow with a little sepia and Vandyke brown.' That was his opinion; he also had a crooked nose and cross eyes, which didn't improve his work. Which shall I choose? A barrel-chested soldier, a round-shouldered lawyer, a poet or a painter with bewildered mien, a poor little coxcomb unworthy of consideration? Which cage shall I choose in this menagerie? I have no idea at all, and I don't feel any more inclination in one direction than another, for they are absolutely equal in stupidity and ugliness.

After that, there would still be something else that I could do, it would be to take someone I loved, even if it were a porter or a horse-dealer; but I don't even love a porter. O what an unhappy heroine I am! A bereaved turtle-dove, condemned to coo eternal elegies!

Oh, how often I've wished I were really a man, as I appeared to be! How many women whom I'd have understood, women whose heart would have understood my heart! Those refinements of love, those noble yearnings of pure passion which I could have answered: how perfectly happy they would have made me! What sweetness, what delights! All the sensitive plants in my soul would have flowered freely, without being forced to contract and close up all the time at some rough touch! What a delightful blossoming of invisible flowers which will never open, flowers whose mysterious perfume would have sweetly scented the fraternal soul! It seems to me that this would have been an enchanting life, a boundless ecstasy with ever-open wings; walks, ever hand-in-hand, down golden-sanded paths, through thickets of rose-trees, for ever blooming, in parks full of fish-ponds where swans were gliding, with alabaster vases standing out against the leaves.

If I had been a young man, how I should have loved Rosette! What adoration it would have been! Our souls were really made for each other, two pearls which were destined to merge together and thenceforth to be one! How perfectly I should have realized her ideas of love! Her character was absolutely right for me, and her kind of beauty pleased me. It is a pity that our love was completely condemned to an indispensable Platonism.

I have recently had an adventure.

I was visiting a house where there was a charming little girl, fifteen years old at most: I have never seen a more adorable miniature. She was fair, but of a fairness which was so delicate and so transparent that ordinary blondes would have seemed excessively brown, or as black as moles, beside her; you would have said she had golden hair powdered with silver; her eyebrows were of a hue so soft and melting that they scarcely had a visible shape; her pale-blue eyes had the most velvet look and the most silken lids that you could possibly imagine; her mouth, so small that you could not put your fingertip into it, added even more to the childlike, dainty character of her beauty, and the dimples and soft roundnesses of her cheeks had an innocent charm beyond expression. The whole of her dear little person enthralled me more than I can possibly say; I loved her frail, white, diaphanous little hands, her bird's feet which scarcely touched the ground, her waist which a breath of wind would have snapped, and her pearl shoulders, still undeveloped, happily revealed by her sash, which was put on askew. Her chatter, in which her innocence added spice to her native wit, held me for hours on end, and it gave me singular pleasure to make her talk; she said a thousand droll and delectable things, sometimes with an extraordinary subtlety of purpose, sometimes without appearing to understand their significance in the very least, which made them a thousand times more attractive.

I gave her sweets and lozenges which I kept specially for her in a pale tortoiseshell box, and this pleased her very much, because she was greedy like the little pussycat that she is. The moment I arrived, she used to run up to me and feel my pockets, to see if the blessed sweetmeat-box was there; I used to pass it from one hand to the other, and that used to start a little battle in which she always ended by getting the best of it and absolutely plundering me.

One day, however, she merely greeted me with a very serious expression, and she didn't come, as usual, to see if the fountain of sweetmeats was still flowing in my pocket; she remained haughtily on her chair, sitting up very straight, with her arms close to her sides.

'Well, Ninon!' I said to her, 'do you like salt nowadays, or are you afraid that sweets may make your teeth fall out?' And, as I spoke, I tapped against the box, which was under my coat, and it gave the sweetest, most honeyed sound in the world.

She put out her little tongue halfway, as if to savour the ideal sweetness of the absent comfit, but she didn't move.

Then I took the box out of my pocket, opened it, and began religiously to eat the pralines which she liked best of all. For a moment, her instinctive greed was stronger than her resolution; she put out her hand to take some, and immediately withdrew it, and said: 'I'm too grown-up to eat sweets!' And she sighed.

'I hadn't noticed that you'd grown up a great deal since last week; are you like the mushrooms which grow up overnight? Come here so that I can measure you.'

'You can laugh as much as you like,' she answered with a delightful pout. 'I'm not a little girl any more, and I want to be very grown-up.'

'Those are excellent resolutions, and you must persevere in them; but may we ask, my dear young lady, why these triumphant ideas have occurred to you? A week ago, you seemed to be very happy to be a little girl, and you munched your pralines without being too afraid that you might compromise your dignity.'

The young girl gave me a singular look, and glanced around her, and, when she was quite sure that no one could hear us, she leant towards me in a mysterious way, and said to me:

'I have a sweetheart.'

'It's getting serious. I'm not surprised if you don't want any more lozenges; but you were wrong not to take them, you could have played at dinner with them, or exchanged them for a shuttlecock.'

The child shrugged her shoulders disdainfully, and looked as if she really took pity on me. As she was still behaving like an insulted queen, I continued:

'What is the name of this glorious personage? Arthur, I imagine, or Henri.' These were two young boys she was in the habit of playing with, and she used to call them her husbands.

'No, it isn't Arthur or Henri,' she said, fixing her clear bright eyes on me. 'It's a man.' She raised her hand above her head to give me an idea of his height.

'As tall as that? But this is a serious matter. Who is this grown-up sweetheart, may I ask?'

'Monsieur Théodore, I'll tell you, but you mustn't talk to anyone about it, not to mama or to Polly (her governess), or to your friends, because they think I'm a child and they'd laugh at me.'

I promised her the most absolute secrecy, because I was very curious to know who this gallant personage was; and the little girl, seeing that I was making the thing into a joke, hesitated to confide in me completely.

I gave her my word of honour that I would take care not to speak. Reassured, she left her chair and came and leant over the back of mine; and very quietly, in my ear, she whispered the name of the beloved prince.

I was astounded: it was the Chevalier de G— – a filthy, boorish animal, with a schoolmaster's mind and a drum-major's physique, the most disgusting rake that it was possible to see – a proper satyr, without the goat's feet and the pointed ears. The prospect filled me with grave anxiety for my dear Ninon, and I promised myself to put a stop to it.

Some people came in, and the conversation ended.

I went into a corner, and tried to think out some means of preventing things from going further, for it would have been real murder to let such a delectable creature fall into the hands of such an arrant scoundrel.

The little girl's mother was a kind of courtesan who gave card parties and presided over a coterie of wits. You read bad verse at her house, and lost good money; which was a compensation. She had small love for her daughter, she found her a kind of living birth certificate who embarrassed her when she falsified her chronology. Besides, the child was growing rather tall, and her budding charms gave occasion for comparisons which were not to the advantage of the prototype, already a little worn by the passage of years and of men. The child was therefore rather neglected and left defenceless against the enterprise of the rascals who frequented the house. If her mother had been concerned with her, it would probably just have been to turn her youth to good account and to exploit her beauty and her innocence. Whatever happened, there was no doubt what fate awaited her. This pained me, for she was a delightful little girl who certainly deserved better, a pearl of the finest water lost in this foul sink of vice; the thought so moved me that I resolved to get her out of this fearful house whatever the cost.

The first thing to do was to prevent the chevalier from continuing his advances. The best and simplest thing, it seemed to me, was to pick a quarrel with him and make him fight me, and I had all the trouble in the world, because he is cowardly in the extreme, and more afraid of sword-wounds than anyone else in existence. In the end I insulted him so much and so bitterly that he was simply compelled to come to the duelling-ground, although he did so much against his will. I even threatened to have him thrashed by my lackey, if he didn't put a better face on it. In fact, he was quite a good swordsman, but he was so frightened that we had hardly crossed swords before I found the means of giving him a nice little wound which sent him to bed for a fortnight. That was enough for me; I didn't want to kill him, and I was quite as glad to let him live so that he could be hanged later on. A touching thought for which he should have shown me more gratitude! Once my villain was laid between two sheets, and duly tied up with bandages, all I had to do was to persuade the little girl to leave the house, which was not excessively difficult.

I told her a story about the disappearance of her sweetheart, for she was uncommonly anxious about him. I told her that he had gone off with an actress from the company which was then performing at C—; this made her indignant, as you can imagine. But I consoled her by saying all sorts of bad things about the chevalier, who was ugly, a drunkard, and already old, and I ended by asking her if she wouldn't rather have me as her gallant. She said that she would indeed prefer to have me, because I was more handsome, and my clothes were new. This innocent remark was made with enormous gravity, and it made me laugh till I cried. I worked up the child to such an extent that I persuaded her to leave the house. A few bouquets, about the same number of kisses, and a string of pearls which I gave her enchanted her to a degree which is difficult to describe, and, in front of the little girls she knew, she assumed an air of importance which could not have been more amusing.

I had a page's costume, very elegant and rich, made to about her size, for I couldn't take her away in her girl's clothes unless I put on my woman's clothes again, which I didn't want to do. I bought a docile little horse, easy to ride, and yet a good enough courser to follow my Barbary horse when I wanted to go fast. Then I told the young girl to come down to the door at dusk, and I told her I should fetch her there. She came down very punctually. I found her on the watch behind the half-open door. I passed very close to the house; she came out, I gave her my hand, she rested her foot on the tip of mine and sprang up very nimbly behind me, for she had wonderful agility. I spurred on my horse and taking seven or eight deserted little by-roads, I managed to return home without anybody seeing us.

I made her take off her clothes to put on her disguise, and I myself served as her lady's maid; she resisted a little, at first, and wanted to get dressed by herself; but I explained that it would lose us a lot of time, and that, besides, as she was my mistress, there was no objection to it, and that it was a common custom between lovers.

She didn't need much convincing, and she submitted with the best grace in the world.

Her body was a little marvel of delicacy. Her arms were rather thin, like those of any young girl, and they had an inexpressible suavity of line. Her budding breasts gave such charming promises that no fuller breasts could have borne comparison. She still had all the graces of the child, she already had all the charm of the woman; she had reached that adorable moment of transition from the little girl to the young girl: a fugitive, imperceptible moment, a delightful time when beauty is full of hope, and every day, instead of taking something from your love, adds new perfections to it.

Her costume couldn't have suited her better. It gave her a slight air of rebellion, which was most curious and most amusing, and made her laugh heartily when I gave her a mirror so that she could see the effect of her dress. Then I made her eat a few biscuits dipped in madeira, to give her courage and make her better able to bear the fatigue of the journey.

The horses were already saddled, and waiting in the courtyard; she mounted hers quite purposefully, I bestrode the other, and we set off. Night had completely fallen, and occasional lights, which went out from one moment to the next, showed that the worthy town of C— was virtuously occupied as every provincial town should be on the stroke of nine.

We couldn't go very fast, for Ninon was not the most accomplished of horsewomen, and, when her horse began to trot, she clung to its mane with all her might. However, next morning we were so far away that no one could have caught us up unless they made the utmost possible haste; but no one followed us, or, at least, if they did so, it was in the opposite direction to the one which we had taken.

I was singularly attached to the lovely child. I no longer had you with me, my dear Graciosa, and I felt an enormous need to love somebody or something, to have a dog or a child with me, something to caress familiarly. Ninon was this for me; she slept in my bed, and she put her little arms round my body when she went to sleep; she quite seriously believed that she was my mistress, and she did not doubt that I was a man; her great youth and her extreme innocence kept her in this error, and I took care not to correct her. The kisses I gave her completed her illusion perfectly, for her ideas didn't go beyond them, and her desires didn't speak loudly enough to make her suspect anything else. Anyway, she was only half mistaken.

And, really, there was between her and me the same difference that there is between me and men. She was so diaphanous, so slight, so small, her nature was so sensitive and rare, that she is a woman even for me, although I am a woman, and I seem like a Hercules beside her. I am tall and dark-haired, she is small and fair; her features are so delicate that they make mine seem almost harsh and austere; her voice is so melodious a murmur that my voice seems hard beside it. Any man who had her would break her in pieces, and I'm always afraid that one fine day the wind may bear her away. I should like to shut her up in a box lined with cottonwool and carry her about, hung round my neck. My dear girl, you can't imagine how much grace and wit she has, what delightful winning ways, what endearing childlike conduct, what pretty gestures and disarming manners. She is indeed the most adorable creature in existence, and it would really have been a pity if she had stayed with her worthless mother.

I took a malicious pleasure in thus concealing this treasure from the rapacity of men. I was the griffon which stopped them from approaching it, and, if I didn't enjoy it myself, at least no one else enjoyed it: a thought which is always consoling, whatever all the fools who slander egoism may say.

I intended to keep her as long as possible in her state of ignorance, and to keep her until she no longer wanted to stay with me, or I had been able to assure her future.

I took her, dressed as a young boy, on all my travels, wherever I went; this kind of life gave her singular satisfaction, and the pleasure she took in it helped her to bear the fatigue which it sometimes caused her. Everywhere I went, people paid me compliments on the exquisite beauty of my page, and I've no doubt that he often made them think what was exactly the opposite of the truth. Several people even tried to enlighten themselves, but I didn't let the little creature talk to anyone, and those who were inquisitive were completely disappointed.

Every day I discovered some new quality in the dear child which made me cherish her still more and congratulate myself on the decision which I had taken. Certainly men were not worthy to possess her, and it would have been deplorable that so many charms of body and soul should have been abandoned to their brutal appetites and their cynical depravity.

Only a woman could love her with enough delicacy and tenderness. There is a certain side of my character which could not have developed in another liaison, and it completely came to light in this one. I need and want to protect, which is usually the man's concern. I should have been extremely displeased if I'd had a lover and he had appeared to look after me, for this is an attention which I myself like to pay to those who please me, and my pride is much better satisfied in the first rôle than the second, although the second is more agreeable. And so I felt happy to give my dear little girl all the attentions which I ought to have liked to receive, such as helping her on an awkward path, holding her bridle and stirrup for her, serving her at table, undressing her and putting her to bed, defending her if someone insulted her, in short by doing for her all that the most impassioned and attentive lover does for a mistress whom he adores.

I was imperceptibly losing the idea of my sex, and I hardly remembered, at long intervals, that I was a woman; at the beginning, I'd often let slip some phrase or other which didn't fit in with the male attire that I was wearing. Nowadays this doesn't happen any more, and even when I'm writing to you – and I have entrusted you with my secret – I sometimes keep my adjectives unnecessarily masculine. If ever the fancy takes me to go and find my skirts again in the drawer where I left them, which I very much doubt, unless I fall in love with some young beau, I shall find it hard to lose this habit, and, instead of a woman disguised as a man, I shall look like a man disguised as a woman. In truth, neither sex is really mine; I don't have the foolish submissiveness, the timidity or the pettiness of the woman; I don't have the vices of men, their disgusting debauchery and their brutal tendencies. I belong to a third sex, a sex apart, which has as yet no name: higher or lower, inferior or superior; I have the body and soul of a woman, the spirit and the strength of a man, and I have too much or too little of either to be able to couple with the other.

O Graciosa! I shall never be able to love anyone completely, man or woman; something unfulfilled still cries out within me, and the lover or the mistress satisfies only one side of my nature. If I had a lover, what is feminine in me would no doubt dominate for a time what is masculine, but that wouldn't last long, and I feel that I should be only half contented; if I have a mistress, the idea of physical pleasure will not let me completely enjoy the pure pleasure of the soul; and so I don't know where to turn, and I drift perpetually from one to the other.

My dream would be to have each sex in turn, and to satisfy my dual nature: man today, woman tomorrow. I should keep for my lovers my languorous tenderness, my submissive and devoted ways, my gentlest caresses, my long drawn-out and melancholy sighs, all the feline and the feminine in my nature; then, with my mistresses, I should be enterprising, bold and impassioned, with a triumphant air, my hat at a rakish angle, the air of a captain and adventurer. My nature would then be completely fulfilled, and I should be perfectly happy, for true happiness is to be able to develop freely in all directions and to be everything that you can be.

But such things are impossible, and one mustn't think of them.

I had carried off the little girl with the idea of misleading my inclinations, and concentrating on one person all this vague tenderness which is overflowing from my soul; I had taken her as a kind of escape for my aptitude for love; but I soon recognized, in spite of all the affection I bore her, what a boundless void, what a bottomless abyss she left in my heart, how little pleasure I derived from her most affectionate caress! . . . I determined to try a lover, but it was a long time before I encountered someone who did not displease me. I forgot to tell you that when Rosette discovered where I'd gone, she wrote to me, and begged and implored me to go back and see her; I couldn't refuse her, and I went to join her on the country estate where she was living. I have since returned there several times, and, indeed, quite recently. Rosette had been in despair that she hadn't had me as a lover, and she had thrown herself into the vortex of society and into dissipation. She was like all tender souls who are not religious and who have been disappointed in first love. She had had many adventures in a brief space of time, and the list of her conquests was already long, for not everyone had the same reasons as I had for resisting her.

She had with her a young man called d'Albert, who was, for the time being, her lover-in-waiting. I seemed to make a very special impression upon him, and from the very first he felt the most ardent friendship for me.

Though he treated her with much respect, and his manner with her was really quite affectionate, he didn't love Rosette – not because of satiety or disgust, but rather because she did not accord with certain ideas of beauty which he had conceived. An ideal cloud interposed itself between them, and prevented him from being happy as he should otherwise have been. His dream was evidently unfulfilled, and he was yearning for something else. But he was not seeking it, and he was still faithful to the bonds which weighed upon him; for he has in his soul a little more honour and delicacy than the majority of mankind, and his heart is far from being as corrupt as his mind. He did not know that Rosette had never been in love, except with me, and that she was so, still, in spite of all her intrigues and follies, and he was afraid to hurt her by letting her see that he did not love her. This consideration held him back, and he sacrificed himself in the most generous way in the world.

The character of my features gave him extraordinary pleasure, for he attaches extreme importance to the outward form, so much so that he fell in love with me, despite my male attire and the formidable rapier at my side. I confess that I was grateful to him for the shrewdness of his instinct, and that I felt a certain esteem for him for having recognized what I was under my deceptive appearance. At the beginning, he thought he was endowed with a taste much more depraved than in fact it was, and I laughed inside myself to see him so tormented. Sometimes, when he approached me, he had a frightened look which I found extremely diverting, and the very natural instinct which drew him towards me seemed to him a diabolical impulse which should have been resisted to the death. On these occasions, he fell back in a fury on Rosette, and struggled to resume more orthodox ways of love; then he returned to me, as was natural, more passionate than ever. Then the luminous idea that I might well be a woman slipped into his mind. In order to convince himself, he began to watch and study me with the most minute attention; he must be aware of every hair of my head and know exactly how many lashes I have on my eyelids; my feet, my hands, my neck, my cheeks, the slightest down at the corners of my mouth: he has examined, compared and analysed it all, and from this investigation, in which the artist helped the lover, it has emerged, as clear as day (when it is clear), that I am well and truly a woman, and, moreover, his ideal, his type of beauty, the realization of his dream. What a wonderful discovery!

It only remained to touch my heart and to have the gift of loving gratitude bestowed on him – to authenticate my sex completely. A play which we were performing, in which I appeared as a woman, decided him at last. I gave him a few equivocal glances, and used a few passages in my part, which resembled our situation, to embolden him and compel him to declare himself. For, if I did not love him with passion, he pleased me enough for me not to let him pine away with love; and as he had been the first since my transformation to suspect that I was a woman, it was only fair that I should enlighten him on this important point, and I was resolved to leave him with no shadow of doubt.

He came to my room several times with his declaration on his lips, but he did not dare to utter it; for, in fact, it is difficult to speak of love to someone who has the same male attire as yourself, and somebody who wears riding-boots. At last, unable to bring himself to speak, he wrote me a long and very Pindaric letter, in which he explained to me at great length what I knew better than he did.

I'm not too sure what I ought to do. Agree to his request, or reject it – that would be excessively virtuous; but he would be too deeply grieved to see himself refused. If we make the people who love us unhappy, what shall we do to those who detest us? Perhaps it would be more strictly correct to play hard-hearted for a while, and to wait for at least a month before one undid the tiger-skin and put on a chemise like a human being. But, since I have resolved to surrender to him, I might as well do so at once as later on; I don't really understand these noble resistances, mathematically graduated, which cede one hand today, the other tomorrow, then a foot, then the leg and knee only as far as the garter; I don't understand those intractable virtues which are always ready to tug at the bell-pull if you exceed by a fraction the ground that they have decided to yield today. It makes me laugh to see those methodical Lucretias who retire with the signs of the most virginal alarm, and from time to time cast a fugitive glance over their shoulder to assure themselves that the sofa they will fall on is exactly behind them. That is a precaution I couldn't take.

I don't love d'Albert, at least in the sense that I understand the word, but I certainly have a liking and an inclination for him; his mind pleases me and his person doesn't repel me; there aren't many men of whom I could say as much. He hasn't got everything, but he has something; what pleases me most about him is that he doesn't try to satisfy himself in a brutal way, like other men; he has a constant aspiration, an ever-present yearning for beauty: for material beauty alone, it's true, but it is still a noble inclination, and it's enough to keep him in the realm of purity. His behaviour with Rosette proves his integrity of heart, an integrity which is more rare than the other, if that is possible.

And then, I must confess to you, I am possessed by the most violent longings, I am pining and dying with desire; for the clothes I wear engage me in all sorts of adventures with women, but they protect me too completely against the enterprise of men; an idea of pleasure which is never realized is floating vaguely in my mind, and this dull and colourless dream tires and vexes me. So many women, in the purest of surroundings, lead the lives of prostitutes! And, by a rather ridiculous contrast, I remain as chaste and virginal as the cold Diana herself, in the midst of the most widespread dissipation and among the greatest rakes of the century. This ignorance of the body without the ignorance of the mind is the most miserable thing there is. I don't want my flesh to put on proud airs in front of my soul, I want to defile it as well, if indeed it is more of a defilement than eating and drinking – which I doubt. In short, I want to know what a man is, and what pleasure he gives. Since d'Albert has recognized me under my disguise, it is only fair that he should be rewarded for his discernment; he is the first to have guessed that I was a woman, and I shall do my best to prove to him that his suspicions were justified. It wouldn't be very kind to let him believe that he has just had a monstrous inclination.

So it is d'Albert who will resolve my doubts and give me my first lesson in love; all that remains now is to contrive things in a really poetical way. I should like not to answer his letter and to look on him coldly for a few days. When I see him really sad and really desperate, reviling the gods, and shaking his fist at creation, and looking at wells to make sure that they're not too deep for him to throw himself into them – then I shall retire like Peau-d'Âne to the end of the corridor, and I shall put on my dress of shot material – that is to say the costume that I wore as Rosalind; for my feminine wardrobe is very restricted. Then I shall go to him, radiant like a strutting peacock, ostentatiously showing what I usually hide with the greatest care; and, wearing only a little lace tucker, very loose and low, I shall say to him in the most moving tone I know:

'O most elegiac, most perspicacious young man! I am indeed a young and chaste and beautiful woman, who adores you into the bargain, and only asks to give you pleasure and give herself pleasure, too. See if that suits you, and if you still have some hesitation, touch this, go in peace, and sin as much as you can.'

After this fine speech, I shall fall half-swooning into his arms, and, as I utter melancholy sighs, I shall deftly unhook my bodice, so as to be in the necessary dress, in other words half naked. D'Albert will do the rest, and I hope that, next morning, I'll know what to make of all those fine things which have been perplexing me for so long. I shall content my curiosity and I shall also have the pleasure of making one person happy.

I also propose to go and pay a visit to Rosette in the same attire, and to show her that, if I haven't responded to her love, it was not out of coldness or disgust. I don't want her to keep this bad opinion of me, and she deserves, as much as d'Albert, that I should betray my incognito for her. How will she countenance this revelation? Her pride will be consoled, but her love will suffer.

Farewell, all-good and all-beautiful; ask the good Lord to grant that pleasure doesn't seem as trivial to me as those who dispense it. I have joked throughout this letter, and yet what I'm going to attempt is a serious matter, and I may feel its effects for the rest of my life.

XVI

It was already more than a fortnight since d'Albert had deposited his love-letter on Théodore's table – and yet nothing seemed to have changed in the latter's manner. D'Albert didn't know how to explain this silence; you would have said that Théodore had no knowledge of the letter; the wretched d'Albert thought that it had gone astray, or been lost; and yet the thing was difficult to explain, for Théodore had gone back to his room a moment later, and it would have been most extraordinary if he hadn't seen a large sheet of paper set all by itself in the middle of the table, in such a way as to attract the most inattentive glance.

Or was it that Théodore was really a man and not a woman at all, as d'Albert had imagined? Or, if she were a woman, did she have such a feeling of aversion for him, such contempt that she did not even deign to take the trouble to answer him? The poor young man had not had the advantage that we've had, and rummaged through the pocket-book which belonged to Graciosa, the confidante of the beautiful Maupin. He was in no position to answer any of these important questions, in the affirmative or the negative, and he wavered wretchedly in the most miserable irresolution.

One evening, he was in his room, his brow sadly pressed against the window-pane, and looking, without seeing them, at the chestnut-trees in the park. They were already tinged with red, and shedding their leaves. A thick mist hid the distance, night was falling, grey rather than black, and carefully setting its velvet feet on the tops of the trees; a big swan was lovingly plunging its neck and shoulders, again and again, in the misty water of the river, and its whiteness made it seem like a big star of snow in the darkness. It was the only living creature which gave a little life to the sombre landscape.

D'Albert was dreaming as sadly as a disappointed man can dream at five o'clock in the evening, in autumn, in misty weather, when he has a rather sharp cold wind for his music, and his vista is the skeleton of a forest without peruke.

He was thinking of throwing himself in the river, but the water seemed to him very black and very cold, and the example of the swan only half persuaded him; he thought of blowing out his brains, but he had no pistol or gunpowder, and he would have been vexed if he'd had them. He thought of taking a new mistress and even of taking two, which was a sinister resolution! He carried despair so far that he wanted to resume relations with women whom he found absolutely unbearable, and had had driven out of his house, with a whip, by his lackey. He finally decided on something much more dreadful . . . to write a second letter.

O sixfold fool!

He had reached this point in his meditation when he felt a hand on his shoulder – like a little dove alighting on a palm-tree. There's a hitch in the comparison since d'Albert's shoulder bore only a slight resemblance to a palm-tree; that doesn't matter, we'll keep it out of pure Orientalism.

The hand was joined to the end of an arm which belonged to a shoulder which was part of a body which belonged to none other than Théodore–Rosalind, Mademoiselle d'Aubigny, or Madelaine de Maupin, to give her her proper name.

Who was surprised? Not you or I, for you and I have long since been prepared for this visit; it was d'Albert, who wasn't expecting it in the very least. He uttered a little cry of surprise somewhere between 'oh!' and 'ah!' However, I have the best reasons for thinking that it was nearer 'ah!' than 'oh!'

It was indeed Rosalind, so beautiful and radiant that she lit up the whole room, – with her ropes of pearls in her hair, her prismatic dress, her great frills of lace, her slippers with red heels, her fine fan of peacock feathers, just in fact as she had been on the day of the performance. Only, an important and decisive difference, she had no ruff, or tucker, or neckerchief or anything at all which hid from sight those two charming fraternal foes – which, alas, tend all too often to be reconciled.

337

An entirely naked bosom, white, transparent, like an antique marble, of the purest and most exquisite shape, boldly emerged from a very open bodice, and seemed to offer a challenge to a kiss. It was a most reassuring sight; and d'Albert reassured himself with the utmost speed, and abandoned himself in all confidence to his wildest emotions.

'Well, Orlando, don't you recognize your Rosalind?' said the fair lady with the most charming smile. 'Or have you left your love hung up with your sonnets on some bushes in the Forest of Arden? Are you really cured of the malady which you so earnestly asked me to cure? I am much afraid that you are.'

'Oh, no, Rosalind, I am suffering more than ever. I am in agony, I'm dead, or very nearly!'

'You're not in too bad a shape for a corpse, and many living people don't look so well.'

'What a week I've had! You can't imagine it, Rosalind. I hope it will be worth at least a thousand years of purgatory to me in the other world. But dare I ask you why you didn't reply to me sooner?'

'Why? I'm not quite sure, unless it's just because. However, if this reason doesn't seem to be valid to you, here are three others which are much less good; you can choose: in the first place because you were carried away by your passion and you forgot to write legibly, and it took me more than a week to guess what your letter was about; and then because my modesty couldn't accustom itself in a shorter time to such a far-fetched idea as taking a dithyrambic poet as a lover; and then because it gave me some pleasure to see whether you would blow your brains out or poison yourself with opium, or if you would hang yourself with your garter. There you are.'

'Malicious wit! Let me assure you that you've done well to come today, you probably wouldn't have found me tomorrow.'

'Really! Poor young man! Don't look so disconsolate, or I should grow maudlin, too, and that would make me a dumber creature than any of the animals which were in the Ark, with the late lamented Noah. If I once unplug my sensibility, you will be submerged, I warn you. A moment ago I gave you three bad reasons, now I shall offer you three good kisses. Do you accept, on condition that you'll forget the reasons for the kisses? I really owe you that and more.'

As she said these words, the beautiful infanta went up to the plaintive suitor, and threw her lovely arms round his neck. D'Albert kissed her effusively on both cheeks and on the mouth. This last kiss lasted longer than the others, and it might have counted as four. Rosalind saw that all she had done until then was mere child's play. Having paid her debt, she sat on d'Albert's lap – he was still much affected – and, passing her fingers through his hair, she said to him:

'All my cruelties are over and done with, my dear one; I had taken that fortnight to satisfy my natural ferocity; I confess that it seemed a long time to me. Don't become vain because I am frank, but that is true. I put myself into your hands, take revenge for my past unkindness. If you were a fool, I shouldn't say that to you, indeed I shouldn't say anything else to you, because I don't like fools. It would have been very easy for me to make you believe that I was prodigiously shocked by your boldness, and that all your Platonic sighs and your most quintessential gibberish wouldn't have been enough to make me forgive you for something which gave me great pleasure; I could, like other people, have been irresolute for a long while and given you piecemeal what I grant you freely and all at once; but I don't think that you would have loved me a single hair's breadth the more. I am not asking you for a vow of eternal love, or for some excessive effusion. Love me as long as the good God wills it so. I shan't call you treacherous and a wretch when you no longer love me. You will also be kind enough to spare me the corresponding odious epithets, if I happen to leave you. I shall only be a woman who has ceased to love you – that's all. It isn't necessary to hate one another for life, because one has spent a night or two together. Whatever happens, and wherever destiny impels me, I promise you, and this is a promise that can be kept, that I shall always keep a charming memory of you, and, if I am no longer your mistress, I shall be your friend as

I have been your companion. For you, tonight, I have abandoned my male attire; tomorrow I shall put it on again for everyone. Remember that I am Rosalind only at night, and that all day I am and can only be Théodore de Sérannes . . .'

The sentence that she was about to utter was put out by a kiss, which was followed by many others. These were no longer counted, and we shan't make an accurate catalogue of them, because it would certainly be rather long and perhaps very immoral – for certain people – for we ourselves find nothing more moral or more sacred in the world than the caresses of man and woman, when both of them are beautiful and young.

As d'Albert's entreaties became more tender and more urgent, Théodore's beautiful face did not light up and shine, instead it took on an expression of proud melancholy which gave some anxiety to her lover.

'Why, my dear sovereign, do you look chaste and serious like some antique Diana? You should have the smile of Venus as she emerges from the sea.'

'You see, d'Albert, it's because I'm more like Diana the huntress than anything else. When I was very young I put on this male attire for reasons which I needn't tell you, reasons which would take a long time to explain. You alone have guessed my sex – and, if I have made conquests, it has only been conquests of women, completely superfluous conquests which have more than once embarrassed me. In short, although it's incredible and ridiculous, I'm a virgin – as virgin as the snow of the Himalayas, the Moon before she had slept with Endymion, or Mary before she had known the dove from heaven, and I feel solemn like anyone who is about to do something irreversible. It is a metamorphosis, a transformation which I am about to undergo. To change the name of a girl for the name of a woman, no longer to possess to give tomorrow what I had yesterday; something which I didn't know and am about to learn, an important page turned in the book of life. That is why I look sad, my dear, and it is not your fault in the least.' As she said this, she parted the young man's long hair with her two lovely hands, and set her gently pursed lips on his brow.

D'Albert, singularly moved by the sweet and solemn tone in which she had recited all this speech, took her hands and kissed all her fingers, one after the other – then very delicately broke the ties of her dress, so that her bodice opened and the two white treasures appeared in all their splendour. On this breast as bright and gleaming as silver there burgeoned the two lovely roses of paradise. He lightly pressed their vermilion tips between his lips, and then he kissed all round them. Rosalind was endlessly obliging, and did not resist – and she tried to return his caresses as faithfully as possible.

'You must find me very clumsy and cold, my poor d'Albert; but I hardly know how to set about it: you will have a great deal to teach me, and I am really giving you a very tedious task.'

D'Albert gave the simplest answer, he didn't answer; and, embracing her more passionately than ever, he covered her bare shoulders and breasts with kisses. The hair of the half-swooning infanta fell about her shoulders, and her dress, as if by enchantment, fell to her feet. She remained standing like a white apparition in a plain shift of the most transparent kind. The happy lover went down on his knees, and had soon thrown the two pretty shoes with red heels into opposite corners of the room; the stockings with embroidered clocks closely followed them.

The shift, endowed with a happy spirit of imitation, quickly went the same way as the dress. To begin with, it slipped from the shoulders, and no one thought of holding it back; then, taking advantage of a moment when the arms were perpendicular, it worked its way out very skilfully and slid down to the hips, whose curving lines half stopped it. At this point Rosalind observed the treachery of her one remaining garment, and raised her knee a little to prevent it from falling to the ground. In this pose, she looked exactly like those marble statues of goddesses, where the intelligent drapery, displeased at hiding so many charms, regretfully envelops the lovely thighs, and, by a fortunate betrayal, stops exactly below the place which it is intended to conceal. But, as the shift was not made of marble and its folds did not hold it up, it continued its triumphal descent, completely subsided on to the dress, and curled itself round its mistress's feet like a big white greyhound.

There was undoubtedly a very simple way of preventing all this disorder, that of holding the fugitive back with the hand. This idea, very natural though it was, did not occur to our chaste heroine.

She remained, then, without any veil, with her fallen clothes making her a kind of plinth, in all the diaphanous brilliance of her lovely nakedness, in the gentle light of an alabaster lamp which d'Albert had lit.

D'Albert, dazzled, gazed on her in rapture.

'I'm cold,' she said, folding her arms.

'Oh, for mercy's sake, a minute more!'

Rosalind unfolded her arms, put a fingertip on the back of a chair and remained motionless; she had slightly turned, to bring into relief all the opulence of the curving line; she did not seem in the least embarrassed, and the imperceptible pink in her cheeks was not a shade deeper: only the rather fast beating of her heart sent a tremor round the contour of her left breast.

The young enthusiast for beauty could not gaze enough at such a sight. We have to say, to the great credit of Rosalind, that this time reality surpassed his dream, and he didn't feel the slightest disappointment.

Everything was united in the lovely body that posed before him: delicacy and strength, form and colour, the lines of a Greek statue of the best period and the tone of a Titian. He saw there, tangible and crystallized, the cloudy dream which he had tried, so often, and in vain, to catch in flight. He was not forced, as he complained so bitterly to his friend Silvio, to limit his attention to a certain part that was quite well made, and not to go beyond it, at the risk of seeing something fearful, and his loving eyes went down from the head to the feet, and rose up again from the feet to the head, always gently caressed by a form which was harmonious and correct.

The knees were wonderfully pure, the ankles elegant and slim, the legs and thighs proud and superb in shape, the belly sleek as agate, and the bosom enough to make the gods descend from heaven to kiss it, the arms and shoulders had the most magnificent distinction; a torrent of beautiful brown hair, slightly crimped, such as you see in portraits by old masters, fell in little waves down an ivory back and marvellously emphasized its whiteness.

The painter had been satisfied, the lover once again was uppermost; for, however much you may love art, there are certain things which you cannot simply look at for long.

He picked the fair lady up in his arms and carried her to the bed; in a trice he had undressed and flown to her side.

The young maiden embraced him tightly and held him close to her, for her breasts were not only as white but as cold as snow. This chill of the skin made d'Albert burn still more, and excited him to the highest degree. The fair lady was soon as warm as he was. He gave her the wildest and the most ardent caresses. Bosom, shoulders, neck and mouth, arms and legs; he would have liked to cover it all in a single kiss: all this lovely body which almost merged into his own, so intimately did they embrace. In this profusion of delightful treasures, he didn't know which to attain.

They no longer separated their kisses, and the sweet lips of Rosalind were just one mouth, now, with d'Albert's; their bosoms heaved, their eyes half closed; their arms, lifeless from pleasure, no longer had the strength for an embrace. The divine moment was approaching: a final obstacle was overcome, an ultimate spasm moved both lovers convulsively – and the inquisitive Rosalind was as enlightened as she could be about this obscure point which so troubled her.

But as a single lesson cannot suffice, however intelligent one may be, d'Albert gave her a second, then a third . . . For the sake of the reader, whom we won't humiliate and drive to despair, we shan't continue our narrative any further. . . .

Our fair lady reader would certainly be sulky with her lover, if we let her know the formidable total which d'Albert reached in love, assisted by Rosalind's curiosity. Let our fair reader recall her best-employed and most delightful night, that night when . . . that night which one would recall for more than a hundred thousand days, if one had not long since died; let her put the book down beside her, and calculate how many times she was loved by the man who loved her the most. In this way she may fill the gap which we have left in this glorious history.

Rosalind had prodigious aptitudes, and on this one night she made enormous progress. This bodily innocence which was surprised by everything, this mental cunning which was not surprised by anything, made the most piquant and the most adorable contrast. D'Albert was delighted, excited, enraptured, and he would have liked this night to last for forty-eight hours, like the night when Hercules was conceived. However, towards morning, despite an infinity of kisses and caresses and pretty ways of the most amorous possible kind, which were well suited to keep him awake after a superhuman effort, he was compelled to take a little rest. A sweet and voluptuous sleep touched his eyes with the tip of its wing, his head sank down, and he fell asleep between the breasts of his beautiful mistress. The latter considered him for some time with an air of melancholy and profound reflection; then, as the dawn cast its whitish rays through the curtains, she gently lifted him up, set him down beside her, got up, and nimbly stepped over his body.

She picked up her clothes and dressed, leant over d'Albert, who was still asleep, and kissed the long and silky lashes on the eyelids. After which she went out, backwards, still looking at him.

Instead of going back to her room, she went to Rosette's. What she said there, what she did there, I have never been able to discover, although I have done the most diligent research. I have found nothing in Graciosa's papers, or in d'Albert's, or in Silvio's, which related to this visit. But a chambermaid of Rosette's informed me of this singular circumstance: although her mistress hadn't slept with her lover that night, the bed was rumpled and disturbed, and it bore the imprint of two bodies. What is more, she showed me two pearls, exactly like the ones which Théodore had worn in his hair when he played the part of Rosalind. She had found them in the bed when she made it. I confide this observation to the sagacity of the reader, and I leave him free to draw whatever conclusions he likes from it; as for me, I've made a thousand conjectures about it, each more preposterous than the other, and so far-fetched that I really don't dare to write them down, even in the most suitable periphrased style.

It was well after noon when Théodore left Rosette's room. He didn't appear at dinner or at supper. D'Albert and Rosette didn't seem in the least surprised. He went to bed very early, and next morning, at dawn, without warning anyone, he saddled his horse and his page's, and left the château, telling a lackey that they shouldn't expect him for dinner, and that he might not come back at all for some days.

D'Albert and Rosette were as surprised as they could be, and didn't know how to explain this strange disappearance: especially d'Albert who, by his prowess on the first night, considered that he had really deserved a second. Towards the end of the week, the unhappy disappointed lover received a letter from Théodore, which we shall transcribe. I am much afraid that it may not satisfy my readers; but in point of fact the letter went like this, and not in any other way, and this glorious novel will have no other conclusion.

XVII

You are no doubt very surprised, my dear d'Albert, by what I have just done after what I did. I understand, you have good reason. I'll wager that you've already given me at least a score of those epithets which we agreed to cross out of our vocabulary: perfidious, unfaithful, villainous – aren't I right? At least, you won't call me cruel or virtuous, and that's always an advantage. You're cursing me, and you are wrong. You wanted me, you loved me. I was your ideal; well and good. I granted you immediately what you were asking; it had only depended on you to have had it sooner. I served to embody your dream in the most obliging manner in the world. I gave you what I shall certainly not give to anyone else, a surprise on which you were hardly counting and for which you should be grateful to me. Now that I have satisfied you, I choose to depart. What is so monstrous about it?

You have had me completely and without reserve for a whole night; what more do you want? Another night, and then yet another; you would even accommodate days, should the need arise. You would go on like this until you were weary of me. I can hear you exclaim, most gallantly, from where I am, that I am not one of the women you tire of. My God, I am! You would tire of me, as you've tired of the rest.

It would last six months, two years, even ten years, if you like, but everything must always have an end. You would keep me out of a sort of sense of propriety, or because you wouldn't be brave enough to discard me. What is the use of waiting for that moment?

And then, it might be I who ceased to love you. I found you charming; perhaps, by dint of seeing you, I should have found you hateful. Forgive me for this supposition. If I had lived very intimately with you, I should no doubt have had occasion to see you

346

in a cotton nightcap or in some ridiculous or comical domestic situation. You would of necessity have lost that romantic and mysterious aspect which seduces me more than anything else, and your character, when I understood it better, would no longer have seemed so strange to me. I should have been less concerned with you when you were beside me, rather as one is with those books which one never opens because one has them in the library. Your nose or your wit would no longer have seemed anything like so well turned; I should have noticed that you coat didn't suit you and that your stockings were wrinkled; I should have had a thousand disappointments of this kind which would have given me singular pain, and in the end I should have reached this conclusion: that you certainly had no heart or soul, and that I was destined not to be understood in love.

You adore me and I reciprocate. You haven't the slightest reproach to make to me, and I have no reason in the world to complain of you. I was perfectly faithful to you all the time that we loved, I haven't deceived you in anything. I didn't have a false bosom or a false virtue; you were so extremely kind as to say that I was even more beautiful than you had imagined. In exchange for the beauty I gave you, you gave me much pleasure; we are quits. I am going on my way, and you on yours, and perhaps we shall meet again in the antipodes. Live in that hope.

Perhaps you believe that I don't love you because I am leaving you. You will later recognize the truth of this. If I had cared about you less, I should have stayed, and I should have poured you out the insipid drink to the dregs. Your love would soon have died of boredom; after a little while, you would have forgotten me completely, and, when you read my name again on your list of conquests, you'd have asked yourself: 'Now who the devil was that?' I have at least the satisfaction of thinking that you will remember me rather than someone else. Your unassuaged desire will still open its wings to fly to me; I shall always be for you something desirable, to which your fancy loves to return, and I hope that in the beds of the mistresses whom you may have, you will sometimes dream of the single night that you spent with me.

You will never be more lovable than you were on that blissful evening, and, even if you were as lovable, you would already be less so; for in love, as in poetry, staying still means falling back. Be content with this impression – you would be wise.

You have made it difficult for the lovers I shall have (if I have other lovers), and no one will be able to surpass my memory of you; they will be the heirs of Alexander.

If you are too desolate at losing me, burn this letter, which is the only proof that you have had me, and you will think that you have had a beautiful dream. What is preventing you? The vision faded before the dawn, at the hour when fantasies go home through the gates of horn or ivory. How many have died, less fortunate than you, who have not even kissed their ideal!

I am not capricious, or mad, or a prude. What I am doing is the result of deep conviction. It isn't to inflame you more, or by some coquettish calculation, that I've left C—; don't try to follow me or find me again: you won't succeed. I have taken too many precautions to hide my tracks from you; for me you will always be the man who opened a world of new sensations for me. Those are things which a woman doesn't easily forget. Though I am absent, I shall often think of you, more often than if you were with me.

Console poor Rosette as well as you can; she must be at least as vexed as you are at my departure. Love one another well in memory of me, whom you have both loved. and sometimes speak my name in a kiss.

MORE ABOUT PENGUINS
AND PELICANS

For further information about books available from Penguins please write to Dept EP, Penguin Books Ltd, Harmondsworth, Middlesex UB7 0DA.

In the U.S.A.: For a complete list of books available from Penguins in the United States write to Dept CS, Penguin Books, 625 Madison Avenue, New York, New York 10022.

In Canada: For a complete list of books available from Penguins in Canada write to Penguin Books Canada Ltd, 2801 John Street, Markham, Ontario L3R 1B4.

In Australia: For a complete list of books available from Penguins in Australia write to the Marketing Department, Penguin Books Australia Ltd, P.O. Box 257, Ringwood, Victoria 3134.

In New Zealand: For a complete list of books available from Penguins in New Zealand write to the Marketing Department, Penguin Books (N.Z.) Ltd, P.O. Box 4019, Auckland 10.

The French genius in Penguin Classics

Benjamin Constant
ADOLPHE
Translated by Leonard Tancock

In *Adolphe* Benjamin Constant (1767–1830) wrote an analysis of passion, recognized but unfelt, that remains unsurpassed in literature. A young man experiments with the love of an older woman: tiring of the passion he creates but cannot answer, he leaves her and she dies. Written in 1815, *Adolphe* remains a unique psychological romance.

Abbé Prévost
MANON LESCAUT
Translated by Leonard Tancock

The masterpiece of the Abbé Prévost (1697–1763), *Manon Lescaut* was based on the author's own experience and tells the story of Des Grieux, a young nobleman at the flamboyant and corrupt court of Louis XV. Des Grieux's overmastering passion for a woman leads him into a morass of crime, degradation, and social ruin. This moving and pitiless study of the human heart has survived as one of the greatest love stories ever written.

Stendhal
LOVE
Translated by Gilbert and Suzanne Sale

Written at a critical time in Stendhal's life when his own love had been rejected, *Love* is a thinly disguised picture of the author's inmost feelings. Though it ranges over a wide variety of topics from courtly love to the emancipation of women, central to the book is Stendhal's account of *amour-passion* – an intense, romantic and generally unrequited love – and his analysis of the power of the imagination to transfigure the image of the loved one.

Also published
Joanna Richardson's translation of
BAUDELAIRE: SELECTED POEMS

PENGUIN CLASSICS

'Penguin continue to pour out the jewels of the world's
classics in translation . . . There are now nearly enough to
keep a man happy on a desert island until the boat comes
in' – Philip Howard in *The Times*

A selection

Shikibu Murasaki
THE TALE OF GENJI
Translated by Edward G. Seidensticker

THE GREEK ANTHOLOGY
Edited by Peter Jay

Three Sanskrit Plays
ŚAKUNTALĀ/RĀKSHASA'S RING
MĀLATĪ AND MĀDAVA
Translated by Michael Coulson

THE ORKNEYINGA SAGA
Translated by Hermann Pálsson and Paul Edwards